"Just by the merest chance, could your name be Mickey?"

Michael O'Halloran

Michael O'Halloran

BY

GENE STRATTON-PORTER

AUTHOR OF "FRECKLES" ETC.

Illustrations by

Frances Rogers

ISBN: 978-93-5128-381-2(HB)

First Published in 1915
Indian Reprint in 2017

Published by

Kalpaz Publications
C-30, Satyawati Nagar,
Delhi – 110052
E-mail: kalpaz@hotmail.com
Website: kalpazpublications.com
Ph.: +91-9212142040

CONTENTS

CHAPTER I

Happy Home in Sunrise Alley

"Aw KID, come on! Be square!"

"You look out what you say to me."

"But ain't you going to keep your word?"

"Mickey, do you want your head busted?"

"Naw! But I did your work so you could loaf; now I want the pay you promised me."

"Let's see you get it! Better take it from me, hadn't you?"

"You're twice my size; you know I can't, Jimmy!"

"Then you know it too, don't you?"

"Now look here kid, it's 'cause you're getting so big that folks will be buying quicker of a little fellow like me; so you've laid in the sun all afternoon while I been running my legs about off to sell your papers; and when the last one is gone, I come and pay you what they sold for; now it's up to you to do what you promised."

"Why didn't you keep it when you had it?"

"'Cause that ain't business! I did what I promised fair and square; I was giving you a chance to be square too."

"Oh! Well next time you won't be such a fool!"

Jimmy turned to step from the gutter to the sidewalk. Two things happened to him simultaneously: Mickey became a projectile. He smashed with the force of a wiry fist on the larger boy's head, while above both, an athletic arm gripped him by the collar.

Douglas Bruce was hurrying to see a client before he should leave his office; but in passing a florist's window his eye was attracted by a sight so beautiful he paused an instant, considering. It was spring; the Indians were coming down to Multiopolis to teach people what the wood Gods had put into their hearts about flower magic.

The watcher scarcely had realized the exquisite loveliness of a milk-white birch basket filled with bog moss of silvery green, in which were set maidenhair and three yellow lady slippers, until beside it was placed another woven of osiers blood red, moss carpeted and bearing five pink moccasin flowers, faintly fined with red lavender; between them rosemary and white ladies' tresses. A flush crept over the lean face of the Scotsman. He saw a vision. Over those baskets bent a girl, beautiful as the flowers. Plainly as he visualized the glory of the swamp, Douglas Bruce pictured the woman he loved above the orchids. While he lingered, his heart warmed, glowing, his wonderful spring day made more wonderful by a vision not adequately describable, on his ear fell Mickey's admonition: "Be square!"

He sent one hasty glance toward the gutter. He saw a sullen-faced newsboy of a size that precluded longer success at paper selling, because public sympathy goes to the little fellows. Before him stood one of these same little fellows, lean, tow-haired, and blue-eyed, clean of face, neat in dress; with a peculiar modulation in his voice that caught Douglas squarely in the heart. He turned again to the flowers, but as his eyes revelled in beauty, his ears, despite the shuffle of passing feet, and the clamour of cars, lost not one word of what was passing in the gutter, while with each, slow anger surged higher. Mickey, well aware that his first blow would be all the satisfaction coming to him, put the force of his being into his punch. At the same instant Douglas thrust forth a hand that had pulled for Oxford and was yet in condition.

"Aw, you big stiff!" gasped Jimmy, twisting an astonished neck to see what was happening above and in his rear so surprisingly. Had that little Mickey

O'Halloran gone mad to hit *him?* Mickey standing back, his face upturned, was quite as surprised as Jimmy.

"What did he promise you for selling his papers?" demanded a deep voice.

"Twen—ty-*five*," answered Mickey, with all the force of inflection in his power. "And if you heard us, Mister, you heard him own up he was owing it."

"I did," answered Douglas Bruce tersely. Then to Jimmy: "Hand him over twenty-five cents."

Jimmy glared upward, but what he saw and the tightening of the hand on his collar were convincing. He drew from his pocket five nickels, dropping them into the outstretched hand of Douglas, who passed them to Mickey, the soiled fingers of whose left hand closed over them, while his right snatched off his cap. Fear was on his face, excitement was in his eyes, triumph was in his voice, while a grin of comradeship curved his lips.

"Many thanks, Boss," he said. "And would you add to them by keeping that strangle hold 'til you give me just two seconds the start of him?" He wheeled, darting through the crowd.

"Mickey!" cried Douglas Bruce. "Mickey, wait!"

But Mickey was half a block away turning into an alley. The man's grip tightened a twist.

"You'll find Mickey's admonition good," he said. "I advise you to take it. 'Be square!' And two things: first, I've got an eye on the Mickeys of this city. If I ever again find you imposing on him or any one else, I'll put you where you can't. Understand? Second, who is he?"

"Mickey!" answered the boy.

"Mickey who?" asked Douglas.

"How'd I know?" queried Jimmy.

"You don't know his name?" pursued Douglas.

"Naw, I don't!" said the boy.

"Where does he live?" continued Douglas.

"I don't know," answered Jimmy.

"If you have a charge to prefer, I'll take that youngster in for you," offered a policeman passing on his beat.

"He was imposing on a smaller newsboy. I made him quit," Douglas explained. "That's all."

"Oh!" said the officer, withdrawing his hand. Away sped Jimmy; with him went all chance of identifying Mickey, but Bruce thought he would watch for him. He was such an attractive little fellow.

Mickey raced through the first alley, down a street, then looked behind. Jimmy was not in sight.

"Got *him* to dodge now," he muttered. "If he ever gets a grip on me he'll hammer me meller! I'm going to have a bulldog if I half starve to buy it. Maybe the pound would give me one. I'll see to-morrow."

He looked long, then started homeward, which meant to jump on a car and ride for miles, then follow streets and alleys again. Finally he entered a last alley that faced due east. A compass could not have pointed more directly toward the rising sun; while there was at least half an hour each clear morning when rickety stairs, wavering fire-escapes, flapping washes, and unkept children were submerged in golden light. Long ago it had been named. By the time of Mickey's advent Sunrise Alley was as much a part of the map of Multiopolis as Biddle Boulevard, and infinitely more pleasing in name. He began climbing interminable stairs. At the top of the last flight he unlocked his door to enter his happy home; for Mickey had a home, and it was a happy one. No one else lived in it, while all it contained was his.

Mickey knew three things about his father: he had had one, he was not square, and he drank himself to death. He could not remember his father, but he knew many men engaged in the occupation of his passing, so he well understood why his mother never expressed any regrets.

Vivid in his mind was her face, anxious and pale, but twinkling; her body frail and overtaxed, but hitting back at life uncomplainingly. Bad things happened, but she explained how they might have been worse; so fed on this sop, and watching her example, Mickey grew like her. The difficult time was while she sat over a sewing machine to be with him. When he grew stout-legged and selfreliant, he could be sent after the food, to carry the rent, and to sell papers, then she could work by the day, earn more, have better health, while what both brought home paid the rent of the top room back, of as bad a shamble as a selfrespecting city would allow; kept them fed satisfyingly if not nourishingly, and allowed them to slip away many a nickel for the rainy day that she always explained would come. And it did.

One morning she could not get up; the following Mickey gave all their savings to a man with a wagon to take her to a nice place to rest. The man was sure about it being a nice place. She had told Mickey so often what to do if this ever happened, that when it did, all that was necessary was to remember what he had been told. After it was over and the nice place had been paid for, with the nickels and the sewing machine, with enough left for the first month's rent, Mickey faced life alone. But he knew exactly what to do, because she had told him. She had even written it down lest he forget. It was so simple that only a boy who did not mind his mother could have failed. The formula worked perfectly.

> *Morning: Get up early. Wash your face, brush your clothes. Eat what was left from supper for breakfast. Put your bed to air, then go out with your papers. Don't be afraid to offer them, or to do work of any sort you have strength for; but be deathly afraid to beg, to lie, or to steal, while if you starve, freeze, or die, never, never touch any kind of drink.*

Any fellow could do that; Mickey told dozens of them so.

He got along so well he could pay the rent each month, dress in whole clothing, have enough to eat, often cooked food on the little gasoline stove, if he were not too tired to cook it, and hide nickels in the old place daily. He had a bed and enough cover; he could get water in the hall at the foot of the flight of stairs leading to his room for his bath, to scrub the floor, and wash the dishes. From two years on, he had helped his mother with every detail of her housekeeping; he knew exactly what must be done.

It was much more dreadful than he thought it would be to come home alone, and eat supper by himself, but if he sold papers until he was almost asleep where he stood, he found he went to sleep as soon as he reached home and had supper. He did not awaken until morning; then he could hurry his work and get ahead of the other boys, and maybe sell to their customers. It might be bad to be alone, but always he could remember her, and make her seem present by doing every day exactly what she told him. Then, after all, being alone was a very wonderful thing compared with having parents who might beat and starve him and take the last penny he earned, not leaving enough to keep him from being hungry half the time.

When Mickey looked at some of the other boys, and heard many of them talk, he almost forgot the hourly hunger for his mother, in thankfulness that he did not have a father and that his mother had been herself. Mickey felt sure that if she had been any one of the mothers of most other boys he knew, he would not have gone home at all. He could endure cold, hunger, and loneliness, but he felt that he had no talent for being robbed, beaten, and starved; while lately he had fully decided upon a dog for company, when he could find the right one.

Mickey unlocked his door, entering for his water bucket. Such was his faith in his environment that he relocked the door while he went to the water tap. Returning to the room he again turned the key, then washed his face and hands. He looked at the slip nailed on the wall where she had put it. He knew every word of it, but always it comforted him to see her familiar writing, to read aloud what to do next as if it were her voice speaking to him. Evening: "Make up your bed." Mickey made his. "Wash any dirty dishes." He had a few so he washed them. "Sweep your floor." He swept. "Always prepare at least one hot thing for supper." He shook the gasoline tank to the little stove. It sounded full enough, so he went to the cupboard his mother had made from a small packing case. There were half a loaf of bread wrapped in its oiled paper, with two bananas discarded by Joe of the fruit stand. He examined his pocket, although he knew perfectly what it contained. Laying back enough to pay for his stock the next day, then counting in his twenty-five cents, he had forty cents left. He put thirty in the rent box, starting out with ten. Five paid for a bottle of milk, three for cheese, two for an egg for breakfast.

Then he went home. At the foot of the fire-escape that he used in preference to the stairs, he met a boy he knew tugging a heavy basket.

"Take an end for a nickel," said the boy.

"Thanks," said Mickey. "It's my time to dine. 'Sides, I been done once to-day."

"If you'll take it, I'll pay first," he offered.

"How far?" questioned Mickey.

"Oh, right over here," said the boy indefinitely.

"Sure!" said Mickey. "Cross my palm with the silver."

The nickel changed hands. Mickey put the cheese and egg in his pocket, the milk in the basket, then started. The place where they delivered the wash made Mickey feel almost prosperous. He picked up his milk bottle and stepped from the door, when a long, low wail that made him shudder, reached his ear.

"What's that?" he asked the woman.

"A stiff was carried past to-day. Mebby they ain't took the kids yet."

Mickey went slowly down the stairs, his face sober. That was what his mother had feared for him. That was why she had trained him to care for himself, to save the pennies, so that when she was taken away, he still would have a home. Sounded like a child! He was halfway up the long flight of stairs before he realized that he was going. He found the door at last, then, stood listening. He heard long-drawn, heart-breaking moaning. Presently he knocked. A child's shriek was the answer. Mickey straightaway opened the door. The voice guided him to a heap of misery in a corner.

"What's the matter kid?" inquired Mickey huskily.

The bundle stirred, while a cry issued. He glanced around the room. What he saw reassured him. He laid hold of the tatters, beginning to uncover what was under them. He dropped his hands, stepping back, when a tangled yellow mop and a weazened, bloated girl-child face peered at him, with wildly frightened eyes.

"If you'd put the wind you're wastin' into words, we'd get something done quicker," advised Mickey.

The tiny creature clutched the filthy covers, still staring.

"Did you come to '*get*' me?" she quavered.

"No," said Mickey. "I heard you from below so I came to see what hurt you. Ain't you got folks?"

She shook her head: "They took granny in a box and they said they'd come right back and '*get*' me. Oh, please, please don't let them!"

"Why they'd be good to you," said Mickey largely. "They'd give you"—he glanced at all the things the room lacked, then enumerated—"a clean bed, lots to eat, a window you could be seeing from, a doll, maybe."

"No! No!" she cried. "Granny always said some day she'd go and leave me; then they'd '*get*' me. She's gone! The big man said they'd come right back. Oh don't let them! Oh hide me quick!"

"Well—well—! If you're so afraid, why don't you cut and hide yourself then?" he asked.

"My back's bad. I can't walk," the child answered.

"Oh Lord!" said Mickey. "When did you get hurt?"

"It's always been bad. I ain't ever walked," she said.

"Well!" breathed Mickey, aghast. "And knowing she'd have to leave you some day, your granny went and scared you stiff about the Home folks taking you, when it's the only place for you to be going? Talk about women having the sense to vote!"

"I won't go! I won't! I'll scratch them! I'll bite them!" Then in swift change: "Oh boy, don't. Please, please don't let them '*get*' me."

Mickey took both the small bony hands reaching for him. He was so frightened with their hot, tremulous clutch, that he tried to pull away, dragging the tiny figure half to light and bringing from it moans of pain.

"Oh my back! Oh you're hurting me! Oh don't leave me! Oh boy, oh *dear* boy, please don't leave me!"

When she said "Oh dear boy," Mickey heard the voice of his mother in an hourly phrase. He crept closer, enduring the touch of the grimy claws.

"My name's Mickey," he said. "What's your?"

"Peaches," she answered. "Peaches, when I'm good. Crippled brat, when I'm bad."

"B'lieve if you had your chance you could look the peaches," said Mickey, "but what were you bad for?"

"So's she'd hit me," answered Peaches.

"But if me just pulling a little hurt you so, what happened when she hit you?" asked Mickey.

"Like knives stuck into me," said Peaches.

"Then what did you be bad for?" marvelled Mickey.

"Didn't you ever get so tired of one thing you'd take something that hurt, jus' for a change?"

"My eye!" said Mickey. "I don't know one fellow who'd do that, Peaches."

"Mickey, hide me. Oh hide me! Don't let them '*get*' me!" she begged.

"Why kid, you're crazy," said Mickey. "Now lemme tell you. Where they'll take you *looks* like a nice place. Honest it does. I've seen lots of them. You get a clean soft bed all by yourself, three big hot meals a day, things to read, and to play with. Honest Peaches, you do! I wouldn't tell you if it wasn't so. If I'll stay with you 'til they come, then go with you to the place 'til you see how nice it is, will you be good and go?"

She burrowed in the covers, screeching again.

"You're scared past all reason," said Mickey. "You don't know anything. But maybe the Orphings' Homes ain't so good as they look. If they are, why was mother frightened silly about them getting *me?* Always she said she just *had* to live until I got so big they wouldn't 'get' me. And I kept them from getting me by doing what she told me. Wonder if I could keep them from getting you? There's nothing of you. If I could move you there, I bet I could feed you more than your granny did, while I know I could keep you cleaner. You could have my bed, a window to look from, and clean covers." Mickey was thinking aloud. "Having you to come home to would be lots nicer than nothing. You'd beat a dog all hollow, 'cause you can talk. If I could get you there, I believe I could be making it. Yes, I believe I could do a lot better than this, and I believe I'd like you, Peaches, you are such a game little kid."

"She could lift me with one hand," she panted. "Oh Mickey, take me! Hurry!"

"Lemme see if I can manage you," said Mickey. "Have you got to be took any particular way?"

"Mickey, ain't you got folks that beat you?" she asked.

"I ain't got folks now," said Mickey, "and they didn't beat me when I had them. I'm all for myself—and if you say so, I guess from now on, I'm for you. Want to go?"

Her arms wound tightly around his neck. Her hot little face pressed against it.

"Put one arm 'cross my shoulders, an' the other round my legs," she said.

"But I got to go down a lot of stairs; it's miles and miles," said Mickey, "and I ain't got but five cents. I spent it all for grub. Peaches, are you hungry?"

"No!" she said stoutly. "Mickey, hurry!"

"But honest, I can't carry you all that way. I would if I could, Peaches, honest I would."

"Oh Mickey, dear Mickey, hurry!" she begged.

"Get down and cover up 'til I think," he ordered. "Say you look here! If I tackle this job do you want a change bad enough to be mean for me?"

"Just a little bit, maybe," said Peaches.

"But I won't hit you," explained Mickey.

"You can if you want to," she said. "I won't cry. Give me a good crack now, an' see if I do."

"You make me sick at my stummick," said Mickey. "Lord, kid! Snuggle down 'til I see. I'm going to get you there some way."

Mickey went back to the room where he helped deliver the clothes basket.

"How much can you earn the rest of the night?" he asked the woman.

"Mebby ten cents," she said.

"Well, if you will loan me that basket and ten cents, and come with me an hour, there's that back and just a dollar in it for you, lady," he offered.

She turned from him with a sneering laugh.

"Honest, lady!" said Mickey. "This is how it is: that crying got me so I went Anthony Comstockin'. There's a kid with a lame back all alone up there, half starved and scared fighting wild. We could put her in that basket, she's just a handful, and take her to a place she wants to go. We could ride most of the way on the cars and then a little walk, and get her to a cleaner, better room, where she'd be taken care of, and in an hour you'd be back with enough nickels in your pocket to make a great, big, round, shining, full-moon cartwheel. Dearest lady, doesn't the prospect please you?"

"It would," she said, "if I had the cartwheel now."

"In which case you wouldn't go," said Mickey. "Dearest lady, it isn't business to pay for undone work."

"And it isn't business to pay your employer's fare to get to your job either," she retorted.

"No, that beats business a mile," said Mickey. "That's an *investment*. You invest ten cents and an hour's time on a gamble. Now look what you get, lady. A nice restful ride on the cars. Your ten cents back, a whole, big, shining, round, ladyliberty bird, if you trust in God, as the coin says the bird does, and more'n that, dearest lady, you go to bed feeling your pinfeathers sprouting, 'cause you've done a kind deed to a poor crippled orphing."

"If I thought you really had the money—" she said.

"Honest, lady, I got the money," said Mickey, "and 'sides, I got a surprise party for you. When you get back you may go to that room and take every scrap that's in it. Now come on; you're going to be enough of a sporting lady to try a chance like that, ain't you? May be a gold mine up there, for all I know. Put something soft in the bottom of the basket while I fetch the kid."

Mickey ran up the stairs.

"Now Peaches," he said, "I guess I got it fixed. I'm going to carry you down; a nice lady is going to put you in a big basket, then we'll take you to the cars and so get you to my house; but you got to promise, 'cross your heart, you won't squeal, nor say a word, 'cause the police will 'get' you sure, if you do. They'll think the woman is your ma, so it will be all right. See?"

Peaches nodded. Mickey wrapped her in the remnants of a blanket, carried her downstairs and laid her in the basket. By turning on her side and drawing up her feet, she had more room than she needed.

"They won't let us on the cars," said the woman.

"Dearest lady, wait and see," said Mickey. "Now Peaches, shut your eyes, also your mouth. Don't you take a chance at saying a word. If they won't stand the basket, we'll carry you, but it would hurt you less, while it would come in handy when we run out of cars. You needn't take coin only for going, dearest lady; you'll be silver plated coming back."

"You little fool," said the woman, but she stooped to her end of the basket.

"Ready, Peaches," said Mickey, "and if it hurts, 'member it will soon be over, and you'll be where nobody will ever hurt you again."

"Hurry!" begged the child.

Down the long stairs they went and to the car line. Crowded car after car whirled past; finally one came not so full, it stopped to let off passengers. Mickey was at the conductor's elbow.

"Please mister, a lame kid," he pleaded. "We want to move her. Please, please help us on."

"Can't!" said the conductor. "Take a taxi."

"Broke my limousine," said Mickey. "Aw come on mister; ain't you got kids of your own?"

"Get out of the way!" shouted the conductor.

"Hang on de back wid the basket," cried the woman.

With Peaches laid over her shoulder, she swung to the platform, and found a seat, while Mickey grabbed the basket and ran to the back screaming after her: "I got my fare; only pay for yourself."

Mickey told the conductor to tell the lady where to leave the car. When she stepped down he was ready with the basket. Peaches, panting and in cold perspiration with pain, was laid in it.

"Lovely part of the village, ain't it, lady?" said Mickey. "See the castles of the millyingaires piercing the sky; see their automobiles at the curb; see the lovely ladies and gents promenading the streets enjoying the spring?"

Every minute Mickey talked to keep the woman from noticing how far she was going; but soon she growled: "How many miles furder is it?"

"Just around a corner, up an alley, and down a side street a step. Nothing at all! Nice promenade for a spry, lovely young lady like you. Evening walk, smell spring in the air. 'Most there now, Peaches."

"Where are ye takin' this kid? How'll I ever get back to the car line?" asked the woman.

Mickey ignored the first question. "Why, I'll be eschorting you of course, dearest lady," he said.

At the point of rebellion, Mickey spoke.

"Now set the basket down right here," he ordered. "I'll be back in no time with the lady-bird."

He returned in a few minutes. Into her outstretched palm he counted twenty-two nickels, picked the child from the basket, darted around a corner calling, "Back in a minute," and was gone.

"Now Peaches, we got some steps to climb," he said. "Grip my neck tight and stand just a little more."

"I ain't hurt!" she asserted. "I like seein' things. I never saw so much before. I ain't hurt—much!"

"Your face, your breathing, and the sweating on your lips, is a little disproving," said Mickey, "but I'll have to take your word for it, 'cause I can't help it; but it'll soon be over so you may rest."

Mickey climbed a flight, then sat down until he could manage another. The last flight he rested three times. One reason he laid Peaches on the floor was because he couldn't reach the bed. After a second's pause he made a light, and opened the milk bottle.

"Connect with that," he said. "I got to take the lady back to the cars."

"Oh!" cried the connected child. "Oh Mickey, how good!"

"Go slow!" said Mickey. "You better save half to have with some bread for your supper. Now I got to leave you a little bit, but you needn't be afraid, 'cause I'll lock you in. Nobody will '*get*' you here."

"Now for the cars," said Mickey to his helper.

"What did them folks say?" she asked.

"Tickled all over," answered Mickey promptly.

"That bundle of dirty rags!" she scoffed.

"They are going to throw away the rags and wash her," said Mickey. "She's getting her supper now."

"Sounds like lying," said the woman, "but mebby it ain't. Save me, I can't see why anybody would want a kid at any time, let alone a reekin' bunch of skin and crooked bones."

"You've known folks to want a dog, ain't you?" said Mickey. "Sure something that can think and talk back must be a lot more amusing. I see the parks are full of the rich folks dolling up the dogs, feeding them candy and sending them out for an airing in their automobiles; so it's up to the poor people to look after the homeless children, isn't it?"

"Do you know the folks that took her?"

"Sure I do!" said Mickey.

"Do you live close?" she persisted.

"Yes! I'm much obliged for your help, dearest lady. When you get home, go up to the last attic back, and if there is anything there you want, help yourself. Peaches don't need it now, while there's no one else. Thank you, and good-bye. Don't fly before your wings grow, 'cause I know you'll feel like trying tonight."

Mickey hurried back to his room. The milk bottle lay on the floor, the child asleep beside it. The boy gazed at her. There were strange and peculiar stirrings in his lonely little heart. She was so grimy he scarcely could tell what she looked like, but the grip of her tiny hot hands was on him. Presently he laughed.

"Well fellers! Look what I've annexed! And I was hunting a dog! Well, she's lots better. She won't eat much more, she can talk, and she'll be something alive waiting when I come home. Gee, I'm *glad* I found her."

Mickey set the washtub on the floor near the sleeping child, and filling the dishpan with water, put it over the gasoline burner. Then he produced soap, a towel, and comb. He looked at the child again, and going to the box that contained his mother's clothing he hunted out a nightdress. Then he sat down to wait for the water to heat. The door slammed when he went after a bucket of cold water, and awakened the girl. She looked at him, then at his preparations. "I ain't going to be washed," she said. "It'll hurt me. Put me on the bed." "Put you on my bed, dirty like you are?" cried Mickey. "I guess not! You are going to be a soaped lady. If it hurts, you can be consoling yourself thinking it will be the last time, 'cause after this you'll be washed every day so you won't need skinning alive but once."

"I won't! I won't!" she cried.

"Now looky here!" said Mickey. "I'm the boss of this place. If I say wash, it's *wash!* See! I ain't going to have a dirty girl with mats in her hair living with me. You begged me and begged me to bring you, now you'll be cleaned up or you'll go back. Which is it, back or soap?"

The child stared at him, then around the room.

"Soap," she conceded.

"That's a lady," said Mickey. "Course it's soap! All clean and sweet smelling like a flower. See my mammy's nice white nightie for you? How bad is your back, Peaches? Can you sit up?"

"A little while," she answered. "My legs won't go."

"Never you mind," said Mickey. "I'll work hard and get a doctor, so some day they will."

"They won't ever," insisted Peaches. "Granny carried me to the big doctors once, an' my backbone is weak, an' I won't ever walk, they all said so."

"Poot! Doctors don't know everything," scorned Mickey. "That was *long* ago, maybe. By the time I can earn enough to get you a dress and shoes, a doctor will come along who's found out how to make backs over. There's one that put different legs on a dog. I read about it in the papers I sold. We'll save our money and get him to put another back on you. Just a bully back."

"Oh Mickey, will you?" she cried.

"Sure!" said Mickey. "Now you sit up and I'll wash you like Mammy always did me."

Peaches obeyed. Mickey soaped a cloth, knelt beside her; then he paused. "Say Peaches, when was your hair combed last?"

"I don't know, Mickey," she answered.

"There's more dirt in it than there is on your face."

"If you got shears, just cut it off," she suggested.

"Sure!" said Mickey.

He produced shears and lifting string after string cut all of them the same distance from her head.

"Girls' shouldn't be short, like boys'," he explained. "Now hang your head over the edge of the tub and shut your eyes so I can wash it," he ordered.

Mickey soaped and scoured until the last tangle was gone, then rinsed and partly dried the hair, which felt soft and fine to his fingers.

"B'lieve it's going to curl," he said.

"Always did," she answered.

Mickey emptied and rinsed the tub at the drain, then started again on her face and ears, which he washed thoroughly. He pinned a sheet around her neck, then she divested herself of the rags. Mickey lifted her into the tub, draped the sheet over the edge, poured in the water, and handed her the soap.

"Now you scour, while I get supper," he said.

Peaches did her best. Mickey locked her in and went after more milk. He wanted to add several extras, but remembering the awful hole the dollar had made in his finances, he said grimly: "No-sir-ee! With a family to keep, and likely to need a doctor at any time and a Carrel back to buy, there's no frills for Mickey. Seeing what she ain't had, she ought to be thankful for just milk."

So he went back, lifted Peaches from the tub and laid her on the floor, where he dried her with the sheet. Then he put the nightdress over her head, she slipped her arms in the sleeves, and he stretched her on his bed. She was so lost in the garment he tied a string under her arms to hold it, and cut off the sleeves at her elbows. The pieces he saved for washcloths. Mickey spread his sheet over her, rolled the bed before the window where she could have air, see sky and housetops, then brought her supper. It was a cup of milk with half the bread broken in, and a banana. Peaches was too tired to eat, so she drank the milk while Mickey finished the remainder. Then he threw her rags from the window, and spread his winter covers on the floor for his bed. Soon both of them were asleep.

CHAPTER II

MOCCASINS AND LADY SLIPPERS

"No messenger boy for those," said Douglas Bruce as he handed the florist the price set on the lady slippers. "Leave them where people may enjoy them until I call."

As he turned, another man was inquiring about the orchids; he too preferred the slippers; but when he was told they were taken, he had wanted the moccasins all the time, anyway. The basket was far more attractive. He refused delivery, returning to his waiting car smiling over the flowers. He also saw a vision of the woman into whose sated life he hoped to bring a breath of change with the wonderful gift. He saw the basket in her hands, and thrilled in anticipation of the favours her warmed heart might prompt her to bestow upon him.

In the mists of early morning the pink orchids surrounded by rosemary and ladies' tresses had glowed and gleamed from the top of a silvery moss mound four feet deep, under a big tamarack in a swamp, through the bog of which the squaw plunged to her knees at each step to uproot them. In the evening glow of electricity, snapped from their stems, the beautiful basket untouched, the moccasins lay on the breast of a woman of fashion, while with every second of contact with the warmth of her body, they drooped lower, until clasped in the arms of her lover, they were quite crushed, then flung from an automobile to be ground to pulp by passing wheels.

The slippers had a happier fate. Douglas Bruce carried them reverently. He was sure he knew the swamp in which they grew. As he went his way, he held the basket, velvet-white, in strong hands, swaying his body with the motion of the car lest one leaf be damaged. When he entered the hall, down the stairs came Leslie Winton.

"Why Douglas, I wasn't expecting you," she said.

Douglas Bruce held up the basket.

"Joy!" she cried. "Oh joy unspeakable! Who has been to the tamarack swamp?"

"A squaw was leaving Lowry's as he put these in his window," answered Douglas.

"Bring them," she said.

He followed to a wide side veranda, set the basket on a table in a cool spot, then drew a chair near it. Leslie Winton seated herself, leaning on the table to study the orchids. Unconsciously she made the picture Douglas had seen. She reached up slim fingers in delicate touchings here and there of moss, corolla and slipper.

"Never in all my days—" she said. "Never in all my days—I shall keep the basket always, and the slippers as long as I possibly can. See this one! It isn't fully open. I should have them for a week at least. Please hand me a glass of water."

Douglas started to say that ice water would be too cold, but with the wisdom of a wise man waited; and as always, was joyed by the waiting. For the girl took the glass and cupping her hands around it sat talking to the flowers, and to him, as she warmed the water with heat from her body. Douglas was so delighted with the unforeseen second that had given him first chance at the orchids, and so this unexpected call, that he did not mind the attention she gave the flowers. He had reasons for not being extravagant; but seldom had a like sum brought such returns. He began drawing interest as he watched Leslie. Never had her form seemed so perfect, her dress so becoming and simple. How could other women make a vulgar display in the same pattern that clothed her modestly? How wonderful were the soft coils of her hair, the tints paling and flushing on her cheeks, her shining eyes! Why could not all women use her low, even, perfectly accented speech and deliberate self-control?

He was in daily intercourse with her father, a high official of the city, a man of education, social position, and wealth. Mr. Winton had reared his only child according to his ideas; but Douglas, knowing these things, believed in blood also. As Leslie turned and warmed the water, watching her, the thought was strong in his mind: what a woman her mother must have been! Each day he was with Leslie, he saw her do things that no amount of culture could instil. Instinct and tact are inborn; careful rearing may produce a good imitation, they are genuine only with blood. Leslie had always filled his ideal of a true woman. To ignore him for his gift would have piqued many a man; Douglas Bruce was pleased.

"You wonders!" she said softly. "Oh you wonders! When the mists lifted in the marshes this morning, and the first ray of gold touched you to equal goldness, you didn't know you were coming to me. I almost wish I could put you back. Just now you should be in such cool mistiness, while you should be hearing a hermit thrush sing vespers, a cedar bird call, and a whip-poor-will cry. But I'm glad I have you! Oh I'm so glad you came to me! I never materialized a whole swamp with such vividness as only this little part of it brings. Douglas, when you caught the first glimpse of these, how far into the swamp did you see past them?"

"To the heart—of the swamp—and of my heart."

"I can see it as perfectly as I ever did," she said. "But I eliminate the squaw; possibly because I didn't see her. And however exquisite the basket is, she broke the law when she peeled a birch tree. I'll wager she brought this to Lowry, carefully covered. And I'm not sure but there should have been a law she broke when she uprooted these orchids. Much as I love them, I doubt if I can keep them alive, and bring them to bloom next season. I'll try, but I don't possess flower magic in the highest degree."

She turned the glass, touching it with questioning palm. Was it near the warmth of bog water? After all, was bog water warm? Next time she was in a swamp she would plunge her hand deeply in the mosses to feel the exact temperature to which those roots had been accustomed. Then she spoke again.

"Yes, I eliminate the squaw," she said. "These golden slippers are the swamp to me, but I see you kneeling to lift them. I am so glad I'm the woman they made you see."

Douglas sat forward and opened his lips. Was not this the auspicious moment?

"Did the squaw bring more?" she questioned.

"Yes," he answered. "Pink moccasins in a basket of red osiers, with the same moss, rosemary and white tresses. Would you rather those?"

She set down the glass, drawing the basket toward her with both hands. As she parted the mosses to drop in the water she slowly shook her head.

"One must have seen them to understand what that would be like," she said. "I know it was beautiful, but I'm sure I should have selected the gold had I been there. Oh I wonder if the woman who has the moccasins will give them a drink to-night! And will she try to preserve their roots?"

"She will not!" said Douglas emphatically.

"How can you possibly know?" queried the girl.

"I saw the man who ordered them," laughed Douglas.

"Oh!" cried Leslie, comprehendingly.

"I'd stake all I'm worth the moccasins are drooping against a lavender dress; the roots are in the garbage can, while the cook or maid has the basket," he said.

"Douglas, how can you!" exclaimed Leslie.

"I couldn't! Positively couldn't! Mine are here!"

The slow colour crept into her cheek. "I'll make those roots bloom next spring; you shall see them in perfection," she promised.

"That would be wonderful!" he exclaimed warmly.

"Tell me, were there yet others?" she asked hastily.

"Only these," he said. "But there was something else. I came near losing them. While I debated, or rather while I possessed these, and worshipped the others, there was a gutter row that almost made me lose yours."

"In the gutter again?" she laughed.

"Once again," he admitted. "Such a little chap, with an appealing voice, while his inflection was the smallest part of what he was saying. 'Aw kid, come on. Be square!' Oh Leslie!"

"Why Douglas!" the girl cried. "Tell me!"

"Of all the wooden-head slowness!" he exclaimed. "I've let him slip again!"

"Let who 'slip again?'" questioned Leslie. "My little brother!" answered he.

"Oh Douglas! You didn't really?" she protested.

"Yes I did," he said. "I heard a little lad saying the things that are in the blood and bone of the men money can't buy and corruption can't break. I heard him plead like a lawyer and argue his case straight. I lent a hand when his eloquence failed, got him his deserts, then let him go! I did have an impulse to keep him. I did call after him. But he disappeared."

"Douglas, we can find him!" she comforted.

"I haven't found either of the others I realized I'd have been interested in, after I let them slip," he answered, "while this boy was both of them rolled into one, and ten more like them."

"Oh Douglas! I'm so sorry! But maybe some other man has already found him," said Leslie.

"No. You can always pick the brothered boys," said Douglas. "The first thing that happens to them is a clean-up and better clothing; then an air of possessed importance. No man has attached this one."

"Douglas, describe him," she commanded. "I'll watch for him. How did he look? What was the trouble?"

"One at a time," cautioned the man. "He was a little chap, a white, clean, threadbare little chap, with such a big voice, so wonderfully intoned, and such a bigger principle, for which he was fighting. One of these overgrown newsboys the public won't stand for unless he is in the way when they are making a car, had hired him to sell his papers while he loafed. Mickey——"

"'Mickey?'" repeated Leslie questioningly.

"The big fellow called him 'Mickey'; no doubt a mother who adored him named him Michael, and thought him 'like unto God' when she did it. The big fellow had loafed all afternoon. When Mickey came back and turned over the money, and waited to be paid off, his employer laughed at the boy for not keeping it when he had it. Mickey begged him 'to be square' and told him that 'was not business'—'*not business*,' mind you, but the big fellow jeered at him and was starting away. Mickey and I reached him at the same time; so I got in the gutter again. I don't see how I can be so slow! I don't see how I did it!"

"I don't either," she said, with a twinkle that might have referred to the first of the two exclamations. "It must be your Scotch habit of going slowly and surely. But cheer up! We'll find him. I'll help you."

"Have you reflected on the fact that this city covers many square miles, of which a fourth is outskirts, while from them three thousand newsboys gathered at the last Salvation Army banquet for them?"

"That's where we can find him!" she cried. "Thanksgiving, or Christmas! Of course we'll see him then."

"Mickey didn't have a Salvation Army face," he said. "I am sure he is a free lance, and a rare one; besides, this is May. I want my little brother to go on my vacation with me. I want him now."

"Would it help any if I'd be a sister to you?"

"Not a bit," said Douglas. "I don't in the very least wish to consider you in the light of a sister; you have another place in my heart, very different, yet all your own; but I do wish to make of Mickey the little brother I never have had. Minturn was telling me what a rejuvenation he's getting from the boy he picked up. Already he has him in his office, and is planning school and partnership with a man he can train as he chooses."

"But Minturn has sons of his own!" protested Leslie.

"Oh no! Not in the least!" exclaimed Douglas. "Minturn has sons of his *wife's*. She persistently upsets and frustrates Minturn's every idea for them, while he is helpless. You will remember she has millions; he has what he earns. He can't separate his boys, splendid physical little chaps, from their mother's money and influence, and educate them to be a help to him. They are to be made into men of wealth and leisure. Minturn will evolve his little brother into a man of brains and efficiency."

"But Minturn is a power!" cried the girl.

"Not financially," explained Douglas. "Nothing but money counts with his wife. In telling me of this boy, Minturn confessed that he was forced, *forced* mind you, to see his sons ruined, while he is building a street gamin as he would them, if permitted."

"How sad, Douglas!" cried Leslie. "Your voice is bitter. Can't he do something?"

"Not a blooming thing!" answered Douglas. "She has the money. She is their mother. Her character is unimpeachable. If Minturn went to extremes, the law would give them to her; she would turn them over to ignorant servants who would corrupt them, and be well paid for doing it. Why Minturn told me—but I can't repeat that. Anyway, he made me eager to try my ideas on a lad who would be company for me, when I can't be here and don't wish to be with other men."

"Are you still going to those Brotherhood meetings?"

"I am. And I always shall be. Nothing in life gives me such big returns for the time invested. There is a world of talk breaking loose about the present 'unrest' among women; I happen to know that the 'unrest' is as deep with men. For each woman I personally know, bitten by 'unrest,' I know two men in the same condition. As long as men and women are forced to combine, to uphold society, it is my idea that it would be a good thing if there were to be a Sisterhood organized; then the two societies frankly brought together and allowed to clear up the differences between them."

"But why not?" asked the girl eagerly.

"Because we are pursuing false ideals, we have a wrong conception of what is *worth while in life*," answered the Scotsman. "Because the sexes except in rare, very rare, instances, do not understand each other, and every day are drifting farther apart, while most of the married folk I know are farthest apart of all. Leslie, what is it in marriage that constrains people? We can talk, argue and agree or disagree on anything, why can't the Minturns?"

"From what you say, it would seem to me it's her idea of what is worth while in life," said Leslie.

"Exactly!" cried Douglas. "But he can sway men! He can do powerful work. He could induce her to marry him. Why can't he control his own blood?"

"If she should lose her money and become dependent upon him for support, he could!" said Leslie.

"He should do it anyway," insisted Douglas.

"Do you think you could?" she queried.

"I never thought myself in his place," said Douglas, "but I believe I will, and if I see glimmerings, I'll suggest them to him."

"Good boy!" said the girl lightly. And then she added: "Do you mind if I think myself in her place and see if I can suggest a possible point at which she could be reached? I know her. I shouldn't consider her happy. At least not with what I call joy."

"What do you call joy?" asked Douglas.

"Being satisfied with your environment."

Douglas glanced at her, then at her surroundings, and looking into her eyes laughed quizzically.

"But if it were different, I am perfectly confident that I should work out joy from life," insisted Leslie. "It owes me joy! I'll have it, if I fight for it!"

"Leslie! Leslie! Be careful! You are challenging Providence. Stronger men than I have wrought chaos for their children," said a warning voice, as her father came behind her chair.

"Chaos or no, still I'd put up my fight for joy, Daddy," laughed the girl. "Only see, Preciousest!"

"One minute!" said her father, shaking hands with Douglas. "Now what is it, Leslie? Oh, I do see!"

"Take my chair and make friends," said the girl.

Mr. Winton seated himself, then began examining and turning the basket. "Indians?" he queried.

"Yes," said Douglas. "A particularly greasy squaw. I wish I might truthfully report an artist's Indian of the Minnehaha type, but alack, it was the same one I've seen ever since I've been in the city, and that you've seen for years before my arrival."

Mr. Winton still turned the basket.

"I've bought their stuff for years, because neither Leslie nor her mother ever would tolerate fat carnations and overgrown roses so long as I could find a scrap of arbutus, a violet or a wake-robin from the woods. We've often motored up and penetrated the swamp I fancy these came from, for some distance, but later in the season; it's so very boggy now. Aren't these rather wonderful?" He turned to his daughter.

"Perfectly, Daddy," she said. "Perfectly!"

"But I don't mean for the Creator," explained Mr. Winton. "I am accustomed to His miracles. Every day I see a number of them. I mean for the squaw."

"I'd have to know the squaw and understand her viewpoint," said Leslie.

"She had it in her tightly clenched fist," laughed Douglas. "One, I'm sure; anyway, not over two."

"That hasn't a thing to do with the *art* with which she made the basket and filled it with just three perfect plants," said Leslie.

"You think there is real art in her anatomy?" queried Mr. Winton.

"Bear witness, O you treasures of gold!" cried Leslie, waving toward the basket.

"There was another," explained Douglas as he again described the osier basket.

Mr. Winton nodded. He looked at his daughter.

"I like to think, young woman, that you were born with and I have cultivated what might be called artistic taste in you," he said. "Granted the freedom of the tamarack swamp, could you have done better?"

"Not so well, Daddy! Not nearly so well. I never could have defaced what you can see was a noble big tree by cutting that piece of bark, while I might have worshipped until dragged away, but so far as art and I are concerned, the slippers would still be under their tamarack."

"You are begging the question, Leslie," laughed her father. "I was not discussing the preservation of the wild, I was inquiring into the state of your artistic ability. If you had no hesitation about taking the flowers, could you have gone to that swamp, collected the material and fashioned and filled a more beautiful basket that this?"

"How can I tell, Daddy?" asked the girl. "There's only one way to learn. I'll forget my scruples, you get me a pair of rubber boots, then we'll drive to the tamarack swamp and experiment."

"We'll do it!" cried Mr. Winton. "The very first half day I can spare, we'll do it. And you Douglas, you will want to come with us, of course."

"Why, 'of course,'" laughed Leslie.

"Because he started the expedition with his golden slippers. When it come to putting my girl, and incidentally my whole family, in competition with an Indian squaw on a question of art, naturally, her father and one of her best friends would want to be present."

"But maybe 'Minnie' went alone, and what chance would her work have with you two for judges?" asked Leslie.

"We needn't be the judges," said Douglas Bruce quietly.

"We can put this basket in the basement in a cool, damp place, where it will keep perfectly for a week. When you make your basket we can find the squaw and bring her down with us. Lowry could display the results side by side. He could call up whomever you consider the most artistic man and woman in the city and get their decision. You'd be willing to abide by that, wouldn't you?"

"Surely, but it wouldn't be fair to the squaw," explained Leslie. "I'd have had the benefit of her art to begin on."

"It would," said Mr. Winton. "Does not every artist living, painter, sculptor, writer, what you will, have the benefit of all art that has gone before?"

"You agree?" Leslie turned to Douglas.

"Your father's argument is a truism."

"But I will know that I am on trial. She didn't. Is it fair to her?" persisted Leslie.

"For begging the question, commend me to a woman," said Mr. Winton. "The point we began at, was not what you could do in a contest with her. She went to the swamp and brought from it some flower baskets. It is perfectly fair to her to suppose that they are her best art. Now what we are proposing to test is whether the finest product of our civilization, as embodied in you, can go to the same swamp, and from the same location surpass her work. Do I make myself clear?"

"Perfectly clear, Daddy, and it would be fair," conceded Leslie. "But it is an offence punishable with a heavy fine to peel a birch tree; while I wouldn't do it, if it were not."

"Got her to respect the law anyway," said Mr. Winton to Douglas. "The proposition, Leslie, was not that you do the same thing, but that from the same source you outdo her. You needn't use birch bark if it involves your law-abiding soul."

"Then it's all settled. You must hurry and take me before the lovely plants have flowered," said Leslie.

"I'll go day after to-morrow," promised Mr. Winton.

"In order to make our plan work, it is necessary that I keep these orchids until that time," said Leslie.

"You have a better chance than the lady who drew the osier basket has of keeping hers," said Mr. Winton. "If I remember I have seen the slippers in common earth quite a distance from the lake, while the moccasins demand bog moss, water and swamp mists and dampness."

"I have seen slippers in the woods myself," said Leslie. "I think the conservatory will do, so they shall go there right now. I have to be fair to 'Minnie.'"

"Let me carry them for you," offered Douglas, arising.

"'Scuse us. Back in a second, Daddy," said Leslie. "I am interested, excited and eager to make the test, yet in a sense I do not like it."

"But why?" asked Douglas.

"Can't you see?" countered Leslie.

"No," said Douglas.

"It's shifting my sense of possession," explained the girl. "The slippers are no longer my beautiful gift from you. They are perishable things that belong to an Indian squaw. In justice to her, I have to keep them in perfect condition so that my work may not surpass hers with the unspeakable art of flower freshness; while instead of thinking them the loveliest thing in the world, I will now lie awake half the night, no doubt, studying what I can possibly find that is more beautiful."

Douglas Bruce opened his slow lips, taking a step in her direction.

"Dinner is served," announced her father. He looked inquiringly toward his daughter. She turned to Douglas.

"Unless you have a previous engagement, you will dine with us, won't you?" she asked.

"I should be delighted," he said heartily.

When the meal was over and they had returned to the veranda, Leslie listened quietly while the men talked, most of the time, but when she did speak, what she said proved that she always had listened to and taken part in the discussions of men, until she understood and could speak of business or politics intelligently.

"Have you ever considered an official position, Douglas?" inquired Mr. Winton. "I have an office within my gift, or so nearly so that I can control it, and it seems to me that you would be a good man. Surely we could work together in harmony."

"It never has appealed to me that I wanted work of that nature," answered Douglas. "It's unusually kind of you to think of me, and make the offer, but I am satisfied with what I am doing, while there is a steady increase in my business that gives me confidence."

"What's your objection to office?" asked Mr. Winton.

"That it takes your time from your work," answered Douglas. "That it changes the nature of your work. That if you let the leaders of a party secure you a nomination, and the party elect you, you are bound to their principles, at least there is a tacit understanding that you are, and if you should happen to be afflicted with principles of your own, then you have got to sacrifice them."

"'Afflict' is a good word in this instance," said Mr. Winton. "It is painful to a man of experience to see you young fellows of such great promise come up and 'kick' yourself half to death 'against the pricks' of established business, parties, and customs, but half of you do it. In the end all of you come limping in, poor, disheartened, defeated, and then swing to the other extreme, by being so willing for a change you'll take almost anything, and so the dirty jobs naturally fall to you."

"I grant much of that," Douglas said, in his deliberate way, "but happily I have sufficient annual income from my father's estate to enable me to live until I become acquainted in a strange city, and have time to establish the kind of business I should care to handle. I am thinking of practising corporation law; I specialized in that, so I may have the pleasure before so very long of going after some of the men who do what you so aptly term the 'dirty' jobs."

"A repetition of the customary chorus," said Mr. Winton, "differing only in that it is a little more emphatic than usual. I predict that you will become an office-holder, having party affiliations, inside ten years."

"Possibly," said Douglas. "But I'll promise you this: it will be a new office no man ever before has held, in the gift of a party not now in existence."

"Oh you dreamers!" cried Mr. Winton. "What a wonderful thing it is to be young and setting out to reform the world, especially on a permanent income. That's where you surpass most reformers."

"But I said nothing about reform," corrected Douglas. "I said I was thinking of corporation law."

"I'm accustomed to it; while you wouldn't scare Leslie if you said 'reform,'" remarked Mr. Winton. "She's a reformer herself, you know."

"But only sweat-shops, child labour, civic improvement, preservation of the wild, and things like that!" cried Leslie so quickly and eagerly, that both men laughed.

"God be praised!" exclaimed her father.

"God be *fervently* praised!" echoed her lover.

Before she retired Leslie visited the slippers.

"I'd like to know," she said softly, as she touched a bronze striped calyx, "I'd like to know how I am to penetrate your location, and find and fashion anything to outdo you and the squaw, you wood creatures you!" Then she bent above the flowers and whispered: "Tuck this in the toe of your slipper! Three times to-night it was in his eyes, and on his tongue, but his slowness let the moment pass. I can 'bide a wee' for my Scotsman, I can bide forever, if I must; for it's he only, and no other."

The moccasins soon had been ground to pulp and carried away on a non-skid tire while at three o'clock in the morning a cross, dishevelled society woman, in passing from her dressing room to her bed, stumbled over the osier basket, kicking it from her way.

CHAPTER III

S.O.S.

Mickey, his responsibility weighing upon him, slept lightly and awakened early, his first thought of Peaches. He slipped into his clothing and advancing peered at her through the grayness. His heart beat wildly.

"Aw you poor kid! You poor little kid!" he whispered to himself as he had fallen into the habit of doing for company. "The scaring, the jolting, the scouring, and everything were too much for you. You've gone sure! You're just like them at the morgue. Aw Peaches! I didn't mean to hurt you, Peaches! I was *trying* to be good to you. Honest I was, Peaches! Aw——!"

As his fright increased Mickey raised his voice until his last wail reached the consciousness of the sleeping child. She stirred slightly, her head moving on the pillow. Mickey almost fell, so great was his relief. He stepped closer, gazing in awe. The sheared hair had dried in the night, tumbling into a hundred golden ringlets. The tiny clean face was white, so white that the blue of the closed eyes showed darkly through the lids, the blue veins streaked the temples and the little claws lying relaxed on the sheet. Mickey slowly broke up inside. A big, hard lump grew in his throat. He shut his lips tight and bored the tears from his eyes with his wiry fists. He began to mutter his thoughts to regain self-control.

"Gee kid, but you had me scared to the limit!" he said. "I thought you were gone, sure. Honest I did! Ain't I glad though! But you're the whitest thing! You're like——I'll tell you what you're like. You're like the lily flowers in the store windows at Easter. You're white like them, and your hair is the little bit of gold decorating them. If I'd known it was like that I wouldn't a-cut it if I'd spent a month untangling it. Honest I wouldn't, kid! I'm awful sorry! Gee, but it would a-been pretty spread over mother's pillow."

Mickey gazed, worshipped and rejoiced as he bent lower from time to time to watch the fluttering breath.

"You're so clean now you just smell good; but I got to go easy. The dirt covered you so I didn't see how sick you were. You'll go out like a candle, that's what you'll do. I mustn't let even the wind blow cold on you. I couldn't stand it if I was to hurt you. I'd just go and lay down before the cars or jump down an elevator hole. Gee, I'm glad I found you! I wouldn't trade you for the smartest dog that's being rode around in the parks. Nor for the parks! Nor the trees! Nor the birds! Nor the buildings! Nor the swimming places! Nor the automobiles! Nor nothing! Not nothing you could mention at all! Not eating! Nor seeing! Nor having! Not no single thing—nothing at all—Lily!

"Lily!" he repeated. "Little snow white lily! Peaches is a good name for you if you're referring to sweetness, but it doesn't fit for colour. Least I never saw none white. Lily fits you better. If you'd been a dog, I was going to name you Partner. But you're mine just as much as if you was a dog, so I'll name you if I want to. Lily! That's what God made you; that's what I'm going to call you."

The God thought, evoked by creation, remained in Mickey's heart. He glanced at the sky clearing from the graying mists of morning, while the rumble of the streets came up to him in a dull roar.

"O God, I guess I been forgetting my praying some, since mother went. I'd nothing but myself and I ain't worth bothering You about. But O God, if You are going to do any *big* things to-day, why not do some for Lily? Can't be many that needs it more. If You saw her yesterday, You must see if You'll look down now, that she's better off, she's worlds better off. Wonder if You sent me to get her, so she would be better off. Gee, why didn't You send one of them millyingaires who could a-dressed her up, fed her and took her to the country where the sun would shine on her. Ain't never touched her, I bet a liberty-bird. But if You did the sending, You sent just me, so she's *my* job, an' I'll do her! But I wish You'd help me, or send me help, O God. It's an awful job to tackle all alone, for I'm going to be scared stiff if she gets sick. I can tell by how I felt when I thought she was gone. So if You sent me God, it's up to You to help me. Come on now! If You see the sparrows when they fall, You jest good naturedly ought to see Lily Peaches, 'cause she's always been down, and she can't ever get up, unless we can help her. Help me all You can O God, and send me help to help her all I can, 'cause she can use all the help she can get, and then some! Amen!"

Mickey took one of Peaches' hands in his.

"I ain't the time now, but to-night I got to cut your nails and clean them, then I guess you'll do to start on," he said as he squeezed the hand. "Lily! Lily Peaches, wake up! It's morning now. I got to go out with the papers to earn supper to-night. Wake up! I must wash you and feed you 'fore I go."

Peaches opened her eyes, drawing back startled.

"Easy now!" cautioned Mickey. "Easy now! Don't be scared. Nobody can 'get' you here! What you want for breakfast, Flowersy-girl? Little Lily white."

An adorable smile illumined the tiny face at the first kindly awakening it ever had known.

"*You* won't let them 'get' me, will you?" she triumphed.

"You know it!" he answered conclusively. "Now I'll wash your face, cook your breakfast, and fix you at the window where maybe you can see birds going across. Think of that, Lily! Birds!"

"My name's Peaches!" said the child.

"So 'tis!" said Mickey. "But since you arrived to such bettered conditions, you got to be a lady of fashion. Now Peaches, every single kid in the Park is named *two* names, these days. Fellow can't have a foot race for falling over Mary Elizabeths, and Louisa Ellens. I can't do so much just to start on, 'cause I can't earn the boodle; fast as I get it, you're going to line up; but nachally, just at starting you must begin on the things that are not expensive. Now names don't cost anything, so I can be giving you six if I like, and you are a lily, so right now I'm naming you Lily, but two's the style; keep your Peaches, if it suits you. Lily just flies out of my mouth when I look at you."

This was wonderful. No cursing! No beating! No wailing over a lame-back brat to feed. Mickey *liked* to give her breakfast! Mickey named her for the wonderful flower like granny had picked up before a church one day, a few weeks ago and in a rare sober moment had carried to her. Mickey had made her feel clean, so rested, and so fresh she wanted to roll over the bed. With child impulse she put up her arms. Mickey stooped to them.

"You goin' to have two names too," she said. "You gotter be fash'nable. I ist love you for everythin', washin', an' breakfast, an' the bed, an' winder, an' off the floor; oh I just love you *sick* for the winder, an' off the floor. You going to be"—she paused in a deep study to think of a word anywhere nearly adequate, then ended in a burst that was her best emanation—"lovest! Mickey-lovest!"

She hugged him closely, then lifted her chin and pursed her lips. Mickey pulled back, a dull colour in his face.

"Now nix on the mushing!" he said. "I'll stand for a hug once a day, but nix on the smear!"

"You'd let a dog," she whimpered. "I ain't kissed nothin' since granny sold the doll a lady gave me the time we went to the doctor's, an' took the money to get drunk on, an' beat me more'n I needed for a change, 'cause I cried for it. I think you might!"

"Aw well, go on then, if you're going to bawl," said Mickey, "but put it there!"

He stepped as far back as he could, leaned over, and swept the hair from his forehead, which he brought in range of her lips. He had to brace himself to keep from flinching at their cold touch and straightened in relief.

"Now that's over!" he said briskly. "I'll wash you, and get your breakfast."

"You do a lot of washin', don't you?" inquired Peaches.

"You want the sleep out of your eyes," coaxed Mickey.

He brought the basin and a cloth, washing the child's face and hands gently as was in his power.

"Flowersy-girl," he said, "if you'd looked last night like you do this morning, I'd never tackled getting you here in the world. I'd thought you'd break sure."

"G'wan kid," she said. "I can stand a lot. I been knocked round somepin awful. She dragged me by one hand or the hair when she was tight, and threw me in a corner an' took the"—Peaches glanced over the bed, refusing to call her former estate by the same name—"took the *place* herself. You ain't hurting me. You can jerk me a lot."

"I guess you've been jerked enough, Lily Peaches," he said. "I guess jerkin' ain't going to help your back any. I think we better be easy with it 'til we lay up the money to Carrel it. He put different legs on a dog, course he can put a new back on you."

"Dogs doesn't count only with rich folks 'at rides 'em, an' feeds 'em cake; but where'll you find 'nother girl 'at ull spare her back for me, Mickey-lovest?" asked Peaches.

"Gee, Lily!" he cried. "I didn't *think* of that—I wish I hadn't promised you. Course he could *change* the backs, but where'd I get one. I'll just have to let him take mine."

"I don't want no boy's back!" flashed Peaches. "I won't go out an' sell papers, an' wash you, an' feed you, an' let you stay here in this nice bed. I don't want no new back, grand like it is here. I won't have no dog's back, even. I won't have no back!"

"Course I couldn't let you work and take care of me, Lily," he said. "Course I couldn't! I was just thinking what I *could* do. I'll write a letter and ask the Carrel man if a dog's back would do. I could get one your size at the pound, maybe."

Peaches arose at him with hands set like claws.

"You fool!" she shrieked. "You big damn fool! '*A dog's back!*' I won't! You try it an' I'll scratch your eyes out! You stop right now on backs an' go hell-bent an' get my breakfast! I'm hungry! I like my back! I will have it! You——"

Mickey snatched his pillow from the floor, using it to press the child against hers. Then he slipped it down a trifle at one corner and spoke:

"Now you cut that out, Miss Chicken, right off!" he said sternly. "I wouldn't take no tantrums from a dog, so I won't from you. You'll make your back worse acting like that, than beating would make it, and 'sides, if you're going to live with me, you must be a lady. No lady says such words as you used, and neither does no gentleman, 'cause I don't myself. Now you'll either say, 'Mickey, please get me my breakfast,' and I'll get you one with a big surprise, or you'll lay here alone and hungry 'til I come back to-night. And it'll be a whole day, see?"

"'F I wasn't a pore crippled kid, you wouldn't say that to me," she wailed.

"And if you wasn't 'a poor crippled kid,' you wouldn't say swearin's to me," said Mickey, "'cause you know I'd lick the stuffin' out of you, and if you could see yourself, you'd know that you need stuffin' in, more than you need it out. I'm 'mazed at you! Forget that you ever heard such stuff, and be a nice lady, won't you? My time's getting short and I got to go, or the other kids will sell to my paper men, then we'll have no supper. Now you say, 'Mickey, please get my breakfast,' like a lady, or you won't get a bite."

"'Mickey, please get my breakfast,'" she imitated.

Mickey advanced threateningly with the pillow.

"Won't do!" he said. "That ain't like no lady! That's like *me*. You'll say it like *yourself*, or you won't get it."

She closed her lips, burying her face in her own pillow.

"All right," said Mickey. "Then I'll get my own. If you don't want any, I'll have twice as much."

He laid the pillow on the foot of the bed, saying politely: "'Scuse me, Lily, till I get *me* a bottle of milk."

Soon he returned and with his first glimpse of the bed stood aghast. It was empty. His eyes searched the room. His pallet on the floor outlined a tiny form. A dismayed half smile flashed over his face. He took a step toward her, and then turned, getting out a cloth he had not used since being alone. Near the bed he set the table and laid a plate, knife, fork and spoon. Because he was watching Peaches he soon discovered she was peeking out at him, so he paid strict attention to the burner he was lighting.

Then he sliced bread, put on a toaster, set the milk on the table, broke an egg in a saucer, and turned the toast. Soon the odours filled the room, also a pitiful sound. Mickey knew Peaches must have hurt herself sliding from the bed, although her arms were strong for the remainder of her body. She had no way to reach his pallet but to roll across the floor. She might have bruised herself badly. He was amazed, disgusted, yet compassionate. He went to her and turned back the comfort.

"You must be speaking a little louder, Lily," he said gently. "I wasn't quite hearing you."

Only muffled sobbing. Mickey dropped the cover.

"I want my breakfast," said a very small voice.

"You mean, 'Mickey, please *get* my breakfast,' Flowersy-girl," he corrected gently.

"Oh I hurt myself so!" Peaches wailed. "Oh Mickey, I fell an' broke my back clear in two. 'Tain't like rollin' off my rags; oh Mickey, it's so *far* to the floor, from your bed! Oh Mickey, even another girl's back, or yours, or a dog's, or anybody's wouldn't fix it now. It'll hurt for days. Mickey, why did I ever? Oh what made me? Mickey-lovest, please, please put me back on the nice fine bed, an' do please give me some of that bread."

Mickey lifted her, crooning incoherent things. He wiped her face and hands, combed her hair, and pushed the table against the bed. He broke toast in a glass and poured milk over it. Then he cooked the egg and gave her that, keeping only half the milk and one slice of bread. He made a sandwich of more bread, and the cheese, put a banana with it, set a cup of water in reach, and told her that was her lunch; to eat it when the noon whistles blew. Then he laid all the picture books he had on the back of the bed, put the money for his papers in his pocket, and locking her in, ran down Sunrise Alley fast as he could.

He was one hour late. He had missed two regular customers. They must be made up and more. Light, air, cleanliness, and kindness would increase Peaches' appetite, which seemed big now for the size of her body. Mickey's face was very sober when he allowed himself to think of his undertaking. How would he make it? He had her now, he simply must succeed. The day was half over before Mickey began to laugh for no apparent reason. He had realized that she had not said what he had required of her, after all.

"Gee, I'm up against it," said Mickey. "I didn't s'pose she'd act like that! I thought she'd keep on being like when she woke up. I never behaved like that."

Then in swift remorse: "But I had the finest mother a fellow ever had to tell me, while she ain't had any one, and only got me now, so I'll have to tell her; course I can't do everything at once. So far as that goes, she didn't do any worse than the millyingaires' kids in the park who roll themselves in the dirt, bump their own heads, and scream and fight. I guess my kid's no worse than other people's. I can train her like mother did me; then we'll be enough alike we can live together, and even when she was the worst, I liked her. I liked her cartloads."

So Mickey shouldered the duties of paternity, and began thinking for his child, his little, neglected, bad, sick child. His wits and feet always had been nimble; that day he excelled himself. Anxiety as to how much he must carry home at night to replace what he had spent in moving Peaches to his room, three extra meals to provide before to-morrow night, something to interest her through the long day: it was a contract, surely! Mickey faced it gravely, but he did not flinch. He did not know how it was to be done, but he did know it must be done. "*Get*" her they should not. Whatever it had been his mother had feared for him, nameless though the horror was, from *that* he must save Lily. Mickey had thought it must be careless nurses or lack of love. Yesterday's papers had said there were some children at one of the Homes, no one ever visited; they were sick for love; would not some kind people come to see them? It must have been *that* she feared. He could not possibly know it was the stigma of having been a charity child she had been combating with all her power.

They had not "got" him; they must not "get" his Lily; yet stirrings in Mickey's brain told him he was not going to be sufficient, alone. There were emergencies he did not know how to manage. He must have help. Mickey revolved the problem in his worried head without reaching a solution. His necessity drove him. He darted, dodged and took chances. Far down the street he selected his victim and studied his method of assault as he approached; for Mickey did victimize people that day. He sold them papers when they did not want them. He bettered that and sold them papers when they had them.

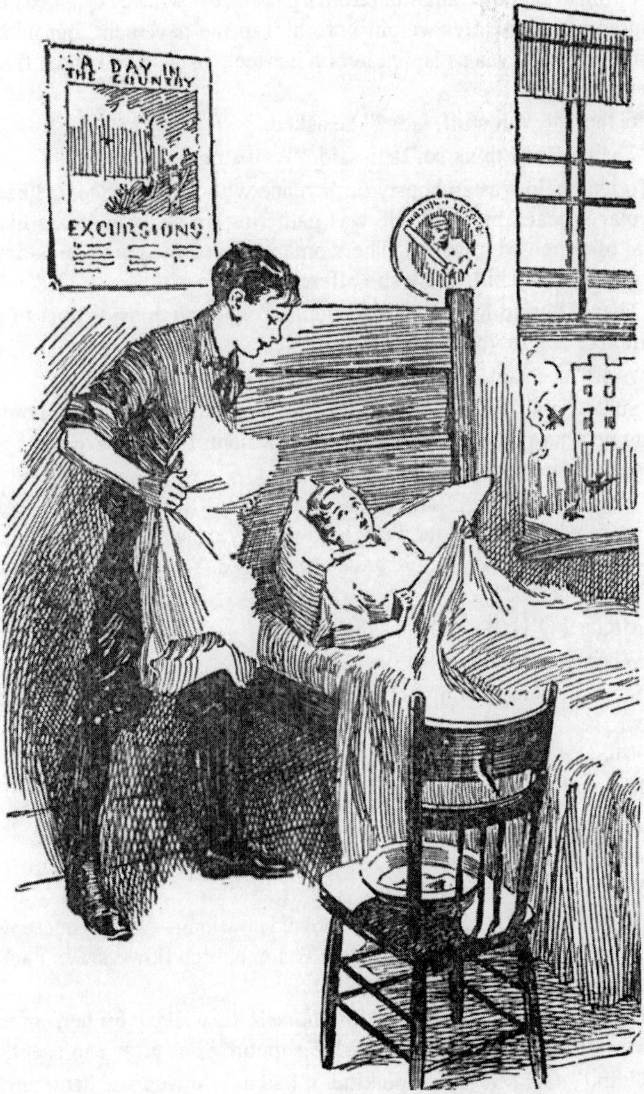

"Now you cut that out, Miss Chicken, right off!" said Mickey.

He snatched up lost papers, smoothed and sold them over. Every gay picture or broken toy dropped from an automobile he caught up and pocketed for her.

A woman stumbled alighting from a passing car. Mickey dropped his papers and sprang forward. Her weight bore him to the pavement, but he kept her from falling, and even as he felt her on her feet, he snatched under the wheels for her purse.

"Is that all your stuff, lady?" he asked.

"Thank you! I think so," she said. "Wait a minute!"

To lend help was an hourly occurrence with Mickey. *She* had been most particular to teach him that. He was gathering up and smoothing his papers several of which were soiled. The woman opened the purse he had rescued, taking therefrom a bill which she offered him.

"Thanks!" said Mickey. "My shoulder is worth considerable to me; but nothing like that to you, lady!"

"Well!" she said. "Are you refusing the money?"

"Sure!" said Mickey. "I ain't a beggar! Just a balance on my shoulder and picking up your purse ain't worth an endowment. I'll take five cents each for three soiled papers, if you say so."

"You amazing boy!" said the woman. "Don't you understand that if you hadn't offered your shoulder, I might now be lying senseless? You saved me a hard fall, while my dress would have been ruined. You step over here a minute. What's your name?"

"Michael O'Halloran," was the answer.

"Where do you live?"

"Sunrise Alley. It's miles on the cars, then some more walking," explained Mickey.

"Whom do you live with?"

"Myself," said Mickey.

"Alone?"

"All but Peaches," said Mickey. "Lily Peaches."

"Who is Lily Peaches?"

"She's about so long"—Mickey showed how long—"and about so wide"—he showed how wide—"and white like Easter church flowers. Her back's bad. I'm her governor; she's my child."

"If you won't take the money for yourself, then take it for her," offered the woman. "If you have a little sick girl to support, you surely can use it."

"Umm!" said Mickey. "You kind of ball a fellow up and hang him on the ropes. Honest you do, lady! I can take care of myself. I know I can, 'cause I've done it three years, but I don't know how I'm goin' to make it with Lily, for she needs a lot. She may get sick any day, so I ain't sure how I'm going to manage well with her."

"How long have you taken care of her?"

"Since last night," explained Mickey.

"Oh! How old is she?" Questions seemed endless.

"I don't know," answered Mickey. "Her granny died and left her lying on rags in a garret. I found her screeching, so I took her to my castle and washed her, and fed her. You should see her now."

"I believe I should!" said the woman. "Let's go at once. You know Michael, you can't care for a *girl*. I'll put her in one of the beautiful Children's Homes—"

"Now nix on the Children's Homes, fair lady!" he cried angrily. "I guess you'll *find* her, 'fore you take her! I found her first, and she's *mine!* I guess you'll *find* her, 'fore you take her to a Children's Home, where the doctors slice up the poor kids for practice so they'll know how to get money for doing it to the rich ones. I've *annexed* Lily Peaches, and you don't '*get*' her! See?"

"I see," said the woman. "But you're mistaken——"

"'Scuse crossing your wire, but I don't think I *am*," said Mickey. "The only way you can know, is to have been there yourself. I don't think you got that kind of a start, or want it for kids of your own. My mother killed herself to keep me out of it, and if it had been so grand, she'd *wanted* me there. Nix on the Orphings' Home talk. Lily ain't going to be raised in droves, nor flocks, nor herds! See? Lily's going to have a home of her own, and a man to take care of her by herself."

Mickey backed away, swallowing a big lump in his throat, and blinking down angry tears.

"'Smorning," he said, "I asked God to help me, and for a minute I was so glad, 'cause I thought He'd helped by sending *you*, so you could tell me how to do; but if God can't beat *you*, I can get along by myself."

"You *can't* take care of a girl by yourself," she insisted. "The *law* won't allow you."

"Oh can't I?" scoffed Mickey. "Well you're mistaken, 'cause I am! And getting along bully! You ought to seen her last night, and then this morning. Next time I yell for help, I won't ask to have anybody sent, I'll ask Him to help me save our souls, myself. Ever see that big, white, wonderful Jesus at the Cathedral door, ma'am, holding the little child in His arms so loving? I don't s'pose He stopped to ask whether it was a girl, or a boy, 'fore He took it up; He just opened his arms to the first *child* that *needed* Him. And if I remember right, He didn't say: 'Suffer little children to be sent to Orphings' Homes.' Mammy never read it to me *that* way. It was suffer them to come to 'Me,' and be took up, and held tender. See? Nix on the Orphings' Home people. They ain't in my class. Beaucheous lady, adoo! Farewell! I depart!"

Mickey wheeled, vanishing. It was a wonderful exhibition of curves, leaps, and darts. He paused for breath when he felt safe.

"So that's the dope!" he marvelled. "I can't take care of a girl? Going to take her away from me? I'd like to know *why?* Men all the time take care of women. I see boys taking care of girls I know their mothers left with them, every day—I'd like to know *why*. Mother said I was to take care of *her*. She said that's what men were made *for*. 'Cause *he didn't* take care of her, was why she was glad my father was *dead*. I guess I know what I'm doing! But I've learned something! Nix on the easy talk after this; and telling anybody you meet all you know. Shut mouth from now on. 'What's your name, little boy?' 'Andrew Carnegie.' 'Where d'you live?' 'Castle on the Hudson!' A mouth just tight shut about Lily, after this! And nix on the Swell Dames! Next one can bust her crust for all I care! I won't touch her!"

On the instant, precisely that thing occurred, at Mickey's very feet. With his lips not yet closed, he knelt to shove his papers under a woman's head, then went racing up the stone steps she had rolled down, his quick eye catching and avoiding the bit of fruit on which she had slipped. He returned in a second with help. As the porter lifted the inert body, Mickey slid his hands under her head, and advised: "Keep her straight!" Into one of the big hospitals he helped carry a blue and white clad nurse, on and on, up elevators and into a white porcelain room where they laid her on a glass table. Mickey watched with frightened eyes. Doctors and nurses came running. He stood waiting for his papers. He was rather sick, yet he remembered he had five there he must sell.

"Better clear out of here now!" suggested a surgeon.

"My papers!" said Mickey. "She fell right cross my feet. I slid them under, to make her head more pillowlike on the stones. Maybe I can sell some of them."

The surgeon motioned to a nurse at the door.

"Take this youngster to the office and pay him for the papers he has spoiled," he ordered.

"Will she—is she going to——?" wavered Mickey.

"I'm not sure," said the surgeon. "From the bleeding probably concussion; but she will live. Do you know how she came to fall?"

"There was a smear of something on the steps she didn't see," explained Mickey.

"Thank you! Go with the nurse," said the surgeon. Then to an attendant: "Take Miss Alden's number, and see to her case. She was going after something."

Mickey turned back. "Paper, maybe," he suggested, pointing to her closed hand. The surgeon opened it and found a nickel. He handed it to Mickey. "If you have a clean one left, let this nurse take it to Miss Alden's case, and say she has been assigned other duty. See to sending a substitute at once."

Every paper proved to be marked.

"I can bring you a fresh one in a second, lady," offered Mickey. "I got the money."

"All right," she said. "Wait with it in the office and then I'll pay you."

"I'm sent for a paper. I'm to be let in as soon as I get it," announced Mickey to the porter. "I ain't taking chances of being turned down," he said to himself, as he stopped a second to clean the step.

He returned and was waiting when the nurse came. She was young and fair faced; her hair was golden, and as she paid Mickey for his papers he wondered how soon he could have Lily looking like her. He took one long survey as he pocketed the money, thinking he would rush home at once; but he wanted to fix in his mind how Lily must appear, to be right, for he thought a nurse in the hospital would be right.

The nurse knew she was beautiful, and to her Mickey's long look was tribute, male tribute; a small male indeed, but such a winning one; so she took the occasion to be her loveliest, and smile her most attractive smile. Mickey surrendered. He thought she was like an angel, that made him think of Heaven, Heaven made him think of God, God made him think of his call for help that morning, the call made him think of the answer, the beautiful woman before him made him think that possibly *she* might be the answer instead of the other one. He rather doubted it, but it might be a chance. Mickey was alert for chances for Peaches, so he smiled again, then he asked: "Are you in such an awful hurry?"

"I think we owe you more than merely paying for your papers," she said. "What is it?"

Again Mickey showed how long and how wide Lily was. "And with hair like yours, and eyes and cheeks that would be, if she had her chance, and nobody to give her that chance but just me," he said. "Me and Lily are all each other's got," he explained hastily. "We're *home* folks. We're a family. We don't want no bunching in corps and squads. We're nix on the Orphings' Home business; but you *must know*, ma'am—would you, oh would you tell me just how I should be taking care of her? I'm doing everything like my mother did to me; but I was well and strong. Maybe Lily, being a girl, should have things different. A-body so beautiful as you, would tell me, wouldn't you?"

Then a miracle happened. The nurse, so clean she smelled like a drug store, so lovely she shone as a sunrise, laid an arm across Mickey's shoulders. "You come with me," she said. She went to a little room, and all alone she asked Mickey questions; with his eyes straight on hers, he answered. She told him surely he could take care of Lily. She explained how. She rang for a basket and packed it full of things he must have, showing him how to use them. She told him to come each Saturday at four o'clock, as she was going off duty, and tell her how he was getting along. She gave him a thermometer, and told him how to learn if the child had fever. She told him about food, and she put in an ointment, instructing him to rub the little back with it, so the bed would not be so tiresome. She showed him how to arrange the pillows; when he left, the tears were rolling down Mickey's cheeks. Both of them were so touched she laid her arm across his shoulder again and went as far as the elevator, while a passport to her at any time was in his pocket.

"I 'spect other folks tell you you are beautiful like flowers, or music, or colours," said Mickey in farewell, "but you look like a window in Heaven to me, and I can see right through you to God and all the beautiful angels;

but what gets me is why the other one had to bust her crust, to make you come true!"

The nurse was laughing and wiping her eyes at the same time. Mickey gripped the basket until his hands were stiff as he sped homeward at least two hours early and happy about it. At the last grocery he remembered every word and bought bread, milk, and fruit with care "for a sick lady" he explained, so the grocer, who knew him, used care. Triumphing Mickey climbed the stairs. He paused a second in deep thought at the foot of the last flight, then ascended whistling to let Peaches know that he was coming, then on his threshold recited:

"One't a little kid named Lily,
Was so sweet she'd knock you silly,
Yellow hair in millying curls,
Beat a mile all other girls."

She was on his bed; she was on his pillow; she had been lonely; both arms were stretched toward him.

"Mickey, hurry!" she cried. "Mickey, lemme hold you 'til I'm sure! Mickey, all day I didn't hardly durst breathe, fear the door'd open an' they'd '*get*' me. Oh Mickey, you won't let them, will you?"

Mickey dropped his bundles and ran to the bed. This time he did not shrink from her wavering clasp. It was delight to come home to something alive, something that belonged to him, something to share with, something to work and think for, something that depended upon him.

"Now nix on the scare talk," he comforted. "Forget it! I've lived here three years alone, and not a single time has anybody come to 'get' me, so they won't you. There's only one thing can happen us. If I get sick or spend too much on eating, and don't pay the rent, the man that owns this building will fire us out. If we, *if we*" Mickey repeated impressively, "pay our rent regular, in advance, nobody will *ever* come, not *ever*, so don't worry."

"Then what's all them bundles?" fretted Peaches. "You ortn't a-got so much. You'll never get the *next* rent paid! They'll 'get' me sure."

"Now throttle your engine," advised Mickey. "Stop your car! Smash down on the brakes! They are things the city you reside in furnishes its taxpayers, or something like that. I pay my rent, so this is my *share*, and it's things for you: to make you comfortable. Which are you worst—tiredest, or hungriest, or hottest?"

"I don't know," she said.

"Then I'll make a clean get-a-way," said Mickey. "Washing is cooling; and it freshens you up a lot."

So Mickey brought his basin again, bathing the tired child gently as any woman could have done it.

"See what I got!" he cried as he opened bundles and explained. "I'm going to see if you have fever."

Peaches rebelled at the thermometer.

"Now come on in," urged Mickey. "Slide straight home to your base! If I'm going to take care of you, I'm going to right. You can't lay here eating wrong things if you have *fever*. No-sir-ee! You don't get to see in any more of these bundles, nor any supper, nor talked to any more, 'til you put this little glass thing under your tongue and hold it there just this way"—Mickey showed how—"three minutes by the clock, then I'll know what to do with you next. I'll sit beside you, and hold your hands, and tell you about the pretty lady that sent it."

Mickey wiped the thermometer on the sheet, then presented it. Peaches took one long look at him and opened her lips. Mickey inserted the tube, set the clock in sight, and taking both her hands he held them closely and talked as fast as he could to keep her from using them. He had not half finished the day when the time was up. If he had done it right, Peaches had very little, if any, fever.

"Now turn over so I can rub your back to make it all nice and rested," he said. "And then I'll get supper."

"I don't want my back rubbed," she protested. "My back's all right now."

"Nothing to do with going to have it rubbed," said Mickey. "It would be a silly girl who would have a back that wouldn't walk, and then wouldn't even try having it doctored, so that it would get better. Just try Lily, and if it doesn't *help*, I won't do it any more."

Peaches took another long look at Mickey, questioning in nature, then turned her back to him.

"Gosh, kid! Your back looks just like horses' going to the fertilizer plant," he said.

"Ain't that swearin's?" asked Peaches promptly.

"First-cousin," answered Mickey. "'Scuse me Lily. If you could see your back, you'd 'scuse worse than that."

"Feelin' ull do fer me," said Peaches. "I live wid it." "Honest kid, I'm scared to touch you," he wavered.

"Aw g'wan!" said Peaches. "I ain't goin' screechin' even if you hurt awful, an' you touch like a sparrer lookin' for crumbs. Mickey, can we put out a few?"

"For the sparrows? Sure!" cried Mickey. "They're the ones that God sees especial when they fall. Sure! Put out some in a minute. Still now!"

Mickey poured on ointment, then began softly rubbing it into the dreadful back. His face was drawn with anxiety and filled with horror. He was afraid, but the nurse said this he should do, while Mickey's first lesson had been implicit obedience. So he rubbed gently as he was fearful; when Peaches made no complaint, a little stronger, and a little stronger, until he was tired. Then he covered her, telling her to lie on it, and see how it felt. Peaches looked at him with wondering eyes.

"Mickey," she said, "nothin" in all my life ever felt like that, an' the nice cool washin' you do. Mickey-lovest, nex' time I act mean 'bout what you want to do to me, slap me good, an' hold me, an' go on an' *do* it!"

"Now nix on the beating," said Mickey. "I never had any from my mother; but the kids who lost sales to me took my nickels, and give me plenty. You ought to know, Lily, that I'm trying hard as I can to make you feel good; and to take care of you. What I want to do, I think will make you *better*, so I'm just nachally going to *do* it, 'cause you're mine, and you got to do what I say. But I won't say anything that'll hurt you and make you worse. If you must take time to think new things over, I can wait; but I can't hit you Lily, you're too little, too sick, and I like you too well. I wish you'd be a lady! I wish you wouldn't ever be bad again!"

"Hoh I feel so good!" Peaches stretched like a kitten. "Mickey, bet I can walk 'fore long if you do that often! Mickey, I just love you, an' *love* you. Mickey, say that at the door over again."

"What?" queried Mickey.

"'One't a little kid named Lily,'" prompted Peaches.

Mickey laughed and obeyed.

Neatly he put away all that had been supplied him; before lighting the burner he gave Lily a drink of milk and tried arranging both pillows to prop her up as he had been shown. When the water boiled he dropped in two bouillon cubes the nurse had given him, and set out some crackers he had bought. He put the milk in two cups, and when he cut the bread, he carefully collected every crumb, putting it on the sill in the hope that a bird might come. The thieving sparrows, used to watching windows and stealing from stores set out to cool, were soon there. Peaches, to whom anything with feathers was a bird, was filled with joy. The odour of the broth was delicious. Mickey danced, turned handsprings, and made the funniest remarks. Then he fixed the bowl on a paper, broke the crackers in her broth, growing unspeakably happy at her delight as she tasted it.

"Every Saturday you get a box of that from the Nurse Lady," he boasted. "Pretty soon you'll be so fat I can't carry you and so well you can have supper ready when I come, then we can——"Mickey stopped short. He had started to say, "go to the parks," but if other ladies were like the first one he had talked with, and if, as she said, the law would not let him keep Peaches, he had better not try to take her where people would see her.

"Can what?" asked Peaches.

"Have the most fun!" explained Mickey. "We can sit in the window to see the sky and birds; you can have the shears and cut pictures from the papers I'll bring you, while I'll read all my story books to you. I got three that She gave me for Christmas presents, so I could learn to read them——"

"Mickey could I ever learn to read them?"

"Sure!" cried Mickey. "Surest thing you know! You are awful smart, Lily. You can learn in no time, and then you can read while I'm gone, so it won't seem long. I'll teach you. Mother taught me. I can read the papers I sell. Honest I can. I often pick up torn ones I can bring to you. It's lots of fun to know what's going on. I sell many more by being able to tell what's in them than kids who can't read. I look all over the front page and make up a spiel on the cars. I always fold my papers neat and keep them clean. To-day it was like this: 'Here's your nice, clean, morning paper! Sterilized! Deodorized! Vulcanized!'"

"Mickey what does that mean?" asked Peaches.

"Now you see how it comes in!" said Mickey. "If you could read the papers, you'd *know*. 'Sterilized,' is what they do to the milk in hot weather to save the slum kids. That's us, Lily. 'Deodorized,' is taking the bad smell out of things. 'Vulcanized,' is something they do to stiffen things. I guess it's what your back needs."

"Is all them things done to the papers?" asked Peaches.

"Well, not *all* of them," laughed Mickey, "but they are starting in on *some* of them, and all would be a good thing. The other kids who can't read don't know those words, so I study them out and use them; it catches the crowd for they laugh, and then pay me for making them. See? This world down on the streets is in such a mix a laugh is the scarcest thing there is; so they *pay* for it. No grouchy, sad-cat-working-on-your-sympathy kid sells many. I can beat one with a laugh every inning."

"What's 'inning,' Mickey?" came the next question.

"Playin' a side at a ball game. Now Ty Cobb——"

"Go on with what you say about the papers," interrupted Peaches.

"All right!" said Mickey. "'Here's your nice, clean morning paper! Sterilized! Deodorized! Vulcanized! I *like* to sell them. You *like* to buy them! *Sometimes* I sell them! Sometimes I *don't!* Latest war news! Japan takes England! England takes France! France takes Germany! Germany takes Belgium! Belgium takes the cake! Here's your paper! Nice clean paper! Rush this way! Change your change for a paper! Yes, I *like* to sell them——' and on and on that way all day, 'til they're gone and every one I pick up and smooth out is gone, and if they're torn and dirty, I carry them back on the cars and sell them for pennies to the poor folks walking home."

"Mickey, will we be slum kids always?" she asked.

"Not on your tin type!" cried Mickey.

"If this is slum kids, I like it!" protested Peaches.

"Well, Sunrise Alley ain't so slummy as where you was, Lily," explained the boy.

"This is grand," said Peaches "Fine an' grand! No lady needn't have better!"

"She wouldn't say so," said Mickey. "But Lily, you got something most of the millyingaire ladies hasn't."

"What Mickey?" she asked interestedly.

"One man all to yourself, who will do what you want, if you ask pretty, and he ain't going to drag you 'round and make you do things you don't like to, and hit you, and swear at you, and get drunk. Gee, I bet the worst you ever had didn't hurt more than I've seen some of the swell dames hurt sometimes. It'd make you sick Lily."

"I guess 'at it would," said the girl, "'cause granny told me the same thing. Lots of times she said 'at she couldn't see so much in bein' rich if you had to be treated like she saw rich ladies. She said all they got out of it was nice dresses an' struttin' when their men wasn't 'round; nelse the money was theirn, an' nen they made the men pay. She said it was 'bout half and half."

"So 'tis!" cried Mickey. "Tell you Lily, don't let's ever *be* rich! Let's just have enough."

"Mickey, what is 'enough?'" asked Peaches.

"Why plenty, but not too much!" explained Mickey judicially. "Not enough to fight over! Just enough to be comfortable."

"Mickey, I'm comf'rable as nangel now."

"Gee, I'm glad, Lily," said Mickey in deep satisfaction. "Maybe He heard my S.O.S. after all, and you just being *comfortable* is the answer."

CHAPTER IV

"Bearer of Morning"

"Douglas," called Leslie over the telephone, "I have developed nerves."

"Why?" inquired he.

"Dad has just come in with a pair of waist-high boots, and a scalping knife, I think," answered Leslie. "Are you going to bring a blanket and a war bonnet?"

"The blanket, I can; the bonnet, I might," said Douglas.

"How early will you be ready?" she asked.

"Whenever you say," he replied.

"Five?" she queried.

"Very well!" he answered. "And Leslie, I would suggest a sweater, short stout skirts, and heavy gloves. Do you know if you are susceptible to poison vines?"

"I have handled anything wild as I pleased all my life," she said. "I am sure there is no danger from that source; but Douglas, did you ever hear of, or see, a massasauga?"

"You are perfectly safe on that score," he said. "I am going along especially to take care of you."

"All right, then I won't be afraid of snakes," she said.

"I have waders, too," he said, "and I'm going into the swamp with you. Wherever you wish to go, I will precede you and test the footing."

"Very well! I have lingered on the borders long enough. To-morrow will be my initiation. By night I'll have learned the state of my artistic ability with natural resources, and I'll know whether the heart of the swamp is the loveliest sight I ever have seen, and I will have proved how I 'line up' with a squaw-woman."

"Leslie, I'm now reading a most interesting human document," said Douglas, "and in it I have reached the place where Indians in the heart of terrific winter killed and heaped up a pile of deer in early day in Minnesota, then went to camp rejoicing, while their squaws were left to walk twenty-eight miles and each carry back on her shoulder a deer frozen stiff. Leslie, you don't line up! You are not expected to."

"Do you believe that, Douglas?" asked the girl.

"It's history dear, not fiction," he answered.

"Douglas!" she warned.

"Leslie, I beg your pardon! That was a slip!" cried he.

"Oh!" she breathed.

"Leslie, will you do something for me?" he questioned.

"What?" she retorted.

"Listen with one ear, stop the other, and tell me what you hear," he ordered.

"Yes," she said.

"Did you hear, Leslie?" he asked anxiously.

"I heard something, I don't know what," she answered.

"Can you describe it, Leslie?"

"Just a rushing, beating sound! What is it Douglas?"

"My heart, Leslie, sending to you each throbbing stroke of my manhood pouring out its love for you."

"Oh-h-h!" cried the astonished girl.

"Will you listen again, Leslie?" begged the man.

"No!" she said.

"You don't want to hear what my heart has to say to you?" he asked.

"Not over a wire! Not so far away!" she panted.

"Then I'll shorten the distance. I'm coming, Leslie!"

"What shall I do?" she gasped. She stared around her, trying to decide whether she should follow her impulse to hide, when her father entered the room.

"Daddy," she cried, "if you want to be nice to me, go away a little while. Go somewhere a few minutes and stay until I call you."

"Leslie, what's the matter?" he asked.

"I've been talking to Douglas, and Daddy, he's coming like a charging Highland trooper. Daddy, I heard him drop the receiver and start. Please, please go away a minute. Even the dearest father in the world can't do anything now! We must settle this ourselves."

"I'm not to be allowed a word?" he protested.

"Daddy, you've had two years! If you know anything to say against Douglas and haven't said it in all that time, why should you begin now? You couldn't help knowing! Daddy, do go! There he is! I hear him!"

Mr. Winton took his daughter in his arms, kissed her tenderly, and left the room. A second later Douglas Bruce entered. Rushing to Leslie he caught her to his breast roughly, while with a strong hand he pressed her ear against his heart.

"Now you listen, my girl!" he cried. "You listen at close range."

Leslie remained quiet a long second. Then she lifted her face, adorable, misty eyed and tenderly smiling.

"Douglas, I never listened to a heart before! How do I know what it is saying? I can't tell whether it is talking about me or protesting against the way you've been rushing around!" "No levity, my lady," he said grimly. "This is serious business. You listen while I interpret. I love you, Leslie! Every beat, every stroke, love for you. I claim you! My mate! My wife! I want you!"

He held her from him, looking into her eyes.

"Now Leslie, the answer!" he cried. "May I listen to it or will you tell me? *Is* there any answer? What is *your* heart saying? May I hear or will you tell me?"

"I want to tell you!" said the girl. "I love you, Douglas! Every beat, every stroke, love for you."

Early the next morning they inspected their equipment carefully, then drove north to the tamarack swamp, where they arranged that Leslie and Douglas were to hunt material, while Mr. Winton and the driver went to the nearest Indian settlement to find the squaw who had made the other basket, and bring her to the swamp.

If you have experienced the same emotions you will know how Douglas and Leslie felt when hand in hand they entered the swamp on a perfect morning in late May. If you have not, mere words are inadequate.

Through fern and brake head high, through sumac, willow, elder, buttonbush, gold-yellow and blood-red osiers, past northern holly, over spongy moss carpet of palest silvery green up-piled for ages, over red-veined pitcher plants spilling their fullness, among scraggy, odorous tamaracks, beneath which cranberries and rosemary were blooming; through ethereal pale mists of dawn, in their ears lark songs of morning from the fields, hermit thrushes in the swamp, bell birds tolling molten notes, in a minor strain a swelling chorus of sparrows, titmice, warblers, vireos, went two strong, healthy young people newly promised for "better or worse." They could only look, stammer, flush, and utter broken exclamations, all about "better." They could not remotely conceive that life might serve them the cruel trick of "worse."

Leslie sank to her knees. Douglas lifted her up, set her on the firmest location he could see, adoring her with his eyes and reverent touch. Since that first rough grasp as he drew her to him, Leslie had felt positively fragile in his hands. She smiled at him her most beautiful smile when wide-eyed with emotion.

"Douglas, why just now, when you've waited two years?" she asked.

"Wanted a degree of success to offer," he answered.

Leslie disdained the need for success.

"Wanted you to have time to know me as completely as possible."

Leslie intimated that she could learn faster.

"Wanted to have the acknowledged right to put my body between yours and any danger this swamp might have to offer to-day."

"Exactly what I thought!" cried she.

"Wise girl," commented the man.

"Douglas, I must hurry!" said Leslie. "It may take a long time to find the flowers I want, while I've no idea what I shall do for a basket. I saw osiers yellow and red in quantities, but where are the orchids?"

"We must make our way farther in and search," he said.

"Douglas, listen!" breathed Leslie.

"I hear exquisite music," he answered.

"But don't you recognize it?" she cried.

"It does seem familiar, but I am not sufficiently schooled in music——"

The girl began softly to whistle.

"By Jove!" cried the man. "What is that Leslie?"

"Di Provenza, from Traviata," she answered. "But I must stop listening for birds Douglas, when I can scarcely watch for flowers or vines. I have to keep all the time looking to make sure that you are really my man."

"And I, that you are my woman. Leslie, that expression and this location, the fact that you are in competition with a squaw and the Indian talk we have indulged in lately, all conspire to remind me that a few days ago, while I was still a 'searcher' myself, I read a poem called 'Song of the Search' that was the biggest thing of its kind that I have yet found in our language. It was so great that I reread it until I am sure I can do it justice. Listen my 'Bearer of Morning,' my 'Bringer of Song——'"

Douglas stood straight as the tamaracks, his feet sinking in "the little moss," while from his heart he quoted Constance Skinner's wonderful poem:

> "*I descend through the forest alone.*
> *Rose-flushed are the willows, stark and a-quiver,*
> *In the warm sudden grasp of Spring;*
> *Like a woman when her lover has suddenly, swiftly taken her.*
> *I hear the secret rustle of little leaves,*
> *Waiting to be born.*
> *The air is a wind of love*
> *From the wings of eagles mating——*
> *O eagles, my sky is dark with your wings!*
> *The hills and the waters pity me,*
> *The pine-trees reproach me.*
> *The little moss whispers under my feet,*
> *"Son of Earth, Brother,*
> *Why comest thou hither alone?"*
> *Oh, the wolf has his mate on the mountain——*
> *Where art thou, Spring-daughter?*
> *I tremble with love as reeds by the river,*

I burn as the dusk in the red-tented west,
I call thee aloud as the deer calls the doe,
I await thee as hills wait the morning,
I desire thee as eagles the storm;
I yearn to thy breast as night to the sea,
I claim thee as the silence claims the stars.
O Earth, Earth, great Earth,
Mate of God and mother of me,
Say, where is she, the Bearer of Morning,
My Bringer of Song?
Love in me waits to be born,
Where is She, the Woman?

"'Where is she, the Woman?' The answer is 'Here!' 'Bearer of Morning,' 'Bringer of Song,' I adore you!"

"Oh Douglas, how beautiful!" cried Leslie. "My Man, can we think of anything save ourselves to-day? Can we make that basket?"

"It would be a bad start to give up our first undertaking together," he said.

"Of course!" she cried. "We must! We simply must find things. Father may call any minute. Let go my hand and follow behind me. Keep close, Douglas!"

"I should go before to clear the way," he suggested.

"No, I may miss rare flowers if you do," she objected.

"Go slowly, so I can watch before and overhead."

"Yes!" she answered. "There! There, Douglas!"

"Ah! There they are!" he exulted.

"But I can't take them!" she protested.

"Only a few, Leslie. Look before you! See how many there are!" he said.

"Douglas, could there be more wonderful flowers than the moccasins and slippers?" she asked.

"Scarcely more wonderful; there might be more delicate and lovely!"

"Farther! Let us go farther!" she urged.

Her cry closed the man's arms around her.

Then there was a long silence during which they stood on the edge of a small open space breathlessly worshipping, but it was the Almighty they were now adoring. Here the moss lay in a flat carpet, tinted deeper green. Water willow rolled its ragged reddish-tan hoops, with swelling bloom and leaf buds. Overflowing pitcher plants grew in irregular beds, on slender stems, lifting high their flat buds. But scattered in groups here and there, sometimes with massed similar colours, sometimes in clumps and variegated patches, stood the rare, early fringed orchis, some almost white, others pale lavender and again the deeper colour of the moccasins; while everywhere on stems, some a foot high, nodded the exquisite lavender and white showy orchis.

"Count!" he commanded.

Leslie pointed a slender finger indicating each as she spoke: "One, two, three—thirty-two, under the sweep of your arms, Douglas! And more! More by the hundred! Surely if we are careful not to kill them, the Lord won't mind if we take out a few for people to see, will He?"

"He must have made them to be seen!" said Douglas.

"And worshipped!" cried the girl.

"Douglas, why didn't the squaw——?" asked Leslie.

"Maybe she didn't come this far," he said. "Perhaps she knows by experience that these are too fragile to remove. You may not be able to handle them, Leslie."

"I'm going to try," she said. "But first I must make my basket. We'll go back to the osiers to weave it and then come here to fill it. Oh Douglas! Did you ever see such flower perfection in all your life?"

"Only in books! In my home country applied botany is a part of every man's education. I never have seen ragged or fringed orchids growing before. I have read of many fruitless searches for the white ones."

"So have I. They seem to be the rarest. Douglas, look there!"

"There" was a group of purple-lavender, white-lipped bloom, made by years of spreading from one root, until above the rank moss and beneath the dark tamarack branch the picture appeared inconceivably delicate.

"Yes! The most exquisite flowers I ever have seen!"

"And there, Douglas!" She pointed to another group. "Just the shade of the lavender on the toe of the moccasin—and in a great ragged mass! Would any one believe it?"

"Not without seeing it," he said emphatically.

"And there, Douglas! Exactly the colour of the moccasins—see that cluster! There are no words, Douglas!"

"Shall you go farther?" he asked.

"No," she answered. "I'm going back to weave my basket. There is nothing to surpass the orchids in rarity and wondrous beauty."

"Good!" he cried. "I'll go ahead and you follow."

So they returned to the osiers. Leslie pondered deeply a few seconds, then resolutely putting Douglas aside, she began cutting armloads of pale yellow osiers. Finding a suitable place to work, she swiftly and deftly selected perfect, straight evenly coloured ones, cutting them the same length, then binding the tip ends firmly with raffia she had brought to substitute for grass. Then with fine slips she began weaving, gradually spreading the twigs while inwardly giving thanks for the lessons she had taken in basketry. At last she held up a big, pointed, yellow basket.

"Ready!" she said.

"Beautiful!" cried Douglas.

Leslie carefully lined the basket with moss in which the flowers grew, working the heads between the open spaces she had left. She bent three twigs, dividing her basket top in exact thirds. One of these she filled with the whitest, one with stronger, and one with the deepest lavender, placing the tallest plants in the centre so that the outside ones would show completely. Then she lifted by the root exquisite showy orchis, lavender-hooded, white-lipped, the tiniest plants she could select and set them around the edge. She bedded the moss-wrapped roots in the basket and began bordering the rim and entwining the handle with a delicate vine. She looked up at Douglas, her face thrilled with triumph, flushed with exertion, her eyes humid with feeling, while he gazed at her stirred to the depth of his heart with sympathy and the wonder of possession.

"'Bearer of Morning,' you win!" he cried triumphantly. "There is no use going farther. Let me carry that to your father, and he too will say so."

"I have a reason for working out our plan," she said.

"Yes? May I know?" he asked.

"Surely!" she answered. "You remember what you told me about the Minturns. I can't live in a city and not have my feelings harrowed every day, and while I'd like to change everything wrong, I know I can't all of it, so what I can't cope with must be put aside; but this refuses, it is insistent. When you really think of it, that is so *dreadful*, Douglas. If they once felt what we do now, could it *all* go? There must be something left! You mention him oftener than any other one man, so you must admire him deeply; I know her as well as any woman I meet in society, better than most; I had thought of asking them to be the judges. She is interested in music and art; it would please her and be perfectly natural for me to ask her; you are on intimate terms with him from your offices being opposite; there could be no suspicion of any ulterior motive in having them. I don't know that it would accomplish anything, but it would let them know, to begin with, that we consider them friends; so it would be natural for them to come with us; if we can't manage more than that to-day, it will give us ground to try again."

"Splendid!" he said. "A splendid plan! It would let them see that at least our part of the world thinks of them together, and expects them to be friends. Splendid!"

"I have finished," said Leslie.

"I quite agree," answered Douglas. "No one could do better. That is the ultimate beauty of the swamp made manifest. There is the horn! Your father is waiting."

A surprise was also waiting. Mr. Winton had not only found the squaw who brought the first basket, but he had made her understand so thoroughly what was wanted that she had come with him, while at his suggestion she had replaced the moccasin basket as exactly as she could and also made an effort at decoration. She was smiling woodenly when Leslie and Douglas approached, but as Leslie's father glimpsed and cried out over her basket, the squaw frowned, drawing back.

"Where you find 'em?" she demanded.

"In the swamp!" Leslie nodded backward.

The squaw grunted disapprovingly. "Lowry no buy 'em! Sell slipper! Sell moccasin! No sell weed!"

Leslie looked with shining eyes at her father.

"That lies with Lowry," he said. "I'll drive you there and bring you back, and you'll have the ride and the money for your basket. That's all that concerns you. We won't come here to make any more."

The squaw smiled again, so they started to the city. They drove straight to the Winton residence for the slippers. While Mr. Winton and the squaw went to take the baskets to Lowry's and leave Douglas at his office, Leslie in his car went to Mrs. Minturn's.

"Don't think I'm crazy," laughed Leslie, as Mrs. Minturn came down to meet her. "I want to use your exquisite taste and art instinct a few minutes. Please do come with me. We've a question up. You know the wonderful stuff the Indians bring down from the swamps to sell on the streets and to the florists?"

"Indeed yes! I often buy of them in the spring. I love the wild white violets especially. What is it you want?"

"Why you see," said Leslie, looking eagerly at Mrs. Minturn, "you see there are three flower baskets at Lowry's. Douglas Bruce is going to buy me the one I want most for a present, to celebrate a very important occasion, and I can't tell which is most artistic. I want you to decide. Your judgment is so unfailing. Will you come? Only a little spin!"

"Leslie, you aren't by any chance asking me to select your betrothal gift, are you?"

Leslie's face was rose-flushed smiling wonderment. She had hastily slipped off her swamp costume. Joy that seemed as if it must be imperishable shone on her brightly illumined face. With tightly closed, smile-curved lips she vigorously nodded. The elder woman bent to kiss her.

"Of course I'll come!" she laughed. "I feel thrilled, and flattered. And I congratulate you sincerely. Bruce is a fine man. He'll make a big fortune soon."

"Oh I hope not!" said Leslie.

"Are you crazy?" demanded Mrs. Minturn. "You said you didn't want me to think you so!"

"You see," said Leslie, "Mr. Bruce has a living income; so have I, from my mother. Fortunes seem to me to work more trouble than they do good. I believe poor folks are happiest, they get most out of life, and after all what gives deep, heart-felt joy, is the thing to live for, isn't it? But we must hurry. Mr. Lowry didn't promise to hold the flowers long."

"I'll be ready in a minute, but I see where Douglas Bruce is giving you wrong ideas," said Mrs. Minturn. "He needs a good talking to. Money is the only thing worth while, and the comfort and the pleasure it brings. Without it you are crippled, handicapped, a slave crawling while others step over you. I'll convince *him!* Back in a minute."

When Mrs. Minturn returned she was in a delightful mood, her face eager, her dress beautiful. Leslie wondered if this woman ever had known a care, then remembered that not long before she had lost a little daughter. Leslie explained as they went swiftly through the streets.

"You won't mind waiting only a second until I run up to Mr. Bruce's offices?" she asked.

He was ready, so together they stopped at Mr. Minturn's door. Douglas whispered: "Watch the office boy. He is Minturn's Little Brother I told you about."

Leslie nodded and entered gaily.

"Please ask Mr. Minturn if he will see Miss Winton and Mr. Douglas Bruce a minute?" she said.

An alert, bright-faced lad bowed politely, laid aside a book and entered the inner office.

"Now let me!" said Leslie.

"Good May, Mr. Minturn!" she cried. "Positively enchanting! Take that forbidding look off your face. Come for a few minutes Maying! It will do you much good, and me more. All my friends are pleasuring me to-day. So I want as good a friend of Mr. Bruce as you, to be in something we have planned. You just must!"

"Has something delightful happened?" asked Mr. Minturn, retaining the hand Leslie offered him as he turned to Douglas Bruce.

"You must ask Miss Winton," he said.

Mr. Minturn's eyes questioned her sparkling face, while again with closed lips she nodded. "My most earnest congratulations to each of you. May life grant you even more than you hope for, and from your faces, that is no small wish to make for you. Surely I'll come! What is it you have planned?"

"Something lovely!" said Leslie. "At Lowry's are three flower baskets that are rather bewildering. I am to have one for my betrothal gift, but I can't decide. I appealed to Mrs. Minturn to help me, and she agreed; she is waiting below. Mr. Bruce named you for him; so you two and Mr. Lowry are to choose the most artistic basket for me, then if I don't agree, I needn't take it, but I want to see what you think. You'll come of course?"

Mr. Minturn's face darkened at the mention of his wife, while he hesitated and looked penetratingly at Leslie. She was guileless, charming, and eager.

"Very well," Mr. Minturn said gravely. "I'm surprised, but also pleased. Beautiful young ladies have not appealed to me so often of late that I can afford to miss the chance of humouring the most charming of her sex."

"How lovely!" laughed Leslie. "Douglas, did you ever know Mr. Minturn could flatter like that? It's most enjoyable! I shall insist on more of it, at every opportunity! Really, Mr. Minturn, society has missed you of late, and it is our loss. We need men who are worth while."

"Now it is you who flatter," smiled Mr. Minturn.

"See my captive!" cried Leslie, as she emerged from the building and crossed the walk to the car. "Mr. Bruce and Mr. Minturn are great friends, so as we passed his door we brought him along by force."

"It certainly would require that to bring him anywhere in my company," said Mrs. Minturn coldly.

The shock of the cruelty of the remark closed Douglas' lips, but it was Leslie's day to bubble, so she resolutely set herself to heal and cover the hurt.

"I think business is a perfect bugbear," she said as she entered the car. "I'm going to have a pre-nuptial agreement as to just how far work may trespass on Douglas' time, and how much belongs to me. I think it can be arranged. Daddy and I always have had lovely times together, and I would call him successful. Wouldn't you?"

"A fine business man!" said Mr. Minturn heartily.

"You could have had much greater advantages if he had made more money," said Mrs. Minturn.

"The advantage of more money—yes," retorted Leslie quickly, "but would the money have been of more advantage to me than the benefits of his society and his personal hand in my rearing? I think not! I prefer my Daddy!"

"When you take your place in society, as the mistress of a home, you will find that millions will not be too much," said Mrs. Minturn.

"If I had millions, I'd give most of them away, and just go on living about as I do now with Daddy," said Leslie.

"Leslie, where did you get bitten with this awful, common—what kind of an idea shall I call it? You haven't imbibed socialistic tendencies have you?"

"Haven't a smattering of what they mean!" laughed Leslie. "The 'istics' scare me completely. Just *social* ideas are all I have; thinking home better than any other place on earth, the way you can afford to have it. Merely being human, kind and interested in what my men are doing and enjoying, and helping any one who crosses my path and seems to need me. Oh, I get such joy, such delicious *joy* from life."

"If I were undertaking wild-eyed reform, I'd sell my car and walk, and do settlement work," said Mrs. Minturn scornfully.

Then Leslie surprised all of them. She leaned forward, looked beamingly into the elder woman's face and cried enthusiastically: "I am positive you'd be stronger, and much happier if you would! You know there is no greater fun than going to the end of the car line and then walking miles into the country, especially now in bloom-time. You see sights no painter ever transferred even a good imitation of to canvas; you hear music—I wish every music lover with your trained ear could have spent an hour in that swamp this morning. You'd soon know where Verdi and Strauss found some of their loveliest themes, and where Beethoven got the bird notes for the brook scene of the Pastoral Symphony. Think how interested you'd be in a yellow and black bird singing the Spinning Song from Martha, while you couldn't accuse the bird of having stolen it from Flotow, could you? Surely the bird holds right of priority!"

"If you weren't a little fool and talking purposely to irritate me, you'd almost cause me to ask if you seriously mean that?" said Mrs. Minturn.

"Why," laughed Leslie, determined not to become provoked on this her great day, "that is a matter you can test for yourself. If you haven't a score of Martha, get one and I'll take you where you can hear a bird sing that strain, then you may judge for yourself."

"I don't believe it!" said Mrs. Minturn tersely, "but if it were true, that would be the *most wonderful experience* I ever had in my life."

"And it would cost you only ten cents," scored Leslie. "You needn't ride beyond the end of the car line for that, while a woman who can dance all night surely could *walk* far enough, to reach any old orchard. That's what I am trying to *tell* you. Money in large quantities isn't necessary to provide the *most interesting* things in the world, while millions don't bring happiness. I can find more in what you would class almost poverty."

"Why don't you try it?" suggested Mrs. Minturn.

"But I *have!*" said Leslie. "And I enjoy it! I could go with a man I love as I do Daddy, and make a home, and get joy I never have found in society, from just what we two could do with our own hands in the woods. I don't like a city. If Daddy's business didn't keep him here, I would be in the country this minute. Look at us poor souls trying to find pleasure in a basket from the swamp, when we might have the whole swamp. I'd be happy to live at its door. Now try a basket full of it. There are three. You are to examine each of them carefully, then write on a slip of paper which you think the *most artistic*. You are not to say things that will influence each other's decisions, or Mr. Lowry's. I want a straight opinion from each of you."

They entered the florist's, and on a glass table faced the orchids, the slippers, the fringed basket, and the moccasins. Mr. Winton and the squaw were waiting, while the florist was smiling in gratification, but the Minturns went to the flowers without a word. They simply stood and looked. Each of the baskets was in perfect condition. The flowers were as fresh as at home in the swamp. Each was a thing of wondrous beauty. Each deserved the mute tribute it was exacting. Mrs. Minturn studied them with gradually darkening face. Mrs. Minturn repeatedly opened her lips as if she would speak, but did not. She stepped closer and gently turned the flowers and lightly touched the petals.

"Beautiful!" she said at last. "Beautiful!"

Another long silence.

Then: "*Honestly Leslie, did you hear a bird sing that strain from Martha?*"

"Yes!" said Leslie, "I did. And if you will go with me to the swamp where those flowers came from, you shall hear one sing a strain that will instantly remind you of the opening chorus, while another renders Di Provenza Il Mar from Traviata."

The lady turned again to the flowers. She was thinking something deep and absorbing, but no one could have guessed exactly what it might be. Finally: "I have decided," she said. "Shall we number these one, two, and three, and so indicate them?"

"Yes," said Leslie a little breathlessly.

"Put your initials to the slips and I'll read them," offered Douglas. Then he smilingly read aloud: "Mr. Lowry, one. Mrs. Minturn, two. Mr. Minturn, three!"

"I cast the deciding vote," cried Leslie. "One!"

The squaw seemed to think of a war-whoop, but decided against it.

"Now be good enough to state your reasons," said Mr. Winton. "*Why* do you prefer the slipper basket, Mr. Lowry?"

"It satisfies my sense of the artistic."

"Why the fringed basket, Mrs. Minturn?"

"Because it contains daintier, more wonderful flowers than the others, and is by far the most pleasing production."

"Now Minturn, your turn. Why do you like the moccasin basket?"

"It makes the deepest appeal to me," he answered.

"But why?" persisted Mr. Winton.

"If you will have it—the moccasins are the colour I once loved on the face of my little daughter."

"Now Leslie!" said Mr. Winton hurriedly as he noted Mrs. Minturn's displeased look.

"Must I tell?" she asked.

"Yes," said her father.

"Douglas selected it for me, so I like it best."

"But Leslie!" cried Douglas, "there were only two baskets when I favoured that. Had the fringed orchids been here then, I most certainly should have chosen them. I think yours far the most exquisite! I claim it now. Will you give it to me?"

"Surely! I'd love to," laughed the girl.

"You have done your most exquisite work on the fringed basket," said Mrs. Minturn to the squaw.

"No make!" said she promptly, pointing to Leslie.

"Leslie Winton, did you go to the swamp to make that basket?" demanded Mrs. Minturn.

"Yes," answered Leslie.

"Did you make all of them?"

"Only that one," replied Leslie.

"Why?" marvelled the lady.

"To see if I could go to the tamarack swamp and bring from it with the same tools and material, a more artistic production than an Indian woman."

"Well, you have!" conceded Mrs. Minturn.

"The majority is against me," said Leslie.

"Majorities mean masses, and masses are notoriously insane!" said Mrs. Minturn.

"But this is a small, select majority," said Leslie.

"Craziest of all," said Mrs. Minturn decidedly. "If you have finished with us, I want to thank you for the pleasure of seeing these, and Leslie, some day I really think I shall try that bird music. The idea interests me more than anything that I have ever heard of. If it were true, it would indeed be wonderful, it would be a new experience!"

"If you want to hear for yourself, make it soon, because now is nesting time; not again until next spring will the music be so entrancing. I can go any day."

"I'll look over my engagements and call you. If one ever had a minute to spare!"

"Another of the joys of wealth!" said Leslie. "Only the poor can afford to 'loaf and invite their souls.' The flowers you will see will delight your eyes, quite as much as the music your ears."

"I doubt your logic, but I'll try the birds. Are you coming Mr. Minturn?"

"Not unless you especially wish me. Are these for sale?" he asked, picking up the moccasins.

"Only those," replied the florist.

"Send your bill," he said, turning with the basket.

"How shining a thing is consistency!" sneered his wife. "You condemn the riches you never have been able to amass, but at the same time spend like a millionaire."

"I never said I was not able to gain millions," replied Mr. Minturn coldly. "I have had frequent opportunities! I merely refused them, because I did not consider them legitimate. As for my method in buying flowers, in this one instance, price does not matter. You can guess what I shall do with them."

"I couldn't possibly!" answered Mrs. Minturn. "The only sure venture I could make is that they will not by any chance come to me."

"No. These go to baby Elizabeth," he said. "Do you want to come with me to take them to her?"

With an audible sneer she passed him. He stepped aside, gravely raising his hat, while the others said good-bye to him and followed.

"Positively insufferable!" cried Mrs. Minturn. "Every one of my friends say they do not know how I endure his insults and I certainly will not many more. I don't, I really don't know what he expects."

Mr. Winton and Douglas Bruce were confused, while Leslie was frightened, but she tried turning the distressing occurrence off with excuses.

"Of course he intended no insult!" she soothed. "He must have adored his little daughter and the flowers reminded him. I am so much obliged for your opinion and I shall be glad to take you to the swamp any time. Your little sons—would they like to go? It is a most interesting and instructive place for children."

"For Heaven's sake don't mention children!" cried Mrs. Minturn. "They are a bother and a curse!"

"Oh Mrs. Minturn!" exclaimed Leslie.

"Of course I don't mean *quite* that; but I do very near! Mine are perfect little devils; all the trouble James and I ever had came through them. His idea of a mother is a combined doctor, wet-nurse and nursery maid, while I must say, I far from agree with him. What are servants for if not to take the trouble of children off your hands?"

Leslie was glad to reach the rich woman's door and deposit her there.

As the car sped away the girl turned a despairing face toward Douglas: "For the love of Moike!" she cried. "Isn't that shocking? Poor Mr. Minturn!"

"I don't pity him half so much as I do her," he answered. "What must a woman have suffered or been through, to warp, twist, and harden her like that?"

"Society life," answered Leslie, "as it is lived by people of wealth who are aping royalty and the titled classes."

"A branch of them—possibly," conceded Douglas. "I know some titled and wealthy people who would be dumbfounded over that woman's ideas."

"So do I," said Leslie. "Of course there are exceptions. Sometimes the exception becomes bigger than the rule, but not in our richest society. Douglas, let's keep close together! Oh don't let's ever drift into such a state as that. I should have asked them to lunch, but I couldn't. If that is the way she is talking before her friends, surely she won't have many, soon."

"Then her need for a real woman like you will be all the greater," answered Douglas. "I suppose you should have asked her; but I'm delighted that you didn't! To-day began so nearly perfect, I want to end it with only you and your father. Will he resent me, Leslie?"

"It all depends on us. If we are selfish and leave him alone he will feel it. If we can make him realize gain instead of loss he will be happier than he is now."

"I wish I hadn't felt obliged to reject his offer the other night. I'm very sorry about it."

"I'm not," said Leslie. "You have a right to live your life in your own way. I have seen enough of running for office, elections and appointments that I hate it. You do the work you educated yourself for and I'll help you."

"Then my success is assured," laughed Douglas. "Leslie, may I leave my basket here? Will you care for it like yours, and may I come to see it often?"

"No. You may come to see me and look at the basket incidentally," she answered.

"Do you think Mrs. Minturn will go to the swamp to listen to those birds?" he asked.

"Eventually she will," answered the girl. "I may have to begin by taking her to an orchard to hear a bird of gold sing a golden song about 'sewing, and mending, and baby tending,' to start on; but when she hears that, she will be eager for more."

"How interesting!" cried Douglas. "'Bearer of Morning,' sing that song to me now."

Leslie whistled the air, beating timc with her hand, then sang the words:

"*I can wash, sir, I can spin, sir,*
I can sew and mend, and babies tend."

"Oh you 'Bringer of Song!'" exulted Douglas. "I'd rather hear you sing that than any bird, but from what she said, Nellie Minturn won't care particularly for it!"

"She may not approve of, or practise, the sentiment," said Leslie, "but she'll love the music and possibly the musician."

CHAPTER V

LITTLE BROTHER

"Now what am I going to do yet to make the day shorter, Lily?" asked Mickey.

"I guess I got everything," she answered. "There's my lunch. Here's my pictures to cut. Here's my lesson to learn. There's my sky and bird crumbs. Mickey, sometimes they hop right in on the sheet. Yest'day one tried to get my lunch. Ain't they sassy?"

"Yes," said Mickey. "They fight worse than rich folks. I don't know why the Almighty pays attention if they fall."

"Mebby nobody else cares," said Peaches, "and He feels obliged to 'cause He made 'em."

"Gee! You say the funniest things, kid," laughed Mickey as he digested the idea. "Wonder if He cares for us 'cause He made us."

"Mebby he didn't make us," suggested Peaches.

"Well we got one consoling thing," said Mickey. "If He made any of them, He made us, and if He didn't make us, He didn't none of them, 'cause everybody comes in and goes out the same way; She said so."

"Then of course it's so," agreed Peaches. "That gives us as good a chance as anybody."

"Course it does if we got sense to take it," said Mickey. "We got to wake up and make something of ourselves. Let me see if you know your lesson for to-day yet. There is the picture of the animal—there is the word that spells its name. Now what is it?"

"Milk!" answered Peaches, her eyes mischievous.

Mickey held over the book chuckling.

"All right! There is the word for that, too. For being so smart, Miss Chicken, you can learn it 'fore you get any more to drink. If I have good luck to-day, I'm going to blow in about six o'clock with a slate and pencil for you; and then you can print the words you learn, and make pictures. That'll help make the day go a lot faster."

"Oh it goes fast enough now," said Peaches. "I love days with you and the window and the birds. I wish they'd sing more though."

"When your back gets well, I'll take you to the country where they sing all the time," promised Mickey, "where there are grass, and trees, and flowers, and water to wade in and——"

"Mickey, stop and go on!" cried Peaches. "Sooner you start, the sooner I'll get my next verse. I want just norful good one to-night."

She held up her arms. Mickey submitted to a hug and a little cold dab on his forehead, counted his money, locked the door and ran. On the car he sat in deep thought, then suddenly sniggered aloud. He had achieved the next installment of the doggerel to which every night Peaches insisted on having a new verse added as he entered. He secured his papers, and glimpsing the headlines started on his beat crying them lustily.

Mickey knew that washing, better air, enough food, and oil rubbing were improving Peaches. What he did not know was that adding the interest of her presence to his life, even though it made his work heavier, was showing on him. He actually seemed bigger, stronger, and his face brighter and fuller. He swung down the street thrusting his papers right and left, crossed and went up the other side, watching closely for a customer. It was ten o'clock and opportunities with the men were almost over. Mickey turned to scan the street for anything even suggesting a sale. He saw none and started with his old cry, watching as he went: "I *like* to sell papers! *Sometimes* I sell them! Sometimes I *don't*——!"

Then he saw her. She was so fresh and joyous. She walked briskly. Even his beloved nurse was not so wonderful. Straight toward her went Mickey.

"I *like* to sell papers! *Sometimes* I sell them! Sometimes I *don't!* Morning paper, lady! Sterilized! Deodorized! Vulcanized! Nice *clean* paper!"

The girl's eyes betokened interest; her smiling lips encouraged Mickey. He laid his chin over her arm, leaned his head against it and fell in step with her.

"*Sometimes* I sell them! Sometimes I *don't!* If I *sell* them, I'm happy! If I don't, I'm *hungry!* If you *buy* them, you're happy! Pa—per?—lady."

"Not to-day, thank you," she said. "I'm shopping, so I don't wish to carry it."

Mickey saw Peaches' slate vanishing. It was a beautiful slate, small so it would not tire her bits of hands, and its frame was covered with red. His face sobered, his voice changed, taking on unexpected modulations.

"Aw lady! I thought *you'd* buy my paper! Far down the street I saw you *coming*. Lady, I like your gentle *voice*. I like your pleasant *smile!* You don't want a nice *sterilized* paper?—lady."

The lady stopped short; she lifted Mickey's chin in a firm grip, looking intently into his face.

"Just by the merest chance, could your name be Mickey?" she asked.

"Sure, lady! Mickey! Michael O'Halloran!"

" 'I can wash, sir, I can spin, sir, I can sew and mend, and babies tend.' "

Her smile became even more attractive.

"I really don't want to be bothered with a paper," she said; "but I do wish a note delivered. If you'll carry it, I'll pay you the price of half a dozen papers."

"Gets the slate!" cried Mickey, bouncing like a rubber boy. "Sure I will! Is it ready, lady?"

"One minute!" she said. She stepped to the inside of the walk, opened her purse, wrote a line on a card, slipped it in an envelope, addressed it and handed it to Mickey.

"You can read that?" she asked.

"I've read worse writing than that," he assured her. "You ought to see the hieroglyphics some of the dimun-studded dames put up!"

Mickey took a last glimpse at the laughing face, then wheeling ran. Presently he went into a big building, studied the address board, then entered the elevator and following a corridor reached the number.

He paused a second, glancing around, when he saw the name on the opposite door. A flash passed over his face. "Ugh!" he muttered. "'Member now—been to this place before! Glad she ain't sending a letter to *that* man." He stepped inside the open door before him, crossed the room and laid the note near a man who was bending over some papers on a desk. The man reached a groping hand, tore open the envelope, taking therefrom a card on which was pencilled: "Could this by any chance be your Little Brother?"

He turned hastily, glancing at Mickey, then in a continuous movement arose with outstretched hand.

"Why Little Brother," he cried, "I'm so glad to see you!"

Mickey's smile slowly vanished as he whipped his hands behind him, stepping back.

"Nothin' doing, Boss," he said. "You're off your trolley. I've no brother. My mother had only me."

"Don't you remember me, Mickey?" inquired Douglas Bruce.

"Sure!" said Mickey. "You made Jimmy pay up!"

"Has he bothered you again?" asked the lawyer.

"Nope!" answered Mickey.

"Sit down, Mickey, I want to talk with you."

"I'm much obliged for helping me out," said Mickey, "but I guess you got other business, and I know I have."

"What is your business?" was the next question.

"Selling papers. What's yours?" was the answer.

"Trying to be a corporation lawyer," explained Douglas. "I've been here only two years, and it is slow getting a start. I often have more time to spare than I wish I had, while I'm lonesome no end."

"Is your mother dead?" asked Mickey solicitously.

"Yes," answered Douglas.

"So's mine!" he commented. "You *do* get lonesome! Course she was a good one?"

"The very finest, Mickey," said Douglas. "And yours?"

"Same here, Mister," said Mickey with conviction.

"Well since we are both motherless and lonesome, suppose we be brothers!" suggested Douglas.

"Aw-w-w!" Mickey shook his head.

"No?" questioned Douglas.

"What's the use?" cried Mickey.

"You could help me with my work and share my play, while possibly I could be of benefit to you."

"I just wondered if you wasn't getting to that," commented Mickey.

"Getting to what?" inquired Douglas.

"Going to do me good!" explained Mickey. "The swell stiffs are always going to do us fellows good. Mostly they do! They do us good and brown! They pick us up a while and make lap dogs of us, then when we've lost our appetites for our jobs and got to having a hankerin' for the fetch and carry business away they go and forget us, so we're a lot worse off than we were before. Some of the fellows come out of it knowing more ways to be mean than they ever learned on the street," explained Mickey. "If it's that Big Brother bee you got in your bonnet, pull its stinger and let it die an unnatural death! Nope! None! Good-bye!"

"Mickey, wait!" cried Douglas.

"Me business calls, an' I must go—'way to my ranch in Idaho!" gaily sang Mickey.

"I'd like to shake you!" said Douglas Bruce.

"Well, go on," said Mickey. "I'm here and you're big enough."

"If I thought it would jolt out your fool notions and shake some sense in, I would," said Douglas indignantly.

"Now look here, Kitchener," said Mickey. "Did I say one word that ain't so, and that you don't know is so?"

"What you said is not even half a truth, young man! I do know cases where idle rich men have tried the Little Brother plan as a fad, and made a failure of it. But for a few like that, I know dozens of sincere, educated men who are honestly giving a boy they fancy, a chance. I can take you into the office of one of the most influential men in this city, right across the hall there, and show you a boy he liked who has in a short time become his friend, an invaluable helper, and hourly companion, and out of it that boy will get a fine education, good business training, and a start in life that will give him a better chance to begin on than the man who is helping him had."

Mickey laughed boisterously, then sobered suddenly.

"'Scuse me, Brother," he said politely, "but that's most *too funny* for any use. Once I took a whirl with that gentleman myself. Whether he does or not, I know the place where he ought to get off. See? Answer me this: why would he be spending money and taking all that time for a 'newsy' when he hardly knows his own kids if he sees them, and they're the wickedest little rippers in the park. Just *why* now?"

Douglas Bruce closed the door; then he came back and placing a chair for Mickey, he took one opposite.

"Sit down Mickey," he said patiently. "There's a reason for my being particularly interested in James Minturn, and the reason hinges on the fact you mention: that he can't control his own sons, yet can make a boy he takes comfort in, of a street gamin."

Mickey's eyes narrowed while he sat very straight in the chair he had accepted.

"If he's made so much of him, it sort of proves that he *wasn't* a gamin. Some of the boys are a long shot closer gentlemen than the guys who are experimenting with them; 'cause they were born rich and can afford it. If your friend's going to train his pick-up to be what *he* is, then that boy would stand a better chance on his own side the curb. See? I've been right up against that gentleman with the documents, so I know him. Also her! Gee! 'Tear up de choild and gimme de papers' was meant for a joke; but I saw that lady and gentleman do it. See? And she was the prettiest little pink and yellow thing. Lord! I can see her gasping and blinking now! Makes me sick! If the boy across the hall had seen what I did, he'd run a mile and never stop. Gee!"

Douglas Bruce stared aghast. At last he said slowly: "Mickey, you are getting mighty close the very thing I wish to know. If I tell you what I know of James Minturn, will you tell me what you know and think?"

"Sure!" said Mickey readily. "I got no reasons for loving him. I wouldn't convoy a millying to the mint for that gentleman!"

"Mickey, shall I go first, or will you?"

"I will," replied Mickey instantly, "'cause when I finish you'll save your breath. See?"

"I see," said Douglas Bruce. "Proceed."

"Well, 'twas over two years ago," said Mickey, leaning forward to look Bruce in the eyes. "I hadn't been up against the game so awful long alone. 'Twas summer and my papers were all gone, and I was tired, so I went over in the park and sat on a seat, just watching folks. Pretty soon 'long comes walking a nice lady with a sweet voice and kind eyes. She sat down close me and says: 'It's a nice day.' We got chummy-like, when right up at the fountain before us stops as swell an automobile as there is. One of the brown French-governess-ladies with the hatchet face got out, and unloaded three kids: two boys and a girl. She told the kids if they didn't sit on the benches she socked them on hard, and keep their clothes clean so she wouldn't have to wash and dress them again that day, she'd knock the livers out of them, and walked off with the entrance policeman. Soon as she and Bobbie got interested, the kids began sliding off the bench and running around the fountain. The girl was only 'bout two or three, a fat toddly thing, trying to do what her brothers did, and taking it like the gamest kid you ever saw when they pushed her off the seat, and tripped her, and 'bused her like a dog.

"Me and the woman were getting madder every minute. 'Go tell your nurse,' says she. But the baby thing just glanced where nurse was and kind of shivered and laughed, and ran on round the fountain, when the big boy stuck his foot out so she fell. Nursie saw and started for her, but she scrambled up and went kiting for the bench, and climbed on it, so nurse told her she'd cut the blood out of her if she did that again, then went back to her policeman. Soon as she was gone those little devils began coaxing their sister to get down and run again. At last she began to smile the cunningest and slipped to the walk, then a little farther, and a little farther, all the time laughing and watching the nurse. The big boy, he said: 'You ain't nothing but a *girl!* You can't step on the edge like I can and then step back!' She says: 'C'n too!' She did to show him, and just as she did she saw that he was going to push her, then she tried to get back, but he did push, and over she went! Not real in, but her arms in, and her dress front some wet.

"She screamed while the little devil that pushed her grabbed her, pretending to be *pulling her out*. Honest he did! Up came nurse just frothing, and in language we couldn't understand she ripped and raved. She dragged little pink back, grabbed her by the hair and cracked her head two or three times against the *stone!* The lady screamed, and so did I, and we both ran at her. The boys just shouted and laughed and the smallest one he up and kicked her while she was down. The policeman walked over laughing too, but he told nurse that was *too rough*. Then my lady pitched in, so he told her to tend to her business, that those kids were too tough to live, and deserved all they got. The nurse laughed at her, and went back to the grass with the policeman. The baby lay there on the stones, and never made a sound. She just kind of gasped, and blinked, and lay there, till my lady went almost wild. She went to her and stooped to lift her up when she got awful sick. The policeman said something to the nurse, so she came and dragged the kid away and said, 'The little pig has gone and eaten too much again, and now I'll have to take her home and wash and dress her all over,' then she gave her an awful shake. The policeman said she'd better cut that out, because it *might* have been the bumping, and she said 'good for her if 'twas.' The driver pulled up just then and he asked 'if the brat had been stuffin' too much again?' She said, 'yes,' and the littlest boy he said, 'she pounded her head on the stone, good,' and the nurse hit him 'cross the mouth till she knocked him against the car, and she said, 'Want to try *that* again? Open your head to say *that* again, and I'll smash you too. *Eating too much made her sick.*' She looked at the big boy fierce like so he laughed and said, 'Course eating too much made her sick!' She nodded at him and said, 'Course! You get two dishes of ice and two pieces of cake for remembering!' then she loaded them in and they drove away.

"My lady was as white as marble and she said, 'Is there any way to find out who they are?' I said, 'Sure! Half a dozen!' 'Boy,' she said, 'get their residence for me and I'll give you a dollar.' Ought to seen me fly. Car was chuffing away, waiting to get the traffic cop's sign when to cut in on the avenue. I just took a dodge and hung on to the extra tire under the top where nobody saw me, and when they stopped, I got the house number they went in. Little pink was lying all white and limber yet, and nurse looked worried as she carried her up. She said something fierce to the boys, the big one rang and they went inside. I saw a footman take the girl. I heard nurse begin that 'eat too much' story, then I cut back to the park. The lady said, 'Get it?' I said, 'Sure! Dead easy.' She said, 'Can you take me?' I said, 'Glad to!'

"She said, 'That was the dreadfullest sight I ever saw. That child's mother is going to know right now what kind of a nurse she is paying to take care of her children. You come show me,' she said, so we went.

"'Will you come in with me?' she asked and I said, 'Yes!'

"Well, we rang and she asked pleasant to see the lady of the house on a little matter of important business, so pretty soon here comes one of the dimun-studded, fashion-paper ladies, all smiling sweet as honey, and asked what the business was. My nice lady she said her name was Mrs. John Wilson and her husband was a banker in Plymouth, Illinois, and she was in the city shopping and went to the park to rest and was talking to me, when an automobile let out a nurse, and two boys and a lovely little pink girl, and she give the number and asked, 'was the car and the children hers?' The dimun-lady slowly sort of began to freeze over, and when the nice lady got that far, she said: 'I have an engagement. Kindly state in a *few* words what you want.'

"My lady sort of stiffened up and then she said: 'I saw, this boy here saw, and the park policeman nearest the entrance fountain saw your nurse take your little girl by the hair, and strike her head against the fountain curb three times, because her brother pushed her in. She lay insensible until the car came, and she has just been carried into your house in that condition.'

"I could see the footman peeking and at that he cut up the stairs. The dimun-lady stiffened up and she said: 'So you are one of those meddling, interfering country jays that come here and try to make us lose our good servants, so you can hire them later. I've seen that done before. Lucette is invaluable,' said she, 'and perfectly reliable. Takes all the care of those dreadful little imps from me. Now you get out of here.' And she reached for the button. My lady just sat still and smiled.

"'Do you really think I'd take the trouble to come here in this way if I couldn't *prove* I had seen the thing happen?' she asked.

"'God only knows what you country women would do!' the woman answered.

"'We would stand between our children and beastly cruelty,' my lady said. 'Your child's *condition* is all the proof my words need. You go examine her head, and feel the welt on it; see hew ill she is and you will thank me. Your nurse is *not* reliable! Keep her and your children will be ruined, if not killed.'

"'Raving!' sneered the dimun-lady. 'But I know your kind so I'll go, as it's the only way to get rid of you.'

"Now what do you think happened next? Well sir, 'bout three minutes in walked the footman and salutes, sneering like a cat, and he said: 'Madam's compliments. She finds her little daughter in perfect condition, sweetly sleeping, and her sons having dinner. She asks you to see how quickly you can leave her residence.'

"The woman looked at me so I said: 'It's all over but burying the kid if it dies; come on, lady, they'd be *glad* to plant it, and get it out of the way.' So I started and she followed, and just as he let me out the door I handed him this: 'I saw you listen and cut to tell, and I bet you helped put the kid to sleep! But you better look out! She gave it to that baby too rough for any use!'

"He started for me, but I flew. When we got on the street, the lady was all used up so she couldn't say anything. She had me call a taxi to take her to her hotel. I set down her name she gave me, and her house and street number. I cut to a Newsies' directory and got the name of the owner of the palace-place and it was Mrs. James Minturn. Next morning coming down on the cars I was hunting headliners to make up a new call, like I always do, and there I saw in big type, 'Mr. and Mrs. James Minturn prostrate over the sudden death of their lovely little daughter from poisoning, from an ice she ate.' I read it every word. Even what the doctors said, and how investigation of the source of the ice came from was to be made. What do you think of it?"

"I have no doubt but it's every word horrible truth," answered Douglas.

"*Sure!*" said Mickey. "I just hiked to the park and walked up to the cop and showed him the paper, and he looked awful glum. I can point him out to you, and give you the lady's address, and there were plenty more who saw parts of it could be found if anybody was on the *kid's* side. Sure it's the truth!

"Well I kept a-thinking it over. One day about three weeks later, blest if the same car didn't stop at the same fountain, and the same nurse got out with the boys and she set them on the same bench and told them the same thing, and then she went into another palaver with the same p'liceman. I looked on pretty much interested, and before long the boys got to running again and one tripped the other, and she saw and come running, and fetched him a crack like to split his head, and pushed him down still and white, so I said to myself: 'All right for you. Lady tried a lady and got nothing. Here's where a gentleman tries a gentleman, and sees what he gets.'

"I marched into the door just across the hall from you here, and faced Mr. James Minturn, and gave him names, and dates, and addresses, even the copper's name I'd got; and I told him all I've told you, and considerable more. He wasn't so fiery as the lady, so I told him the whole thing, but he never opened his trap. He just sat still and stony, listened till I quit, and finally he heaved a big breath and looked at me sort of dazed like and he said: 'What do you want, boy?'

"That made me red hot so I said: 'I want you to know that I saw the same woman bust one of your *boys* a good crack, over the head, a few minutes ago.'

"That made him jump, but he didn't say or do anything, so I got up and went—and—the same woman was in the park with the same boys yesterday, and they're the biggest little devils there. What's the answer?"

"A heartbroken man," said Douglas Bruce. "Now let me tell you, Mickey."

Then he told Mickey all he knew of James Minturn.

"All the same, he ought to be able to do something for his own kids, 'stead of boys who don't need it *half* so bad," commented Mickey. "Why honest, I don't know one street kid so low that he'd kick a little girl—after she'd been beat up scandalous, for his meanness to start on. Honest, I don't! I don't care what he is doing for the boy he has got, that boy doesn't need help half so much as his *own*; I can prove it to you, if you'll come with me to the park 'most any morning."

"All right, I'll come," said Douglas promptly.

"Well I couldn't say that they would be there this minute," said Mickey, "but I can call you up the first time I see they are."

"All right, I'll come, if it's possible. I'd like to see for myself. So this gives you a settled prejudice against the Big Brother movement, Mickey?"

"In my brogans, what would it give you?"

"A hard jolt!" said Douglas emphatically.

"Then what's the answer?"

"That it is more unfair than I thought you could be, to deprive me of my Little Brother, because you deem the man across the hall unfit to have one. Do I look as if you couldn't trust me, Mickey?"

"No, you don't! But neither does Mr. James Minturn. He *looks* as if a fellow could get a grip on him and pull safe across Belgium hanging on. But you know I said the *same woman*——"

"I know Mickey; but that only proves that there are times when even the strongest man can't help himself."

"Then like Ulhan I'd trot 1:54-1/2 to the judge of the Juvenile Court," said Mickey, "and I'd yell long and loud, and I'd put up the *proof*. That would get the lady down to brass tacks. See?"

"But with Mrs. Minturn's position and the stain such a proceeding would put on the boys——"

"Cut out the boys," advised Mickey. "They're gold plated, staining wouldn't stick to them."

"So you are going to refuse education, employment and a respectable position because you disapprove of one man among millions?" demanded Douglas.

"That lets me out," said Mickey. "*She* educated me a lot! No day is long enough for the work I do right now; you can take my word for it that I'm respectable, same as I'm taking yours that you are."

"All right!" said Douglas. "We will let it go then. Maybe you are right. At least you are not worth the bother it requires to wake you up. Will you take an answer to the note you brought me?"

"Now the returns are coming in," said Mickey. "Sure I will; but she is in the big stores shopping."

"I'll find out," said Douglas.

He picked up the telephone and called the Winton residence; on learning Leslie was still away, he left a request that she call him when she returned.

"I would spend the time talking with you," he said to Mickey, "if I could accomplish anything; as I can't, I'll go on with my work. You busy yourself with anything around the rooms that interests you."

Mickey grinned half abashed. He took a long survey of the room they were in, arose and standing in the door leading to the next he studied that. To him "busy" meant work. Presently he went into the hall and returned with a hand broom and dust pan he had secured from the janitor. He carefully went over the floor, removing anything he could see that he thought should not be there, and then began on the room adjoining. Next he appeared with a cloth and dusted the furniture and window seats. Once he met Douglas' eye and smiled. "Your janitor didn't have much of a mother," he commented. "I could beat him to his base a rod."

"Job is yours any time you want it."

"Morning papers," carrolled Mickey. "Sterilized, deodorized, vulcanized. I *like* to sell them——"

Defeated again Bruce turned to his work and Mickey to his. He straightened every rug, pulled a curtain, set a blind at an angle that gave the worker more light and better air. He was investigating the glass when the telephone rang.

"Hello, Leslie! It certainly was! How did you do it? Not so hilarious as you might suppose. Leslie, I want to say something, not for the wire. Will you hold the line a second until I start Mickey with it? All right!

"She is there now, Mickey. Can you find your way?"

"Sure!" laughed Mickey. "If you put the address on. She started me from the street."

"The address is plain. For straightening my rooms and carrying the note, will that be about right?"

"A lady-bird! Gee!" cried Mickey. "I didn't s'pose you was a plute! And I don't s'pose so yet. You want a Little Brother bad if you're willing to *buy* one. This number ain't far out, and I wouldn't have sold more than three papers this time of day—twenty-five is about right."

"But you forget cleaning my rooms," said Douglas.

Mickey grinned, his face flushed.

"Me to you!" he said. "Nothing! Just a little matter of keeping in practice. Good-bye and be good to yourself!"

Douglas turned to the telephone.

"Leslie!" he said, "I'm sending Mickey back to you with a note, not because I had anything to say I couldn't say now, but because I can't manage him. I pretended I didn't care, and let him go. Can't you help me? See if you can't interest him in something that at least will bring him back, or show us where to find him. Certainly! Thank you very much!"

When Mickey delivered the letter the lovely young woman just happened to be in the hall. She told him to come in until she read it, to learn what Mr. Bruce wanted. Mickey followed into a big room, looked around, then a speculative, appreciative gleam crossed his face. He realized the difference between a home and a show room. He did not know what he was seeing or why it affected him as it did. Really the thought that was in his mind was that this woman was far more attractive, but had less money to spend on her home, than many others. He missed the glitter, but enjoyed the comfort, for he leaned back against the chair offered him, thinking what a cool, restful place it was. The girl seemed in no hurry to open the letter.

"Have trouble finding Mr. Bruce?" she asked.

"Easy! I'd been to the same building before."

"And I suppose you'll be there many times again," she suggested.

"I'm going back right now, if you want to send an answer to that letter," he said.

"And if it requires none?" she questioned.

"Then I'm going to try to sell the rest of these papers, get a slate for Lily and go home."

"Is Lily your little sister?" she asked.

Mickey straightened, firmly closing his lips. He had done it again.

"Just a little girl I know," he said cautiously.

"A little bit of a girl?" she asked.

"'Bout the littlest girl you ever saw," said Mickey, unconsciously interested in the subject.

"And you are going to take her a slate to draw pictures on? How fine! I wish you'd carry her a package for me, too. I was arranging my dresser this morning and I put the ribbons I don't want into a box for some child. Maybe Lily would like them for her doll."

"Lily hasn't any doll," he said. "She had one, but her granny sold it and got drunk on the money."

Mickey stopped suddenly. In a minute more he would have another Orphans' Home argument on his hands.

"Scandalous!" cried Leslie. "In my room there is a doll just begging to go to some little girl. If you took it to Lily, would her granny sell it again?"

"Not this morning," said Mickey. "You see Miss, a few days ago she lost her breath. Permanent! No! If Lily had a doll, nobody would take it from her now."

"I'll bring it at once," she offered "and the ribbons."

"Never mind," said Mickey. "I can get her a doll."

"But you haven't seen this one!" cried Leslie. "You save your money for oranges."

Without waiting for a reply she left the room, presently returning with a box and a doll that seemed to Mickey quite as large as Peaches. It had a beautiful face, hair, real hair that could be combed, and real clothes that could be taken off. Leslie had dressed it for a birthday gift for the little daughter of one of her friends; but by making haste she could prepare another. Mickey gazed in bewilderment. He had seen dolls, even larger and more wonderful than that, in the shop windows, but connecting such a creation with his room and Peaches required mental adjustments.

"I guess you better not," he said with conviction.

"But why not?" asked Leslie in amazement.

"Well for 'bout fifty reasons," replied Mickey. "You see Lily is a poor kid, and her back is bad. That doll is so big she couldn't dress it without getting all tired out; and what's the use showing her such dresses, when she can't have any herself. She's got the best she ever had, and the best she can have right now; so that ain't the kind of a doll for Lily—it's too big—and too—too gladsome!"

"I see," laughed Leslie. "Well Mickey, you show me what would be the right size of a doll for Lily. I'll get another, and dress it as you say. How would that do?"

"You needn't!" said Mickey. "Lily is happy now."

"But wouldn't she *like* a doll?" persisted Leslie. "I never knew a girl who didn't love a doll. Wouldn't she *like* a doll?"

"'Most to death I 'spect," said Mickey. "I know she said she cried for the one her granny sold, 'til she beat her. Yes I guess she'd *like* a doll; but I can get her one."

"But you can't make white nighties for Lily to put on it to take to bed with her, and cunning little dresses for morning, and a street dress for afternoon, and a party dress for evening," tempted the girl.

"Lily has been on the street twice, and she never heard of a party. Just nighties and the morning dress would do, and there's no use for me to be sticking. If you like to give away dolls, Lily might as well have one, for she'd just—I don't know what she would do about it," conceded Mickey.

"All right," said Leslie. "I'll dress it this afternoon, and tomorrow you can come for it in the evening before you go home. If I am not here, the package will be ready. Take the ribbons now. She'd like them for her hair."

"Her hair's too short for a ribbon," said Mickey.

"Then a headband! This way!" said Leslie.

She opened a box and displayed a wonderment of ribbon bands, and bits of gay colour.

"Gee!" gasped Mickey. "I couldn't pick up that much brightness for her in a year!"

"You save what you find for her?" asked Leslie.

"Sure!" said Mickey. "You see Miss, things are pretty plain where she is, so all the brightness I can take her ain't going to hurt her eyes. Thank you heaps. Is there going to be any answer to the letter?"

"Why I haven't read it yet!" cried the girl.

"No! A-body can see that some one else is rustling for your grub!" commented Mickey.

"That's so too," laughed Leslie. "Darling old Daddy!"

"Just about right is he?" queried Mickey, interestedly.

"Just exactly right!" said Leslie.

"Gur-ur-and!" said Mickey. "Some of them ain't so well fixed! And he that wrote the note, I guess he's about as fine as you make them, too!"

"He's the finest man I ever have known, Mickey!" said the girl earnestly.

"Barring Daddy?" suggested Mickey.

"Not barring anybody!" cried she. "Daddy is lovely, but he's Daddy! Mr. Bruce is different!"

"No letter?" questioned Mickey, rising.

"None!" said the girl. "Come to-morrow night. You are sure Lily is so very little, Mickey?"

"You wouldn't call me big, would you?" he asked. "Well! I can lift her with one hand! Such a large doll as that would be tiring and confusing. Please make Lily's *more like she's used to*. See?"

"Mickey, I do see!" said Leslie. "I beg your pardon. Lily's doll shall not tire her or make her discontented with what she has. Thank you for a good idea."

Mickey returned to the street shortly after noon, with more in his pocket than he usually earned in a day, where by expert work he soon disposed of his last paper. He bought the slate, then hurried home carrying it and the box. At the grocery he carefully selected food again. Then he threw open his door and achieved this:

"*Once a little kid named Peaches,*
Swelled my heart until it eatches.
If you think I'd trade her for a dog,
Your think-tank has slipped a cog!"

Peaches laughed, stretching her hands as usual. Mickey stooped for her caress, scattering the ribbons over her as he arose. She gasped in delighted amazement.

"Oh! Mickey! Where did you ever? Mickey, where did you get them? Mickey, you didn't st——?"

"You just better choke on that, Miss!" yelled Mickey. "No I didn't st——! And I don't st——! And nothing I ever bring you will be st——! And you needn't ever put no more st's—— at me. See?"

"Mickey, I didn't *mean* that! Course I know you *wouldn't!* Course I know you *couldn't!* Mickey, that's the best poetry piece yet! Did you bring the slate?"

"Sure!" said Mickey, somewhat mollified, but still injured. "I must have dropped it with the banquet!"

Peaches pushed away the billow of colour, taking the slate. Her fingers picking at the string reminded Mickey of sparrow feet; but he watched until she untied and removed the paper which he folded to lay away. She picked up the pencil, meditating.

"Mickey!" she said. "Make my hand do a word!"

"Sure!" said Mickey. "What do you want to write first, Flowersy-girl?"

Peaches looked at him reproachfully.

"Course there wouldn't be but *one* I'd want to do first of all," she said. "Hold my hand tight, and big and plain up at the top make it write, 'Mickey-lovest.'"

"Sure," said the boy in a hushed voice. He gripped the hand, bending above her, but suddenly collapsed, buried his face in her hair and sobbed until he shook.

Peaches crouched down, lying rigidly. She was badly frightened. At last she could endure it no longer.

"Mickey!" she gasped. "Mickey, what did I do? Mickey, don't write it if you don't *want* to!"

Mickey arose, wiping his face on the sheet.

"You just bet I want to write that, Lily!" he said. "I never wanted to do anything *more* in all my life!"

"Then why——?" she began.

"Never you mind 'why' Miss!" said Mickey.

Grasping her hand, he traced the words. Peaches looked at them a long time, then carefully laid the slate aside. She began fingering the ribbons.

"Let me wash you," said Mickey, "and rub your back to rest you from all this day, then I'll comb your hair and you pick the prettiest one. I'll put it on the way she showed me, so you'll be a fash'nable lady."

"Who showed you Mickey, and gave you such pretties?"

"A girl I carried a letter to. After you're bathed and have had supper I'll tell you."

Then Mickey began work. He sponged Peaches, rubbed her back, laid her on his pallet, putting fresh sheets on her bed and carefully preparing her supper. After she had eaten he again ran the comb through her ringlets, telling her to select the ribbon he should use.

"No you!" said Peaches.

Mickey squinted, so exacting was the work of deciding. Red he discarded with one sweep against her white cheeks; green went with it; blue almost made him shudder, but a soft warm pink pleased him, so Mickey folded it into the bands in which it had been creased before, binding it around Peaches' head as Leslie had shown him, then with awkward fingers did his best on a big bow. He crossed the room and picked up a mirror which he held before her reciting: "Once a little kid named Peaches, swelled my heart——"

Peaches took the mirror, studying the face intently. She glanced over her shoulder so Mickey piled the pillows higher. Then she looked at him. Mickey scrutinized her closely.

"You're clean kid, clean as a plate!" he assured her. "Honest you are! You needn't worry about that. I'll always keep you washed clean. *She* was more particular about that than anything else. Don't you fret about my having a dirty girl around! You're clean, all right!"

Peaches sighed as she returned the mirror. Mickey replaced it, laid the slate and ribbons in reach, washed the dishes, then the sheets he had removed, and their soiled clothing. Peaches lay folding and unfolding the ribbons; asking questions while Mickey worked, or with the pencil tracing her best imitations of the name on the slate. By the time he had finished everything to be done and drawn a chair beside the bed, to see if she had learned her lesson for the day, it was cool evening. She knew all the words he had given her, so he proceeded to write them on the slate. Then told her about the big man named Douglas Bruce and the lovely girl named Leslie Winton, also every word he could remember about the house she lived in; then he added: "Lily, do you like to be surprised better or do you like to think things over?"

"I don't know," said Peaches.

"Well, before long, I'll know," said Mickey. "What I was thinking was this: you are going to have something. I just wondered whether you'd rather know it was coming, or have me walk in with it and surprise you."

"Mickey, you just walk in," she decided.

"All right!" said Mickey.

"Mickey, write on the other side of my slate what you said at the door to-night," she coaxed. "Get a little book an' write 'em all down. Mickey, I want to learn all of them, when I c'n read. Lemme tell you. You make all you c'n think of. Nen make more. An' make 'em, an' make 'em! An' when you get big as you're goin' to be, make books of 'em, an' be a poet-man 'stead of sellin' papers."

"Sure!" said Mickey. "I'd just as lief be a poet-man as not! I'd write a big one all about a little yellow-haired girl named Lily Peaches, and I'd put it on the front page of the *Herald!* Honest I would! I'd like to!"

"Gee!" said Peaches. "You go on an' grow hel—wope! I mean hurry! Hurry an' grow up!"

CHAPTER VI

The Song of a Bird

"Leslie," said the voice of Mrs. James Minturn over the telephone, "is there any particular time of the day when that bird of yours sings better than at another?"

"Morning, Mrs. Minturn; five, the latest. At that time one hears the full chorus, and sees the perfect beauty. Really, I wouldn't ask you, if I were not sure, positively sure, that you'd find the trip worth while."

"I'll be ready in the morning, but that's an unearthly hour!" came the protest.

"It is almost unearthly sights and sounds to which you are going," answered Leslie. "And be sure you wear suitable clothing."

"What do you call suitable clothing?"

"High heavy shoes," said Leslie, "short stout skirts."

"As if I had such things!" laughed Mrs. Minturn.

"Let me send you something of mine," offered Leslie. "I've enough for two."

"You're not figuring on really going in one of those awful places, are you?" questioned Mrs. Minturn.

"Surely!" cried Leslie. "The birds won't sing to an automobile. And you wouldn't miss seeing such flowers on their stems as you saw at Lowry's for any money. It will be something to tell your friends about."

"Send what I should have. I'd ride a llama through a sea of champagne for a new experience."

Mrs. Minturn turned from the telephone with a contemptuous sneer on her face; but Leslie's gay laugh persisted in her ears. Restlessly she moved through her rooms thinking what she might do to divert herself, and shrinking from all the tiresome things she had been doing for years until there was not a drop of the fresh juice of life to be extracted from them.

"I'm going to take a bath, go to bed early and see if I can sleep," she muttered. "I don't know what it is that James is contemplating, but his face haunts me. Really, if he doesn't be more civil, and stop his morose glowering when I do see him, I'll put him or myself where we won't come in contact.

He makes it plain every day that he blames me about Elizabeth. Why should he? He couldn't possibly know of the call of that wild-eyed reformer. So unfortunate that she should come just at that time too! Of course hundreds of children die from spoiled milk every summer, the rich as well as the poor. I'll never get over regretting that I didn't finish what I started to do; but I'd scarcely touched her in her life. She always was so pink and warm, and that awful whiteness chilled me to the soul. I wish I had driven, forced myself! Then I could defy James with more spirit. That's what I lack—*spirit!* Maybe this trip to the swamp will steady my nerves! Something must be done soon, and I believe, actually I believe he is thinking of doing it! Pooh! What *could* he do? There isn't an irregularity in my life he can lay his fingers on!"

She rang for her maid and cancelling two engagements for the evening, went to bed, but not to sleep. When she was called early in the morning, she gladly arose, and was dressed in Leslie Winton's short skirts, a waist of khaki, and high shoes near enough her size to be comfortable. Her bath had refreshed her, a cup of hot coffee stimulated her, and despite the lack of sleep she felt better than she had that spring as she went down to the car. On the threshold she met her husband. Evidently he had been out all night on strenuous business. His face was haggard, his eyes bloodshot, while in both hands he gripped a small, square paper-wrapped package. They looked at each other a second that seemed long to both, then the woman laughed.

"Evidently an accounting is expected," she said. "Leslie Winton at the door and the roll of music I carry should be sufficient to prove why I am going out at this hour. You heard us make the arrangement. Thank Heaven I've no interest in knowing where you have been, or what your precious package contains."

His expression and condition frightened her.

"For the weight of a straw overbalance," he said, "only for a hint that you have a soul, I'd freeze it for all time with the contents of this package."

"A threat? You to me?" she cried in amazement.

"Verily, Madam," he said. "I wish you all the joy of the birds and flowers this morning."

"You've gone mad!" she cried.

"Contrarily, I have come to my senses after years of insanity," he said. "I will see you when you return."

She stood bewildered, watching him go down the hall and enter his library. That and his sleeping room were the only places in the house sacred to him. No one entered, no one, not even the incorrigible children, touched anything there. She slowly went to the car, trying to rally to Leslie's greeting, struggling to fix her mind on anything pointed out to her as something she might enjoy.

At last she said: "I don't know what is the matter with me Leslie. James is planning something, I haven't an idea what; but his grim, reproachful face is slowly driving me wild. I'm getting so I can't sleep. You saw him come home as I left. He talked positively crazy, as if he had the crack of doom in his hands and were prepared to crack it. He said he 'would see me when I came back.' Indeed he will—to his sorrow! He will be as he used to be, or we will separate. The idea, with scarcely a cent to his name, of him undertaking to dictate to me, *to me!* Do you blame me Leslie? You heard him the other day! You know how he insulted me!"

Leslie leaned forward, laying a firm hand in a grip on Mrs. Minturn's arm.

"Since you ask me," she said, "I will answer. If you find life with Mr. Minturn insufferable, an agony to both of you, I *would* separate, and *speedily*. If it has come to the place where you can't see each other or speak without falling into unpleasantness, then I'd keep apart."

"That is exactly the case!" cried Mrs. Minturn. "Oh Leslie, I am so glad you agree with me!"

"But I haven't finished," said Leslie, "you interrupted me in the middle. If you are absolutely sure you can't go on peaceably, I would stop; but if I once had loved a man enough to give my life and my happiness into his keeping, to make him the father of my children, I would not separate from him, until I had exhausted every resource, to see if I couldn't in some possible way end with credit."

"If you had been through what I have," said Mrs. Minturn, "you wouldn't endure it any longer."

"Perhaps," said Leslie. "But you see dear Mrs. Minturn, I am handicapped by not knowing *what* you have been through. To your world you appear to be a woman of great wealth, who does exactly as she pleases and pays her own bills. You seem to have unlimited money, power, position, leisure for anything you fancy. I'll wager you don't know the names of half the servants in your house; a skillful housekeeper takes the responsibility off your hands. You never are seen in public with your children; competent nurses care for them. You don't appear with your husband any more; yet he is a man of fine brain, unimpeachable character, who handles big affairs for other men, and father says he believes his bank account would surprise you. He has been in business for years; surely all he makes doesn't go to other men."

"You know I never thought of that!" cried Mrs. Minturn. "He had nothing to begin on and I've always kept our establishment; he's never paid for more than his clothing. Do you suppose that he has made money?"

"I know that he has!" said Leslie. "Not so fast as he might! Not so much as he could, for he is incorruptible; but money, yes! He is a powerful man, not only in the city, but all over the state. Some of these days you're going to wake up to find him a Senator, or Governor. You seem to be the only person who doesn't know it, or who doesn't care if you do. But when it comes about, as it will, you'll be so proud of him! Dear Mrs. Minturn, please, please go slowly! Don't, oh don't let anything happen that will make a big regret for both."

"Leslie, where did you get all this?" asked Mrs. Minturn in tones of mingled interest and surprise.

"From my father!" answered Leslie. "And from Douglas Bruce. Douglas' office is across the hall from Mr. Minturn's; they meet daily, and from the first they have been friends. Mr. Minturn took Douglas to his clubs, introduced him and helped him into business, so often they work together. Why only yesterday Douglas came to me filled with delight. Mr. Minturn secured an appointment for him to make an investigation for the city which will be a great help to Douglas. It will bring him in contact with prominent men, give him big work and a sample of how mercenary I am—it will bring him big pay and he knows how to use the money in a big way. Douglas knows Mr. Minturn so well, and respects him so highly, yet no one can know him as you do——"

"That is quite true! I live with him! I know the real man!" cried Mrs. Minturn.

"How mean of you!" laughed Leslie, "to distort my reasoning like that! I don't ask you to think up all the little things that have massed into one big grievance against him; I mean stop that for to-day, out here in the country where everything is so lovely, and go back where I am."

"He surely has an advocate! Leslie, when did you start making an especial study of Mr. Minturn?"

"When Douglas Bruce began speaking to me so frequently of him!" answered Leslie. "Then I commenced to watch him and to listen to what people were saying about him, and to ask Daddy."

"It's very funny that every one seems so well informed and so enthusiastic just at the time when I feel that life is unendurable with him," said Mrs. Minturn. "I can't understand it!"

"Mrs. Minturn, try, oh do try to get my viewpoint before you do anything irreparable," begged Leslie. "Away up here in the woods let's think it out! Let's discuss James Minturn in every phase of his nature and see if the big manly part doesn't far outweigh the little irritations. Let's see if you can't possibly go to the meeting he wants when we return with a balance struck in his favour. A divorced woman is always—well, it's disagreeable. Alone you'd feel stranded. Attempt marrying again, where would you find a man with half the points that count for good, to replace him? In after years when your children realize the man he is, how are you going to explain to them why you couldn't live with him?"

"From your rush of words, it is evident you have your arguments at hand," said Mrs. Minturn. "You've been thinking more about my affairs than I ever did. You bring up points I never have thought of; you make me see things that would not have occurred to me; yet as you put them, they have awful force. You haven't exactly said it, but what you mean is that you believe *me* in the wrong; so do all my friends. All of you sympathize with Mr. Minturn! All of you think him a big man worthy of every consideration and me deserving none."

"You're putting that too strong," retorted Leslie. "You are right about Mr. Minturn; but I won't admit that I find you 'worthy of no consideration at all,' or I wouldn't be imploring you to give yourself a chance at happiness."

"'Give myself a chance at happiness!'"

"Dear Mrs. Minturn, yes!" said Leslie. "All your life, so far, you have lived absolutely for yourself; for your personal pleasure. Has happiness resulted?"

"Happiness?" cried Mrs. Minturn in amazement. "You little fool! With my husband practically a madman, my children incorrigible, my nerves on edge until I can't sleep, because one thought comes over and over."

"Well you achieved it in society!" said Leslie. "It's the result of doing exactly what you *wanted to!* You can't say James Minturn was to blame for what you had the money and the desire to do. You can't think your babies would have preferred their mother to the nurses and governesses they have had——"

"If you say another word about that I'll jump from the car and break my neck," threatened Mrs. Minturn. "No one sympathizes with me!"

"That is untrue," said Leslie. "I care, or I wouldn't be doing what I am now. And as for sympathy, I haven't a doubt but every woman of your especial set will weep tears of condolence with you, if you'll tell them what you have me. There is Mrs. Clinton and Mrs. Farley, and a dozen women among your dearest friends who have divorced their husbands, and are free lances or remarried; you can have friends enough to suit you in any event."

"Fools! Shallow-pated fools!" cried Mrs. Minturn. "They never read anything! Their idea of any art would convulse you! They don't know a note of real music!"

"But they are your best friends," interposed Leslie. "What then is their attraction?"

"I am sure I don't know!" said Mrs. Minturn. "I suppose it's unlimited means to follow any fad or fancy, to live extravagantly as they choose, to dress faultlessly as they have taste, freedom to go as they please! Oh they do have a good time!"

"Are you sure that they didn't go through the same 'good time' you are having right now, before they lost the men they loved and married, and then became mothers who later deliberately orphaned their own children?"

"Leslie, for God's sake where did you learn it?" cried Mrs. Minturn. "How can you hit like that? You make me feel like a—like a——! Oh Lord!"

"Don't let's talk any more, Mrs. Minturn," suggested Leslie. "You know what all refined, home-loving people think. You know society and what it has to offer. You're making yourself unhappy, while I am helping you, but if some one doesn't stop you, you may lose the love of a good man, the respect of the people worth while, and later of your own children! See, here is the swamp and this is as close as we can go with the car."

"Is this where you found the flowers for your basket?"

"Yes," said Leslie.

"No snakes, no quicksands?"

"Snakes don't like this kind of moss," answered Leslie; "this is an old lake bed grown up with tamaracks and the bog of a thousand years."

"Looks as if ten thousand might come closer!"

"Where you ever in such a place?" asked Leslie.

"Never!" said Mrs. Minturn.

"Well to do this to perfection," said Leslie, "we should go far enough for you to see the home life of our rarest wild flowers and to get the music full effect. We must look for a high place to spread this waterproof sheet I have brought along, then nestle down and keep still. The birds will see us going in, but if we make ourselves inconspicuous, they will soon forget us. Have you the score?"

"Yes," answered Mrs. Minturn. "Go ahead!"

Leslie had not expected Mrs. Minturn's calm tones and placid acceptance of the swamp. The girl sent one searching look the woman's way, then came enlightenment. This was a stunt. Mrs. Minturn had been doing stunts in the hope of new sensations all her life. What others could do, she could, if she chose; in this instance she chose to penetrate a tamarack swamp at six o'clock in the morning, to listen to the notes of a bird.

"I'll select the highest places and go as nearly where we were as I can," said Leslie. "If you step in my tracks you'll be all right."

"Why, you're not afraid, are you?" asked Mrs. Minturn.

"Not in the least," said Leslie. "Are you?"

"No!" said Mrs. Minturn. "One strikes almost everything motoring through the country, in the mountains or at sea, and travelling. This looks interesting. How deep could one sink anyway?"

"Deeply enough to satisfy you," laughed Leslie. "Come quietly now!"

Grasping the score she carried, Mrs. Minturn unconcernedly plunged after Leslie. Purposely the girl went slowly, stooping beneath branches, skirting too wet places, slipping over the high hummocks, turning to indicate by gesture a moss bed, a flower, or glancing upward to try to catch a glimpse of some entrancing musician.

Once Leslie turned to look back and saw Mrs. Minturn on her knees separating the silvery green moss heads and thrusting her hand deeply to learn the length of the roots. She noticed the lady's absorbed face, and the wet patches spreading around her knees. Leslie fancied she could see Mrs. Minturn entering the next gathering of her friends, smiling faintly and crying: "Dear people, I've had a perfectly new experience!" She could hear every tone of Mrs. Minturn's voice saying: "Ferns as luxuriant as anything in Florida! Moss beds several feet deep. A hundred birds singing, and all before sunrise, my dears!" When Mrs. Minturn arose Leslie went forward slowly until she reached the moccasin flowers, but remembering, she did not stop. The woman did. She stooped and Leslie winced as she snapped one to examine it critically. She held it up in the gray light, turning it.

"Did you ever see—little Elizabeth?" she asked.

"Yes," said Leslie.

"Do you think——?" She stopped abruptly.

"That one is too deep," said Leslie. "The colour he saw was on a freshly opened one like that."

She pointed to a paler moccasin of exquisite pink with red lavender veining. Mrs. Minturn assented.

"He can't forget anything," she said, "or let any one else. He always will keep harping."

"We were peculiarly unfortunate that day," said Leslie. "He really had no intention of saying anything, if he hadn't been forced."

"Oh he doesn't require forcing," said Mrs. Minturn. "He's always at the overflow point about her."

"Perhaps he was very fond of her," suggested Leslie.

"He was perfectly foolish about her," said Mrs. Minturn impatiently. "I lost a nurse or two through his interference. When I got such a treasure as Lucette I just told her to take complete charge, make him attend his own affairs, and not try being a nursery maid. It really isn't done these days!"

Leslie closed her lips, moving forward until she reached the space where the ragged boys and the fringed girls floated their white banners, where lacy yellow and lavender blooms caressed each other, there on the highest place she could select, across a moss-covered log, she spread the waterproof sheet, and seating herself, motioned Mrs. Minturn to do the same. She reached for the music and opening it ran over the score. Her finger paused on the notes she had whistled, while with eager face she sat waiting.

Mrs. Minturn dropped into an attitude of tense listening. The sun began dissipating the gray mists and heightening the exquisite tints on all sides. Every green imaginable was there from palest silver to the deepest, darkest shades; all dew wet, rankly growing, gold tinted and showing clearer each minute. Gradually Mrs. Minturn relaxed, made herself comfortable as possible, then turned to the orchids of the open space. The colour flushed and faded on her tired face, she nervously rolled the moccasin stem in her fingers, or looked long at the delicate flower. She was thinking so intently that Leslie saw she was neither seeing the swamp, nor hearing the birds.

It was then that a little gray singer straying through the tamaracks sent a wireless to his mate in the bushes of borderland, in which he wished to convey to her all there was in his heart about the wonders of spring, the joy of mating, the love of her, and their nest. He waited a second, then tucking his tail, swelled his throat, and made sure he had done his best.

At the first measure, Leslie thrust the sheet before Mrs. Minturn, pointing to the place. Instantly the woman scanned the score, then leaned forward listening. As the bird flew, Leslie faced Mrs. Minturn with questioning eyes. She cried softly: "He did it! Perfectly! If I hadn't heard I never would have believed."

"There is another that can do this from Verdi's *Traviata*." Leslie whistled the notes. "We may hear him also."

Again they waited. Leslie realized that Mrs. Minturn was not listening, and would have to be recalled if the bird sang. Leslie sat silent. The same bird sang, and others, but to the girl had come the intuition that Mrs. Minturn was having her hour in the garden, so wisely she remained silent. After an interminable time she arose, making her way forward as far as she could penetrate and still see the figure of the woman, then hunting an old stump, climbed upon it and did some thinking herself.

At last she returned to the motionless figure. Mrs. Minturn was leaning against the tamarack's scraggy trunk, her head resting on a branch, lightly sleeping. A rivulet staining her cheeks from each eye showed where slow tears had slipped from under her closed lids. Leslie's heart ached with pity. She thought she never had seen any one seem so sad, so alone, so punished for sins of inheritance and rearing. She sat beside Mrs. Minturn, waiting until she awakened.

"Why I must have fallen asleep!" she cried.

"For a minute," said Leslie.

"But I feel as if I had rested soundly a whole night," said Mrs. Minturn. "I'm so refreshed. And there goes that bird again. Verdi to take his notes! Who ever would have thought of it? Leslie, did you bring any lunch? I'm famished."

"We must go back to the car," said Leslie.

They spread the waterproof sheet on the ground where it would be bordered with daintily traced partridge berry, and white-lined plantain leaves, and sitting on it ate their lunch. Leslie did what she could to interest Mrs. Minturn and cheer her, but at last that lady said: "Thank you dear, you are very good to me; but you can't entertain me to-day. Some other time we'll come back and bring the scores you suggest, and see what we can really hear from these birds. But to-day, I've got the battle of my life to fight. Something is coming; I should be in a measure prepared, and as I don't know what to expect, it takes all the brains I have to figure things out."

"You don't know, Mrs. Minturn?" asked Leslie.

"No," she said wearily. "I know James hates the life I lead; he thinks my time wasted. I know he's a disappointed man, because he thought when he married me he could cut me out of everything worth while in the world, and set me to waiting on him, and nursing his children. Every single thing I have done since, or wanted or had, has been a disappointment to him. I know now he never would have married me, if he hadn't figured he was going to make me over; shape me and my life to suit his whims, and throw away my money to please his fancies. He's been utterly discontented since Elizabeth was born.

Why Leslie, we haven't lived together since then. He said if I were going to persist in bringing 'orphans' into the world, babies I wouldn't mother myself, or wouldn't allow him to father, there would be no more children. I laughed at him, because I didn't think he meant it; but he did, so that ended even a semblance of content. Half the time I don't know where he is, or what he is doing; he seldom knows where I am; if we appear together it is accidental; I thought I had my mind made up to leave him, and soon; but what you say, coupled with doubts I had myself, have set me to thinking, till I don't know. I hate a scandal. You know how careful I always have been. All my closest friends have jeered me for a prude; there isn't a flaw he can find, there has been none!"

"Certainly not," said Leslie. "Every one knows that."

"Leslie, you don't know, do you?" asked Mrs. Minturn. "He didn't say anything to Bruce, did he?"

"You want an honest answer?" questioned Leslie.

"Of course I do!" cried Mrs. Minturn.

"Douglas did tell me in connection with Mr. Minturn joining the Brotherhood and taking a gamin from the streets into his office, that he said he was scarcely allowed to see his own sons, not to exercise the slightest control, so he was going to try his theories on a Little Brother. But Douglas wouldn't mention it, only to me, and of course I wouldn't repeat it to any one. Mr. Minturn seemed to feel that Douglas thought it peculiar for a man having sons, to take so much pains with a newsboy; they're great friends, so he said that much to Bruce."

"'He said that much——'" scoffed Mrs. Minturn.

"Well, even so, that is very little compared with what you've said about him to me," retorted Leslie. "You shouldn't complain on that score."

"I suppose, in your eyes, I shouldn't complain about anything," said Mrs. Minturn.

"A world of things, Mrs. Minturn, but not the ones you do," said Leslie.

"Oh!" cried Mrs. Minturn.

"I think your grievance is that you were born in, and reared for, society," said Leslie, "and in your extremity it has failed you. I believe I can give you more help to-day than any woman of your age and intimate association."

"That's true Leslie, quite true!" exclaimed Mrs. Minturn eagerly. "And I need help! Oh I do!"

"You poor soul, you!" comforted Leslie. "Turn where you belong! Turn to your own blood!"

"My mother would jeer me for a weakling," said Mrs. Minturn. "She has urged me to divorce James, ever since Elizabeth was born."

"I didn't mean your mother," said Leslie. "I meant closer relatives, I meant your husband and sons."

"My husband would probably tell me he had lost all respect for me, while my sons would very likely pull my hair and kick my shins if I knelt to them for sympathy," said Mrs. Minturn. "They are perfect little animals."

"Oh Mrs. Minturn!" cried Leslie amazed. "Then you simply must take them in charge and save them; they are so fine looking, while you're their mother, you are!"

"It means giving up life as I have known it always, just about everything!" said Mrs. Minturn.

"Look at yourself now!" said Leslie. "I should think you would be glad to give up your present state."

"Leslie, do you think it wrong to gather those orchids?"

"I think it unpardonable sin to *exterminate* them," answered Leslie. "If you have any reason for wanting a few, and merely gather the flowers, leaving the roots to spread and bloom another year, I should say take them."

"Will you wait in the car until I go back?" she asked.

"But I wish to be alone," said Mrs. Minturn.

"You're not afraid? You won't become lost?"

"I am not afraid, and I will not lose myself," said Mrs. Minturn. "Must I hurry?"

"Take all the time you want," said Leslie.

It was mid-afternoon when she returned, her hands filled with a dripping moss ball in which she had embedded the stems of a mass of feathery pink-fringed orchids. Her face was flushed with tears, but her eyes were bright, her step quick and alert.

"Leslie, what do you think I am going to do?" she cried. Then without awaiting a reply: "I'm going to ask James to go with me to take these to Elizabeth, to beg him to forgive my neglect of her; to pledge the rest of my life to him and the boys."

Leslie caught Mrs. Minturn in her arms. "Oh you darling!" she exulted. "Oh you brave, wonderful girl!"

"After all, it's no more than fair," Mrs. Minturn said. "I have had everything my way since we were married. And I did love James. He's the only man I have ever really wanted. Leslie, he will forgive me and start over, won't he?"

"He'll be at your feet!" cried Leslie.

"Fortunately, I have decided to be at his," said Mrs. Minturn. "I've reached the place where I will even wipe James Jr.'s nose and dress Malcolm, and fix James' studs if it will help me to sleep, and have only a tinge of what you seem to be running over with. Leslie, you are the most joyous soul!"

"You see, I never had to think about myself," said Leslie. "Daddy always thought for me, so there was nothing left for me to spend my time and thought on but him. It was a beautiful arrangement."

"Leslie, this is your car, but won't you dear, drive fast!" begged Mrs. Minturn.

"Of course Nellie!" exclaimed the girl.

"Leslie, will you stand by me, and show me the way, all you can?" asked Mrs. Minturn anxiously. "I'll lose every friend I have got; my house must be torn down and built up from the basement on a new system, as to management; and I haven't an idea *how* to do it. Oh, I hope James can help me."

"You may be sure James will know and can help you," comforted Leslie. "You'll be leaving for the seashore in a few days; install a complete new retinue, and begin all fresh. Half the servants you keep, really interested in their work, would make you far more comfortable than you are now."

"Yes, I think that too!" agreed Mrs. Minturn eagerly. "Some way I feel as if I were turning against Lucette. I never want to see her again, after I tell her to go; not that I know what I shall do without her. The boys will probably burn down the house, and where I'll find a woman who will tolerate them, I don't know."

"Employ a man until you get control," suggested Leslie. "They are both old enough; hire a man, and explain all you want to him. They'd be afraid of a man."

"Afraid!" cried Mrs. Minturn. "They are afraid of Lucette! I can't understand it. I wonder if James——"

"Poor James!" laughed Leslie. "Honestly Nellie, don't impose too much of your—your work on him. Undertake it yourself. Show him what a woman you are."

"Great Heavens, Leslie, you don't know what you are saying!" cried Mrs. Minturn. "My only hope lies in deceiving him. If I showed him the woman I am, as I saw myself back there in that swamp an hour ago, he'd take one look, and strangle me for the public good."

"How ridiculous!" exclaimed Leslie. "Why must a woman always rush from one extreme to the other? Choose a middle course and keep it."

"That's what I am telling you I must do," said Mrs. Minturn. "Leslie, it is wonderful how I feel. I'm almost flying. Do you honestly think it is possible that there is going to be something new, something interesting, something really worth while in the world for me?"

"I know it," said Leslie. "Such interest, such novelty, such joy as you never have experienced!"

With that hope in her heart, her eyes filled with excitement, Nellie Minturn rang her bell, ran past her footman and hurried up the stairs. She laid her flowers on a table, summoned her maid, then began throwing off her hat and outer clothing.

"Do you know if Mr. Minturn is here?"

"Yes. He——" began the maid.

"Never mind what 'he.' Get out the prettiest, simplest dress I own, and the most becoming," she ordered. "Be quick! Can't you see I'm in a hurry?"

"Mrs. Minturn, I think you will thank me for telling you there is an awful row in the library," said the maid.

"'An awful row?'" Mrs. Minturn paused.

"Yes. I think they are killing Lucette," explained the maid. "She's shrieked bloody murder two or three times."

"Who? What do you mean?" demanded Mrs. Minturn.

She slipped on the bathrobe she had picked up, and stood holding it together, gazing at the maid.

"Mr. Minturn came with two men. One was a park policeman we know. They went into the library and sent for Lucette. There she goes again!"

"Is there any way I could see, could hear, what is going on, without being seen?"

"There's a door to the den from the back hall, and that leads to the library," suggested the maid.

"Show me! Help me!" begged Mrs. Minturn.

As they passed the table the orchids hanging over the edge caught on the trailing robe and started to fall. Mrs. Minturn paused to push them back, then studied the flowers an instant, and catching up the bunch carried it along. She closed the den door after her without a sound, and creeping beside the wall, hid behind the door curtain and peeped into the library. There were two men who evidently were a detective and a policeman. She saw Lucette backed against the wall, her hands clenched, her eyes wild with fear. She saw her husband's back, and on the table beside him a little box, open, its wrappings near, its contents terrifying to the woman.

"To sum up then," said Mr. Minturn in tones she never before had heard: "I can put on oath this man, who will be forced to tell what he witnessed or be impeached by others who saw it at the same time, and*are ready to testify to what he said;* I can produce the boy who came to tell me the part he took in it; I have the affidavit and have just come from the woman who interfered and followed you here in an effort to save Elizabeth; I have this piece of work in my hands, done by one of the greatest scientists and two of the best surgeons living. Although you shrink from it, I take pleasure in showing it to you. This ragged seam is an impress of the crack you made in a tiny skull lying in a vault out at Forest Hill."

He paused, holding a plaster cast before the woman.

"It's a little bit of a thing," he said deliberately. "She was a tiny creature to have been done to death at your hands. I hope you will see that small pink face as I see it, and feel the soft hair in your fingers, and—after all, I can't go on with that. But I am telling you, and showing you exactly what you are facing, because you must go from this house with these men; your things will be sent. You must leave this city and this country on the boat they take you to, and where you go you will be watched; if ever you dare take service handling a *child* again, I shall have you promptly arrested and forced to answer for the cold-blooded murder of my little daughter. Live you must, I suppose, but not longer by the torture of children. Go, before I strangle you as you deserve!"

How Mrs. Minturn came to be standing beside her husband, she never afterward knew; only that she was, pulling down his arm to stare at the white cast. Then she looked up at him and said simply: "But Lucette didn't murder her; it was I. I was her mother. I knew she was beaten. I knew she was abused! I didn't stop my pleasure to interfere, lest I should lose a minute by having to see to her myself! A woman did come to me, and a boy! I knew they were telling the truth! I didn't know it was so bad, but I knew it must have been dreadful, to bring them. I had my chance to save her. I went to her as the woman told me to, and because she was quiet, I didn't even turn her over. I didn't run a finger across her little head. I didn't call a surgeon. I preferred an hour of pleasure to taking the risk of being disturbed. I am quite as guilty as Lucette! Have them take me with her."

James Minturn stepped back, gazing at his wife. Then he motioned the men toward the door, so with the woman they left the room.

"Lucette just had her sentence," he said, "now for yours! Words are useless! I am leaving your house with my sons. They *are* my sons, and with the proof I hold, you will not claim them. If you do, you will not get them. I am taking them to the kind of a house I deem suitable for them, and to such care as I can provide. I shall keep them in my presence constantly as possible until I see just what harm has been done, and how to remedy what can be changed. I shall provide such teachers as I see fit for them, and devote the remainder of my life to them. All I ask of you is to spare them the disgrace of forcing me to*prove* my right to them, or ever having them realize just *what* happened to their sister, and *your* part in it."

She held the flowers toward him.

"I brought these——" she began, then paused. "You wouldn't believe me, if I should tell you. You are right! Perfectly justified! Of course I shall not bring this before the public. Go!"

At the door he looked back. She had dropped into a chair beside the table, holding the cast in one hand, the fringed orchids in the other.

CHAPTER VII

PEACHES' PREFERENCE IN BLESSINGS

"God ain't made a sweeter girl
'An Lily, at keeps my heart a-whirl.
If I was to tell an awful whopper,
I'd get took by the cross old copper." – *Mickey*

Thus chanted Mickey at his door, his hands behind him. Peaches stretched both hers toward him as usual; but he stood still, swinging in front of him a beautiful doll, for a little sick girl. A baby doll in a long snowy dress and a lace cap; it held outstretched arms, but was not heavy enough to tire small wavering hands. Peaches lunged forward until only Mickey's agility saved her from falling. He tossed the doll on the bed, and caught the child, the lump in his throat so big his voice was strained as he cried: "Why you silly thing!"

With her safe he again proffered it. Peaches shut her eyes and buried her face on his breast.

"Oh don't let me see it! Take it away!"

"Why Lily! I thought you'd be crazy about it," marvelled Mickey. "Honest I did! The prettiest lady sent it to you. Let me tell you!"

"Giving them up is worser 'an never having them. Take it away!" wailed Peaches.

"Well Lily!" said Mickey. "I never was stuck up about my looks, but I didn't s'pose I looked so like a granny that you'd think *that* of me. Don't I seem man enough to take care of a little flowersy-girl 'thout selling her doll? There's where I got your granny skinned a mile. I don't booze, and I never will. Mother hammered that into me. Now look what a pretty it is! You'll just love it! I wouldn't take it! I'd lay out anybody who would. Come on now! Negotiate it! Get your flippers on it!"

He was holding the child gently and stroking her tumbled hair. When he put her from him to see her face, Mickey was filled with envy because he had been forced to admit the gift was not from him. He shut his lips tight, but his face was grim as he studied Peaches' flushed cheeks and wet eyes, and noted the shaking eagerness for the doll she was afraid to look at. He reached over and put it into her arms, then piled the pillows so she could see better, talking the while to comfort her.

"Course it is yours! Course nobody is going to take it! Course you shall *always* have it, and maybe a grown-up lady doll by Christmas. Who knows?"

In utter content Peaches sank against the pillows, watching Mickey, while she gripped the baby.

"Thank you, Mickey-lovest," she said. "Oh thank you for this Precious Child!"

"You got to thank a lady about twice my height, with dark hair, pink cheeks, and beautiful dresses. She's got a big rest house, a lover man, and an automobile I wish you could see, Lily," he said.

"If I was on the rags in the corner, I'd have this child—wouldn't I?" scoffed Peaches, still clutching the doll, but her gaze on Mickey. "What happened was, 'at she *liked you* for something, and *give* you the baby, so you brought it to me. Thank you Mickey, for this Precious Child!"

Peaches lifted her lips. Mickey met them more obsessed than before. Then she turned away, clasping the doll. Mickey could see that the tears were slipping from under the child's closed lids, but her lips were on the doll face, so he knew she was happy. He stole out to bring in his purchases for supper, and begin his evening work. He gave Peaches a drink, her daily rub, cleaned the room without making dust as the nurse had shown him, and brought water. He shook his fist at the faucet.

"Now hereafter, nix on the butting in!" he said belligerently. "Mebby I couldn't have got *that* doll, but I could have got one she'd have *liked* just as well, and earned it extra, in one day. There's one feature of the Big Brother business that I was a little too fast on. He's the finest man that ever wanted me, while his rooms are done shameful. I could put a glitter on them so he could see himself with the things he has to work with, and he said any time I wanted it, the job was mine. It wouldn't be cheating him any if I took it, and did better work than he's getting, and my steady papers are sure in the morning; that would be sure in the afternoon, and if I cut ice with a buzz saw, I might get through in time to pick up something else before coming home, and being sure beats *hoping* a mile, yes ten miles! Mebby I'll investigate that business a little further, 'cause hereafter I provide for my own family. See? Lily was grand about it. Gee! she's smart to think it out that way all in a minute. But by and by she's going to have a lot of time to think. Then she'll be remembering about the lady I got to tell her of 'stead of *me*, as she *should!* Guess I'll run my own family! I'll take another look at cleaning that office. There ain't any lap-dog business in a job, and being paid for it, if you do it well."

Mickey turned the faucet and marched up the stairs with head high and shoulders square. His face was grave while he worked, but Peaches was so happy she did not notice. When he came with her supper she kissed the doll, then insisted on Mickey kissing it also. Such was the state of his subjugation he commenced with "Aw!" and ended by doing as he was told. He even helped lay the doll beside Peaches exactly as her fancy dictated, and covered it with her sheet, putting its hands outside. Peaches was enchanted. She insisted on offering it a drink of her milk first, and was so tremulously careful lest she spill a drop that Mickey had to guide her hand. He promised to wash the doll's dress if she did have an accident, or when it became soiled, and bowed his head meekly to the crowning concession by sitting on the edge of the bed, after he had finished his evening work, and holding the doll where she could see it, exactly as instructed, while he told her about his wonderful adventure.

"Began yesterday," explained Mickey. "You know I told you there was going to be a surprise. Well this is it. When the lady gave me the ribbons for you, she told me to come back to-night, and get it. Course I *could* a-got it myself. I *would* a-got it for Christmas——"

"Oh Mickey-lovest, does Christmas come here?"

"Surest thing you know!" said Mickey. "A fat stocking full of every single thing the Nurse Lady tell Santa Claus a little—a little flowersy-girl that ain't so strong yet, may have, and a big lady doll and a picture book."

"But I never had no stockings," said Peaches.

"Well you'll have by *that* time," promised Mickey.

"Oh Mickey, I'm so glad I want to say a prayin's 'at you found *me*, 'stead of some other kid!" exulted Peaches.

"Yes Miss, and that's one thing I forgot!" said Mickey. "We'll *begin* to-night. You ain't a properly raised lady unless you say your prayers. I know the one *She* taught me. To-night will be a good time, 'cause you'll be so thankful for your pretty ribbons and your baby, that you'll just love to say a real thankful prayer." "Mickey, I ain't goin' to say prayin's! I just *said* I was," explained Peaches. "I never said none for granny, 'cause she only told me to when she was drunk."

"No and you never had a box of ribbons to make you look so sweet, or a baby to stay with you while I'm gone. If you ain't thankful enough for them to say your prayers, you shouldn't have them, nor any more, nor Christmas, nor anything, but just—*just like you was*."

Peaches blinked, gasped, digested the statements, then yielded wholly.

"I guess I'll say them. Mickey when shall I?"

"To-night 'fore you go to sleep," said Mickey.

"Now tell me about the baby," urged Peaches.

"Sure! I *was!* I *could* a-got it myself, like I was telling you; but the ones in the stores have such funny clothes. They look so silly. I knew I couldn't wash them and of course they'd get dirty like everything does, and we couldn't *have* them dirty, so I thought it over, and I said to Mickey-boy, 'if the Joy Lady is so anxious to get the baby, and sew its clothes herself, why I'll just let her,' so I did *let* her, but it took some time to make them, so I had to wait to bring it 'til tonight. I was to go to her house after it, and when I got there she was coming home in her car from a long drive, and gee, Lily, I wish you could have seen her! She's the prettiest lady, and the most joyous lady I ever saw."

"Prettier than the Nurse Lady?" asked Peaches.

"Well different," explained Mickey. "Nurse Lady is all gold like the end of Sunrise Alley at four o'clock in the morning. This lady has dark hair and eyes. Both of them are as pretty as women are made, but they are not the same. Nurse Lady is when the sun comes up, and warms and comforts the world; but the doll-lady is like all the stars twinkling in the moonlight on the park lake, and music playing, and everybody dancing. The doll-lady is joy, just the Joy Lady. Gee, Lily, you should have seen her face when the car stopped, while I was coming down the steps."

"Was she so glad to see you?" asked Peaches.

"'Twasn't me!" said Mickey. "'Twas on her face *before* she saw me. She was just gleaming, and shining, and spilling over joy! She isn't the kind that would dance on the street, nor where it ain't nice to dance; but she was dancing inside just the same. She pulled me right into that big fine car, so I sat on the seat with her, and we went sailing, and skating, and flying along and all the boys guying me, but I didn't care! I like to ride in her car! I never rode in a car like that before. She went a-whizzing right to the office of the big man, where maybe I'll work; I guess I'll go see him tomorrow, I got a hankering for knowing what I'm going to *do*, and *where* I'm going to be paid for it. Well she went spinning there, and she said 'you wait a minute,' then she ran in and pretty soon out she came with him. His name is Mr. Douglas Bruce, and I guess it would be a little closer what *She'd* think right if I'd use it. And hers he calls her by, is Leslie. Ain't that pretty? When he says 'Leslie' sounds as if he kissed the name as it came through. Honest it does!"

"I bet he says it just like you say 'Lily!'"

"I wonder now!" grinned Mickey. "Well he came out and what she had told him, set him crazy too. They just talked a streak, but he shook hands with me, and she said, 'You tell the driver where to go Mickey,' and I said, 'Go where, Miss?' and she said, 'To take you home,' and I said, 'You don't need!' and she said, 'I'd like to!' and I saw she didn't care *what* she did, so I just sent him to the end of the car line and saved my nickel, and then I come on here, and both of them——"

"What?" asked Peaches eagerly.

Mickey changed the "wanted to come to see you" that had been on his lips. If he told Peaches that, and she asked for them to come, and they came, and then thought he was not taking care of her right, and took her away from him—then what?

"Said good-bye the nicest," he substituted. "And I'm going to see if she wants any more letters carried as soon as my papers are gone in the morning, and if she does, I'm going to take them, and if one is to him, I'm going to ask him more about the job he offered me, and if we can agree, I'm going to take it. Then I can buy you what you want myself, because I'll know every day exactly what I'll have, and when the rent is counted out, and for the papers, all the rest will be for eating, and what you need, and to save for your new back."

"My, I wisht I had it now!" cried Peaches. "I wisht I could a-rode in that car too! Wasn't it perfeckly grand Mickey?"

"Grand as any king," said Mickey.

"What is a king?" asked Peaches.

"One of the big bosses across the ocean," explained Mickey. "You'll learn them when you get farther with your lessons. They own most all the money, and the finest houses, and *all the people*. Just *own* them. Own them so's they can tell good friends to go to it, and *kill* each other, even *relations*."

"And do they *do* it?" marvelled Peaches.

"Sure they do it!" cried Mickey. "Why they are doing it *right now!* I could bring a paper and read you things that would make you so sick you couldn't sit up!"

"What kind of things, Mickey?"

"About kings making all the fathers kill each other, and burn down each other's houses, and blow up the cities, and eat all the food themselves, and leave the mothers with no home, and no groceries, and no stove, and no beds, and the bullets flying, and the cities burning, and no place to go, and the children starving and dying—Gee, I ain't ever going to tell you any more, Lily! It's too awful! You'd feel better not to know. Honest you would! Wish I hadn't told you anything about it at all. Where's your slate? We got to do lessons 'fore it gets so dark and we are so sleepy we can't see."

Peaches proudly handed him the slate. In wavering lines and tremulous curves ran her first day's work alone, over erasures, and with relinings, in hills and deep depressions, which it is possible Mickey read because he knew what it had to be, he proudly translated, "Mickey-lovest." Then the lines of the night before, then "cow" and "milk." And then Mickey whooped because he faintly recognized an effort to draw a picture of the cow and the milk bottle.

"Grand Lily!" he cried. "Gee, you're the smartest kid I ever knew! You'll know all I do 'fore long, and then you'll need your back, so's you can get ready to go to a Young Ladies' Sem'nary."

"What's that?" interestedly asked Peaches.

"A school. Where other *nice* girls go, and where you learn all that I don't know to teach you," said Mickey.

"I won't go!" said Peaches.

"Oh yes you will, Miss," said Mickey. "'Cause you're my family, so you'll do as I say."

"Will you go with me?" asked Peaches.

"Sure! I'll take you there in a big au——Oh, I don't know as I will either. We'll have to save our money, if we *both* go. We'll go on a *street* car, and walk up a grand av'noo among trees, and I'll take you in, and see if your room is right, and everything, and all the girls will like you 'cause you're so smart, and your hair's so pretty, and then I'll go to a boys' school close by, and learn how to make poetry pieces that beat any in the papers. Every time I make a new one I'll come and ask, 'Is Miss Lily—Miss Lily Peaches——' Gee kid, *what's your name?*"

Mickey stared at Peaches, while she stared back at him.

"I don't know," she said. "Do you care, Mickey?"

"What was your granny's?" asked Mickey.

"I don't know," answered Peaches.

"Was she your mother's mother?" persisted Mickey.

"Yes," replied Peaches.

"Did you ever see your father?" Mickey went on.

"I don't know nothing about fathers," she said.

Mickey heaved a deep sigh.

"Well! *That's* over!" he said. "*I* know something about fathers. I know a lot. I know that you are no worse off, not knowing *who* your father was than to know he was so *mean* that you are *glad* he's dead. Your way leaves you *hoping* that he was just awful nice, and got killed, or was taken sick or something; my way, there ain't no doubts in your mind. You are plumb sure he wasn't decent. Don't you bother none about fathers!"

"My I'm glad, Mickey!" cried Peaches joyously.

"So am I," said Mickey emphatically. "We don't want any fathers coming here to butt in on us, just as we get your back Carreled and you ready to start to school."

"Can I go without a *name* Mickey?" asked Peaches.

"Course not!" said Mickey. "You have to put your name on a roll the first thing, then you must be interdooced to the Head Lady and all the girls."

"What'll I do Mickey?" anxiously inquired Peaches.

"Well, for smart as you are in some spots, you're awful dumb in others," commented Mickey. "What'll you do, saphead? Gee! Ain't you *mine?* Ain't you my *family?* Ain't *my name* good enough for you? Your name will be Miss Lily Peaches O'Halloran. That's a name good enough for a Queen Lady!"

"What's a Queen?" inquired Peaches.

"Wife of those kings we were just talking about."

"Sure!" said Peaches. "None of them have a nicer name than that! Mickey, is my bow straight?"

"Naw it ain't!" said Mickey. "Take the baby 'til I fix it! It's about slipped off! There! That's better."

"Mickey, let me see it!" suggested Peaches.

Mickey brought the mirror. She looked so long he grew tired and started to put it back, but she clung to it.

"Just lay it on the bed," she said.

"Naw I don't, Miss Chicken—O'Halloran!" he said. "Mirrors cost money, and if you pull the sheet in the night, and slide ours off, and it breaks, we got seven years of bad luck coming, and we are nix on changing the luck we have right now. It's good enough for us. Think of them Belgium kids where the kings are making the fathers fight. This goes where it belongs, then you take your drink, and let me beat your pillow, and you fix your baby, and then we'll say our prayers, and go to sleep."

Mickey replaced the mirror and carried out the program he had outlined. When he came to the prayer he ordered Peaches to shut her eyes, fold her hands and repeat after him:

"'Now I lay me down to sleep'"——

Peaches' eyes opened.

"Oh, is it a poetry prayer, Mickey?" she asked.

"Yes. Kind of a one. Say it," answered Mickey.

Peaches obeyed, repeating the words lingeringly and in her sweetest tones. Mickey thrilled to his task.

"'I pray the Lord my soul to keep'"——he proceeded.

"What's my soul, Mickey?" she asked.

"The very nicest thing inside of you," explained Mickey. "Go on!"

"Like my heart?" questioned Peaches.

"Yes. Only nicer," said Mickey. "Shut your eyes and go on!"

Peaches obeyed.

"'If I should die before I wake'"——continued Mickey.

Peaches' eyes flashed open; she drew back in horror.

"I won't!" she cried. "I won't *say* that. That's what happened to granny, an' I saw. She was the awfullest, an' then—the men came. I *won't!*"

Mickey opened his eyes, looking at Peaches, his lips in a set line, his brow wrinkled in thought.

"Well I don't know what they went and put *that* in for," he said indignantly. "Scaring little kids into fits! It's all right when you don't *know* what it means, but when kids has been through what we have, it's different. I wouldn't say it either. You wait a minute. I can beat that myself. Let me think. Now I got it! Shut your eyes and go on:

"If I should come to live with Thee——"

"Well I ain't goin'!" said Peaches flatly. "I'm goin' to stay right here with you. I'd a lot rather than anywhere. King's house or anywhere!"

"I never saw such a kid!" wailed Mickey. "I think that's pretty. I like it heaps. Come on Peaches! Be good! Listen! The next line goes: 'Open loving arms to shelter me.' Like the big white Jesus at the Cathedral door. Come on now!"

"I *won't!* I'm goin' to live right here, and I don't want no big white Jesus' arms; I want *yours*. 'F I go anywhere, you got to lift me yourself, and let me take my Precious Child along."

"Lily, you're the worst kid I ever saw," said Mickey. "No you ain't either! I know a lot worse than you. You just don't understand. I guess you better pray something you *do* understand. Let me think again. Now try this: Keep me through the starry night——"

"Sure! I just love that," crooned Peaches.

"Wake me safe with sunrise bright," prompted Mickey, and the child smilingly repeated the words. "Now comes some 'Blesses,'" said Mickey. "I don't know just how to manage them. You haven't a father to bless, and your mother got what was coming to her long ago; blessing her now wouldn't help any if it wasn't pleasant; same with your granny, only more recent. I'll tell you! Now I know! 'Bless the Sunshine Lady for all the things to make me comfortable, and bless the Moonshine Lady for the ribbons and the doll.'"

"Aw!" cried Peaches, staring up at him in rebellion.

"Now you go on, Miss Chicken," ordered Mickey, losing patience, "and then you end with 'Amen,' which means, 'So be it,' or 'Make it happen that way,' or something like that. Go to it now!"

Peaches shut her eyes, refolded her hands and lifted her chin. After a long pause Mickey was on the point of breaking, she said sweetly: "Bless Mickey-lovest, an' bless him, an' bless him million times; an' bless him for the bed, an' the window, an' bless him for finding the Nurse Lady, an' bringing the ribbons, an' the doll, an' bless him for the slate, an' the teachin's, an' bless him for everything I just love, an' love. Amen—hard!"

When Peaches opened her eyes she found Mickey watching her, a commingling of surprise and delight on his face. Then he bent over and laid his cheek against hers.

"You fool little kid," he whispered tenderly. "You precious fool little flowersy-kid! You make a fellow love you 'til he nearly busts inside. Kiss me good-night, Lily."

He slipped the ribbon from her hair, straightened the sheets, arranged as the nurse had taught him, laid the doll as Peaches desired, and then screened by the foot of the bed, undressed and stretched himself on the floor. The same moon that peeped in the window to smile her broadest at Peaches and her Precious Child, and touched Mickey's face to wondrous beauty, at that hour also sent shining bars of light across the veranda where Leslie sat and told Douglas Bruce about the trip to the swamp.

"I never knew I could be so happy over anything in all this world that didn't include you and Daddy. But of course this does in a way; you, at least. Much as you think of, and are with, Mr. Minturn, you can't help being glad that joy has come to him at last. Why don't you say something, Douglas?"

"I have been effervescing ever since you came to the office after me, and I find now that the froth is off, I'm getting to the solid facts in the case, and, well I don't want to say a word to spoil your joyous day, but I'm worried, 'Bringer of Song.'"

"Worried?" cried Leslie. "Why? You don't think he wouldn't be pleased? You don't think he might not be—responsive, do you?"

"Think of the past years of neglect, insult and humiliation!" suggested Douglas.

"Think of the future years of loving care, reparation and joy!" commented Leslie.

"Please God they outweigh!" said Douglas. "Of course they will! It must be a few things I've seen lately that keep puzzling me."

"What have you seen, Douglas?" questioned Leslie.

"Deals in real estate," he answered. "Consultations with detectives and policemen, scientists and surgeons."

"But what could that have to do with Nellie Minturn?"

"Nothing, I hope," said Douglas, "but there has been a grimness about Minturn lately, a going ahead with jaws set that looks ugly for what opposes him, and you tell me they have been in opposition ever since they married. I can't put him from my thoughts as I saw him last."

"And I can't her," said Leslie. "She was a lovely picture as she came across the silver moss carpet, you know that gray green, Douglas, her face flushed, her eyes wet, her arms full of those perfectly beautiful, lavender-pink fringed orchids. She's a handsome woman, dearest, and she never looked quite so well to me as when she came picking her way beneath the dark tamarack boughs. She was going to ask him to go with her to take her flowers to Elizabeth, and over that little white casket she intended—Why Douglas, he couldn't, he simply couldn't!"

"Suppose he had something previously worked out that cut her off!"

"Oh Douglas! What makes you think such a thing?"

"What Minturn said to me this morning with such bitterness on his face and in his voice as I never before encountered in man," Douglas answered.

"He said——?" prompted Leslie.

"This is my *last* day as a *laughing-stock* for my fellowmen! To-morrow I shall hold up my head!"

"Why didn't you tell me that *before?*"

"Didn't realize until just now that you and she hadn't *seen* him—that you were acting on presumption.

"I'm going to call her!" cried Leslie.

"I wouldn't!" advised Douglas.

"Why not?"

"After as far as she went to-day, if she had anything she wanted you to know, wouldn't she feel free to call you?"

"You are right," conceded Leslie. "Even after to-day, for me to call would be an intrusion. Let's not talk of it further! Don't you wish we could take a peep at Mickey carrying the doll to the little sick girl?"

"I surely do!" answered Douglas. "What do you think of him, Leslie?"

"Great! Simply great!" cried the girl. "Douglas you should have heard him educate me on the doll question."

"How?" he asked interestedly.

"From the first glimpse I had of him, the thought came to me, 'That's Douglas' Little Brother'" she explained. "When you telephoned and said you were sending him to me, just one idea possessed me: to get what you wanted. Almost without thought at all I tried the first thing he mentioned, which happened to be a little sick neighbour girl he told me about. All girls like a doll, and I had one dressed for a birthday gift for a namesake of mine, and time plenty to fix her another. I brought it to Mickey and thought he'd be delighted."

"Was he rude?" inquired Douglas anxiously.

"Not in the least!" she answered. "Only casual! Merely made me see how thoughtless and unkind and positively vulgar my idea of pleasing a poor child was."

"Leslie, you shock me!" exclaimed Douglas.

"I mean every word of it," said the girl. "Now listen to me! It *is* thoughtless to offer a gift headlong, without considering a second, is it not?"

"Merely impulsive," replied Douglas.

"Identically the same thing!" declared Leslie. "Listen I said! Without a thought about suitability, I offered an extremely poor child the gift I had prepared for a very rich one. Mickey made me see in ten words that it would be no kindness to fill his little friend's head with thoughts that would sadden her heart with envy, make her feel all she lacked more keenly than ever; give her a gift that would breed dissatisfaction instead of joy; if that isn't vulgarity, what is? Mickey's Lily has no business with a doll so gorgeous the very sight of it brings longing, instead of comfort. It was unkind to offer a gift so big and heavy it would tire and worry her."

"There *are* some ideas there on giving!"

"Aren't there though!" said Leslie. "Mickey took about three minutes to show me that Lily was *satisfied* as she was, so no one would thank me for awakening discontent in her heart. He measured off her size and proved to me that a small doll, that would not tire her to handle, would be suitable, and so dressed that its clothes could be washed and would be plain as her own. Even further! Once my brain began working I saw that a lady doll with shoes and stockings to suggest outdoors and walking, was not a kind gift to make a bedridden child. Douglas, after Mickey started me I arose by myself to the point of seeing that a little cuddly baby doll, helpless as she, one that she could nestle, and play with lying in bed would be the proper gift for Lily. Think of a 'newsy' making me see *that!* Isn't he wonderful?"

"You should have heard him making me see things!" said Douglas. "Yours are faint and feeble to the ones he taught me. Refused me at every point, and marched away leaving me in utter rout! Outside wanting you for my wife, more than anything else on earth, I wanted Mickey for my Little Brother."

"You have him!" comforted the girl. "The Lord arranged that. You remember He said, 'All men are brothers,' and wasn't it Tolstoy who wrote: 'If people would only understand that they are not the sons of some fatherland or other, nor of governments, but are sons of God?' You and Mickey will get your brotherhood arranged to suit both of you some of these days."

"Exactly!" conceded Douglas. "But I wanted Mickey at hand now! I wanted him to come and go with me. To be educated with what I consider education."

"It will come yet," prophesied Leslie. "Your ideas are splendid! I see how fine they are! The trouble is this: you had a plan mapped out at which Mickey was to jump. Mickey happened to have preconceived ideas on the subject, so he didn't jump. You wanted to be the king on the throne and stretch out a royal hand," laughed Leslie. "You wanted to lift Mickey to your level, and with the inherent fineness in him, have him feel eternal love and gratitude toward you?"

"That sounds different, but it is the real truth."

"And Mickey doesn't care to be brother to kings, he doesn't perceive the throne even; he wants you to understand at the start that you will *take*, as well as *give*. Refusing pay for tidying your office was his first inning. That 'Me to you!' was great. I can see the accompanying gesture. It was the same one he used in demolishing my doll. Something vital and inborn. Something loneliness, work, the crowd, and raw life have taught Mickey, that we don't know. Learn all you can from him. I've had one good lesson, I'm receptive and ready for the next. Let's call the car and drive an hour."

"That will be pleasant," agreed Douglas.

"Anywhere in the suburbs to avoid the crowds," was Leslie's order to her driver.

Slowly, under traffic regulations, the car ran through the pleasant spring night; the occupants talking without caring where they were so long as they were together, in motion, and it was May. They were passing residences where city and country met. The dwellings of people city bound, country determined. Homes where men gave so many hours to earning money, then sped away to train vines, prune trees, dig in warm earth and make things grow. Such men now crossed green lawns and talked fertilizers, new annuals, tree surgery, and carried gifts of fragrant, blooming things to their friends. Here the verandas were wide and children ran from them to grassy playgrounds; on them women read or sat with embroidery hoops or visited in small groups.

"Let's move," said Leslie. "Let's coax Daddy to sell our place and come here. One wouldn't ever need go summering, it's cool and pleasant always. I'd love it! There's a new house and a lawn under old trees, to shelter playing children; isn't it charming?"

"Quite! But that small specimen seems refractory."

Leslie leaned forward to see past him. In an open door stood a man clearly silhouetted against the light. Down the steps sped a screaming boy about nine. After him ran another five or six years older. When the child saw he would be overtaken, he headed straight for the street; as the pursuer's hand brushed him, he threw himself kicking and clawing. The elder boy hesitated, looking for an opening to find a hold. The car was half a block away when Leslie turned a white face to Douglas and gasped inarticulately. He understood something was wrong so signalled the driver to stop.

"Turn and pass those children again!" ordered Leslie.

As the car went by slowly the second time, the child still fought, the boy stepped back, while James Minturn with grim face, bent under the light and by force took into his arms the twisting, fighting boy.

"Heaven help him!" cried Douglas. "Not a sign of happy reconciliation there!"

Leslie tried to choke down her sobs.

"Oh Nellie Minturn! Poor woman!" she wailed.

"So *that's* what he was doing!" marvelled Douglas. "A house he has built to suit himself; training his sons personally, with the assistance of his Little Brother. That boy was William. I see him in Minturn's office every day."

"Oh I think he might have given her a chance!" protested Leslie. "Remember how she was reared! Think what a struggle it was for her even to contemplate trying to be different."

"Evidently she was too late!" said Douglas. "He must have been gone before you returned from the swamp."

"I'm going back there and tell him a few things! I think he might have waited. Douglas, I'm afraid he did wait! She said he told her he wanted to talk with her when she came back—and oh Douglas, she said he had a small box and he threatend to 'freeze her soul with its contents!' Douglas, *what* could he have had?"

"'Freeze her soul!' Let me think!" said Douglas. "I met Professor Tickner and Dr. Wills coming from his offices a few days ago, while he's just back from a trip that he didn't tell me he was taking——

"You mean Tickner, the scientist; Wills, the surgeon?"

"Yes," answered Douglas.

"But those children! Aren't they perfectly healthy?"

"They look it! Lord, Leslie!" cried Douglas, "I have it! He *has* made good his threat. He has frozen her soul! What you want to do is to go to her, Leslie!"

"Douglas, tell me!" she demanded.

"I can't!" said Douglas. "I may be mistaken. I think I am not, but there is always a chance! Drive to the Minturn residence," he ordered.

They found a closed dark pile of stone.

"Go past that place where the children were again!" said Leslie.

The upper story was quiet. Outlined by veranda lights the massive form of James Minturn paced back and forth under the big trees, his hands clasped behind him, his head bowed, and he walked alone.

"Douglas, I'm going to speak to him. I'm going to tell him!" declared Leslie.

"But you're now conceding that *she* saw him!" Douglas pointed out. "Then what have you to tell him that she would not? If she couldn't move him with what she said, and while you don't know his side, what could you say to him?"

"Nothing," she conceded.

"Precisely my opinion," said Douglas. "Remember Leslie I am a little ahead of you in this. You know *her* side. I know all you have told me of her, also I know what he has told me; while putting what I have seen, and heard at the office, and him here with the boys, in a house she would consider too plebeian for words——"

"No Douglas. No! She is changed!" cried Leslie. "Completely changed, I tell you! She said she would wipe Malcolm's nose and fix James' studs——"

"Mere figures of speech!" remarked Douglas.

"They meant she was ready to work with her own hands for happiness," said Leslie indignantly.

"I think she's too late!" said Douglas. "I am afraid she is one of the unhappiest women in the world to-night!"

"Douglas, it wrings my heart!" cried Leslie.

"Mine also, but what can we do?" he answered. "For ten years, she has persisted in having her way, you tell me; what could she have expected?"

"That he would have some heart," protested Leslie. "That he would forgive when he was asked, as all of us are commanded to."

"Does it occur to you that he might have confronted her with something that prevented her from asking?" suggested Douglas. "She may never have reached her flowers and her proposed concessions."

"What makes you think so?" queried Leslie.

"What I see and surmise, and a thing I know."

"What can I do?" asked Leslie.

"Nothing!" Douglas said with finality. "If either of them wants you, they know where to find you. But you're tired now. Let's give the order for home."

"Shan't sleep a wink to-night!" prophesied Leslie.

"I was afraid of that!" exclaimed Douglas. "There may be a message there for you that will be a comfort."

"So there may be! Let's hurry!" urged the girl.

There was. They found a brief, pencilled note.

DEAR LESLIE:

After to-day, it was due you to send a word. You tried so hard dear, and you gave me real joy for an hour. Then James carried out his threat. He did all to me he intended, and more than he can ever know. I have agreed to him taking full possession of the boys, and going into a home such as he thinks suitable. They will be far better off, and since they scarcely know me, they can't miss me. Before you receive this, I shall have left the city. I can't state just now where I am going or what I shall do. You can realize a little of my condition. If ever you are tired of home life and faintly tempted to neglect it for society, use me for your horrible example. Good-bye,

NELLIE MINTURN.

Leslie read this aloud.

"It's a relief to know that much," she said with a deep breath. "I can't imagine myself ever being 'faintly tempted," but if I am, surely she is right about the 'horrible example.' Douglas, whatever did James Minturn have in that box?"

"I could tell you what I surmise, but so long as I don't *know* I'd better not," he answered.

"As our mutual friend Mickey would say, 'Nix on the Swell Dames,' for me!" said Leslie determinedly.

"Thank God with all my heart!" cried Douglas Bruce.

CHAPTER VIII

BIG BROTHER

"I've no time to talk," said Douglas Bruce, as Mickey appeared the following day; "my work seems too much for one man. Can you help me?"

"Sure!" said Mickey, wadding his cap into his back pocket. Then he rolled his sleeves a turn higher, lifted his chin a trifle and stepped forward. "Say what!"

It caught Douglas so suddenly there was no time for concealment. He laughed heartily.

"That's good!" he cried. Mickey grinned in comradeship. "First, these letters to the box in the hall."

"Next?" Mickey queried as he came through the door.

"This package to the room of the Clerk in the City Hall, and bring back a receipt bearing his signature."

Mickey saluted, laid the note inside the cover of a book, put it in the middle of the package, and a second later his gay whistle receded down the hall.

"'Train up a child in the way he should go, and when he is old he will not depart from it,'" Douglas quoted. "Mickey has been trained until he would make a good trainer himself."

In one-half the time the trip had taken the messenger boys Douglas was accustomed to employing, Mickey was back like the Gulf in the Forum, demanding "more."

"See what you can do for these rooms, until the next errand is ready," suggested Douglas.

Mickey began gathering up the morning papers, straightening the rugs, curtains and arranging the furniture.

"Hand this check to the janitor," said Douglas. "And Mickey, kindly ask him if two dollars was what I agreed to pay him for my extras this week."

"Sure!" said Mickey.

Douglas would have preferred "Yes sir," but "Sure!" was a permanent ejaculation decorating the tip of Mickey's tongue. The man watching closely did not fail to catch the flash of interest and the lifting of the boy figure as he paused for instructions. When he returned Douglas said casually: "While I am at it, I'll pay off my messenger service. Take this check to the address and bring a receipt for the amount."

Mickey's comment came swiftly: "Gee! that boy would be sore, if he lost his job!"

"Messenger Service Agency," Douglas said, busy at his desk. "No boy would lose his job."

"Oh!" exclaimed Mickey comprehendingly. His face lighted at the information. Next he carried a requisition for books to another city official and telephoned a café to deliver a pitcher of lemonade and some small cakes, and handed the boy a dime.

"Why didn't you send me and save your silver?"

"I did not think," answered Bruce. "Some one gets the tip, you might as well have had it."

"I didn't mean me *have* it, I meant you *save* it."

"Mickey," said Douglas, "you know perfectly I can't take your time unless you accept from me what I am accustomed to paying other boys."

"Letting others bleed you, you mean," said Mickey indignantly. "Why I'd a-been glad to brought the juice for five! You never ought to paid more."

"Should have paid more," corrected Douglas.

"'Should have paid more,'" repeated Mickey. "Thanks!"

"Now try this," said Douglas, filling two glasses.

"'Tain't usual!" said Mickey. "You drink that yourself or save it for friends that may drop in."

"Very well!" said Douglas. "Of course you might have it instead of the boy who comes after the pitcher, but if you don't like it——"

"All right if that's the way!" agreed Mickey.

He retired to a window seat, enjoyed the cool drink and nibbled the cake, his eyes deeply thoughtful. When offered a second glass Mickey did not hesitate.

"Nope!" he said conclusively. "A fellow's head and heels work better when his stomach is running light. I can earn more not to load up with a lot of stuff. I eat at home when my work is finished. She showed me that."

"She showed you a good many things, didn't She?"

"Sure!" said Mickey. "She was my mother, so we had to look out for ourselves. When you got nothing but yourself between you and the wolf, you learn to fly, and keep your think-tank in running order. She knew just what was coming to me, so She *showed* me, and *every single thing She said has come, and then some!*"

"I see!" said Douglas. "A wise mother!"

"Sure!" agreed Mickey. "But I guess it wouldn't have done either of us much good if I hadn't remembered and kept straight on doing what she taught me."

"You are right, it wouldn't," conceded Douglas.

"That's where I'm going to climb above some of the other fellows," announced Mickey confidently. "Either they didn't have mothers to teach them or else they did, and forget, or think the teaching wasn't worth anything. Now me, I *know* She was right! She always *proved* it! She had been up against it longer than I had and She knew, so I am going to go right along doing as She said. I'll beat them, and carry double at that!"

"How double, Mickey?" inquired Douglas.

"I didn't mean to say that," he explained. "That was a slip. There's a—there's something——something I'm trying to do that costs more than it does to live. I'm bound to do it, so I got to run light and keep my lamps polished for chances. What next, sir?"

"Call 9-40-X, and order my car here," said Douglas.

He bent over his papers to hide his face when from an adjoining room drifted Mickey's voice in clear enunciation and suave intonation: "Mr. Douglas Bruce desires his car to be sent immediately to the Iroquois Building."

His mental comment was: "The little scamp has drifted to street lingo when he lacked his mother to restrain him. He can speak a fairly clean grade of English now if he chooses."

"Next?" briskly inquired Mickey.

"Now look here," said Douglas. "This isn't a horse race. I earn my living with my brains, not my heels. I must have time to think things out; when your next job arrives I'll tell you. If you are tired, take a nap on that couch in there."
"Asleep at the switch!" marvelled Mickey.

He went to the adjoining room but did not sleep. He quietly polished and straightened furniture, lingered before bookcases and was at Douglas' elbow as he turned to call him. Then they closed the offices and went to the car, each carrying a load of ledgers.

"You do an awful business!" commented Mickey. "Your car?"

"Yes," answered Douglas.

"You're doing grand, for young as you are."

"I haven't done it all myself, Mickey," explained Douglas. "I happened to select a father who was of an acquisitive turn of mind. He left me enough that I can have a comfortable living in a small way, from him."

"Gee! It's lucky you got the Joy Lady then!" exclaimed Mickey. "Maybe you wouldn't ever work if you didn't have her to scratch for!"

"I always have worked and tried to make something of myself," said Douglas.

"Yes, I guess you have," conceded Mickey. "I think it shows when a man does. It just shows a lot on you."

"Thank you, Mickey! Same to you!"

"Aw, nix on me!" said Mickey. "I ain't nothing on looks! I ain't ever looked at myself enough that if I was sent to find Michael O'Halloran I mightn't bring in some other fellow."

"But you're enough acquainted with yourself that you wouldn't bring in a dirty boy with a mouth full of swearing and beer," suggested Douglas.

"Well not this evening!" cried Mickey. "On a gamble that ain't my picture!"

"If it were, you wouldn't be here!" said Douglas.

"No, nor much of any place else 'cept the gutters, alleys, and the police court," affirmed Mickey. "That ain't my style! I'd like to be—well—about like you."

"You are perfectly welcome to all I have and am," said Douglas. "If you fail to take advantage of the offer, it will be your own fault."

"Yes, I guess it will," reflected Mickey. "You gave me the chance. I am to blame if I don't cop on to it, and get in the game. I like you fine! Your work is more interesting than odd jobs on the street, and you pay like a plute. You're being worked though. You pay too much. If I work for you it would save you money to let me manage that; I could get you help and things a lot cheaper, then you could spend what you save on the Joy Lady, making her more joyous."

"You are calling Miss Winton the Joy Lady?"

"Yes," said Mickey. "Doesn't she just look it?"

"She surely does," agreed Douglas. "It's a good title. I know only two that are better. She sows happiness everywhere. What about your Lily girl and her doll?"

"Doll doesn't go. That's a Precious Child!"

"I see! Lily is a little girl you like, Mickey?"

"Lily is the littlest girl you ever saw," answered Mickey, "with a bad back so that she hasn't ever walked; and she's so sweet—she's the only thing I've got to love, so I love her 'til it hurts. Her back is one thing I'm saving for. I'm going to have it Carreled as soon as I get money, and she grows strong enough to stand it."

"'Carreled?'" queried Douglas wonderingly.

"You know the man who put different legs on a dog?" said Mickey. "I often read about him in papers I sell. I think he can fix her back. But not yet. A Sunshine Nurse I know says nobody can help her back 'til she grows a lot stronger and fatter. She has to have milk and be rubbed with oil, and not be jerked for a while before it's any use to begin on her back."

"And has she the milk and the oil and the kindness?"

"You just bet she has," said Mickey. "Her family tends to that. And she has got a bed, and a window, and her Precious Child, and a slate, and books."

"That's all right then," said Douglas. "Any time you see she needs anything Mickey, I'd be glad if you would tell me or Miss Winton. She loves to do kind things to little sick children to make them happier."

"So do I," said Mickey. "And Lily is *my* job. But that isn't robbing Miss Joy Lady. She can love herself to death if she wants to on hundreds of little, sick, cold, miserable children, in every cellar and garret and tenement of the east end of Multiopolis. The only kind thing God did for them out there was to give them the first chance at sunrise. Multiopolis hasn't ever followed His example by giving them anything."

"You mean Miss Winton can find some other child to love and care for?" asked Douglas.

"Sure!" said Mickey emphatically. "It's hands off Lily. Her family is taking care of her, so she's got all she needs right now."

"That's good!" said Bruce. "Here we unload."

They entered a building and exchanged the books they carried for others which Douglas selected with care, then returning to the office, locked them in a safe.

"Now I am driving to the golf grounds for an hour's play," said Douglas. "Will you go and caddy for me?"

"I never did. I don't know how," answered Mickey.

"You can learn, can't you?" suggested Douglas.

"Sure!" said Mickey. "I've seen boys carrying golf clubs that hadn't enough sense to break stone right. I can learn, but my learning might spoil your day's sport."

"It would be no big price to pay for an intelligent caddy," replied Douglas.

"Mr. Bruce, what price is an intelligent caddy worth?"

"Our Scotch Club pays fifty cents a game and each man employs his own boy if he chooses. The club used to furnish boys, but since the Big Brother movement began, so many of the men have boys in their offices they are accustomed to, and want to give a run over the hills after the day's work, that the rule has been changed. I can employ you, if you want to serve me."

"I'd go to the *country* in the car with you, every day you play, and carry your clubs?" asked Mickey wonderingly.

"Yes," answered Douglas.

"Over real hills, where there's trees, grass, cows and water?" questioned Mickey.

"Yes," repeated Douglas.

"What time would we get back?" he asked.

"Depends on how late I play, and whether I have dinner at the club house, say seven as a rule, maybe ten or later at times."

"Nothing doing!" said Mickey promptly. "I got to be home at six by the clock every day, even if we were engaged in 'hurling back the enemy.' See?"

"But Mickey! That spoils everything!" cried Douglas. "Of course you could work for me the remainder of the day if you wanted to, and I could keep my old clubhouse caddy, but I want *you*. You want the ride in the country, you want the walk, you *need* the change and recreation. You are not a real boy if you don't want that!"

"I'm so real, I'm two boys if *wanting* it counts, but it doesn't!" said Mickey. "You see I got a *job* for evening. I'm promised. I'd rather do what you want than anything I ever saw or heard of, except just this. I've given my word, and I'm depended on. I couldn't give up this work, and I wouldn't, if I could. Even golf ain't in it with this job that I'm on."

"What is your work Mickey?"

"Oh I ain't ever exactly certain," said Mickey. "Sometimes it is one thing, sometimes it is another, but always it's something, and it's work for a party I couldn't disappoint, not noways, not for all the golf in the world."

"You are sure?" persisted Douglas.

"Dead sure with no changing," said Mickey.

"All right then. I'm sorry!" exclaimed Douglas.

"So am I," said Mickey. "But not about the job!"

Douglas laughed. "Well come along this evening and look on. I'll be back before six and I'll run you where we did last night, if that is close your home."

"Thanks," said Mickey. "I'd love to, but you needn't bother about taking me home. I can make it if I start at six. Shall I take the things back to the café?"

"Let them go until morning," said Douglas.

"What becomes of the little cakes?"

"Their fate is undecided. Have you any suggestions?"

"I should worry!" he exclaimed. "They'd fit my pocket. I could hike past the hospital and ask the Sunshine Lady; if she said so, I could take them to Lily. Bet she never tasted any like them. If it's between her and the café selling them over, s'pose she takes the cake?"

Mickey's face was one big insinuating, suggestive smile. Douglas' was another.

"Suppose she does," he agreed.

"I must wrap them," said Mickey. "Have to be careful about Lily. If she's fed dirty, wrong stuff, it will make fever so her back will get worse instead of better."

"Will a clean envelope do?" suggested Douglas.

"That would cost you two cents," said Mickey. "Haven't you something cheaper?"

"What about a sheet of paper?" hazarded Douglas.

"Fine!" said Mickey, "and only half as expensive."

So they wrapped the little cakes and closed the office. Then Douglas said: "Now this ends work for the day. Next comes playtime."

"Then before we begin to play we ought to finish business," said Mickey. "I have been thinking over what you said the other day, and while I was right about some of it, I was mistaken about part. I ain't changing anything I said about Minturn men and his sort, and millyingaire men and their sort; but you ain't that kind of a man——"

"Thank you, Mickey," said Douglas.

"No you ain't that *kind* of a man," continued Mickey. "And you are just the kind of a man I'd *like* to be; so if the door ain't shut, guess I'll stick around afternoons."

"Not all day?" inquired Douglas.

"Well you see I am in the paper business and that takes all morning," explained Mickey. "I can always finish my first batch by noon, lots of times by ten; from that on to six I could work for you."

"Don't you think you could earn more with me, and in the winter at least, be more comfortable?" asked Douglas.

"Winter!" cried Mickey, his face whitening.

"Yes," said Douglas. "The newsboys always look frightfully cold in winter."

"Winter!" It was a piteous cry.

"What is it, Mickey?" questioned Bruce kindly.

"You know I *forgot* it," he said. "I was so took up with what I was doing, and thinking right now, that I forgot a time ever was coming when it gets blue cold, and little kids freeze. Gee! I almost wish I hadn't thought of it. I guess I better sell my paper business, and come with you all day. I *know* I could earn more. I just sort of *hate* to give up the papers. I been at them so long. I've had such a good time. 'I like to sell papers!' That's the way I always start my cry, and I do. I just love to. I sell to about the same bunch every morning, and most of my men know me, and they always say a word, and I like the rush and excitement and the things that happen, and the looking for chances on the side——"

"There's messenger work in my business."

"I see! I like that! I like your work all right," said Mickey. "Gimme a few days to sell my route to the best advantage I can, and I'll come all day. I'll come for about a half what you are paying now."

"But you admit you need money urgently."

"Well not so urgently as to skin a friend to get it—not even with the winter I hadn't thought of coming. Gee—I don't know just what I am going to do about that."

"For yourself, Mickey?" inquired Douglas.

"Well in a way, yes," hesitated Mickey. "There are things to *think* about! Gee I got to hump myself while the sun shines! If you say so, then I'll get out of the paper business as soon as I can; and I'll begin work for you steady at noon to-morrow. I've seen you pay out over seven to-day. I'll come for six. Is it a bargain?"

"No," said Douglas, "it isn't! The janitor bill was for a week of half-done work. The messenger bill was for two days, no caddying at all. If you come you will come for not less than eight and what you earn extra over that. I don't agree to better service for less pay. If you will have things between us on a commercial basis, so will I."

"Oh the Big Brother business would be all right—with you," conceded Mickey, "but I don't just like the way it's managed, mostly. God didn't make us brothers no more than he did all men, so we better not butt in and try to fix things over for Him. Looks to me like we might cut the brother business and just be *friends*. I could be an awful good *friend* to you, honest I could!"

"And I to you Mickey," said Douglas Bruce, holding out his hand. "Have it as you will. Friends, then! Look for you at noon to-morrow. Now we play. Hop in and we'll run to my rooms and get my clubs."

"Shall I sit up with your man?" asked Mickey.

"My friends sit beside me," said Douglas. Mickey spoke softly: "Yes, but if I watched him sharp, maybe I could get the hang of driving for you. Think what a lump that would save. When I'm going, I'd love to drive, just for the fun of it."

"And I wouldn't allow you to drive for less than I pay him," said Douglas.

"I don't see why!" exclaimed Mickey.

"When you grow older and know me better, you will."

While the car was running its smoothest, while the country Mickey had not seen save on rare newsboy excursions, flashed past, while the wonder of the club house, the links, and the work he would have loved to do developed, he shivered and cried in his tormented little soul: "Gee, how will I ever keep Lily warm?" Douglas noticed his abstraction and wondered. He had expected more appreciation of what Mickey was seeing and doing; he was coming to the realization that he would find out what was in the boy's heart in his own time and way. On the home run, when Douglas reached his rooms, he told the driver to take Mickey to the end of the car line; the boy shyly interposed to ask if he might go to the "Star of Hope Hospital," so Douglas changed the order.

Mickey's passport held good at the hospital. The Sunshine Nurse inspected the cakes and approved them. She was so particular she even took a tiny nibble of one and said: "Sugar, flour, egg and shortening—all right Mickey, those can't hurt her. And how is she to-day?"

"Fine!" cried Mickey. "She is getting a lot stronger already. She can sit up longer and help herself better, and she's got ribbons, the prettiest you ever laid eyes on, that a lady gave me for her hair, and they make her pink and nicer; and she's got a baby doll in long clean white dresses to snuggle down and stay with her all day; and she's got a slate, and a book, and she knows 'cow' and 'milk' and my name, and to-day she is learning 'bread.' To-morrow I am going to teach her 'baby,' and she can say her prayer too nice for anything, once we got it fixed so she'd say it at all."

"What did you teach her, Mickey?"

"'Now I lay me,' only Lily wouldn't say it the way She taught me. You see Lily was all alone with her granny when she winked out and it scared her most stiff, so when I got to that 'If I should die before I wake,' line, she just went into fits, and remembering what I'd seen myself, I didn't blame her; so I changed it for her 'til she liked it."

"Tell me about it, Mickey?" said the nurse.

"Well you see she has a window, so she can see the stars and the sun. She knows them, so I just shifted the old sad, scary lines to:

"*Guard me through the starry night,*
Wake me safe with sunshine bright!"

"But Mickey, that's lovely!" cried the nurse. "Wait till I write it down! I'll teach it to my little people. Half of them come here knowing that prayer and when they are ill, they begin to think about it. Some of them are old enough to worry over it. Why you're a poet, Mickey!"

"Sure!" conceded Mickey. "That's what I'm going to be when I get through school. I'm going to write a poetry piece about Lily for the first sheet of the *Herald* that'll be so good they'll pay me to write one every day, but all of them will be about her."

"Mickey, is there enough of such a little girl to furnish one every day?" asked the nurse.

"Surest thing you know!" cried Mickey enthusiastically. "Why there are the hundred gold rings on her head, one for each; and her eyes, tender and teasy, and sad and glad, one for each; and the colour of them different a dozen times a day, and her little white face, and her lips, and her smile, and when she's good, and when she's bad; why Miss, there's enough of Lily for a book big as Mr. Bruce's biggest law book."

"Well Mickey!" cried the girl laughing. "There's no question but you will write the poetry, only I can't reconcile it with the kind of a hustler you are. I thought poets were languid, dreamy, up-in-the-clouds kind of people."

"So they are," explained Mickey. "*That* comes later. First I got to hustle to get Lily's back Carreled and us through school, and ready to *write* the poetry; then it will take so much dreaming to think out what is nicest about her, and how to say it best, that it would make any fellow languid—you can see how that would be!"

"Yes, I see!" conceded the nurse. "Mickey, by Carreling her back, do you mean Dr. Carrel?"

"Sure!" cried Mickey. "You see I read a lot about him in the papers I sell. He's the biggest man in the *world! He's bigger than emperors and kings!* They—why the biggest thing they can *do* is to kill all their strongest, bravest men. He's so much bigger than kings, that he can take men they shoot to pieces and put them together again. Killing men ain't much! Anybody can do killing! Look at him making folks live! *Gee, he's big!*"

"And you think he can make Lily's back better?"

"Why I *know* he can!" said Mickey earnestly. "That wouldn't be a patching to what he *has* done! Soon as you say she is strong enough, I'm going to write to him and tell him all about her, and when I get the money saved, he'll come and fix her. Sure he will!"

"If you could get to him and tell him yourself, I really believe he would," marvelled the nurse. "But you see it's like this, Mickey: when men are as great as he is, just thousands of people want everything of them, and write letters by the hundreds, and if all of them were read there would be time for nothing else, so a secretary opens the mail and decides what is important, and that way the big people don't always know about the ones they would answer if they were doing it. He's been here in this very hospital; I've seen him operate once. Next time a perfectly wonderful case comes in, that is in his peculiar line, no doubt he will be notified and come again. Then if I could get word to you, and you could get Lily here, possibly—just possibly he would listen to you and look at her—of course I can't say surely he would—but I think he would!"

"Why of course he would!" triumphed Mickey. "Of course he would! He'd be tickled to pieces! He'd just love to! Any man would! Why a white little flowersy-girl who can't walk——!"

"If you could reach him, I really think he would," said the nurse positively.

"Well just you gimme a hint that he's here, and see if I don't get to him," said Mickey.

"Is there any place I'd be certain to find you quickly, if a chance should come?" she asked. "One never can tell. He might not be here in years, but he might be called, and come, to-morrow."

"Why yes!" cried Mickey. "Why of course! Why the telephone! Call me where I work!"

"But I thought you were a 'newsy!'" said the nurse.

"Well I was," explained Mickey lifting his head, "but I've give up the papers. I've graduated. I'm going to sell out tomorrow. I'm going to work permanent for Mr. Douglas Bruce. He's the biggest lawyer in Multiopolis. He's got an office in the Iriquois Building, and his call is 500-X. Write that down too and put it where you can't lose it. He's just a grand man. He asked about Lily to-day. He said any time he'd do things for her. Sure he would! He'd stop saving the taxpayers of Multiopolis, and take his car, and go like greased lightning for a little sick girl. He's the grandest man and he's got a Joy Lady that puts in most of her time making folks happy. Either of them would! Why it's too easy to talk about! You call me, I take a car and bring her scooting! If I'd see Lily standing on her feet, stepping right out like other folks, I'd be so happy I'd almost bust wide open. Honest I would! If he *does* come, you'd try *hard* to get me a chance, wouldn't you?"

"I'd try as hard for you as I would for myself Mickey; I couldn't promise more," she said.

"Lily's as good as fixed," exulted Mickey. "Why there is that big easy car standing down in the street waiting to take me home right now."

"Does Douglas Bruce send you home in his car?"

"Oh no, not regular! This is extra! Work is over for to-day so we went to the golf links; then he lets his man take me while he bathes and dresses to go to his Joy Lady. Gee, I got to hurry or I'll make the car late; but I can talk with you all you will. I can send the car back and walk or hop a 'tricity-wagon."

"Which is a street car?" queried the nurse.

"Sure!" said Mickey.

"Well go hop it!" she laughed. "I can't spare more time now, but I won't forget, Mickey; and if he comes I'll keep him till you get here, if I have to chain him."

"You go to it!" cried Mickey. "And I'll begin praying that he comes soon, and I'll just pray and pray so long and so hard, the Lord will send him quick to get rid of being asked so constant. No I won't either! Well wouldn't that rattle your slats?"

"What, Mickey?" asked the nurse.

"Why don't you *see?*" cried Mickey.

"No, I don't see," admitted the girl.

"Well I do!" said Mickey. "What would be square about that? Why that would be asking the Lord to make maybe some other little girl so sick, the Carrel man would be sent for, so I'd get my chance for Lily. That ain't business! I wouldn't have the cheek! What would the Lord *think* of me? He wouldn't come in a mile of *doing* it. I wouldn't come in ten miles of having the nerve to ask him. I do get up against it 'til my head swims. And there is *winter* coming, too!"

The nurse put her arm around Mickey again, and gently propelled him toward the elevator.

"Mickey," she said softly, her lips nipping his fair hair, "God doesn't give many of us your clear vision and your big heart. I'd have asked him that, with never a thought of who would have to be ill to bring Dr. Carrel here. But I'll tell you. You can pray *this* with a clean conscience: you can ask God if the doctor *does* come, to put it into his heart to hear you, and to examine Lily. That wouldn't be asking ill for anyone else so that you might profit by it. And dear laddie, don't worry about *winter*. This city is still taking care of its taxpayers. You do your best for Lily all summer, and when winter comes, if you're not fixed for it, I will see what your share is and you can have it in a stove that will burn warm a whole day, and lots of coal, *plenty* of it. I know I can arrange that."

"Gee, you're great!" he cried. "This is the biggest thing that ever happened to me! I see now what I can ask Him on the square; so it's *business* and all right; and Mr. Bruce or Miss Leslie will loan me a car, and if you see about the stove and the coal the city has for me"—in came Mickey's royal flourish—"why dearest Nurse Lady, Lily is as good as walking right now! Gee! In my place would you tell her?"

"I surely would," said the nurse. "It will do her good. It will give her hope. Dr. Carrel isn't the only one who can perform miracles; if he *doesn't* come by the time Lily is strong enough to bear the strain of being operated, we can try some other great man; and if she is shy, and timid from having been alone so much, expecting it will make it easier for her. By the way, wait until I bring some little gifts, I and three of my friends have made for her in our spare time. I think your mother's night dresses must be big and uncomfortable for her, even as you cut them off. Try these. Give her a fresh one each day. It is going to be dreadfully hot soon. When she has used two, bring them here and I'll have them washed for you."

"Now nix on that!" said Mickey. "You're a shining angel bright to sew them for her, I'm crazy over them, but I wash them. Mother showed me. That will be *my* share. I can do it fine. And they *will* be better! She's so lost in mother's, I have to shake them to find her!"

They laughed together, then Mickey sped to the sidewalk and ordered the car back.

"I've been too long," he said. "Nurse Lady had some things to tell me about a little sick girl and I was glad to miss my ride for them. Mr. Bruce will be ready by now. You go where he told you."

"I got twenty-seven minutes yet," said the driver. "I can take you at least almost there. Hop in."

"Mither o' Mike!" cried Mickey. "Is *that* all there is to it? Gee, how I'd like to have a try at it."

"Are you going to be in Mr. Bruce's office from now on?" asked the driver.

"If I can sell my paper line," answered Mickey.

"Got a good route?" inquired the man.

"Best of any boy in my district," said Mickey. "I *like* to sell papers. I got it down fine!"

"I guess you have," said the driver. "I know your voice, and everybody on your street knows that cry. Your route ought to be worth a fair price. I got a kid that wants a paper start. What would you ask to take him over your round and tell the men you are turning your business over to him, and teach him your cries?"

"Hum-m-m-m!" said Mickey. "My cry is whatever has the biggest headlines on the front page, mixed in with a lot of joyous fooling, and I'd have to see your boy 'fore I'd say if I could teach him. Is he a clean kid with a joyous face, and his anatomy decorated with a fine large hump? That's the only kind that gets my job. I won't have my nice men made sore all day 'cause they start it by seeing a kid with a boiled-owl face."

"You think a happy face sells most papers?"

"Know it!" said Mickey, "'cause I wear it on the job, and I get away with the rest of them three times and coming. Same everywhere as with the papers. A happy face would work with your job, if you'd loosen up a link or two, and tackle it. It may crack your complexion, if you start too violent, but taking it by easy runs and greasing the ways 'fore you cut your cable, I believe you'd survive it!"

Mickey flushed and grinned in embarrassment when people half a block away turned to look at his driver, and the boy's mouth opened as a traffic policeman smiled in sympathy when he waved his club, signalling them to cross. Mickey straightened up reassured.

"*Did you get that?*" he inquired.

"I got it!" said the driver. "But it won't ever happen again. McFinley has been on that crossing for five years and that's his first smile on the job."

"Then make it your business to see that it ain't his *last!*" advised Mickey. "There's no use growing morgue lines on your mug; with all May running wild just to please you and the man in the moon; loosen up, if you have to tickle your liver with a torpedo to start you!"

"You brass monkey!" said the driver. "You climb down right here, before I'm arrested for a plain drunk."

"Don't you think it," called Mickey. "If you like your job, man, cotton up to it; chuckle it under the chin, and get real familiar. See? Try grin, 'stead of grouch just one day and watch if the whole world doesn't look better before night."

"Thanks kid, I'll think it over!" promised the driver.

Mickey hurried home to Peaches. He hid the cake and the hospital box under the things he bought for supper and went to her with empty hands. He could see she was tired and hungry, so he gave her a drink of milk, and proceeded to the sponge bath and oil rub. These rested and refreshed her so that Mickey demanded closed eyes, while he slipped the dainty night-robe over her head, and tied the pink ribbon on her curls. Then he piled the pillows, leaned her against them and brought the mirror.

"Now open your peepers, Flowersy-girl, and tell me how Miss O'Halloran strikes you!" he exulted.

Peaches took one long look. She opened her mouth. Then she turned to Mickey and shut her mouth; shut it and clapped both hands over it; so that he saw the very act of strangling a phrase he would have condemned.

"That's a nice lady!" he commented in joy. "Now let me tell you! You got four of these gorgeous garments, each one made by a different nurse-lady, while she was resting. Every day you get a clean one, and I wash the one you wore last, careful and easy not to tear the lacy places. Ain't they the gladdest rags you ever saw!"

Peaches gasped: "Mickey, I'll bust!"

"Go on and bust then!" conceded Mickey. "Bust if you must; but don't you dare say no words that ain't for the ladiest of ladies, in that beautiful, softy, white dress."

Peaches set her lips, stretching her arms widely. She sat straighter than Mickey ever had seen her, lifting her head higher. Gradually a smile crept over her face. She was seeing a very pinched, white little girl, with a shower of yellow curls bound with a pink ribbon tied in a big bow; wearing a dainty night dress with a fancy yoke run with pink ribbons tied under her chin and at her elbows. She crooked an arm, primped her mouth, and peered at the puffed sleeves, then hastily gulped down whatever she had been tempted to say.

Again Mickey approved. Despite protests he removed the mirror, then put the doll in her arms. "Now you line up," he said. "Now you look alike! After you get your supper, comes the joy part for sure."

"More joyous than this?" Peaches surveyed herself.

"Yes, Miss! The joyousest thing of all the world that could happen to you," he said.

"But Mickey-lovest!" she cried in protest. "You know—*you know*—what *that* would be!"

"Sure I know!" said Mickey.

"I don't believe it! It never could!" she cried.

"There you go!" said Mickey in exasperation. "You make me think of them Texas bronchos kicking at everything on earth, in the Wild West shows every spring. Honest you do!"

"Mickey, you forgot my po'try piece to-night!" she interposed hastily.

"What you want a poetry piece for with such a dress and ribbon as you got?" he demanded.

"I like the po'try piece *better* than the dress or the ribbon," she asserted positively.

"You'll be saying better than the baby, next!"

"Yes, an' better than the baby!"

"You look out Miss," marvelled Mickey. "You got to tell true or you can't be my family."

"Sure and true!" said Peaches emphatically.

"Well if I ever!" cried Mickey. "I didn't think you was *that* silly!"

"'Tain't silly!" said Peaches. "The po'try pieces is *you!* 'Tain't silly to like *you* better than a dress, and a ribbon, or a Precious Child. I want my piece now!"

"Well I've been so busy to-day, I forgot your piece, said Mickey. "'Nough things have happened to make me forget my head, if 'twasn't fast. I forgot your piece. I thought you'd like the dress and the joyous thing better."

"Then you *didn't* forget it!" cried Peaches. "You thought something else, and you thought what ain't! So there! I *want* my po'try piece!"

"Well do you want it worse than your supper?" demanded Mickey.

"Yes I do!" said Peaches.

"Well use me for a mop!" cried Mickey. "Then you'll have to wait 'til I make one."

"Go on and make it!" ordered the child.

"Well how do you like this?"

"*Once a stubborn little kicker,*
Kicked until she made me snicker.
If she had wings, she couldn't fly,
'Cause she'd be too stubborn to try."

A belligerent look slowly spread over Peaches' face.

"*That's* no po'try piece," she scoffed, "an' I don't like it at all, an' I won't write it on my slate; not if I never learn to write anything. Mickey-lovest, please make a *nice* one to save for my book. It's going to have three on ev'ry page, an' a nice piece o' sky like right up there for backs, and mebby—mebby a cow on it!"

"Sure a cow on it," agreed Mickey. "I saw a lot to-day! I'll tell you after supper. Gimme a little time to think. I can't do nice ones right off."

"You did that one right off," said Peaches.

"Sure!" answered Mickey. "I was a little—a little—per_voked!_ And you said that wasn't a *nice* one."

"And so it wasn't!" asserted Peaches positively.

"If I have a nice one ready when I bring supper, will that do?" questioned Mickey.

"Yes," said Peaches. "But I won't eat my supper 'til I have it."

"Now don't you get too bossy, Miss Chicken," warned Mickey. "There's a surprise in this supper like you never had in all your life. I guess you'd eat it, if you'd see it."

"I wouldn't 'til I had my po'try piece."

In consideration of the poetry piece Mickey desisted. The inference was too flattering. Between narrowed lids he looked at Lily. "You fool sweet little kid," he muttered. Then he prepared supper. When he set it on the table he bent over and taking both hands he said gently:

"*Flowersy-girl of moonbeam white,*
Golden head of sunshine bright,
Dancing eyes of sky's own blue,
No other flower in the world like you."

"Get the slate!" cried Peaches. "Get the slate! Now *that's* a po'try piece. That's the best one yet. I'm going to put that right under the cow!"

"Sure!" said Mickey. "I think that's the best yet myself. You see, you make them come better every time, 'cause you get so much sweeter every day."

"Then why did you make the bad one?" she pouted.

"Well every time you just yell 'I won't,' without ever giving me a chance to tell you *what* I'm going to do, or why," explained Mickey. "If only you'd learn to wait a little, you'd do better. If I was to tell you that Carrel man was at the door with a new back for you, if you turn over and let him put it in, I s'pose you'd yell: 'I won't!'"

The first tinge of colour Mickey had seen, almost invisibly faint, crept to the surface of Peaches' white cheek.

"Just you try it, Mickey-lovest!" she exclaimed.

"Finish your supper, and see what I try."

Peaches obeyed. She had stopped grabbing and cramming. She ate slowly, masticating each morsel as the nurse told Mickey she should. To-night he found her so dainty and charming, as she instinctively tried to be as nice as her dress and supper demanded, that he forgot himself, until she reminded him. Then he rallied and ate his share. He presented the cakes, and while they enjoyed them he described every detail of the day he thought would interest her, until she had finished. He told her of the nurse and the dresses and when she wanted to see the others he said: "No sir! You got to wait till you are bathed and dressed each evening, and then you can see yourself, and that will be more fun than taking things all at once. You needn't think I'm coming in here *every* night with a great big lift-the-roof surprise for you. Most nights there won't be anything for you only me, and your supper."

"But Mickey, them's the nicest nights of all!" said Peaches. "I like thinking about you better than nurse-ladies, or joy-ladies, or my back, even; if it wasn't for having supper ready to *help* you."

"There you go again!" exclaimed Mickey. "Cut that stuff out, kid! You'll get me so broke up, I won't be fit for nothing but poetry, and that's tough eating; there's a lot must come, 'fore I just make a business of it. Now Miss, you brace up, and get this: the Carrel man has been in this very burg. See! Our Nurse Lady at the 'Star of Hope' has watched him making some one over. Every time anybody is brought there with a thing the matter with them, that he knows best how to cure, the big head knifers slip it over to him, so he comes and does it to get practice on the job. He *may* not come for a long time; he *might* come to-morrow. See?"

"Oh Mickey! Would he?" gasped Peaches.

"Why sure he would!" cried Mickey with his most elaborate flourish. "Sure he would! That's what he lives for. He'd be tickled to pieces to make over the back of a little girl that can't walk. Sure he would! What I ain't sure of is that you wouldn't gig back and say, 'I won't!' if you had a chance to be fixed."

Peaches spoke with deliberate conviction: "Mickey, I'm most *sure* I've *about* quit that!"

"Well, it's time!" said Mickey. "What you got to do is to eat, and sleep, and be bathed, and rubbed, and get so big and strong that when I come chasing up the steps and say, 'He's here, Lily, clap your arms around my neck and come to the china room and the glass table and be fixed,' you just take a grip and never open your head. See! You can be a game little kid, the gamest I ever saw, you will then, Lily, won't you?"

"Sure!" she promised. "I'll just grab you and I'll say, 'Go Mickey, go h——!"

"Wope! Wope there lady!" interposed Mickey. "Look out! There's a subm'rine coming. Sink it! Sink it!"

"Mickey what's a subm'rine?" asked Peaches.

"Why it's like this," explained Mickey. "There's places where there's water, like I bring to wash you, only miles and miles of it, such a lot, it's called an ocean——"

"Sure! 'Crost it where the kings is makin' people kill theirselves," cried Peaches.

"Yes," agreed Mickey. "And on the water, sailing along like a lady, is a big, beautiful ship. Then there's a nasty little boat that can creep under the water. It slips up when she doesn't know it's coming, and blows a hole in the fine ship and sinks her all spoiled. But if the nice ship sees the subm'rine coming and sinks it, why then she stays all nice, and isn't spoiled at all. See?"

"Subm'rines spoil things?" ventured Peaches.

"They were just *invented* for that, and nothing else."

"Mickey, I'll just say, 'Hurry! Run fast!' Mickey, can you carry me that far?" she asked anxiously.

"No, I can't carry you that far," admitted Mickey. "But Mr. Douglas Bruce, that we work for after this, will let me take his driver and his nice, easy car, and it will beat streetcars a mile, and we'll just go sailing for the 'Star of Hope' and get your back made over, and then comes school and everything girls like. See?"

"Mickey, what if he never comes?" wavered Peaches.

"Yes, but he *will!*" said Mickey positively.

"Mickey, what if he should come, an' wouldn't even *look* at my back?" she pursued.

"Why, he'd be *glad* to!" cried Mickey. "Don't be silly. Give the man some chance!"

CHAPTER IX

JAMES JR. AND MALCOLM

Nellie Minturn returned to her room too dazed to realize her suffering. She had intended doing something; the fringed orchids reminded her. She rang for water to put them in, while her maid with shaking fingers dressed her, then ordered the car. The girl understood that some terrible thing had happened and offered to go with the woman who moved so mechanically she proved she scarcely knew what she was doing.

"No," said Mrs. Minturn. "No, the little soul has been out there a long time alone, her mother had better go alone and see how it is."

She entered the car, gave her order and sank back against the seat. When the car stopped, she descended and found the gates guarding the doors of the onyx vault locked. She pushed her flowers between the bars, dropping them before the doors, then wearily sank on the first step, leaning her head against the gate, trying to think, but she could not. Near dawn her driver spoke to her.

"It's almost morning," he said. "You've barely time to reach home before the city will be stirring."

She paid no attention, so at last he touched her.

"You, Weston?" she asked.

"Yes, Madam," he said. "I'm afraid for you. I ventured to come closer than you said. Excuse me."

"Thank you Weston," she answered.

"Let me drive you home now, Madam," he begged.

"Just where would you take me if you were taking me home, Weston?"

"Where we came from," he replied.

"Do you think that has ever been a home, Weston?"

"I have thought it the finest home in Multiopolis, Madam," said the driver in surprise.

She laughed bitterly. "So have I, Weston. And to-day I have learned what it really is. Help me, Weston! Take me back to the home of my making."

When he rang for her, she gave him an order: "Find Mr. John Haynes and bring him here immediately."

"Bring him now, Madam?" he questioned.

"Immediately, I said," she repeated.

"I will try, Madam," said Weston.

"You will bring him at once if he is in Multiopolis," she said with finality.

Weston knew that John Haynes was her lawyer; he had brought him from his residence or office at her order many times; he brought him again. At once John Haynes dismissed all the servants in the Minturn household, arranged everything necessary, and saw Mrs. Minturn aboard a train in company with a new maid of his selection; then he mailed a deed of gift of the Minturn residence to the city of Multiopolis for an endowed Children's Hospital. The morning papers briefly announced the departure and the gift. At his breakfast table James Minturn read both items, then sat in deep thought.

"Not like her!" was his mental comment. "I can understand how that place would become intolerable to her; but I never knew her to give a dollar to the suffering. Now she makes a princely gift, not because she is generous, but because the house has become unbearable; and as usual, with no thought of any one save herself. If the city dares accept, how her millionaire neighbours will rage at disease and sickness being brought into the finest residence district! Probably the city will be compelled to sell it and build somewhere else. But there is something fitting in the reparation of turning a building that has been a place of torture to children, into one of healing. It proves that she has a realizing sense."

He glanced around the bright, cheerful breakfast room, with its carefully set, flower-decorated table, at his sister at its head, at a son on either hand, at a pleasant-faced young tutor on one side, and his Little Brother on the other; for so had James Minturn ordered his household.

Mrs. Winslow had left a home she loved to come at her brother's urgent call for help to save his boys. The tutor had only a few hours of his position, and thus far his salary seemed the attractive feature. James Jr. and Malcolm were too dazed to be natural for a short time. They had been picked up bodily, and carried kicking and screaming to this place, where they had been dressed in plain durable clothing. Malcolm's bed stood beside Little Brother's in a big sunny room; James' was near the tutor's in a chamber the counterpart of the other, save for its bookcases lining one wall.

There was a schoolroom not yet furnished with more than tables and chairs, its floors and walls bare, its windows having shades only. When worn out with the struggle the amazed boys had succumbed to sleep on little, hard, white beds with plain covers; had awakened to a cold bath at the hands of a man, and when they rebelled and called for Lucette and their accustomed clothing, were forcibly dressed in linen and khaki.

In a few minutes together before they were called to breakfast, James had confided to Malcolm that he thought if they rushed into William's back with all their strength, on the top step, they could roll him downstairs and bang him up good. Malcolm had doubts, but he was willing to try. William was alert, because as many another "newsy" he had known these boys in the park; so when the rush came, a movement too quick for untrained eyes to follow swung him around a newel post, while both boys bumping, screaming, rolled to the first landing and rebounded from a wall harder than they. When no one hastened at their screams to pick them up, they arose fighting each other. The tutor passed and James tried to kick him, merely because he could. He was not there either, but he stopped for this advice to the astonished boy: "If I were you I wouldn't do that. This is a free country, and if you have a right to kick me, I have the same right to kick you. I wouldn't like to do it. I'd rather allow mules and vicious horses to do the kicking; still if you're bound to kick, I can; but my foot is so much bigger than yours, and if I forgot and took you for a football, you'd probably have to go to the hospital and lie in a plaster cast a week or so. If I were you, I wouldn't! Let's go watch the birds till breakfast is called, instead."

The invitation was not accepted. The tutor descended alone. As he stepped to the veranda he met Mr. Minturn.

"Well?" that gentleman asked tersely.

Mr. Tower shook his head. He was studying law. He needed money to complete his course. He needed many things he could acquire from James Minturn.

"It's a problem," he said guardedly.

"You draw your salary for its solution," Mr. Minturn said tartly. "Work on the theory I outlined; if it fails after a fair test, we'll try another. Those boys have got to be saved. They are handsome little chaps with fine bodies and good ancestry. What happened just now?"

"They tried to rush William on the top step. William evaporated, so they took the fall themselves."

"Exactly right," commented Mr. Minturn. "Get the idea and work on it. Every rough, heartless thing they attempt, if at all possible, make it a boomerang to strike them their own blow; but you reserve blows as a last resort. There is the bell." Mr. Minturn called: "Boys! The breakfast bell is ringing. Come!"

There was not a sound. Mr. Minturn nodded to the tutor. Together they ascended the stairs. They found the boys hidden in a wardrobe. Mr. Minturn opened the door, gravely looking at them.

"Boys," he said, "you're going to live with me after this, so you're to come when I call you. You're going to eat the food that makes *men* of boys, where I can see what you get. You are going to do what I believe best for you, until you are so educated that you are capable of thinking for yourselves. Now what you must do, is to come downstairs and take your places at the table. If you don't feel hungry, you needn't eat; but I would advise you to make a good meal. I intend to send you to the country in the car. You'll soon want food. With me you will not be allowed to lunch at any hour, in cafes and restaurants. If you don't eat your breakfast you will get nothing until noon. It is up to you. Come on!"

Neither boy moved. Mr. Minturn smiled at them.

"The sooner you quit this, the sooner all of us will be comfortable," he said casually. "Observe my size. See Mr. Tower, a college athlete, who will teach you ball, football, tennis, swimming in lakes and riding, all the things that make boys manly men; better stop sulking in a closet and show your manhood. With one finger either of us can lift you out and carry you down by force; and we will, but why not be gentlemen and walk down as we do?"

Both boys looked at him; then at each other, but remained where they were.

"Time is up!" said Mr. Minturn. "They've had their chance, Mr. Tower. If they won't take it, they must suffer the consequences. Take Malcolm, I'll bring James."

Instantly both boys began to fight. No one bribed them to stop, struck them, or did anything at all according to precedent. They raged until they exposed a vulnerable point, then each man laid hold, lifted and carefully carried down a boy, placing him on a chair. James instantly slid to the floor.

"Take James' chair away!" ordered Mr. Minturn. "He prefers to be served on the floor."

Malcolm laughed.

"I don't either. I slipped," cried James.

"Then excuse yourself, resume your chair, and be mighty careful you don't slip again."

James looked at his father sullenly, but at last muttered, "Excuse me," and took the chair. With bright inflamed eyes they stared at their almost unknown father, who now had them in his power; at a woman they scarcely knew, whom they were told to call Aunt Margaret; at a strange man who was to take Lucette's place, and who had a grip that made hers seem feeble, and who was to teach them the things of which they knew nothing, and therefore hated; and at a boy nearer their own size and years, whom their father called William. Both boys refused fruit and cereal, rudely demanding cake and ice cream. Margaret Winslow looked at her brother in despair. He placidly ate his breakfast, remarking that the cook was a treasure. As he left the table Mr. Minturn laid the papers before his sister, indicating the paragraphs he had read, then calling for his car he took the tutor and the boys and left for his office. He ordered them to return for him at half-past eleven, and with minute instructions as to how they were to proceed, Mr. Tower and William drove to the country to begin the breaking in of the Minturn boys.

They disdained ball, did not care for football, improvised golf clubs and a baseball were not interesting, further than the use of the clubs on each other, which was not allowed. They did not care what the flowers were, they jerked them up by the roots when they saw it annoyed Mr. Tower, while every bird in range flew from a badly aimed stone. They tried chasing a flock of sheep, which chased beautifully for a short distance, then a ram declined to run farther and butted the breath from Malcolm's small body until it had to be shaken in again. They ran amuck and on finding they were not pursued, gave up, stopping on the bank of a creek. There they espied tiny shining fish swimming through the water and plunged in to try to capture them. When Mr. Tower and William came up, both boys were busy chasing fish. From a bank where they sat watching came a proposal from William.

"I'll tell you fellows, I believe if we could build a dam we could catch them. Gather stones and pile them up till I get my shoes off."

Instantly both boys obeyed. Mr. Tower and William stripped their feet, and rolled their trousers. Into the creek they went setting stones, packing with sod and muck, using sticks and leaves until in a short time they had a dam before which the water began rising, then overflowing.

"Now we must wait until it clears," said William.

So they sat under a tree to watch until in the clean pool formed they could see little fish gathering. Then the boys lay on the banks and tried to catch them with their hands, and succeeded in getting a few. Mr. Tower suggested they should make pools, one on each side of the creek, for their fish, so they eagerly went to work. They pushed and slapped each other, they fought over the same stone, but each constructed with his own hands a stone and mud enclosed pool in which to pen his fish. They were really interested in what they were doing, they really worked, also soon they were really tired, they were really hungry. With imperative voice they demanded food.

"You forget what your father told you at breakfast," said Mr. Tower. "He knew you were coming to the country where you couldn't get food. William and I are not hungry. We want to catch these little fish, and see who can get the most. We think it's fun. We can't take the car back until your father said to come."

"You take us back right now, and order meat, and cake, and salad and ice cream, lots of it!" stormed James.

"I have to obey your father!" said Mr. Tower.

"I just hate fathers!" cried James.

"I'll wager you do!" conceded Mr. Tower.

James stared open mouthed.

"I can see how you feel," said Mr. Tower companionably. "When a fellow has been coddled by nurses all his life, has no muscle, no appetite except for the things he shouldn't have, and never has done anything but silly park-playing, it must be a great change to be out with men, and doing as they do."

Both boys were listening, so he went on: "But don't feel badly, and don't waste breath hating. Save it for the grand fun we are going to have, and next time good food is before you, eat like men. We don't start back for an hour yet; see which can catch the most fish in that time."

"Where is Lucette?" demanded James.

"Gone back to her home across the ocean; you'll never see her again," said Mr. Tower.

"Wish I could a-busted her head before she went!" said James regretfully.

"No doubt," laughed Mr. Tower. "But break your own and see how it feels before you try it on any one else."

"I wish I could break yours!" cried James angrily.

"No doubt again," agreed the tutor, "but if you do, the man who takes my place may not know how to make bows and arrows, or build dams, or anything that's fun, while he may not be so patient as I am."

"Being hungry ain't fun," growled Malcolm.

"That's your own fault," Mr. Tower reminded him. "You wouldn't eat. That was a good breakfast."

"Wasn't a thing Lucette gave us!" scoffed James.

"But you don't like Lucette very well," said Mr. Tower. "After you've been a man six months, you won't eat cake for breakfast; or much of it at any time."

"Lucette is never coming back?" marvelled Malcolm.

"Never!" said Mr. Tower conclusively.

"How soon are we going home?" demanded James.

"Never!" replied Mr. Tower. "You are going to live where you were last night, after this."

"Where is Mamma?" cried Malcolm.

"Gone for the summer," explained Mr. Tower.

"I know. She always goes," said James. "But she took us before. I just hate it. I like this better. We make no difference to her anyway. Let her go!"

"Ain't we rich boys any more?" inquired Malcolm.

"I don't know," said Mr. Tower. "That is your father's business. I think you have as much money as ever, but from now on, you are going to live like men."

"We won't live like men!" cried both boys.

"Now look here," said Mr. Tower kindly, "you may take my word for it that a big boy almost ten years old, and another nearly his age, who can barely read, who can't throw straight, who can't swim, or row, or walk a mile without puffing like an engine, who begins to sweat over lifting a few stones, is a mighty poor specimen. You think you are wonders because you've heard yourself called big, fine boys; you are soft fatties. I can take you to the park and pick out any number of boys half your size and age who can make either of you yell for mercy in three seconds. You aren't boys at all; if you had to get on your feet and hike back to town, before a mile you'd be lying beside the road bellowing worse than I've heard you yet. You aren't as tough and game as half the girls of your age I know."

"You shut your mouth!" cried James in rage. "Mother'll fire you!"

"It is you who are fired, young man," said the tutor. "Your mother is far away by this time. She left you boys with your father, who pays me to make *men* of you, so I'm going to do it. You are big enough to know that you'll never be men, motoring around with nurses, like small babies; eating cake and ice cream when your bones and muscles are in need of stiffening and toughening. William, peel off your shirt, and show these chaps how a man's muscle should be."

William obeyed, swelling his muscles.

"Now you try that," suggested Mr. Tower to James, "and see how much muscle you can raise."

"I'm no gutter snipe," he sneered. "I'm a gentleman! I don't need muscle. I'm never going to work."

"But you've just been working!" cried the tutor. "Carrying those stones was work, and you'll remember it took both of you to lift one that William, who is only a little older than you, James, moved with one hand. You can't *play* without working. You've got to pull to row a boat, or hold a horse. You must step out lively to play tennis, or golf, or to skate, while if you try to swim without work, you'll drown."

"I ain't going to do those things!" retorted James.

"No, you are going to spend your life riding in an automobile with a nurse, feeding you cake!" scoffed the tutor.

William shouted and turned a cart wheel so flashingly quick that both boys jumped, James' face coloured a slow red, so the tutor took hope.

"I see that makes you blush," he said. "No wonder! You should be as tough as leather, and spinning along this creek bank like William. Instead you are a big, bloated softy. You carry too much fat for your size, while you are mushy as pudding! If I were you, I'd show my father how much of a man I could be, instead of how much of a baby."

"Father isn't a gentleman!" announced Malcolm. "Lucette said so!"

"Hush!" cried Mr. Tower. "Don't you ever say that again! Your father is one of the big men of this great city: one of the men who think, plan, and make things happen, that result in health, safety and comfort for all of us. One of the men who is going to rule, not only his own home, but this city, and this whole state, one of these days. You don't *know* your father. You don't know what men say and think of him. You do know that Lucette was fit for nothing but to wash and dress you like babies, big boys who should have been *ashamed* to let a woman wait on them. You do know that she is on her way back where she came from, because she could not do her work right. And you have the nerve to tell me what she said about a fine man like your father. I'm amazed at you!"

"Gentlemen don't work!" persisted Malcolm. "Mother said so!"

"I'm sorry to contradict your mother, but she forgot something," said Mr. Tower. "If the world has any gentlemen it surely should be those born for generations of royal and titled blood, and reared from their cradles in every tradition of their rank. Europe is full of them, and many are superb men. I know a few. Now will you tell me where they are to-day? They are down in trenches six feet under ground, shivering in mud and water, half dead for sleep, food, and rest, trying to save the land of their birth, the homes they own, to protect the women and children they love. They are marching miles, being shot down in cavalry rushes, and blown up in boats they are manning, in their fight to save their countries. *Gentlemen don't work!* You are too much of an idiot to talk with, if you don't know how gentlemen of birth, rank and by nature are working this very day."

The descent on him was precipitate and tumultuous.

"The war!" shouted both boys in chorus. "Tell us about the war! Oh I just love the war!" cried Malcolm. "When I'm a man I'm going to have a big shiny sword, and ride, and fight, and make the enemy fly! You ought to seen Gretchen and Lucette fight! They ain't either one got much hair left."

The tutor could not help laughing; but he made room for a boy on either side of him, and began on the war. It was a big subject, there were phases of it that shocked and repulsed him; but it was his task to undo the wrong work of ten years, he was forced to use the instrument that would accomplish that end. With so much material he could tell of things unavoidable, that men of strength and courage were doing, not forgetting the boys and the *women*. William stretched at his feet and occasionally made a suggestion, or asked a question, while James and Malcolm were interested in something at last. When it was time to return, neither wanted to go.

"Your father's orders were to come for him at half-past eleven," reminded Mr. Tower. "I work for him, so I must obey!"

"Nobody pays any attention to father," cried James. "I order you to stay here and tell of the fighting. Tell about the French boy who wouldn't show where the troops were."

"Oh, I am to take orders from you, am I?" queried Mr. Tower. "All right! Pay my salary and give me the money to buy our lunch!"

James stood thinking a second. "I have all the money I want," he said. "I go to Mrs. Ranger for my money. Mother always makes her give me what I ask for."

"You have forgotten that you have moved, and brought only yourselves," said Mr. Tower. "Your mother and the money are gone. Your father pays the bills now, and if you'll watch sharp, you'll see that things have changed since this time yesterday. Every one pays all the attention there is to *father* now. What we have, and do, and want, must come from him, and as it's a big contract, and he's needed to help manage this city, we'd better begin thinking about father, and taking care of him as much as we can. Now we are to obey him. Come on William. It's lunch time, and I'm hungry."

The boys climbed into the car without a word, and before it had gone a mile Malcolm slipped against the tutor and shortly thereafter James slid to the floor, tired to insensibility and sound asleep. So Mr. Minturn found them when he came from his office. He looked them over carefully, wet, mud-stained, grimy, bruised and sleeping in exhaustion.

"Poor little soldiers," he said. "Your battle has been a hard one I see. I hope to God you gained a victory."

He entered the car, picked up James and taking him in his arms laid the tired head on his breast, leaning his face against the boy's hair. When the car stopped at the new house, the tutor waited for instructions.

"Wake them up, make them wash themselves, and come to lunch," said Mr. Minturn. "Afterward, if they are sleepy, let them nap. They must establish regular habits at the beginning. It's the only way."

Dashes of cold water helped, so William and the tutor telling each other how hungry they were, brought two boys ready to eat anything, to the table. Cake and cream were not mentioned. Bread and milk, cold meat, salad, and a plain pudding were delicious. Between bites James studied his father, then suddenly burst forth: "Are you a gentleman?"

"I try to be," answered Mr. Minturn.

"Are you running this city?" put in Malcolm.

"I am doing what I can to help," said his father.

"Make Johnston take me home to get my money."

"You have no home but this," said Mr. Minturn. "Your old home now belongs to the city of Multiopolis. It is to be torn up and made over into a place where sick children can be cured. If you are ever too ill for us to manage, we'll take you there to be doctored."

"Will mother and Lucette be there?" asked James.

Malcolm nudged his brother.

"Can't you remember?" he said. "Lucette has gone across the ocean, and she is never coming back, goody! goody! And you know about how much mother cares when we are sick. She's *coming* the other *way*, when anybody is *sick*. She just hates sick people. Let *them* go, and get your *money!*"

Thus reminded, James began again, "I want to get my money."

"Your money came from your mother, so it went with your home, your clothes, and your playthings," explained Mr. Minturn. "You have none until you *earn* some. I can give you a home, education, and a fine position when you are old enough to hold it; but I *can't give you money. No one ever gave me any. I always had to work for mine. From now on you are going to live with me, so if you have money you'll have to go to work and earn it.*"

Both boys looked aghast at him. "Ain't we rich any more?"

"No," said Mr. Minturn. "Merely comfortable!"

James leaned back in his chair, twisting his body in its smooth linen covering. He looked intently at the room, table and people surrounding it. He glanced from the window at the wide green lawn, the big trees, and for an instant seemed to be listening to the birds singing there. He laid down his fork, turning to his brother. Then he exploded the bomb that shattered the family.

"Oh damn being rich!" he cried. "I like being *comfortable* a *lot* better! Malcolm, being rich has put us about ten miles behind where we ought to be. We're baby-girl softies! We wouldn't a-faced the guns and*not* told where the soldiers were, *we'd* a-bellered for cake. Brace up! Let's get in the game! Father, have we got to go on the street and hunt work, or can you give us a job?"

James Minturn tried to speak, then pushing back his chair left the table precipitately. James Jr. looked after him doubtfully. He turned to Aunt Margaret.

"Please excuse me," he said. "I guess he's choked. I'd better go pound him on the back like Lucette does us."

Malcolm looked at Aunt Margaret. "Mother won't let us work," he announced.

"It's like this Malcolm," said Aunt Margaret gently. "Mother had charge of you for ten years. The women she employed didn't train you as boys should be, so mother has turned you over to father. For the next ten years you will try *another* plan; after that, you will be big enough to decide how you want to live; but now I think you will just love father's way, if you will behave yourself long enough to find out what fun it is."

"Mother won't like it," said Malcolm positively.

"I think she does dear, or she wouldn't have gone and left you to try it," said Aunt Margaret. "She knew what your father would think you should do; if she hadn't thought he was *right* she would have taken you with her, as before."

"I just hate being taken on trains and boats with her. So does James! We like the dam, the fish, and we're going to have bows and arrows, to shoot at mark.

"And we are going to swim and row," added William.

"And we are going to be soldiers, and hurl back the enemy," boasted Malcolm, "ain't we Mr. Tower?"

"Indian scouts are more fun," suggested the tutor.

"And there is the money we must earn, if we've *got* to," said Malcolm. "I guess father is telling James how. I'll go ask him too. Excuse me, Aunt Margaret!"

"Of all the surprises I ever did have, this is the biggest one!" said Aunt Margaret. "I was afraid I never could like them. I thought this morning it would take years."

"There is nothing like the receptivity and plasticity of children," said the tutor.

Later James Minturn appeared on his veranda with a small boy clinging to each hand. The trio came forth with red eyes, but firmly allied.

"Call the car, if you please, William," said Senior. "I am going to help build that dam higher, and see how many fish I can catch for my pool."

Malcolm walked beside him, rubbing his head caressingly across an arm. "We don't have to go on the streets and hunt," he announced. "Father is going to find us work. While the war is so bad, we'll drink milk, and send what we earn to boys who have no father. The war won't take our father, will it?"

"To-night we will pray God not to let that happen," said Aunt Margaret. "Is there room in the car for me too, James? I haven't seen one of those little brook fish in years!"

James Jr. went to her and leaned against her chair. "I got three in my pool. You may see mine! I'll give you one."

"I'd love to see them," said Aunt Margaret. "I'll go bring my hat. But I think you shouldn't give the fish away, James. They belong to God. He made their home in the water. If you take them out, you will kill them, and He won't like that. Let's just look at them, and leave them in the water."

"Malcolm, the fish 'belong to God,'" said James, turning to his brother. "We may play with them, but we mustn't take them out of the water and hurt them."

"Well, who's going to take them out of the water?" cried Malcolm. "I'm just going to scoot one over into father's pool to start him. Will you give him one too?" "Yes," said James Jr.

"The next money I earn, I shall send to the war; but the first time I rake the lawn, and clean the rugs, I'll give what I earn to father, so he will have more time to play with us. Father is the biggest man in this city!"

"It may take a few days to get a new régime started," said father, "I've lived only for work so long; but as soon as it's possible, my day will be so arranged that some part of it shall be yours, boys, to show me what you are doing. I think one day can be given wholly to going to the country."

With an ecstatic whoop they rushed James Minturn, whose wide aching arms opened to them.

CHAPTER X

THE WHEEL OF LIFE

"What are your plans for this summer, Leslie?" asked Mr. Winton over his paper at breakfast.

"The real question is, what are yours?"

"I have none," said Mr. Winton. "I can't see my way to making any for myself. Between us, strictly, Swain has been hard hit. He gave me my chance in life. It isn't in my skin to pack up and leave for the sea-shore or the mountains on the results of what he helped me to, and allow him to put up his fight *alone*. If you understood, you'd be ashamed of me if I did, Leslie."

"But I do understand, Daddy!" cried the girl. "What makes you think I don't? All my life you've been telling me how you love Mr. Swain and what a splendid big thing he did for you when you were young. Is the war making business awfully hard for you men?"

"Close my girl," said Mr. Winton. "Bed rock close!"

"That is what cramps Mr. Swain?" she continued.

"It is what cramps all of us," said Mr. Winton. "It hit him with peculiar force because he had made bad investments. He was running light anyway in an effort to recoup. All of us are on a tension brought about by the result of political changes, to which we were struggling to adjust ourselves, when the war began working greater hardships and entailing millions of loss and expenses."

"I see, and that's why I said the real question was, 'what are your plans?'" explained Leslie, "because when I find out, if perchance they should involve staying on the job this summer, why I wanted to tell you that I'm on the job too. I've thought out the grandest scheme."

"Yes, Leslie? Tell me!" said Mr. Winton.

"It's like this," said Leslie. "Everybody is economizing, shamelessly—and that's a bully word, Daddy, for in most instances it is shameless. Open faced 'Lord save me and my wife, and my son John and his wife.' In our women's clubs and lectures, magazines and sermons, we've had a steady dose all winter of hard times, and economy, and I've tried to make my friends see that their efforts at economy are responsible for the very hardest crux of the hard times."

"You mean, Leslie—?" suggested Mr. Winton eagerly.

"I mean all of us quit using eggs, dealers become frightened, eggs soar higher. Economize on meat, packers buy less, meat goes up. All of us discharge our help, army of unemployed swells by millions. It works two ways and every friend I've got is economizing for herself, and with every stroke for herself she is weakening her nation's financial position and putting a bigger burden on the man she is trying to help."

"Well Leslie—" cried her father.

"The time has come for women to find out what it is all about, then put their shoulders to the wheel of life and push. But before we gain enough force to start with any momentum, women must get together and decide what they want, what they are pushing for."

"Have you decided what you are pushing for?"

"Unalterably!" cried the girl.

"And what is it?" asked her father.

"My happiness! My joy in life!" she exclaimed.

"And exactly in what do you feel your happiness consists, Leslie?" he asked.

"You and Douglas! My home and my men and what they imply!" she answered instantly. "As I figure it, it's *homes* that count, Daddy. If the nation prospers, the birth rate of Americans has got to keep up, or soon the immigrants will be in control everywhere, as they are in places, right now. Births imply homes. Homes suggest men to support them, women to control them. If the present unrest resolves itself into a personal question, so far as the women are concerned at least, if you are going to get to primal things, whether she realizes it or no, what each woman really *wants* she learns, as Nellie Minturn learned when she took her naked soul into the swamp and showed it to her God—what each woman *wants* is her man, her cave, and her baby. If the world is to prosper, *that* is woman's work, why don't you men who are doing big things *realize* it, and do yourselves what women are going to be forced from home to *do*, mighty soon now, if you don't!"

"Well Leslie!" cried Mr. Winton.

"You said that before Daddy!" exclaimed the girl. "Yet what you truly want of a woman is a home and children. Children imply to all men what I am to you. If some men have not reared their children so that they receive from them what you get from me, it is time for the men to *realize* this, and change their methods of *rearing* their daughters and sons. A home should mean to every man what your home does to you. If all men do not get from their homes what you do, in most cases it is *their own fault*. Of course I know there are women so abominably obsessed with self, they refuse to become mothers, and prefer a café, with tangoing between courses, to a home; such women should have first the ducking stool, and if that isn't efficacious, extermination; they are a disgrace to our civilization and the weakest spot we have. They are at the bottom of the present boiling discontent of women who really want to be home loving, home keeping. They are directly responsible for the fathers, sons, brothers, and lovers with two standards of morals. A man reared in the right kind of a home, by a real mother, who goes into other homes of the same kind, ruled by similar mothers, when he leaves his, and marries the right girl and establishes for himself a real home, is not going to go *wrong*. It is the sons, lovers, and husbands of the women who refuse home and children, and carry their men into a perpetual round of what they deem pleasure in their youth, who find life desolate when age begins to come, and who instantly rebel strongest against the very conditions they have made. I've been listening to you all my life, Daddy, and remembering mother, reading, thinking, and watching for what really pays, and believe me, *I've found out*. I gave Nellie Minturn the best in my heart the other day, but you should see what I got back. Horrors, Daddy! Just plain horrors! I said to Douglas that night when I read him the letter I afterward showed you, that if, as she suggested, I was 'ever faintly tempted to neglect home life for society,' in her I would have all the 'horrible example' I'd ever need, and rest assured I shall."

"Poor woman!" exclaimed Mr. Winton.

"Exactly!" cried Leslie. "And the poorest thing about it is that *she* is not to *blame* in the least. You and my mother could have made the same kind of a woman of me. If you had fed me cake instead of bread; if you had given me candy instead of fruit; if you had taken me to the show instead of entertaining me at home; if you had sent me to summer resorts instead of summering with me in the country, you'd have had another Nellie on your hands. The world is full of Nellies, but where one woman flees too strict and monotonous a home, to make a Nellie out of herself, ten are taken out and deliberately moulded, drilled and fashioned into Nellies by their own parents. I have lain awake at nights figuring this, Daddy; some woman is urging me every day to join different movements, and I've been forced to study this out. I know the cause of the present unrest among women."

"And it is—?" suggested Mr. Winton.

"It is the rebound from the pioneer lives of our grandmothers! They and their mothers were at one extreme; we are at the widest sweep of the other. They were forced to enter the forest and in most cases defend themselves from savages and animals; to work without tools, to live with few comforts. In their determination to save their children from hardships, they lost sense, ballast and reason. They have saved them to such an extent they have *lost* them. By the very method of their rearing, they have robbed their children of love for, and interest in, home life, and with their own hands sent them to cafés and dance halls, when they should be at their homes training their children for the fashioning of future homes. I tell you, Daddy——"

"Leslie, tell me this," interposed Mr. Winton. "Did you get any small part of what you have been saying to me, from me? Do you feel what I have tried to teach you, and the manner in which I have tried to rear you, have put your love for me into your heart and such ideas as you are propounding into your head?"

"Of course, Daddy!" cried the girl. "Who else? Mother was dear and wonderful, but I scarcely remember her. What you put into the growth of me, that is what is bound to come out, when I begin to live independently."

"This is the best moment of my life!" said Mr. Winton. "From your birth you have been the better part of me, to me; and with all my heart I have *tried* to fashion you into such a woman for a future home, as your mother began, and you have completed for me. Other things have failed me; I count you my success, Leslie!"

"Oh Daddy!" cried the happy girl.

"Now go back to our start," said Mr. Winton. "You have plans for the summer, of course! I realized that at the beginning. Are you ready to tell me?"

"I am ready to ask you," she said.

"Thank you," said Mr. Winton. "I appreciate the difference. Surely a man does enjoy counting for something with his women."

"Spoiled shamelessly, dearest, that's what you are," said Leslie. "A spoiled, pampered father! But to conclude. Mr. Swain helped you. Pay back, Daddy, no matter what the cost; pay *back*. You help *him*, I'll help *you!* My idea was this: for weeks I've foreseen that you wouldn't like to leave business this summer. Douglas is delving into that investigation Mr. Minturn started him on and he couldn't be dragged away. He's perfectly possessed. Of course where my men are, like Ruth, 'there will be I also,' so for days I've been working on a plan, and now it's all finished and waiting your veto or approval."

"Thrilling, Leslie! Tell quickly. I'm all agog!"

"It's this: let's not go away and spend big sums on travel, dress, and close the house, and throw our people out of work. Do you realize, Daddy, how long you've had the same housekeeper, cook, maid and driver? Do you know how badly I'd feel to let them go, and risk getting them back in the fall? My scheme is to rent, for practically nothing, a log cabin I know, a little over an hour's run from here—a log cabin with four rooms and a lean-to and a log stable, beside a lake where there is grand fishing and swimming."

"But Leslie——" protested Mr. Winton.

"Now listen!" cried the girl. "The rent is nominal. We get the house, stable, orchard, garden, a few acres and a rented cow. The cabin has two tiny rooms above, one for you, the other for Douglas. Below, it has a room for me, a dining-room and a kitchen. The big log barn close beside has space in the haymow for the women, and in one side below for our driver, the other for the cars. Over the cabin is a grapevine. Around it there are fruit trees. There is a large, rich garden. If I had your permission I could begin putting in vegetables tomorrow that would make our summer supply. Rogers——"

"You are not going to tell me Rogers would touch a garden?" queried Mr. Winton.

"I am going to tell you that Rogers has been with me in every step of my investigations," replied Leslie. "Yesterday I called in my household and gave them a lecture on the present crisis; I found them a remarkably well-informed audience. They had a very distinct idea that if I economized by dismissing them for the summer, and leaving the house with a caretaker, what it would mean to *them*. Then I took my helpers into the car and drove out the Atwater road—you know it well Daddy, the road that runs smooth over miles of country and then instead of jumping into a lake as it seems to be going to, it swings into corduroy through a marsh, runs up on a little bridge spanning the channel between two lakes, lifts to Atwater lake shore, than which none is more lovely—you remember the white sand floor and the clean water for swimming—climbs another hill, and opposite beautiful wood, there stands the log cabin I told you of, there I took them and explained. They could clean up in a day; Rogers could plant the garden and take enough on one truck load, for a beginning. We may have wood for the fireplace by gathering it from the forest floor. Rogers again!"

"Are you quite *sure* about Rogers?"

"Suppose you ride with him going down and ask him yourself," suggested Leslie. "Rogers is anxious to hold his place. You see it's like this: all of them get regular wages, have a chance at the swimming, rowing, gardening and the country. The saving comes in on living expenses. Out there we have the cow, flour, fish, and poultry from the neighbours, fresh eggs, butter and the garden—I can cut expenses to one-fourth; lights altogether. Moonshine and candles will serve; cooking fuel, gasoline. Daddy will you go to-night and see?"

"No, I won't go to-night and see, I'll go swim and fish," said Mr. Winton. "Great Heavens, Leslie, do you really mean to live all *summer* beside a lake, where a man can expand, absorb and exercise? I must get out my fishing tackle. I wonder what Douglas has! I've tried that lake when bass were slashing around wild thorn and crab trees shedding petals and bugs. It is man's sport there! I like black bass fishing. I remember that water. Fine for swimming! Not the exhilaration of salt, perhaps, but grand, clean, old northern Indiana water, cooled by springs. I love it! Lord, Leslie! Why don't we *own* that place? Why haven't we homed there, and been comfortable for years?"

"I shall go ahead then?" queried Leslie.

"You shall go a-hurry, Miss, hurry!" cried Mr. Winton. "I'll give you just two days. One to clean, the other to move; to-morrow night send for me. I want a swim; and cornbread, milk, and three rashers of bacon for my dinner and nothing else; and can't the maids have my room and let me have a blanket on the hay?"

"But father, the garden!" cautioned Leslie.

"Oh drat the garden!" cried Mr. Winton.

"But if you go dratting things, I can't economize," the girl reminded him. "Rogers and I have that garden down on paper, and it's *late* now."

"Leslie, don't the golf links lie half a mile from there?"

"Closer Daddy," said the girl, "right around the corner."

"I don't see why you didn't think of it before," he said. "Have you told Douglas?"

"Not a word!" exclaimed Leslie. "I'm going to invite him out when everything is in fine order."

"Don't make things fine," said Mr. Winton. "Let's have them rough!"

"They will be rough enough to suit you, Daddy," laughed Leslie, "but a few things have got to be done."

"Then hurry, but don't forget the snake question."

"People are and have been living there for generations; common care is all that is required," said Leslie. "I'll be careful, but if you tell Bruce until I am ready, I'll never forgive you."

Mr. Winton arose. "'Come to me arms,'" he laughed, spreading them wide. "I wonder if Douglas Bruce knows what a treasure he is going to possess!"

"Certainly not!" said Leslie emphatically. "I wouldn't have him know for the world! I am going to be his progressive housekeeping party, to which he is invited every day, after we are married, and each day he has got a new surprise coming, that I hope he will like. The woman who endures and wears well in matrimony is the one who 'keeps something to herself.' It's my opinion that modern marriage would be more satisfactory if the engaged parties would not come so nearly being married, for so long before they are. There is so little left for afterward, in most cases, that it soon grows monotonous."

"Leslie, where did you get all of this?" he asked.

"I told you. From you, mostly," explained the girl, "and from watching my friends. Go on Daddy! And send Rogers back soon! I want to begin buying radish seed and onion sets."

So Leslie telephoned Douglas Bruce that she would be very busy with housekeeping affairs the coming two days. She made a list of what would be required for that day, left the maids to collect it, and went to buy seeds and a few tools; then returning she divided her forces and leaving part to pack the bedding, old dishes and things absolutely required for living, she took the loaded car and drove to Atwater Lake.

The owner of the land, a cultured, refined gentleman, who spoke the same brand of English used by the Wintons, and evinced a knowledge of the same books, was genuinely interested in Leslie and her plans. It was a land owner's busiest season, but he spared a man an hour with a plow to turn up the garden, and came down himself and with practiced hand swung the scythe, and made sure about the snakes. Soon the maids had the cabin walls swept, the floors scrubbed, the windows washed, and that was all that could be done. The seeds were earth enfolded in warm black beds, with flower seeds tucked in for borders. The cut grass was raked back, and spread to dry for the rented cow.

When nothing further was to be accomplished there, they returned to Multiopolis to hasten preparations for the coming day. It was all so good Leslie stopped at her father's office and poured a flood of cloverbloom, bird notes and water shimmer into his willing ears.

She seldom went to Douglas Bruce's offices, but she ran up a few moments to try in person to ease what she felt would be disappointment in not spending the evening with her. The day would be full far into the night with affairs at home, he would notice the closing of the house, and she could not risk him spoiling her plans by finding out what they were, before she was ready. She found him surrounded with huge ledgers, delving and already fretting for Mickey. She stood laughing in his doorway, half piqued to find him so absorbed in his work, and so full of the boy he was missing, that he seemed to take her news that she was too busy to see him that night with quite too bearable calmness; but his earnestness about coming the following night worked his pardon, so Leslie left laughing to herself over the surprise in store for him.

Bruce bent over his work, praying for Mickey. Everything went wrong without him. He was enough irritated by the boy who was not Mickey, that when the boy who was Mickey came to his door, he was delighted to see him. He wanted to say: "Hello, little friend. Come get in the game, quickly!" but two considerations withheld him: Mickey's manners were a trifle too casual; at times they irritated Douglas, and if he took the boy into his life as he hoped to, he would come into constant contact with Leslie and her friends, who were cultured people of homing instincts. Mickey's manners must be polished, and the way to do it was not to drop to his level, but to improve Mickey. And again, the day before, he had told Mickey to sit down and wait until an order was given him. To invite him to "get in the game" now, was good alliteration; it pleased the formal Scotch ear as did many another United States phrase of the street, so musical, concise and packed with meaning as to become almost classic; but in his heart he meant as Mickey had suspected, "to do him good"; so he must lay his foundations with care. What he said was a cordial and cheerful, "Good morning!"

"Noon," corrected Mickey. "Right ye are! Good it is! What's my job? 'Scuse me! I won't ask that again!"

"Plenty," Douglas admitted, "but first, any luck with the paper route?"

"All over but killing the boy I sold it to, if he doesn't do right. I ain't perfectly crazy about him. He's a papa's boy and pretty soft; but maybe he'll learn. It was a fine chance for me, so I soaked it."

"To whom did you sell, Mickey?" asked Douglas.

"To your driver, for his boy," answered Mickey. "We talked it over last night. Say, was your driver 'the same continued,' or did you detect glimmerings of beefsteak and blood in him this morning?"

"Why?" asked Douglas curiously.

"Oh he's such a stiff," explained Mickey. "He looks about as lively as a salted herring."

"And did you make an effort to enliven him, Mickey?"

"Sure!" cried Mickey. "The operation was highly successful! The patient made a fine recovery. Right on the job, right on the street, right at the thickest traffic corner, right at 'dead man's crossing,' he let out a whoop that split the features of a copper who hadn't smiled in years. It was a double play and it worked fine. What I want to know is whether it was fleeting or holds over."

"It must be 'over,' Mickey," said Douglas. "Since you mention it, he opened the door with the information that it was a fine morning, while I recall that there was colour on his face, and light in his usually dull eyes."

"Good!" cried Mickey. "Then there's some hope that his kid may go and do likewise."

"The boy who takes your route has to smile, Mickey?"

"Well you see most of my morning customers are regulars, so they are used to it," said Mickey. "The minute one goes into his paper, he's lost 'til knocking off time; but if he starts on a real-wide-a-wake-soulful smile, he's a chance of reproducing it, before the day is over, leastwise he has *more* chance than if he never smiles."

"So it is a part of the contract that the boy smiles at his work?" questioned Douglas.

"*It is so!*" exclaimed Mickey. "I asked Mr. Chaffner at the *Herald* office what was a fair price for my route. You see I've sold the *Herald* from the word go, and we're pretty thick. So he told me what he thought. It lifted my lid, but when I communicated it to Henry, casual like, he never batted an eye, so I am going to try his boy 'til I'm satisfied. If he can swing the job it's a go."

"Your customers should give you a vote of thanks!"

"And so they will!" cried Mickey. "You see the men who buy of me are the top crust of Multiopolis, the big fine men who can smile, and open their heads and say a pleasant word, and they like to. It does them good! I live on it! I always get my papers close home as I can so I have time coming down on the cars to take a peep myself, and nearly always there are at least three things on the first page that hit you in the eye. Once long ago I was in the *Herald* office with a note to Chaffner the big chief, and I gave him a little word jostle as I passed it over. He looked at me and laughed good natured like, so I handed him this: 'Are you the big stiff that bosses the make-up?' He says, 'Mostly! I can control it if I want to.' 'All right for you,' I said. 'I live by selling your papers, but I could sell a heap more if I had a better chance.' 'Chance in what way?' said he. 'Building your first page,' said I. He said, 'Sure. What is it that you want?' 'I'll show you,' said I. 'I'll give you the call I used this morning.' Then I cut loose and just like on the street I cried it, and he yelled some himself. 'What more do you want?' he asked me. 'A lot,' I said. 'You see I only got a little time on the cars before my men begin to get on, and my time is precious. I can't read second, third, and forty-eleventh pages hunting up eye-openers. I must get them *first* page, 'cause I'm short time, and got my pack to hang on to.

Now makin'-up, if you'd a-put that "Germans driven from the last foot of Belgian soil," first, it would a-been better, 'cause that's what every living soul wants. Then the biggest thing about *ourselves*. Place it prominent in big black letters, where I get it quick and easy, and then put me in a scream. Get me a laugh in my call, and I'll sell you out all by myself. Folks are spending millions per annum for the glad scream at night, they'll pay just the same morning, give them a chance. I live on a laugh,' said I, to Chaffner. He looked me over and he said: 'When you get too big for the papers, you come to me and I'll make a top-notch reporter out of you.' 'Thanks Boss,' said I, 'you couldn't graft that job on to me, with asphaltum and a buzz saw. I'm going to be on your front page 'fore you know it, but it's going to be a poetry piece that will raise your hair; I ain't going to frost my cake, poking into folks' private business, telling shameful things on them that half kills them. Lots of times I see them getting their dose on the cars, and they just shiver, and go white, and shake. Nix on the printing about shame, and sin, and trouble in the papers for me!' I said, and he just laughed and looked at me closer and he said, 'All right! Bring your poetry yourself, and if they don't let you in, give them this,' and he wrote a line I got at home yet."

"Is that all about Chaffner?" asked Douglas.

"Oh no!" said Mickey. "He said, 'Well here is a batch of items being written up for first page to-morrow. According to you, I should give "Belgian citizens flocking back to search for devastated homes," the first place?' 'That's got the first place in the heart of every man in God's world. Giving it first place is putting it where it belongs.' 'Here's the rest of it,' said he, 'what do you want next?' 'At the same glance I always take, *this*,' said I, pointing to where it said, 'Movement on foot to eliminate graft from city offices.' 'You think that comes next?' said he. 'Sure!' said I. 'Hits the pocketbook! Sure! Heart first! Money next!' 'Are you so sure it isn't exactly the reverse?' asked he. 'Know it!' said I. 'Watch the crowds any day, and every clip you'll see that loving a man's country, and his home, and his kids, and getting fair play, comes *before* money.' 'Yes, I guess it does!' he said thoughtful like, 'least it *should*. We'll make it the policy of this paper to put it that way anyhow. What next?' 'Now your laugh,' said I. 'And while you are at it, make it a scream!' 'All right,' he said, 'I haven't anything funny in yet, but I'll get it. Now show me where you want these spaced.' So I showed him, and every single time you look, you'll see Mr. *Herald* is made up that way, and you ought to hear me trolling out that Belgian line, soft and easy, snapping in the graft quicklike, and then yelling out the scream. You bet it catches them! If I can't get that kid on to his job, 'spect I'll have to take it back myself; least if he can't get on, he's doomed to get off. I gave him a three days' try, and if he doesn't catch by that time, he never will."

"But how are you going to know?" asked Douglas.

"I'm going down early and follow him and drill him like a Dutch recruit, and he'll wake up my men, and interest them and fetch the laugh or he'll stop!"

"You think you got a fair price?" asked Douglas.

"Know it! All it's worth, and it looks like a margin to me," said Mickey.

"That's all right then, and thank you for telling me about the papers," said Douglas. "I enjoyed it immensely. I see you are a keen student of human nature."

"'Bout all the studying I get a chance at," said Mickey.

"You'll have opportunity at other things now," said Douglas. "Since you mention it, I see your point about the papers, and if that works on business men going to business, it should work on a *jury*. I think I've had it in mind, that I was to be a compendium of information and impress on a judge or jury what I know, and why what I say is *right*. You give me the idea that a better way would be to impress on them what *they* know. Put it like this: first soften their hearts, next touch their pockets, then make them laugh; is that the idea?"

"Duck again! You're doing fine! I ain't made my living selling men papers for this long not to know the big boys *some*, and more. Each man is different, but you can cod him, or bluff him, or scare him, or let down the floodgates; some way you can put it over if you take each one separate, and hit him where he lives. See? Finding his dwelling place is the trouble."

"Mickey, I do see," cried Douglas. "What you tell me will be invaluable to me. You know I am from another land so I have personal ways of thinking and the men I'm accustomed to are different. What I have been centring on is myself, and what I can do."

"Won't work here! What you got to get a bead on here is the *other fellow*, and how to *do* him. See?"

"Take these books and fly," said Douglas. "I've spent one of the most profitable hours of my life, but concretely it is an hour, and we're going to the Country Club to-night and may stay as long as we choose and we're going to have a grand time. You like going to the country, don't you?"

"Ain't words for telling," said Mickey, gathering his armload of books and racing down the hall.

When the day's work was finished, with a load of books to deliver before an office closed, they started on the run to the club house. Bruce waited in the car while Mickey sped in with the books, and returning, to save opening the door and crossing before the man he was fast beginning to idolize, Mickey took one of his swift cuts across the back end of the car. While his hand was outstretched and his foot uplifted to enter, from a high-piled passing truck toppled a box, not a big box, but large enough to knock Mickey senseless and breathless when it struck him between the shoulders. Douglas had Mickey in the car with orders for the nearest hospital, toward which they were hurrying, when the boy opened his eyes and sat up. He looked inquiringly at Douglas, across whose knees he had found himself.

"Wha—what happened?" he questioned with his first good indrawing of recovered breath.

"A box fell from a truck loaded past reason and almost knocked the life out of you!" cried Douglas.

"'Knocked the life out of me?'" repeated Mickey.

"You've been senseless for three blocks, Mickey."

A slow horror spread over Mickey's face.

"Wha—what was you going to do?" he wavered.

"Running for a hospital," said Douglas.

"S'pose my head had been busted, and I'd been stretched on the glass table and maybe laid up for days or knocked out altogether?" demanded Mickey.

"You'd have had the best surgeon in Multiopolis, and every care, Mickey," assured Douglas.

"Ugh!" Mickey collapsed utterly.

"Must be hurt worse than I thought," was Douglas' mental comment. "He couldn't be a coward!"

But Mickey almost proved that very thing by regaining his senses again, and immediately falling into spasms of long-drawn, shuddering sobbing. Douglas held him carefully, every moment becoming firmer in his conviction of one of two things: either he was hurt worse or he was——He would not let himself think it; but never did boy appear to less advantage. Douglas urged the driver to speed. Mickey heard and understood.

"Never mind," he sobbed. "I'm all right Mr. Bruce; I ain't hurt. Not much! I'll be all right in a minute!"

"If you're not hurt, what *is* the matter with you?"

"A minute!" gasped Mickey, as another spasm of sobbing caught him.

"I am amazed!" cried Douglas. "A little jolt like that! You are acting like a coward, Mickey!"

The word straightened Mickey.

"Coward! Who? Me!" he cried. "Me that's made my way since I can remember? Coward, did you say?"

"Of course not, Mickey!" cried Douglas. "Excuse me. I shouldn't have said that. But it is unlike you. What the devil *is* the matter with you?"

"I helped carry in a busted head and saw the glass table once," he cried. "Inch more and it would a-been my head—and I might have been knocked out for days. O Lord! What will I *do?*"

"Mickey you're not afraid?" asked Douglas.

"'Fraid? Me? 'Bout as good as coward!"

"What is the matter with you?" demanded Douglas.

Mickey stared at him amazedly.

"O Lord!" he panted. "You don't s'pose I was thinking about *myself*, do you?"

"I don't know what to think!" exclaimed Douglas.

"Sure! How could you?" conceded Mickey.

He choked back another big dry sob.

"Gimme a minute to think!" he said. "O God! What have I been doing? I see now what I'm up against!"

"Mickey," said Douglas Bruce, suddenly filled with compassion, "I am beginning to understand. Won't you tell me?"

"I guess I got to," panted Mickey. "But I'm afraid! O Lord, I'm so afraid!"

"Afraid of me, Mickey?" asked Douglas gently now.

"Yes, afraid of you," said Mickey, "and afraid of her. Afraid of her, more than you."

"You mean Miss Winton?" pursued Douglas.

"Yes, I mean Miss Winton," replied Mickey. "I guess I don't risk her, or you either. I guess I go to the Nurse Lady. She's used to folks in trouble. She's trained to know what to do. Why sure! That's the thing!"

"Your back hurts, Mickey?" questioned Douglas.

"My back hurts? Aw forget my back!" cried Mickey roughly. "I ain't hurt, honest I ain't."

Douglas took a long penetrating look at the small shaking figure, then he said softly: "I wish you wanted to confide in me, Mickey! I can't tell you how glad I'd be if you'd trust me; but if you have some one else you like better, where is it you want to be driven?"

"*Course* there ain't any one I *like* better than you, 'cept——" he caught a name on the tip of his tongue and paused. "You see it's like this: I've been to this Nurse Lady before, and I know exactly what she'll say and think. If you don't think like I do, and if you go and take——"

"Gracious Heaven Mickey, you don't think I'd try to take anything you wanted, do you?" demanded Douglas.

"I don't know *what* you'd do," said Mickey. "I only know what one Swell Dame I struck wanted to do."

"Mickey," said Douglas, "when I don't know what you are thinking about, I can't be of much help; but I'd give considerable if you felt that you had come to trust me."

"Trust you? Sure I trust you, about myself. But this is——" cried Mickey.

"This is about some one else?" asked Douglas casually.

Mickey leaned forward, his elbows on his knees, his head bent with intense thinking.

"Much as you are doing for me," he muttered, "if you really care, if it makes a difference to you—of course I can *trust* you, if you *don't* think as I do!"

"You surely can!" cried Douglas Bruce. "Now Mickey, both of us are too shaken to care for the country; take me home with you and let's have supper together and become acquainted. We can't know each other on my ground alone. I must meet you on yours, and prove that I'm really your friend. Let's go where you live and have supper."

"Go where I live? You?" cried Mickey.

"Yes! You come from where you live fresh and clean each day, so can I. Take me home with you. I want to go dreadfully, Mickey. Please?"

"Well, I ain't such a cad I'm afraid for you to see how I live," he said. "Though you wouldn't want to come more than once; that ain't what I was thinking about."

"Think all you like, Mickey," said Douglas. "Henry, drive to the end of the car line where you've gone before."

On the way he stopped at a grocery, then a café, and at each place piles of tempting packages were placed in the car. Mickey's brain was working fast. One big fact was beginning to lift above all the others. His treasure was slipping from him, and for her safety it had to be so. If he had been struck on the head, forced to undergo an operation, and had lain insensible for hours—Mickey could go no further with that thought. He had to stop and proceed with the other part of his problem. Of course she was better off with him than where she had been; no sane person could dispute that; she was happy and looking improved each day but—could she be made happier and cared for still better by some one else, and cured without the long wait for him to earn the money? If she could, what would be the right name for him, if he kept her on what he could do? So they came at last as near as the car could go to Mickey's home in Sunrise Alley. At the foot of the last flight Mickey paused, package laden.

"Now I'll have to ask you to wait a minute," he said.

He ascended, unlocked the door and stepped inside. Peaches' eyes gleamed with interest at the packages, but she waved him back. As Mickey closed the door she cried: "My po'try piece! Say it, Mickey!"

"You'll have to wait again," said Mickey. "I got hit in the back with a box and it knocked the poetry out of me. You'll have to wait 'til after supper to-night, and then I'll fix the grandest one yet. Will that do?"

"Yes, if the box hit hard, Mickey," conceded Peaches.

"It hit so blame hard, Miss Chicken, that it knocked me down and knocked me out, and Mr. Bruce picked me up and carried me three blocks in his car before I got my wind or knew what ailed me."

Peaches' face was tragic; her hands stretched toward him. Mickey was young, and his brain was whirling so it whirled off the thought that came first.

"And if it had hit me *hard* enough to bust my head, and I'd been carried to a hospital to be mended and wouldn't a-knowed what hurt me for days, like sometimes, who'd a-fed and bathed you, Miss?"

Peaches gazed at him wordless.

"You close your mouth and tell me, Miss," demanded Mickey, brutal with emotion. "If I hadn't come, what would you have done?"

Peaches shut her mouth and stared while it was closed. At last she ventured a solution.

"You'd a-told our Nurse Lady," she said.

Mickey made an impatient gesture.

"Hospitals by the dozen, kid," he said, "and not a chance in a hundred I'd been took to the 'Star of Hope,' and times when your head is busted, you don't know a thing for 'most a *week*. What would you *do* if I didn't come for a week?"

"I'd have to slide off the bed if it killed me, and roll to the cupboard, and make the things do," said Peaches.

"You couldn't get up to it to save your life," said Mickey, "and there's never enough for a week, and you couldn't get to the water—what would you *do?*"

"Mickey, what would I do?" wavered Peaches.

"Well, I know, if you don't," said Mickey, "and I ain't going to tell you; but I'll tell you this much: you'd be scared and hurt worse than you ever was yet; and it's soon going to be too hot for you here, so I got to move you to a cooler place, and I don't risk being the only one knowing where you are another day; or my think-tank will split. It's about split now. I don't want to do it, Miss, but I got to, so you take your drink and lemme straighten you, and wash your face, and put your pretties on; then Mr. Douglas Bruce, that we work for now, is coming to see you and he's going to stay for supper—Now cut it out! Shut right up! Here, lemme fix you, and you see, Miss, that you act a *lady* girl, and don't make me lose my job with my boss, or we can't pay our rent. Hold still 'til I get your ribbon right, and slip a fresh nightie on you. There!"

"Mickey——" began Peaches.

"Shut up!" said Mickey in desperation. "Now mind this, Miss! You belong to *me!* I'm taking care of you. You answer what he says to you pretty or you'll not get any supper this night, and look at them bundles he got. Sit up and be nice! This is a party!"

Mickey darted around arranging the room, then he flung the door wide and called: "Ready!"

Douglas Bruce climbed the stairs and entered the door. As Mickey expected, his gaze centred and stopped. Mickey began taking packages from his hands; still gazing Douglas yielded them. Then he stepped forward when Mickey placed the chair, and said: "Mr. Douglas Bruce, this is Lily. This is Lily Peaches O'Halloran. Will you have a chair?" He turned to Peaches, putting his arm around her as he bent to kiss her.

"He's all right, Flowersy-girl," he said. "We *like* to have him come. He's our friend. Our big, nice friend who won't let a soul on earth get us. He doesn't even want us himself, 'cause he's got *one* girl. His girl is the Moonshine Lady that sent you the doll. Maybe she will come some day too, and maybe she'll make the Precious Child a new dress."

Peaches clung to Mickey and past him peered at her visitor, and the visitor smiled his most winning smile. He recognized Leslie's ribbon, and noted the wondrous beauty of the small white face, now slowly flushing the faintest pink with excitement. Still clinging she smiled back. Wordless, Douglas reached over to pick up the doll. Then the right thought came at last.

"Has the Precious Child been good to-day?" he asked.

Peaches released Mickey, dropping back against her pillows, her smile now dazzling. "Jus' as *good!*" she said.

"Fine!" said Douglas, straightening the long dress.

"An' that's my slate and lesson," said Peaches.

"Fine!" he said again as if it were the only adjective he knew. Mickey glanced at him, grinning sympathetically, "She does sort of knock you out!" he said.

"'Sort' is rather poor. Completely, would be better," said Douglas. "She's the loveliest little sister in all the world, but she doesn't resemble you. Is she like your mother?"

"Lily isn't my sister, only as you wanted me for a brother," said Mickey. "She was left and nobody was taking care of her. She's my find and you bet your life I'm going to *keep* her!"

"Oh! And how long have you had her, Mickey?"

"Now that's just what the Orphings' Home dame asked me," said Mickey with finality, "and we are nix on those dames and their askings. Lily is *mine*, I tell you. My family. Now you visit with her, while I get supper."

Mickey pushed up the table, then began opening packages and setting forth their contents. Watching him as he moved swiftly and with assurance, his head high, his lips even, a slow deep respect for the big soul in the little body began to dawn in the heart of Douglas Bruce. Understanding of Mickey came in rivers swift and strong, so while he wondered and while he watched entranced, over and over in his head went the line: "Fools rush in where angels fear to tread." With every gentle act of Mickey for the child Douglas' liking for him grew. When he went over the supper and with the judgment of a nurse selected the most delicate and suitable food for her, in the heart of the Scotsman swelled the marvel and the miracle that silenced criticism.

CHAPTER XI

THE ADVENT OF NANCY AND PETER

When Leslie began the actual work of closing her home, and loading what would be wanted for the country, she found the task too big for the time allotted, so wisely telephoned Douglas that she would be compelled to postpone seeing him until the following day.

"Leslie," laughed Douglas over the telephone, "did you ever hear of the man who cut off his dog's tail an inch at a time, so it wouldn't hurt so badly?"

"I have heard of that particular dog."

"Well this process of cutting me out of seeing you a day at a time reminds me of 'that particular dog,' and evokes my sympathy for the canine as never before."

"It's a surprise I am getting ready for you Douglas!"

"It *is* a surprise all right," answered Douglas, "and 'Bearer of Morning,' I have got a surprise for you too."

"Oh goody!" cried Leslie. "I adore surprises."

"You'll adore this one!"

"You might give me a hint!" she suggested.

"Very well!" he laughed. "Since last I saw you I have seen the loveliest girl of my experience."

"Delightful! Am I to see her also?"

"Undoubtedly!" explained Douglas. "And you'll succumb to her charms just as I did."

"When may I meet her?" asked Leslie eagerly.

"I can't say; but soon now."

"All right!" agreed the girl. "Be ready at four tomorrow."

Leslie sat in frowning thought a moment, before the telephone; then her ever-ready laugh bubbled. "Why didn't I think of it while I was talking?" she wondered. "Of course Mickey has taken him to visit his Lily. I must see about that wrong back before bone and muscle harden."

Then she began her task. By evening she had a gasoline stove set up, the kitchen provisioned, her father's room ready and arrangements sufficiently completed that she sent the car to bring him to his dinner of cornbread and bacon under an apple tree scattering pink petals beside the kitchen door, with every lake breeze. Then they went fishing and landed three black bass.

Douglas Bruce did not mind one day so much, but he resented two. When he greeted Mickey that morning it was not with the usual salutation of his friends, so the boy knew there was something not exactly right. He was not feeling precisely jovial himself. He was under suspended judgment. He knew that when Mr. Bruce had time to think, and talk over the situation with Miss Winton, both of them might very probably agree with the woman who said the law would take Lily from him and send her to a charity home for children.

Mickey, with his careful drilling on the subject, was in rebellion. *How* could the law take Lily from him? Did the law know anything *about* her? Was she in the *care* of the law when he found her? Wouldn't the law have allowed her to *die* grovelling in filth and rags, inside a few more hours? He had not infringed on the law in any way; he had merely saved a life the law had forgotten to save. Now when he had it in his possession and in far better condition than he found it, how had the law *power* to step in and rob him?

Mickey did not understand, while there was nothing in his heart that could teach him. He had found her: he would keep her. The Orphans' Home should not have her. The law should not have her. Only one possibility had any weight with Mickey: if some one like Mr. Bruce or Miss Winton wanted to give her a home of luxury, could provide care at once, for which he would be forced to wait years to earn the money; if they wanted her and the Carrel man of many miracles would come for them; did he dare leave her lying an hour, when there was even hope she might be on her feet? There was only one answer to that with Mickey, but it pained his heart. So his greeting lacked its customary spontaneity.

By noon Bruce was irritable, while Mickey was as nearly sullen as it was in his nature to be. At two o'clock Bruce surrendered, summoned the car, and started to the golf grounds. He had played three holes when he overtook a man who said a word that arrested his attention, so both of them stopped, and with notebooks and pencils, under the shade of a big tree began discussing the question that meant more to Douglas than anything save Leslie. He dismissed Mickey for the afternoon, promising him that if he would be ready by six, he should be driven back to the city.

Mickey wanted to be alone to concentrate on his problem, but people were everywhere and more coming by the carload. He could see no place that was then, or would be, undisturbed. The long road with grassy sides gave big promises of leading somewhere to the quiet retreat he sought. Telling the driver that if he were not back by six, he would be waiting down the road, Mickey started on foot, in thought so deep he scarcely appreciated the grasses he trod, the perfume in his nostrils, the concert in his ears. What did at last arouse him was the fact that he was very thirsty. That made him realize that this was the warmest day of the season. Instantly his mind flew to the mite of a girl, lying so patiently, watching the clock for his coming, living for the sound of his feet.

Mickey stopped, studying the landscape. A cool gentle breeze crossed the clover field beside the way, refreshing him in its passing. He sucked his lungs full, then lifted his cap, shaking the hair from his forehead. He stuffed the cap into his pocket, walking slowly along, intending to stop at the nearest farmhouse to ask for water. But the first home was not to Mickey's liking. He went on, passing another and another.

Then he came to land that attracted him. The fences were so straight. The corners so clean where they were empty, so delightful where they were filled with alder, wild plum, hawthorn; attractive locations for the birds of the bushes that were field and orchard feeders. Then the barn and outbuildings looked so neat and prosperous; grazing cattle in rank meadows were so sleek; then a big white house began to peep from the screen of vines, bushes and trees.

"Well if the water here gives you fever, it will anywhere," said Mickey, and turning in at the open gate started up a walk having flower beds on each side. There was a wide grassy lawn where the big trees scattered around afforded almost complete shade. Mickey never had seen a home like it closely. He scarcely could realize that there were places in the world where families lived alone like this. He tried to think how he would feel if he belonged there. When he reached the place where he saw Lily on a comfort under a big bloom-laden pear tree, his throat grew hard, his eyes dry and his feet heavy. Then the screen to the front door swung back as a smiling woman in a tidy gingham dress came through and stood awaiting Mickey.

"I just told Peter when he came back alone, I bet a penny you'd got off at the wrong stop!" she cried. "I'm so glad you found your way by yourself. But you must be tired and hot walking. Come right in and have a glass of milk, then strip your feet and I'll ring for Junior."

For one second Mickey was dazed. The next, he knew what it must mean. These people were the kind whom God had made so big and generous they divided home and summer with tenement children from the big city thirty miles away. Some boy was coming for a week, maybe, into what exactly filled Mickey's idea of Heaven, but he was not the boy.

"'Most breaks my heart to tell you," he said, "but I ain't the boy you're expecting. I'm just taking a walk and I thought maybe you'd let me have a drink. I've wanted one past the last three houses, but none looked as if they'd have half such good, cool water as this."

"Now don't that beat the nation!" exclaimed the woman. "The Multiopolis papers are just oozing sympathy for the poor city children who are wild for woods and water; and when I'd got myself nerved up to try one and thought it over till I was really anxious about it, and got my children all worked up too, here for the second time Peter knocks off plowing and goes to the trolley to meet one, and he doesn't come. I've got a notion to write the editor of the *Herald* and tell him my experience. I think it's funny! But you wanted water, come this way."

Mickey followed a footpath white with pear petals around the big house and standing beside a pump waited while the woman stepped to the back porch for a cup. He took it, drinking slowly.

"Thank you ma'am," he said as he handed it back, turning to the path.

Yesterday had weakened his nerve. He was going to cry again. He took a quick step forward, but the woman was beside him, her hand on his shoulder.

"Wait a minute," she said. "Sit on this bench under the pear tree. I want to ask you something. Excuse me and rest until I come back."

Mickey leaned against the tree, shutting his eyes, fighting with all his might. He was too big to cry. The woman would think him a coward as Mr. Bruce had. Then things happened as they actually do at times. The woman hurriedly came from the door, sat on the bench beside him, and said: "I went in there to watch you through the window, but I can't stand this a second longer. You poor child you, now tell me right straight what's the matter!"

Mickey tried but no sound came. The woman patted his shoulder. "Now doesn't it beat the band?" she said, to the backyard in general. "Just a little fellow not in long trousers yet, and bearing such a burden he can't talk. I guess maybe God has a hand in this. I'm not so sure my boy hasn't come after all. Who are you, and where are you going? Don't you want to send your ma word you will stay here a week with me?"

Mickey lifted a bewildered face.

"Why, I couldn't, lady," he said brokenly, but gaining control as he went on. "I must work. Mr. Bruce needs me. I'm a regular plute compared with most of the 'newsies'; you wouldn't want to do anything for me who has so much; but if you're honestly thinking about taking a boy and he hasn't come, how would you like to have a little girl in his place? A little girl about *so* long, and *so* wide, with a face like Easter church flowers, and rings of gold on her head, and who wouldn't be half the trouble a boy would, because she hasn't ever walked, so she couldn't get into things."

"Oh my goodness! A crippled little girl?"

"She isn't crippled," said Mickey. "She's as straight as you are, what there is of her. She had so little food, and care, her back didn't seem to stiffen, so her legs won't walk. She wouldn't be half so much trouble as a boy. Honest, dearest lady, she wouldn't!"

"Who are you?" asked the woman.

Mickey produced a satisfactory pedigree, and gave unquestionable references which she recognized, for she slowly nodded at the names of Chaffner and Bruce.

"And who is the little girl you are asking me to take?"

Mickey studied the woman and then began to talk, cautiously at first. Ashamed to admit the squalor and the awful truth of how he had found the thing he loved, then gathering courage he began what ended in an outpouring.

The woman watched him, listening, and when Mickey had no further word: "She is only a tiny girl?" she asked wonderingly.

"The littlest girl you ever saw," said Mickey.

"Perfectly helpless?" marvelled the woman.

"Oh no! She can sit up and use her hands," said Mickey. "She can feed herself, write on her slate, and learn her lessons. It's only that she stays put. She has to be lifted if she's moved."

"You lift her?" queried the woman.

"Could with one hand," said Mickey tersely.

"You say this young lawyer you work for, whose name I see in the *Herald* connected with the investigation going on, is at the club house now?" she asked.

"Yes," answered Mickey.

"He's coming past here this evening?" she pursued.

Mickey explained.

"About how much waiting on would your little girl take?" she asked next.

"Well just at present, she does the waiting on me," said Mickey. "You see, dearest lady, I have to get her washed and fix her breakfast and her lunch beside the bed, and be downtown by seven o'clock, and I don't get back 'til six. Then I wash her again to freshen her up and cook her supper. Then she says her lesson, her prayers and goes to sleep. So you see it's mostly *her* waiting on *me*. A boy couldn't be less trouble than that, could he?"

"It doesn't seem like it," said the woman, "and no matter how much bother she was, I guess I could stand it for a week, if she's such a little girl, and can't walk. The difficulty is this: I promised my son Junior a boy and his heart is so set. He's wild about the city. He's going to be gone before we know it. He doesn't seem to care for anything we have, or do. I don't know just what he hoped to get out of a city boy; but I promised him one. Then I felt scared and wrote Mr. Chaffner how it was and asked him to send me a real nice boy who could be trusted. If it were not for Junior—Mary and the Little Man would be delighted."

"Well never mind," said Mickey. "I'll go see the Nurse Lady and maybe she can think of a plan. Anyway I don't know as it would be best for Lily. If she came here a week, seems like it would kill me to take her back, and I don't know how she'd bear staying alone all day, after she had got used to company. And pretty soon now it's going to get so hot, top floors in the city, that if she had a week like this, going back would make her sick."

"You must give me time to think," said the woman. "Peter will soon be home to supper. I'll talk it over with him and with Junior and see what they think. Where could you be found in Multiopolis? We drive in every few days. We like to go ourselves, and there's no other way to satisfy the children. They get so tired and lonesome in the country."

Mickey was aghast. "They *do?* Why it doesn't seem possible! I wish I could trade jobs with Junior for a while. What is his work?"

"He drives the creamery wagon," answered the woman.

"O Lord!" Mickey burst forth. "Excuse me ma'am, I mean——Oh my! Drives a real live horse along these streets and gathers up the cream cans we pass at the gates, and takes them to the trolley?"

"Yes," she said.

"And he'd give up *that* job for blacking somebody's shoes, or carrying papers, or running errands, or being shut up all summer in a big hot building! Oh my!"

"When will you be our way again?" asked the woman. "I'll talk this over with Peter. If we decided to try the little girl and she did the 'waiting' as you say, she couldn't be much trouble. I should think we could manage her, and a boy too. I wish you could be the boy. I'd like to have *you*. I've been thinking if we could get a boy to show Junior what it is he wants to know about a city, he'd be better satisfied at home, but I don't know. It's just possible it might make him worse. Now such an understanding boy as you seem to be, maybe you could teach Junior things about the city that would make him contented at *home*. Do you think you could?"

"Dearest lady, I *get* you," said Mickey. "*Do I think I could?* Well if you really wished me to, I could take your Junior to Multiopolis with me for a week and make him so sick he'd never want to see a city again while his palpitator was running."

"Hu'umh!" said the lady slowly, her cycs on far distance. "Let me think! I don't know but that would be a fine thing for all of us. We have land enough for a nice farm for both boys, and the way things look now, land seems about as sure as anything; we could give them a farm apiece when we are done with it, and the girl the money to take to her home when she marries—I would love to know that Junior was going to live on land as his father does; but all his life he's talked about working in the city when he grows up. Hu'umh!"

"Well if you want him cured of that, gimme the job," he grinned. "You see lady, I know the city, inside out and outside in again. I been playing the game with it since I can remember. You can't tell me anything I don't know about the lowest, poorest side of it. Oh I could tell you things that would make your head swim. If you want your boy dosed just sick as a horse on what a workingman gets in Multiopolis 'tween Sunrise Alley and Biddle Boulevard, just you turn him over to me a week. I'll fix him. I'll make the creamery job look like 'Lijah charioteering for the angels to him, honest I will lady; and he won't ever *know* it, either. He'll come through with a lump in his neck, and a twist in his stummick that means home and mother. See?"

The woman looked at Mickey in wide-eyed and open-mouthed amazement: "Well if I ever!" she gasped.

"If you don't believe me, try it," said Mickey.

"Well! Well! I'll have to think," she said. "I don't know but it would be a good thing if it could be done."

"Well don't you have any misgivings about it being done," said Mickey. "It's being *done* every day. I know men, hundreds of them, just scraping, and slaving and half starving to get together the dough to pull out. I hear it on the cars, on the streets, and see it in the papers. They're jumping their jobs and going every day, while hundreds of Schmeltzenschimmers, O'Laughertys, Hansons, and Pietros are coming in to take their places. Multiopolis is more than half filled with crowd-outs from across the ocean now, instead of home folks' cradles, as it should be. If Junior has got a hankering for Multiopolis that is going to cut him out of owning a place like this, and bossing his own job, dearest lady, cook him! Cook him quick!"

"Would you come here?" she questioned.

"Would I?" cried Mickey. "Well try me and see!"

"I'm deeply interested in what you say about Junior," she said. "I'll talk it over to-night with Peter."

"Well I don't know," said Mickey. "He might put the grand kibosh on it. Hard! But if Junior came back asking polite for his mush and milk, and offering his Christmas pennies for the privilege of plowing, or driving the cream wagon, believe me dear lady, then Peter would fall on your neck and weep for joy."

"Yes, in that event, he would," said the lady, "and the temptation is so great, that I believe if you'll give me your address, I'll look you up the next time I come to Multiopolis, which will be soon. I'd like to see your Lily before I make any promises. If I thought I could manage, I could bring her right out in the car. Tell me where to find you, and I'll see what Peter thinks."

Mickey grinned widely. "You ain't no suffragette lady, are you?" he commented.

"Well I don't know about that," said the lady. "There are a good many things to think of these days."

"Yes I know," said Mickey, "but as long as everything you say swings the circle and rounds up with Peter, it's no job to guess what's most important in your think-tank. Peter must be some pumpkins!"

"Come to think of it, he is, Mickey," she said. "Come to think of it, I do sort of revolve around Peter. We always plan together. Not that we always *think* alike: there are some things I just *can't* make Peter see, that I wish I *could;* but I wouldn't trade Peter——"

"No I guess he's top crust," laughed Mickey.

"He is so!" said the woman. "How did you say I could reach you?"

"Well, the easiest way would be this. Here, I'll write the number for you."

"Fine!" said the woman. "I'll hurry through my shopping and call you—when would it suit you best?"

"Never mind me," said Mickey. "For this, I'll come when you say."

"What about three in the afternoon, then?"

"Sure!" cried Mickey. "Suits me splendid! Mostly quit for the day then. But ma'am, I don't know about this. Lily isn't used to anybody but me, she may be afraid to come with you."

"And I may think I would scarcely want to try to take care of her for a week, when I see her," said the woman.

"You may think that now, but you'll change your mind when you see her," said Mickey. "Dearest lady, when you see a little white girl that hasn't ever walked, smiling up at you shy and timid, you won't be any more anxious for Orphings' Homes and Charity Palaces to swallow her up than I am; not a bit! All I must think of is what Lily will say about coming. She's never been out of my room since I found her, and she hasn't seen any one but Mr. Bruce, so she'll be afraid, and worried. *Seeing her* is all I ask of *you!* What I'm up against is what she's going to say; and how I'm going to take her *back* after a week here, when it will be hotter there and lonesomer than ever."

"You surely give one things to think about," commented the woman.

"Do I?" queried Mickey. "Well I don't know as I should. Probably with Peter, and three children of your own, and this farm to run, you are busy enough without spending any of your time on me."

"The command in the good book is plain: 'Bear ye one another's burdens,'" quoted the woman.

"Oh yes! 'Burdens,' of course!" agreed Mickey. "But that couldn't mean Lily, 'cause she's nothing but joy! Just pure joy! All about her is that a fellow loves her so, that it keeps him laying awake at nights thinking how to do what would be *best* for her. She's mine, and I'm going to *keep* her; that's the surest thing you know. If I take you to see Lily, and if I decide to let you have her a few days to rest her and fresh her up, you wouldn't go and want to put her 'mong the Orphings' Home kids, would you? You wouldn't think she ought to be took from me and raised in a flock of every kind, from every place. Would you lady?"

"No, I wouldn't," said the lady. "I see how you feel, and I am sure I wouldn't want that for one of mine."

"Well, there's no question about her being *mine!*" said Mickey. "But I like you so, maybe I'll let you *help* me a *little*. A big boy that can run and play doesn't need you, dearest lady, half so much as my little girl. Do you think he does?"

"No, I think the Lord sent you straight here. If you don't stop I'll be so worked up I can't rest. I may come to-morrow."

Mickey arose, holding out his hand.

"Thank you dearest lady," he said. "I must be getting out where the car won't pass without my seeing it."

"You wait at the gate a minute," she said, "I want to send in a little basket of things to-night. I'll have it ready in a jiffy."

Mickey slowly walked to the gate. When the woman came with a basket covered with a white cloth, he thanked her again; as he took it he rested his head against her arm, smiling up at her with his wide true eyes.

"A thing I can't understand is," he said, "why when the Lord was making mothers, he didn't cut all of them from the same piece he did you. I'll just walk on down the road and smell June beside this clover field. Is it yours?"

"Yes," she said.

"Would you care if I'd take just a few to Lily? I know she never saw any."

"Take a bunch as big as your head if you want them."

"Lily is so little, three will do her just as well; besides, she's got to remember how we are fixed, so she needn't begin to expect things to come her way by baskets and bunches," said Mickey. "She's bound to be spoiled bad enough as it is. I can't see how I'm going to come out with her, but she's mine, and I'm going to keep her."

"Mickey," laughed the woman, "don't you think you swing around to Lily just about the way I do to Peter?"

"Well maybe I do," conceded Mickey.

"What kind of a car did you say Mr. Bruce has?"

"Oh the car is dark green, and the driver has sandy hair; and Mr. Bruce—why you'd know him anywhere! Just look for the finest man you ever saw, if you are out when he goes by, and that will be Mr. Douglas Bruce."

"I guess I'll know him if I happen to be out."

"Sure lady, you couldn't miss him," replied Mickey.

Carefully holding his basket he went down the road. The woman made supper an hour late standing beside the gate watching for a green car. Many whirled past, then at last one with the right look came gliding along; so she stepped out and raised her hand for a parley. The car stopped.

"Mr. Douglas Bruce?" she asked.

"At your service, Madam!" he answered.

"Just a word with you," she said.

He arose instantly, swung open the car door, and stepping down walked with her to the shade of a big widely branching maple. The woman looked at him, and said flushing and half confused: "Please to excuse me for halting you, but I had a reason. This afternoon such an attractive little fellow stopped here to ask for a drink in passing. Now Peter and I had decided we'd try our hand at taking a city boy for a week or so for his vacation, and twice Peter has left his work and gone to the trolley station to fetch him, and he failed us. I supposed Peter had missed him, so when I saw the boy coming, just the first glimpse my heart went right out to him——"

"Very likely——" assented Mr. Bruce.

"Mickey had the best of three or four boys concealed in his lean person."

"He surely is the most winning little chap I ever saw with his keen blue eyes and that sort of light on his forehead," said the woman.

"I've noticed that," put in the man.

"Yes," she said, "anybody would see that almost the first thing. So I thought he was the boy I was to mother coming, and I went right at the job. He told me quick enough that I was mistaken, but I could see he was in trouble. Someway I'd trust him with my character or my money, but I got to be perfectly sure before I trust him with my children. You see I have three, and if ever any of them go wrong, I don't want it to be because I was *careless*. I thought I'd like to have him around some; my oldest boy is bigger, but just about his age. He said he might be out this way with you this summer and I wanted to ask him in, and do what I could to entertain him; but first I wanted to inquire of you——"

"I see!" said Douglas Bruce. "I haven't known Mickey so long, but owing to the circumstances in which I met him, and the association with him since, I feel that I know him better than I could most boys in a longer time. The strongest thing I can say to you is this: had I a boy of my own, I should be proud if Mickey liked him and would consider being friends with him. He is absolutely trustworthy, that I know."

"Then I won't detain your further," she said.

Mickey, cheered in mind and heart, had walked ahead briskly with his basket, while as he went he formulated his plans. He would go straight to the Sunshine Nurse, tell her about the heat and this possible chance to take Lily to the country for a week, and consult with her as to what the effect of the trip might be, and what he could do with her afterward, then he would understand better. He kept watching the clover field beside the way. When he decided he had reached the finest, best perfumed place, he saw a man plowing on the other side of the fence and thought it might be Peter and that Peter would wonder what he was doing in his field, so Mickey set the basket in a corner and advanced.

He was wonderfully elated by what had happened to him and the conclusions at which he had arrived, as he came across the deep grasses beside the fence where the pink of wild rose and the snow of alder commingled, where song sparrows trilled, and larks and quail were calling. He approached smiling in utter confidence. As he looked at the man, at his height, his strong open face, his grip on the plow, he realized why the world of the little woman revolved around Peter. Mickey could have conceived of few happier fates than being attached to Peter, so he thought in amazement of the boy who wanted to leave him. Then a slow grin spread over his face, for by this time Peter had stopped his horses and was awaiting him with an answering smile and hand outstretched.

"Why son, I'm glad to see you!" he cried. "How did I come to miss you? Did you get off at the wrong stop?"

Mickey shook his head as he took the proffered hand.

"You are Peter?" he asked.

"Yes, I'm Peter," confirmed the man.

"Well you're making the same mistake your pleasant lady did," explained Mickey. "She thought I was the boy who had been sent to visit you, so she gave me the glad hand too. I wish I was in his shoes! But I'm not your boy. Gee, your lady is a nice gentle lady."

"You're all correct there," agreed Peter. "And so you are not the boy who was to be sent us. Pshaw now! I wish you were. I'm disappointed. I've been watching you coming down the road, and the way you held together and stepped up so brisk and neat took my eye."

"I been 'stepping up brisk and neat' to sell papers, run errands, hop cars, dodge cars and automobiles, and climbing fire-escapes instead of stairs, and keeping from under foot since I can remember," laughed Mickey. "You learn on the streets of Multiopolis to step up, and watch sharp without knowing you are doing it."

"You're a newsboy?" asked Peter.

"I was all my life 'til a few days ago," said Mickey. "Then I went into the office of Mr. Douglas Bruce. He's a corporation lawyer in the Iriquois Building."

"Hum, I've been reading about him," said Peter. "If I ever have a case, I'm going to take it to him."

"Well you'll have a man that will hang on and dig in and *sweat* for you," said Mickey. "Just now he's after some of them big office-holders who are bleeding the taxpayers of Multiopolis. Some of these days if you watch your *Herald* sharp, you're going to see the lid fly off of two or three things at once. He's on a hot trail now."

"Why I have seen that in the papers," said Peter. "He was given the job of finding who is robbing the city, by James Minturn; I remember his name. And you work for him? Well, well! Sit down here and tell me about it."

"I can't now," said Mickey. "I must get back to the road. His car may pass any minute, and I'm to be ready. Your pleasant lady said I might take a few clover flowers to my little sick girl, and just as I came to the finest ones in the field, I saw you so I thought maybe I'd better tell you what I was doing before you fired me."

"Take all you want," said Peter. "I'd like to send the whole field, larks and all, to a little sick girl. I'd like especial to send her some of these clowny bobolink fellows to puff up and spill music by the quart for her; I guess nothing else runs so smooth except water."

"I don't know what she'd say," said Mickey gazing around him. "You see she hasn't ever walked, so all she's seen in her life has been the worst kind of bare, dark tenement walls, 'til lately she's got a high window where she can see sky, and a few sparrows that come for crumbs. This!"—Mickey swept his arm toward the landscape—"I don't know what she'd say to this!"

"Pshaw, now!" cried Peter. "Why bring her out! You bring her right out! That's what we been wanting to know. Just what a city child would *think* of country things she'd never seen before. Bring her to see us!"

"She's a little bit of a thing and she can't walk, you know," explained Mickey.

"Poor little mite! That's too bad," lamented Peter. "Wonder if she couldn't be doctored up. It's a shame she can't walk, but taking care of her must be easy!"

"Oh she takes care of herself," said Mickey. "You see she is alone all day from six 'til six; she must take care of herself, so she studies her lesson, and plays with her doll—I mean her Precious Child."

"Too bad!" said Peter. "By jacks that's a sin! Did you happen to speak to Ma about her?"

"We did talk a little," admitted Mickey. "She was telling me of the visitor boy who didn't come, and your son who doesn't think he'll want to stay; so we got to talking. She said just what you did about wanting to see how a city child who hadn't ever seen a chicken, or a cow, or horse would act——"

"Good Lord!" cried Peter. "*Is* there a child in Multiopolis who hasn't ever seen a little chicken, or a calf?"

"Hundreds of them!" said Mickey. "I've scarcely seen a cow myself. I've seen hens and little chickens in shop windows at Easter time——"

"But not in the orchard in June?" queried Peter.

"No, 'not in the orchard in June!'" said Mickey.

"Well, well!" marvelled Peter. "There's nothing so true as that 'one half doesn't know how the other half lives.' I've heard that, but I didn't quite sense it, and I don't know as I do yet. You bring her right out!"

"Your pleasant lady talked about that; but you see bringing her out and showing her these things, and getting her used to them is *one* thing; then taking her back to a room so hot I always sleep on the fire-escape, and where she has to stay all day alone, is *another*. I don't know but so long as she must go *back* to what she has now, it would be better to *leave* her there."

"Humph! I see! What a pity!" exclaimed Peter. "Well, if you'll be coming this way again, stop and see us. I'll talk to Ma about her. We often take a little run to Multiopolis. Junior wouldn't be satisfied till we got a car, and I can't say we ain't enjoying it ourselves. What was that you were saying about my boy not thinking he'll stay?"

"*She* told me," said Mickey, "about the city bug he had in his system. Why don't you swat it immediate?"

"What do you mean?" inquired Peter.

"Turn him over to me a week or two," suggested Mickey. "I can give him a dose of working in a city that will send him hiking back to home and father."

"It's worth considering," said Peter.

"I know that what I got of Multiopolis would make me feel like von Hindenberg if I had the job of handling the ribbons of your creamery wagon; and so I know about what would put sonny back on the farm, tickled 'most to death to be here."

"By gum! Well, I'll give you just one hundred dollars if you'll do it!" exclaimed Peter. "You see my grandfather and father owned this land before me. We've been on the plowing job so long we have it reduced to a system, so it comes easy for me, and I take pride and pleasure in it; I had supposed my boys would be the same. Do you really think you could manage it?"

"Sure," said Mickey. "Only, if you really mean it, not now, nor ever, do you want son to *know* it. See! The medicine wouldn't work, if he knew he took it."

"Well I'll be jiggered!" laughed Peter. "I guess you could do it, if you went at it right."

"Well you trust me to do it right," grinned Mickey. "Loan me sonny for a week or two, and you can have him back for keeps."

"Well it's worth trying," said Peter. "Say, when will you be this way again?"

"'Most any day," said Mickey. "And your lady said she'd be in Multiopolis soon, so we are sure to have a happy meeting before long. I think that is Mr. Bruce's car coming. Goodbye! Be good to yourself!"

With a spring from where he was standing Mickey arose in air, alighted on the top rail of the division fence, then balancing, he raced down it toward the road. Peter watched him in astonishment, then went back to his plowing with many new things on his mind. Thus it happened that after supper, when the children were in bed, and he and his wife went to the front veranda for their usual evening visit, and talk over the day, she had very little to tell him.

As was her custom, she removed her apron, brushed her waving hair and wore a fresh dress. She rocked gently in her wicker chair, while her voice was moved to unusual solicitude as she spoke. Peter also had performed a rite he spoke of as "brushing up" for evening. He believed in the efficacy of soap and water, so his body, as well as his clothing, was clean. He sat on the top step leaning against the pillar where the moonlight emphasized his big frame, accented the strong lines of his face and crowned his thick hair, as Nancy Harding thought it should be, with glory.

"Peter," she said, "did you notice anything about that boy, this afternoon, different from other boys?"

"Yes," answered Peter slowly, "I did Nancy. He didn't strike me as being *one* boy. He has the best of three or four concealed in his lean person."

"He's had a pretty tough time, I judge," said Nancy.

"Yet you never saw a boy who took your heart like he did, and neither did I," answered Peter.

Mickey holding his basket and clover flowers was waiting when the car drew up, and to Bruce's inquiry answered that a lady where he stopped for a drink had given him something for Lily. He left the car in the city, sought the nurse and luckily found her at leisure. She listened with the greatest interest to all he had to say.

"It's a problem," she said, as he finished. "To take her to such a place for a week, and then bring her back where she is, would be harder for her than never going."

"I got that figured," said Mickey; "but I've about made up my mind, after seeing the place and thinking over the folks, that it wouldn't *happen* that way. Once they see her, and find how little trouble she is, they're not people who would send her back 'til it's cool, if they'd want to then. And there's this, too: there are other folks who would take her now, and see about her back. Have I got the right to let it go a day, waiting to earn the money myself, when some one else, maybe the Moonshine Lady, or Mr. Bruce, would do it *now*, and not put her in an Orphings' Home, either?"

"No Mickey, you haven't!" said the nurse.

"Just the way I have it figured," said Mickey. "But she's mine, and I'm going to *keep* her. If her back is fixed, I'm going to have it done. I don't want any one else meddling with my family. You haven't heard anything from the Carrel man yet?"

"No," she said.

"My, I wish he'd come!" cried Mickey.

"So do I," said the nurse. "But so far Mickey, I think you are doing all right. If she must be operated, she'd have to be put in condition for it; and while I suspect I could beat you at your job, I am positive you are far surpassing what she did have."

"Well I know that too," said Mickey. "But surpassing nothing at all isn't going either far or fast. I must do something."

"If you could bring yourself to consent to giving her up——" suggested the nurse.

"Well I can't!" interposed Mickey.

"Just for a while!" continued the nurse.

"Not for a minute! I found her! She's mine!"

"Yes, I know; but——" began the nurse.

"I know too," said Mickey. "Gimme a little time." He studied the problem till he reached his grocery. There he thriftily lifted the cloth to peep, and with a sigh of satisfaction pursued his way. Presently he opened his door, to be struck by a wave of hot air and to note a flushed little face and drawn mouth as he went into Peaches' outstretched arms. Then he delivered the carefully carried clover and the following:

"*I got these from a big, pink field bewildering,*
That God made a-purpose for cows and childering.
Her share is being consumed by the cow,
Let's go roll in ours right now."

"Again!" demanded Peaches.

Mickey repeated slowly.

"How could we?" asked Peaches.

"Easy!" said Mickey.

"'Easy?'" repeated Peaches.

"Just as easy!" reiterated Mickey.

"Did you see it?" demanded Peaches.

"Yes, I saw it to-day," said Mickey. "It's like this: you see some folks live in houses all built together, and work at selling things to eat, and wear, and making things, and doing other work that must be done like doctors, and lawyers, and hospitals; *that's a city*. Then to *feed them*, other folks live on big pieces of land; the houses are far apart, with streets between, and beside them the big fields where the wheat grows for our bread, and our potatoes, and the grass, and the clover like this to feed the cows. To-day Mr. Bruce didn't play long, so I went walking and stopped at a house for a drink, and there was the nicest lady; we talked some and she give me our supper in that pretty basket; and she sent you the clovers from a big pink field so sweet smelly it would 'most make you sick; and there are trees through it, and lots of birds sing, and there are wild roses and fringy white flowers; and it's quiet 'cept the birds, and the roosters crowing, and the wind comes in little perfumery blows on you, and such milk!"

"Better 'an our milk?" asked Peaches.

"Their milk is so rich it makes ours look like a poorhouse relation," scoffed Mickey.

"Tell me more," demanded Peaches.

"Wait 'til I get the water to wash you, you are so warm."

"Yes, it's getting some hot; but 'tain't nothing like on the rags last summer. It's like a real lady here."

"A pretty warm lady, just the same," said Mickey.

Then he brought water and leaving the door ajar for the first time, he soon started a draft; that with the coming of cooler evening lowered the child's temperature, and made her hungry. As he worked Mickey talked. The grass, the blooming orchard, the hen and her little downy chickens, the big cool porch, the wonderful woman and man, the boy whom they expected and who did not come; and then cautiously, slowly, making sure she understood, he developed his plan to take her to the country. Peaches drew back and opened her lips. Mickey promptly laid the washcloth over them.

"Now don't begin to say you 'won't' like a silly baby," he said. "Try it and see, then if you don't like it, you can come right back. You want to ride in a grand automobile like a millyingaire lady, don't you? All the swells go away to the country for the summer, you got to be a swell lady! I ain't going to have you left way behind!"

"Mickey, would you be there?" she asked.

"Yes lady, I'd be right on the job!" said Mickey. "I'd be there a lot more than I am here. You go the week they wanted that boy, and he didn't come; then if you like it, I'll see if they won't board you, and you can have a nice little girl to play with, and a fat, real baby, and a boy bigger than me—and you should see Peter!"

Peaches opened her lips, Mickey reapplied the cloth.

"Calm down now!" he ordered. "I've decided to do it. We got to hump ourselves. This is our *chance*. Why there's milk, and butter, and eggs, and things to eat there like you never tasted, and to have a cool breeze, and to lie on the grass——"

"Oh Mickey, could I?" cried Peaches.

"Sure silly! Why not?" said Mickey. "There's big fields of it, and the cows don't need it all. You can lie on the grass, or the clover, and hear the birds, and play with the children. I'll take a day and get things started right before I leave you to come to work, like I'll have to. When I come at night, I'll carry your outdoors; why I'll take you down to the water and you can kick your feet in it, where it's nice and warm; all the time you can have as many flowers as your hands will hold; and such bird singing, why Lily Peaches O'Halloran, there are birds as red as blood, yes ma'am, and yellow as orange peel and light blue like this ribbon and dark blue like that—hold still 'til I fix you—and such singing!"

"Mickey, would you hold me?" wavered Peaches.

"Smash anybody that lays a finger on you, unless you say so," said Mickey promptly.

"And you'd stay a whole day?" she asked anxiously.

"Sure!" cried Mickey.

"An' if I was afraid you'd bring me back?" she went on.

"Sure! Right away!" he promised.

"An' they wouldn't anybody 'get' me there?"

"'Way out there 'mong the clover?" scoffed Mickey. "Why it's *here* they'll '*get*' you if they are going to. Nobody out there *wants* you, but me."

"Mickey, when will you take me?" she asked eagerly.

"Before so very long," promised Mickey. "You needn't be surprised to hear me coming with the nice lady to see you any day now, and to be wrapped in a sheet, and put in a big car, and just scooted right out to the very place that God made especial for little girls. To-night we put in another blesses, Lily. We'll pray, 'Bless the nice lady who sent our supper,' won't we?"

"Yes Mickey, and 'fore you came I didn't want any supper at all, and now I *do*," said Peaches.

"You were too warm honey," said Mickey. "We'll just fix this old hot city. We'll run right away from it. See? Now we'll have the grandest supper we ever had."

Mickey brought water, plates, and forks, and opened the basket. Peaches bolstered with her pillows cried out and marvelled. There was a quart bottle of milk wrapped in a wet cloth. There was a big loaf of crusty brown country bread. There was a small blue bowl of yellow butter, a square of honey even yellower, a box of strawberries, and some powdered sugar, and a little heap of sliced, cold boiled ham. Mickey surveyed the table.

"Now Miss Chicken, here's how!" he warned. "I found you all warm and feverish. If you load up with this, you'll be sick sure. You get a cup of milk, a slice of bread and butter, some berries and a teeny piece of meat. We can live from this a week, if the heat doesn't spoil it."

"You fix me," said Peaches.

Then they had such a supper as they neither one ever had known, during which Mickey explained wheat fields and bread, bees and honey, cows and clover, pigs and ham, as he understood them. Peaches repeated her lesson and her prayers and then as had become her custom, demanded that Mickey write his last verse on the slate, so she might learn and copy it on the morrow. She was asleep before he finished. Mickey walked softly, cleared the table, placed it before the window, and taking from his pocket an envelope Mr. Bruce had given him drew out a sheet of folded paper on which he wrote long and laboriously, then locking Peaches in, he slipped down to the mail-box and posted this letter:

DEAR MISTER CARREL:

I saw in papers I sold how you put different legs on a dog. I have a little white flowersy-girl that hasn't ever walked. It's her back. A Nurse Lady told me at the "Star of Hope" how you came there sometimes, and the next time you come, I guess I will let you see my little girl; and maybe I'll have you fix her back. When you see her you will know that to fix her back would be the biggest thing you ever did or ever could do. I got a job that I can pay her way and mine, and save two dollars a week for you. I couldn't pay all at once, but I could pay steady; and if you'd lose all you have in any way, it would come in real handy to have that much skating in steady as the clock every week for as long as you say, and soon as I can, I'll make it more. I'd give all I got, or ever can get, to cure Lily's back, and because you fixed the dog, I'd like you to fix her. I do hope you will come soon, but of course I don't wish anybody else would get sick so you'd have to. You can ask if I am square of Mr. Douglas Bruce, Iriquois Building, Multiopolis, Indiana, or of Mr. Chaffner, editor of the Herald, *whose papers I've sold since I was big enough.*

MICHAEL O'HALLORAN.

CHAPTER XII

FEMININE REASONING

With vigour renewed by a night of rest Leslie began her second day at Atwater Cabin. She had so many and such willing helpers that before noon she could find nothing more to do. After lunch she felt a desire to explore her new world. Choosing the shady side, she followed the road toward the club house, but one thought in her mind: she must return in time to take the car and meet Douglas Bruce as she had promised.

She felt elated that she had so planned her summer as to spend it with her father, while of course it was going to be delightful to have her lover with her. So going she came to a most attractive lane that led from the road between tilled fields, back to a wood on one side, and open pasture on the other. Faintly she heard the shouts of children, and yielding to sudden impulse she turned and followed the grassy path. A few more steps, then she stopped in surprise. An automobile was standing on the bank of a brook. On an Indian blanket under a tree sat a woman of fine appearance holding a book, but watching with smiling face the line of the water, which spread in a wide pool above a rudely constructed dam, overflowing it in a small waterfall.

On either bank lay one of the Minturn boys, muddy and damp, trying with his hands to catch something in the water. Below the dam, in a blue balbriggan bathing suit, stood James Minturn, his hands filled with a big piece of sod which he bent and applied to a leak. Leslie untied the ribbons of her sunshade and rumpling her hair to the light breeze came forward laughing.

"Well Mr. Minturn!" she cried. "What is going to become of the taxpayers of Multiopolis while their champion builds a sod dam?"

Whether the flush on James Minturn's face as he turned to her was exertion, embarrassment, or unpleasant memory Leslie could not decide; but she remembered, after her impulsive greeting, that she had been with his wife in that early morning meeting the day of the trip to the swamp. She thought of many things as she went forward. James Minturn held out his muddy hands as he said laughingly: "You see I'm not in condition for our customary greeting."

"Surely!" cried Leslie. "It is going to wash off, isn't it? If from you, why not from me?"

"Of course if you want to play!" he said.

"Playing? You? Honestly?" queried Leslie.

"Honestly playing," answered the man. "The 'honestest' playing in all the world; not the political game, not the money game, not anything called manly sport, just a day off with my boys, being a boy again. Heavens Leslie, I'm wild about it. I could scarcely sleep last night for eagerness to get started. But let me make you acquainted with my family. My sister, Mrs. Winslow, a friend of mine, Miss Leslie Winton; my sons' tutor, Mr. Tower; my little brother, William Minturn; my boys, Junior and Malcolm."

"Anyway, we can shake hands," said Leslie to Mrs. Winslow. "The habit is so ingrained I am scandalized on meeting people if I'm forced to neglect it."

"Will you share my blanket?" asked Mrs. Winslow.

"Thanks! Yes, for a little time," said Leslie. "I am greatly interested in what is going on here."

"So am I," said Mrs. Winslow. "We are engaged in the evolution of an idea. A real 'Do-the-boy's-hall.'"

"It seems to be doing them good," commented Leslie.

"Never mind the boys," said Mr. Minturn. "I object to such small men monopolizing your attention. Look at the 'good' this is doing me. And would you please tell me why you are here, instead of disporting yourself at, say Lenox?"

"How funny!" laughed Leslie. "I am out in search of amusement, and I'm finding it. I think I'm perhaps a mile from our home for the summer."

"You amaze me!" cried Mr. Minturn. "I saw Douglas this morning, and told him where I was coming, but he never said a word."

"He didn't know one to say on this subject," explained Leslie. "You see I rented a cabin over at Atwater and had my plans made before I told even father what a delightful thing was in store for him."

"But how did it happen?"

"Through my seeing how desperately busy Daddy and Douglas have been all spring, Daddy especially," replied Leslie. "Douglas is bad enough, but father's just obsessed, so much so that I think he's carrying double."

"I know he is," said Mr. Minturn. "And so you made a plan to allow him to proceed with his work all day and then have the delightful ride, fishing and swimming in Atwater morning and evening. How wonderful! And of course Douglas will be there also?"

"Of course," agreed Leslie. "At least he shall have an invitation. I'm going to surprise him with it this very evening. How do you think he'll like it?"

"I think he will be so overjoyed he won't know how to express himself," said James Minturn. "But isn't it going to be lonely for you? Won't you miss your friends, your frocks, and your usual summer round?"

"You forget," said Leslie. "My friends and my frocks always have been for winter. All my life I have summered with father."

"How will you amuse yourself?" he asked.

"It will take some time each day to plan what to do the next that will bring most refreshment and joy; I often will be compelled to drive in of mornings with orders for my house-keeping, and when other things are exhausted, I am going to make an especial study of wild-bird music."

"That is an attractive subject," said Mr. Minturn. "Have you really made any progress?"

"Little more than verifying a few songs already recorded," replied Leslie. "I hear smatterings and snatches, but they are elusive, while I'm not always sure of the identity of the bird. But the subject is thrillingly tempting."

"It surely is," conceded Mr. Minturn. "I could see that Nellie was alert the instant you mentioned it. Come over here to the shade and tell me how far you have gone. You see I've undertaken the boys' education. Malcolm inherits his mother's musical ability to a wonderful degree. It is possible that he could be started on this, and so begin his work while he thinks he's playing."

Leslie walked to the spot indicated, far enough away that conversation would not interrupt Mrs. Winslow's reading, and near enough to watch the boys; she and Mr. Minturn sat on the grass and talked.

"It might be the very thing," said Leslie. "Whatever gives even a faint hope of attracting a boy to an educational subject is worth testing."

"One thing I missed, I always have regretted," said Mr. Minturn, "I never had educated musical comprehension. Nellie performed and sang so well, and in my soul I knew what I could understand and liked in music she scorned. Sometimes I thought if I had known only enough to appreciate the right thing at the right time, it might have formed a slender tie between us; so I want the boys both to recognize good music when they hear it; but they have so much to learn all at once, poor little chaps, I scarcely see where to begin, and in a musical way, I don't even know how to begin. Tell me about the birds, Leslie. Just what is it you are studying?"

"The strains of our famous composers that are lifted bodily for measures at a time, from the song of a bird or indisputably based upon it," answered Leslie.

"Did you and Nellie have any success?"

"Indeed yes! We had the royal luck to hear exactly the song I had hoped; and besides we talked of many things and Nellie settled her future course in her mind. When she went into the swamp alone and came out with an armload of lavender fringed orchids she meant to carry to Elizabeth, and her heart firmly resolved to begin a new life with you, she told me she felt like flying; that never had she been so happy."

Leslie paused, glancing at James Minturn. He seemed puzzled: "I don't understand. But nothing matters now. Tell me about the birds," he said.

"And it is what you admit you don't understand that I must tell you of," said Leslie. "I've been afraid, horribly afraid you didn't understand, and that you took some course you wouldn't have taken if you did. What happened in the swamp was all my fault!"

"The birds, Leslie, tell me of the birds," commanded James Minturn. "You can't possibly know what occurred that separated Nellie and me."

"No, I don't know your side of it; but I do know hers, and I don't think you do," persisted Leslie. "Now if you would be big enough to let me tell you how it was with her that day, and what she said to me, your mind would be perfectly at rest as to the course you have taken."

"My mind is 'perfectly at rest now as to the course I have taken,'" said Mr. Minturn. "I realize that a man should meet life as it comes to him. I endured mine in sweating humiliation for years, and I would have gone on to the end, if it had been a question of me only, but when the girl was sacrificed and the boys in a fair way to meet a worse fate than hers, the question no longer hinged on me. You have seen my sons during their mother's régime, when they were children of wealth in the care of servants; look at them now and dare to tell me that they are not greatly improved."

"Surely they are!" said Leslie. "You did right to rescue them from their environment; all the fault that lies with you so far is, that you did not do from the start what you are now doing. The thing that haunts me is this, Mr. Minturn, and I must get it out of my mind before I can sleep soundly again—you will let me tell you—you won't think me meddling in what must be dreadful heartache? Oh you won't will you?"

"No, I won't," said Mr. Minturn, "but it is prolonging heartache to discuss this matter, and wasting time better used in the building of a sod dam—indeed Leslie, tell me about the birds."

"I will, if you'll answer one question," said Leslie.

"Dangerous, but I'll risk it," replied Mr. Minturn.

"I must ask two or three minor ones to reach the real one," explained the girl.

"Oh Leslie," laughed Mr. Minturn. "I didn't think you were so like the average woman."

"A large number of men are finding 'the average woman' quite delightful," said Leslie. "Men respect a masculine, well-balanced, argumentative woman, but every time they love and marry the impulsive, changeable, companionable one."

"Provided she be endowed with truth, character, and common mother instinct enough to protect her young—yes—I grant it, and glory in it," said Mr. Minturn. "I can furnish logic for one family, and most men I know feel qualified to do the same."

"Surely!" agreed Leslie. "You were waiting for Nellie the night she came from the tamarack swamp with me, and she told me you had a little box, and that with its contents you had threatened to 'freeze her soul,' if she had a soul. I'll be logical and fair, and ask but the *one* question I first stipulated. Here it is:

did you wait until you made sure she had a soul, worthy of your consideration, before you froze it?"

James Minturn's laugh was ugly to hear.

"My dear girl," he said. "I made sure she had *not* three years ago."

"And I made equally sure that she had," said Leslie, "in the tamarack swamp when she wrestled as Jacob at Peniel against her birth, her environment, her wealth, and triumphed over all of them for you and her sons. I can't go on with my own plan for personal happiness, until I know for sure if you perfectly understand that she came to you that night to confess to you her faults, errors, mistakes, sins, if need be, and ask you to take the head of your household, and to help her fashion each hour of her life anew. Did she have a chance to tell you all this?"

"No," said Mr. Minturn. "But it would have made *no difference,* if she had. It came too late."

"You have not the right to say that to any living, suffering human being!" protested Leslie.

"I have a perfect right to say it to her," said Mr. Minturn. "A right that would be justified in any court in the world, either of lawyers or people."

"Then thank God, Nellie gets her trial higher. He will understand, and forgive her."

"You don't know what she did," said Mr. Minturn. "What she stood before me and the officers of the law, and admitted she did."

"I don't care what she did! There were men forgiven on the cross; because they sincerely repented, God had mercy on them, so He will on her, and what's more, He won't have any on *you*, unless you follow His example and forgive when you are asked, by a woman who is as deeply repentant as she was."

"Her repentance comes too late," said Mr. Minturn with finality. "Her error is *not reparable*."

"There is no such thing as true repentance being too late," insisted Leslie. "You are distinctly commanded to forgive; you have got to do it! There is no error that is reparable. Since you hint tragedy, I will concede it. If she had been directly responsible for the death of her child, it was a mistake, criminal carelessness, but not a thing purposely planned; so she could atone for it by doing her best for you and the boys."

"Any mother who once did the things she did is not fit to be trusted again!"

"What nonsense! James Minturn, you amaze me!" said Leslie. "That is a little too cold masculine logic. That is taking from the whole human race the power to repent of and repair a mistake."

"There are some mistakes that cannot be repaired!"

"I grant it," said Leslie. "There are! *You are making one right now!*"

"That's the most strictly feminine utterance I ever heard," said Mr. Minturn, with a short laugh.

"Thank you," retorted Leslie. "The compliment is high, but I accept it. I ask nothing better at the hands of fate than to be the most feminine of women. And I've told you what I feel forced to. You can now go on with your plans, knowing they are exactly what she had mapped out, hastily, but surely. She said to me that she must build from the foundations, which meant a new home."

"You are fatuously mistaken!" said Mr. Minturn.

"She said to me," reiterated Leslie forcefully, "that for ten years she had done exactly what she pleased, lived only for her own pleasure, now she would do as *you* dictated for a like time, live your way—I never was farther from a mistake in my life. If you think it doesn't take courage to tell you this, and if you think I enjoy it, and if you think I don't wish I were a mile away——"

"I still maintain I know the lady better than you do," said Mr. Minturn. "But you are wonderful Leslie, and I always shall respect and honour you for your effort in our behalf. It does credit to your head and heart. I envy Douglas Bruce. If ever an hour of trial comes to you, I would feel honoured for a chance to prove to you how much I appreciate——"

"Don't talk like that!" wailed Leslie. "It's all a failure if you do! Promise me that you will *think this over*. Let me send you the note Nellie wrote me before she went away. Won't you try to imagine what she is suffering to-day, in the change from what she went to you hoping, and what she received at your hands?"

"Let me see," said James Minturn. "At this hour she is probably enduring the pangs of wearing the most tasteful afternoon gown on the veranda of whatever summer resort suits her variable fancy, also the discomfiture of the woman she induced to bid high and is now winning from at bridge. I am particularly intimate with her forms of suffering; you see I judge them by my own and my children's during the past years."

"Then you think I'm not sincere?" asked Leslie.

"Surely, my dear girl!" said Mr. Minturn. "With all my heart I believe you! I know you are loyal to her, and to me! It isn't *you* I disbelieve, child, it is my wife."

"But I've told you over and over that she's changed."

"And I refuse to believe in her power to undergo the genuine and permanent change that would make her an influence for good with her sons, or anything but an uncontrollable element in my home," said Mr. Minturn. "Why Leslie, if I were to hunt her up and ask her to come to my house, do you think she would do it?"

"I know she would be most happy," said Leslie.

"Small plain rooms, wait on herself, children over the house and lawn at all times—Nellie Minturn? You amuse me!" he said.

"There's no amusement in it for me, it is pitiful tragedy," said Leslie. "She is willing, she has offered to change, you are denying her the opportunity."

"You don't think deeply enough!" said the man. "Suppose, knowing her as I do, I agreed to her coming to my house. Suppose I filled it with servants to wait on her, and ruin and make snobs of the boys; it could only result in a fiasco all around, and bring me again to the awful thing I have been through once, in forcing a separation. The present is too good for the boys, and now they are my first consideration."

"So I see," said Leslie. "Nellie isn't getting a particle and she *is* their mother, and once she really awakened to the situation, she was hungry to mother them, and to take her place in their hearts. I don't know where she is, but feeling as she did when we parted, I know she's not at any summer resort playing bridge at this minute."

"You are a friend worth having, Leslie; I congratulate my wife on so staunch an advocate," said James Minturn. "And I'll promise you this: I'll go back to the hateful subject, just when I felt I was free from it. I'll think on both sides, and I'll weigh all you've said. If I see a glimmering, I will do this much—I will locate her, and learn how genuine was the change you witnessed, and I rather think I'll manage for you to see also. Will that satisfy you?"

"That will make me radiant, because the change I witnessed was genuine. I know that wherever Nellie is to-day and whatever she is doing, she is still firm as when she left me in her desire for reparation toward you and her sons. Please think fast, and find her quickly."

"Leslie, you're incorrigible! Go bring Douglas to his surprise. He has a right to be happy."

"So have you," insisted Leslie. "More than he, because you have had such deep sorrow. Good-bye."

Then Leslie took leave of the others, returned to the cabin, and hurried to her room to dress for her trip to bring her lover. Douglas Bruce was waiting when she stopped at the Iriquois and his greeting was joyous. Mr. Winton was cordial, but Douglas noticed that he seemed tired and worried, and inquired if he were working unusually hard. He replied that he was, and beginning to feel the heat a little.

"Then we will drive to the country before dinner to cool off," said Leslie, seeing her opportunity.

Both men agreed that would be enjoyable. After a few minutes of casual talk they relaxed while making smooth passage over city streets and the almost equally level highways of the country. At the end of half an hour Douglas sat upright, looking around him.

"I don't recognize this," he said. "Have we been here before, Leslie?"

"I think not," she answered. "I don't know why. It is one of my best loved drives. Always before we have taken the road to the club house, or some of its branches."

They began a gentle ascent, when directly across their way stretched the blue water of a lake.

"Is here where we take the plunge?" inquired Douglas.

"No indeed!" answered Leslie. "Here we speed until we gather such momentum that we shoot across the water and alight on the opposite bank without stopping. Make your landing neatly, Rogers!"

"Why have we never been here before?" marvelled Douglas. "I don't remember any other road one-half so inviting. Just look ahead here! See what a beautiful picture!" He indicated a vine of creeping blackberry spreading over gold sand, its rough, deeply serrated leaves of most artistic cutting, with tufts of snowy bloom surrounding dark-tipped stamens in their centres.

"Isn't it!" answered Mr. Winton. "You know what Whitman said of it?"

"I'm not so well read in Whitman as you are."

"Which is your distinct loss," said Mr. Winton. "It was he who wrote, 'A running blackberry would adorn the parlours of Heaven.'"

"And so it would!" exclaimed Douglas. "What a frieze that would make for a dining-room! Have you ever seen it used?"

"Never," answered Leslie, "or many other of our most exquisite forms of wild growth."

"What beautiful country!" Douglas commented a minute later as the car sped from the swamp, ran uphill, and down a valley between stretches of tilled farm land on either side, sloping back to the lakes now growing distant, then creeping up a gradual incline until Atwater flashed into sight.

"Man! That's fine!" he said, rising in the car to better admire the view, at which Leslie signalled the driver to run slower. "I don't remember that I ever saw anything quite so attractive as this. And if ever water invited a swimmer—that white sand bed seems to extend as far into the lake as you can see. Jove! Wasn't that a black bass under that thorn bush?"

Leslie's eyes were shining while her laugh was as joyous as any of the birds. He need not say more. There was a bathing suit in his room; in ten minutes he could be cleaving the water to the opposite shore and have time to return before dinner. The car sped down where the road ran level with the water. A flock of waders arose and circled the lake. On the right was the orchard, the newly made garden, the tiny cabin with green lawn, hammocks swinging between trees, Indian blankets spread, and the odour of cooking food in the air. The car stopped, Douglas sprang out and offered his hand as he saw Leslie intended descending. She took the hand and kept it in her left. With her right she included woods, water, orchard and cabin.

"These are my surprise for you," she said. "I am going to live here this summer, and keep house for you and Dad while you run and reform the world. Welcome home, Douglas!"

He slowly looked around, then at Mr. Winton.

"Do you believe her?" he asked incredulously.

"Yes indeed! Leslie has the faculty of making good. And I'm one day ahead of you. She tried this on me last night. Hurry into your bathing suit;

we'll swim before dinner, and then we'll fish. It was great going in this morning! I'm sure you'll enjoy it!"

"Enjoy it!" cried Douglas. "Here is where the paucity of our language is made manifest."

Too happy herself for the right word, Leslie showed Douglas to his room, with its white bed, and row of hooks, on one of which hung the bathing suit; then she went to put on her own, and they hurried to the lake.

"You are happy here, Leslie?" asked Douglas.

"Never in my life have I been so happy as I am this moment," said Leslie, skifting the clear water with her hands while she waited for her father before starting the swim to the opposite shore. "I've got the most joyous thing to tell you."

"Go on and tell, 'Bearer of Morning,'" he said. "I am so delighted I'm maudlin."

"Right over there, on the road to the club house, while 'seeking new worlds to conquer' this afternoon, I ran into James Minturn wearing a bathing suit, to his knees in mud and water, building a sod dam for his boys."

"You did?" cried Douglas.

"I did!" said Leslie. "Here's the picture: a beautiful winding stream, big trees like these on the banks, shade and flowers, birds, and air a-plenty, a fine appearing woman he introduced as his sister, a Minturn boy catching fish with his bare hands on either bank, the brother Minturn must have adopted legally, since he gave him his name——"

"He did," interrupted Douglas. "He told me so——"

"I was sure of it," said Leslie. "And an interesting young man, a tutor, bringing up more sod; the boys acted quite like any other agreeably engaged children—but Minturn himself, looking like a man I never saw before, down in the sand and water building a sod dam—a sod dam I'm telling you——"

"I notice what you are telling me," cried Douglas. "It is duly impressing me. 'Dam' is all I can think of."

"It's no wonder!" exclaimed Leslie.

"What did he say to you?" queried Douglas.

"It wasn't necessary for him to say anything," said Leslie. "I could see. He is making over his boys and in order to do it sympathetically, and win their confidence and love, he is being a boy himself again. He has the little chaps under control now. There are love and admiration in their tones when they speak to him, while they *obey* him. Think of it!"

"It is something worth thinking of," said Douglas. "He was driven to action, but his methods must have been heroic; for they seem to have worked."

"Yes, for him and the boys," said Leslie, "but they are not all his family."

"The remainder of his family always has looked out for herself to the exclusion of everything else in life, you have told me; I imagine she is still doing it with wonderful success," hazarded Douglas.

"It amazes me how men can be so unfeeling."

"So you talked to him about her?"

"I surely did!" asserted Leslie.

"And I'll wager you wasted words," said Douglas.

"Not one!" cried the girl. "He will remember each one I spoke. If I don't hear of him taking some action soon, I'll find another occasion, and try again. He shall divide the joy of remaking those boys with their mother."

"She will respectfully—I mean disdainfully, decline!"

"You don't believe she was in earnest in what she said to me then?" asked the girl.

"I am quite sure she was," he answered, "but a few days of her former life with her old friends will take her back to her previous ways with greater abandon than ever. You mark my words."

"Bother your words!" cried Leslie emphatically. "I tell you Douglas, I went through the fire with her. I watched her soul come out white. Promise me that if ever he talks to you, you won't say anything against her."

"It would be a temptation," he said. "Minturn is a different man."

"So is she a different woman! Come on Dad, we are waiting for you," called Leslie. "What kept you so?"

"A paper fell from my pocket, so I picked it up and in glancing at it I became interested in a thought that hadn't occurred to me before, and I forgot. You must forgive your old Daddy; his hands are about full these days. Between my job for the city, and my own affairs, and those of a friend, I have all I can carry. Now let me forget business. I call this great of the girl. And one of the biggest appeals to me is the bill of fare. I had a dinner for a king last night. What have we to-night?"

"But won't anticipation spoil it?" she asked.

"Not a particle," he declared.

"It's the fish we caught last night, baked potatoes, cress salad from Minturn's brook, strawberries from Atwaters, cream from our rented cow, real clover cream, Mrs. James says, and biscuit. That's all."

"Glory!" cried Mr. Winton. "Doesn't that thrill you? Let's head for the tallest tamarack of the swamp and then have a feast."

On the opposite bank they rested a few minutes, then returned to dinner. Afterward, with Rogers rowing for Mr. Winton, and Leslie for Douglas, they went bass fishing. When the boats passed on the far shore Leslie and Douglas had three, and Mr. Winton five. This did not prove that he was the better fisherman, only that he worked constantly; they lost much time in conversation which interested them; but as they enjoyed what they had to say more than the sport, while Leslie only wished them to take the fish they would use, it was their affair. The girl soon returned to the Minturns and secured a promise from Douglas that if Mr. Minturn talked with him, at least he would say nothing to discourage his friend about the sincerity of his wife's motives. Leslie's thoughts then turned to the surprise Douglas had mentioned.

"Oh, that pretty girl?" he inquired casually.

"Yes, Lily," she said. "Of course Mickey took you to see her! Is she really a lovable child, and attractive? Could you get any idea of what is her trouble?"

Douglas carefully reeled while looking at Leslie with a speculative smile. "You refuse to consider an attractive young lady of greater beauty than I have previously seen?" he queried.

"Absolutely! Don't waste time on it," she said.

"You'll have to begin again and ask me one at a time," he laughed. "What was your first?"

"Is she really a lovable child?" repeated Leslie.

"She most certainly is," said Douglas. "I could love her dearly. It's plain that Mickey adores her. Why when a boy gives up trips to the country, the chance to pick up good money, in order to stand over, wash, and cook for a little sick girl, what is the answer?"

"The one you have given—that he adores her," conceded Leslie. "The next was, 'Is she attractive?'"

"Wonderfully!" cried Douglas. "And what she would be in health with flesh to cover her bones and colour on her lips and cheeks is now only dimly foreshadowed."

"She must have her chance," said Leslie. "I was thinking of her to-day. I'll go to see her at once and bring her here. I will get the best surgeon in Multiopolis to examine her and a nurse if need be; then Mickey can come out with you."

"Would you really, Leslie?" asked Douglas.

"But why not?" cried she. "That's one of the things worth while in the world."

"I'd love to go halvers with you," proposed Douglas. "Let's do it! When will you go to see her?"

"In a few days," said Leslie. "The last one was, 'Could you get any idea of what is the trouble?'"

"Very little," said Douglas. "She can sit up and move her hands. He is teaching her to read and write. She had her lesson very creditably copied out on her slate. She practises in his absence on poems Mickey makes."

"Poems?"

"Doggerel," explained Douglas. "Four lines at a time. Some of it is pathetic, some of it is witty, some of it presages possibilities. He may make a poet. She requires a verse each evening, so he recites it, then writes it out, and she uses it for copy the next day. The finished product is to have a sky-blue cover and be decorated either with an English sparrow, the only bird she has seen, or a cow.

She likes milk, and the pictures of cows give her an idea that she can handle them like her doll——"

"Oh Douglas!" protested Leslie.

"I believe she thinks a whole herd of cows could be kept on her bed, while she finds them quite suitable to decorate Mickey's volume," said Douglas.

"Why, hasn't she seen anything at all?"

"She has been on the street twice in her life that she knows of," answered Douglas. "It will be kind of you to take her, and cure her if it can be done, but you'll have to consult Mickey. She is his find, so he claims her, belligerently, I might warn you!"

"Claims her! *He has her?*" marvelled Leslie.

"Surely! In his room! On his bed! Taking care of her himself, and doing a mighty fine job of it! Best she ever had I am quite sure," said Douglas.

"But Douglas!" cried Leslie in amazement.

"'But me no buts,' my lady!" warned Douglas. "I know what you would say. Save it! You can't do anything that way. Mickey is right. She *is* his. He found her in her last extremity, in rags, on the floor in a dark corner of an attic. He carried her home in that condition, to a clean bed his mother left him. Since, he has been her gallant little knight, lying on the floor on his winter bedding, feeding her first and most, not a thought for himself. God, Leslie! I don't stand for anything coming between Mickey and his child, his 'family' he calls her. He's the biggest small specimen I ever have seen. I'll fight his cause in any court in the country, if his right to her is questioned, as it will be the minute she is taken to a surgeon or a hospital."

"How old is she?" asked Leslie.

"Neither of them knows. About ten, I should think."

"How has he managed to keep her hidden this long?"

"He lives in an attic. The first woman he tried to get help from started the Home question, and frightened him; so he appealed to a nurse he met through being connected with an accident; she gave him supplies, instructions and made Lily gowns."

"But why didn't she——?" began Leslie.

"She may have thought the child was his sister," said Douglas. "She's the loveliest little thing, Leslie!"

"Very little?" asked Leslie.

"Tiny is the word," said Douglas. "It's the prettiest sight I ever saw to watch him wait on her, and to see her big, starved, scared eyes follow him with adoring trust."

"Adoration on both sides, then," laughed Leslie.

"You imply I'm selecting too big words," said Douglas. "Wait till you see her, and see them together."

"It's a problem!" said Leslie.

"Yes, I admit that!" conceded Douglas, "but it isn't *your* problem."

"But they can't go on that way!" cried Leslie.

"I grant that," said Douglas. "All I stipulate is that Mickey shall be left to plan their lives himself, and in a way that makes him happy."

"That's only fair to him!" said Leslie.

"Now you are grasping and assimilating the situation properly," commented Douglas.

When they returned to the cabin they found Mr. Winton stretched in a hammock smoking. Douglas took a blanket and Leslie a cushion on the steps, while all of them watched the moon pass slowly across Atwater.

"How are you progressing with the sinners of Multiopolis?" asked Mr. Winton of Douglas.

"Fine!" he answered. "I've found what I think will turn out to be a big defalcation. Somebody drops out in disgrace with probably a penitentiary sentence."

"Oh Douglas! How can you?" cried Leslie.

"How can a man live in luxury when he is stealing other people's money to pay the bills?" he retorted.

"Yes I know, but Douglas, I wish you would buy this place and plow corn, or fish for a living."

"Sometimes I have an inkling that before I finish with this I shall wish so too," replied he.

"What do you think, Daddy?" asked Leslie.

"I think the 'way of the transgressor is hard,' and that as always he pays in the end. Go ahead son, but let me know before you reach my office or any of my men. I hope I have my department in perfect order, but sometimes a man gets a surprise."

"Of course!" agreed Douglas. "Look at that water, will you? Just beyond that ragged old sycamore! That fellow must have been a whale. Isn't this great?"

"The best of life," said Mr. Winton, stooping to kiss Leslie as he said good-night to both.

CHAPTER XIII

A Safe Proposition

When Mickey posted his letter, in deep thought he slowly walked home. That night his eyes closed with a feeling of relief. He was certain that when Peter and his wife and children talked over the plan he had suggested they would be anxious to have such a nice girl as Lily in their home for a week. He even went so far as the vague thought that if they kept her until fall, they never would be able to give her up, and possibly she could remain with them until he could learn whether her back could be cured, and make arrangements suitable for her. In his heart he felt sure that Mr. Bruce or Miss Leslie would help him take care of her, but he had strong objections to them. He thought the country with its clean air, birds, flowers and quiet the best place for her; if he allowed them to take her, she would be among luxuries which would make all he could do unappreciated.

"She wasn't born to things like that; what's the use to spoil her with them?" he argued. "Course they haven't spoiled Miss Leslie, but she wasn't a poor kid to start on, and she has a father to take care of her, and Mr. Bruce. Lily has only me and I'm going to manage my family myself. Pretty soon those nice folks will come, and if she likes them, maybe I'll let them take her 'til it's cooler."

Mickey had thought they would come soon, but he had not supposed it would be the following day. He went downtown early, spent some time drilling his protégé in the paper business, and had the office ready when Douglas Bruce arrived an hour late. During that hour, Mickey's call came. He made an appointment to meet Mr. and Mrs. Peter Harding at Marsh & Jordan's at four o'clock.

"Peter must have wanted to see her so bad he quit plowing to come," commented Mickey, as he hung up the receiver. "He couldn't have finished that field last night! They're just crazy to see Lily, and when they do, they'll be worse yet; but of course they wouldn't want to take her from me, 'cause they got three of their own. I guess Peter is the safest proposition I know. Course he wouldn't ever put a little flowersy-girl in any old Orphings' Home. Sure he wouldn't! He wouldn't put his own there, course he wouldn't mine!"

"Mickey, what do you think?" asked Douglas as he entered. "I've moved to the country!"

Mickey stared. Then came his slow comment: "Gee! The cows an' the clover gets all of us!"

"I can beat that," said Douglas. "I'm going to live beside a lake where I can swim every night and morning, and catch big bass, and live on strawberries from the vines and cream straight from the cow——"

"I thought you'd get to the cow before long."

"And you are invited to go out with me as often as you want to, and you may arrange to have Lily out too! Won't that be fine?"

Mickey hesitated while his eyes grew speculative, before he answered with his ever ready: "Sure!"

"Miss Winton made a plan for her father and me," explained Douglas. "She knew we would lose our vacations this summer, so she took an old cabin on Atwater, and moved out. We are to go back and forth each morning and evening. I never was at the lake before, but it's not far from the club house and it's beautiful. I think most of all I shall enjoy the swimming and fishing."

"I haven't had experience with water enough to swim in," said Mickey. "A tub has been my limit. You'll have a fine time all right, and thank you for asking me. I think Miss Winton is great. Ain't it funny how many fine folks there are in the world? 'Most every one I meet is too nice for any use; but I don't know any Swell Dames, my people are just common folks."

"You wouldn't call Miss Winton a 'Swell Dame,' then?"

"Well I should say nix!" cried Mickey. "You wouldn't catch her motoring away to a party and leaving her baby to be slapped and shook out of its breath by a mad nurselady, 'cause she left it herself where the sun hurt its eyes. She wouldn't put a little girl that couldn't walk in any Orphings' Home where no telling what might happen to her! She'd fix her a Precious Child and take her for a ride in her car and be careful with her."

"Are you quite sure about that Mickey?"

"Surest thing you know," said Mickey emphatically. "Why look her straight in the eyes, and you can tell. I saw her coming away down the street, and the minute I got my peepers on her I picked her for a winner. I guess you did too."

"I certainly did," said Douglas. "But it is most important that I be perfectly sure, so I should like to have your approval of my choice."

"I guess you're kidding now," ventured Mickey.

"No, I'm in earnest," said Douglas Bruce. "You see Mickey, as I have said before, your education and mine have been different, but yours is equally valuable."

"What shall I do now? 'Scuse me, I mean—what do I mean?" asked Mickey.

"To wait until I'm ready for you," suggested Douglas.

"Sure!" conceded Mickey. "It's because I'm used to hopping so lively on the streets."

"Do you miss the streets?" inquired Douglas.

"Well not so much as I thought I would," said Mickey, "'sides in a way I'm still on the job, but I guess I'll get Henry's boy so he can go it all right. He seems to be doing fairly well; so does the old man."

"Have you got him in training too?" asked Douglas.

"Oh it's his mug," explained Mickey impatiently. "S'pose you do own a grouch, what's the use of displaying it in your show window? Those things are dangerous. They're contagious. Seeing a fellow on the street looking like he'd never smile again, makes other folks think of their woes, so pretty soon everybody gets sorry for themselves. I'd like to see the whole world happy."

"Mickey, what makes *you* so happy to-day?"

"I scent somepin' nice in the air," said Mickey. "I hear the rumble of the joy wagon coming my way."

"You surely look it," declared Douglas. "It's a mighty fine thing to be happy. I am especially thinking that, because it looks like this last batch you brought me has a bad dose in it for a man I know. He won't be happy when he sees his name in letters an inch high on the front page of the *Herald*."

"No, he won't," agreed Mickey, his face dulling. "That *comes in my line*. I've seen men forced to take it right on the cars. Open a paper, slide down, turn white, shiver, then take a brace and try to sit up and look like they didn't care, when you could see it was all up with them. Gee, it's tough! I wish we were in other business."

"But what about the men who work hard for their money, not to mince matters, that these men you are pitying steal?" asked Douglas.

"Yes, I know," said Mickey. "But there's a big bunch of taxpayers, so it doesn't hit any *one* so hard. It's tough on them, but honest, Mr. Bruce, it ain't as tough to lose your coin as it is to lose your glad face. You can earn more money or slide along without so much; but once you get the slick, shamed look on your show window, you can't ever wash it off. Since your face is what your friends know you by, it's an awful pity to spoil it."

"That's so too, Mickey," laughed Bruce, "but keep this clearly in your mind. *I'm not spoiling any one's face*. If any man loses his right to look his neighbour frankly in the eye, from the job we're on, it is *his* fault, not *ours*. If men have lived straight we can't find defalcations in their books, can we?"

"Nope," agreed Mickey. "Just the same I wish we were plowing corn, 'stead of looking for them. That plowing job is awful nice. I watched a man the other day, the grandest big bunch of bone and muscle, driving a team it took a gladiator to handle. First time I ever saw it done at close range and it got me. He looked like a man you'd want to tie to and stick 'til the war is over. If he ever has a case he is going to bring it to you. But where he'll get a case out there ten miles from anybody, with the bluest sky you ever saw over his head, and black fields under his feet, I can't see. Yes, I wish we were plowing for corn 'stead of trouble."

"You little dunce," laughed Douglas. "We'd make a fortune plowing corn."

"What's the difference how much you make if something black keeps ki-yi-ing at your heels 'bout how you make it?" asked Mickey.

"There's a good strong kick in my heels, and the 'ki-yi-ing' is for the feet of the man I'm after."

"Yes, I know," said Mickey, "but 'fore we get through with this I just got a hunch that you'll wish we had been plowing corn, too."

"What makes you so sure, Mickey?" said Douglas.

"Oh things I hear men say when I get the books keep me thinking," replied Mickey.

"What things?" queried Douglas.

"Oh about who's going to get the axe next!" said Mickey.

"But what of that?" asked Douglas.

"Why it might be somebody you know!" he cried. "When you find these wrong entries you can't tell who made them."

"I know that the man who made them deserves what he gets," said Douglas.

"Yes, I guess he does," agreed Mickey. "Well go on! But when I grow up I'm going to plow corn."

"What about the poetry?" queried Douglas.

"They go together fine," explained Mickey. "When the book is finished, I'd like clover on the cover better than the cow; but if Lily wants the live stock it goes!"

"Of course," assented Douglas. "But when she sees a real cow she may change her mind."

"Right in style! Ladies do it often," conceded Mickey. "I've seen them so changeful they couldn't tell when they called a taxi where they wanted to be taken." "Mickey, your observations on human nature would make a better book than your poetry."

"Oh I don't know," said Mickey. "You see I ain't really got *at* the poetry job yet. I have to be educated a lot to do it right. What I do now I wouldn't show to anybody else, it's just fooling for Lily. But I got an address that gives me a look-in on the paper business if I ever want it. I ain't got at the poetry yet, but I been on the human-nature job from the start. When you go cold and hungry if you don't know human nature—why you *know* it, that's all!"

"You surely do," said Douglas. "Now let's hustle this forenoon, and then you may have the remainder of the day. I am going fishing."

"Thank you," said Mickey, "I hope you get a bass as long as your arm, and I hope the man you are chasing breaks his neck before you get him."

Mickey grinned at Douglas' laugh, and went racing about his work, then he helped on his paper route until four, when he hurried to his meeting with Nancy and Peter.

"When everybody is so nice if you give them any show at all, I can't understand where the grouchers get their grouch," muttered Mickey, as he hopped from one toe to the other and tried to select the car at the curb which would be Peter's.

"Hey you!" presently called a voice from one of them. Mickey sent a keen glance over a boy who had come up and entered the car.

"Straw you!" retorted Mickey, landing on the curb in a flying leap.

"Is your name Mickey?" inquired the boy.

"Yep. Is your father's name Peter?" asked Mickey.

"Yep. And mine is Peter too. So to avoid two Peters I am Junior. Come on in 'til the folks come."

Formalities were over. Mickey laughed as he entered the car and straightway began an investigation of its machinery. Now any boy is proud to teach another something he wants to know and does not, so by the time the car was thoroughly explained any listener would have thought them acquaintances from birth.

"Hurry!" cried Junior when his parents came. "I want to get home with Mickey. I want him to show me——"

"Don't you hurry your folks, Junior," said Mickey, "I'll show you all right!"

"Well it's about time I was seeing something."

"Sure it is," agreed Mickey. "Come on with me here, and I'll show you what real boys are!"

"Say father, I'm coming you know," cried Junior. "I'm tired poking in the country. Just look what being in the city has made of Mickey."

"Yes, just look!" cried Mickey, waving both hands and bracing on feet wide apart. "Do look! Your age or more, and about *half* your beefsteak and bone."

"But you got muscle. I bet I couldn't throw you!"

"I bet you couldn't either," retorted Mickey, "'cause I survived Multiopolis by being Johnny *not* on the spot! I've dodged for my life and my living since I can remember. I'm champeen on that. But you come on with me, and I'll get you a job and let you try yourself."

"I'm coming," said Junior. Then remembering he was not independent he turned to his mother. "Can't I take a job and work here?"

Mrs. Harding braced herself and succumbed to habit. "That will be as your father says."

Junior turned toward his father, doubt in his eye, to receive a shock. There was not a trace of surprise or disapproval on the face of Peter.

"Now maybe that would be the best way in the world for you to help me out," he said. "You see me through planting and harvest and then I'll arrange to spare you, and you can see how you like it till fall. But you are too young to give up school and I don't agree to interrupting your education."

Mrs. Harding entered the car. "Now Mickey," she said as she distributed parcels, "you sit up there with Peter and show him the way, and we will go see if we want to undertake the care of your little girl for a week."

"Drop the anchor, furl the sail, right here," directed Mickey when they reached Sunrise Alley. "You know I told you dearest lady, about how scared my little girl is, having seen so few folks and not expecting you; so I'll have to ask you to wait a few minutes 'til I go up and get her used to your being here and then I'll have to sort of work her up to you one at a time. I 'spect you can't hardly believe that there's anything in all the world so small, and so white, that's lived to have the brains she has, and yet hasn't seen the streets of this city but for a short ride on a street-car twice in her life, and hasn't talked to half a dozen people. She may take you for a bear, Peter; you will be quiet and easy, won't you?"

"Why Mickey," said Peter, "why of course, son!"

Mickey bounded up the stairs and swung wide his door. Again the awful heat hit him in the face. He swallowed a mouthful, hastily shutting the door. "It's hard on Lily," was his mental comment, "but I guess I'll just *save* that for Mr. and Mrs. Peter. I think a few gulps of it will do them good; it will show them better than talking why, once she's *out* of it, she shouldn't come back 'til cold weather at least, if at all. Yes I guess!"

"Most baked honey?" he asked, taking her hot hands.

"Mickey, 'tain't near six," she panted.

"No it's two hours early," said Mickey. "But you know Flowersy-girl, I'm going to take *care* of you. It's getting too hot for you. Don't you remember what I told you last night?"

"'Bout laying on the grass an' the clover flowers?"

"Exactly yes!" said Mickey. "'Fore we melt let's roll up in this sheet and go, Lily! What do you say?"

"Has—has the red-berry folks come?" she cried.

"They're downstairs, Lily. They're waiting."

Peaches began climbing into his arms.

"Mickey, Mickey-lovest, hold me tight," she panted. "Mickey, I'm scairt just God-damned!"

"Wope! Wope lady! None of that!" cried Mickey aghast. "The place where you're going there's a *nice little girl* that never said such a word in all her life, and if she did her mammy would wash the badness out of her mouth with soap, just like I'll have to wash out yours, if you don't watch. You can't go in the big car, being held tight by me, else you promise cross your heart never, not never to say that again."

"Mickey, will soapin' take it out?" wailed Peaches.

"Well my mammy took it out of *me* that way!"

"Mickey get the soap, an' wash, an' scour it all out now, so's I can't ever. Mickey, quick before the nice lady comes that has flower fields, an' red berries, an' honey 'lasses. Mickey, hurry!"

"Oh you fool little sweet kid," he half laughed, half sobbed. "You fool little precious child-kid—I can't! There's a better way. I'll just put on a kiss so tight that no bad swearin's will ever pop out past it. There, like that! Now you won't ever say one 'fore the nice little girl, and when I want you not to so bad, will you?"

"Not never Mickey! Not never, never, never!"

"The folks can't wait any longer," said Mickey. "Here quick, I'll wash your face and comb you, and get a clean nightie on you, and your sweetest ribbon."

"Then it's pink," declared Peaches, "an' Mickey, make me a pretty girl, so's the nice lady will like me to drink her milk."

"Greedy!" said Mickey. "How can I make you pretty when the Lord didn't!"

"Ain't I pretty any at all?" queried Peaches.

"Mebby you would be if you'd fatten up a little," said Mickey judicially. "Can't anybody be pretty that's got bones sticking out all over them."

"Mickey, is the girl where we are going pretty?"

"I don't know," said Mickey. "I haven't seen her. She's a fine little girl, for she's at home taking care of her baby brother so's that her mammy can come and see if you are *nice enough* to go to her house and not *spoil* her children. See?"

Peaches nodded comprehendingly.

"Mickey, I won't again!" she insisted. "I said not never, never, never. Didn't you *hear* me?"

"Yes I heard you," said Mickey, applying the washcloth, slipping on a fresh nightdress, brushing curls, and tying the ribbon with fingers shaking with excitement and haste. "Yes I heard you, but that stuff seems to come awful easy, Miss. You got to be careful no end. Now, I'm going to bring them. You just smile at them, and when they ask you, tell them the right answer *nice*. Will you honey? Will you *sure?*"

"Surest thing you know," quoted Peaches promptly.

"Aw-w-w-ah!" groaned Mickey. "That ain't right! Miss Leslie wouldn't ever said that! You got that from me, too! I guess I better soap out my mouth 'fore I begin on you. 'Yes ma'am,' is the answer. Now you remember! I'll just bring in the lady first."

"I want to see Peter first!" announced Peaches.

"Well if I ever!" cried Mickey. "Peter is a great big man, 'bout twice as big as Mr. Bruce. You don't either! You want to see the nice lady first, 'cause it's up to *her* to say if she'll take care of you. She may get mad and not let you go at all, if you ask to see Peter *first*. You want to see the nice lady first, don't you Lily?"

"Yes, if I got to, to see the cow. But I don't!" said Lily. "I want to see Peter. I like Peter the *best*."

"Now you look here Miss Chicken, don't you start a tantrum!" cried Mickey. "If you don't see this nice lady first and be pretty to her, I'll just go down and tell them you *like* lying here roasting, and they can go back to their flower-fields and berries. See?"

Peaches drew a deep breath but her eyes were wilful. A wave of heat seemed to envelop them.

"Sweat it out right now!" ordered Mickey. "When people do things for you 'cause they are sorry for you, it's up to you to be polite, to pay back with manners at least. See?"

Peaches' smile was irresistible: "Mickey, I feel so p'lite! I'll see the nice lady first."

"Now there's a real, sure-enough lady!"

Mickey stooped to kiss Peaches again, take a last look at the hair ribbon, and straighten the sheet, then he ran; but he closed in the heat quickly as he slipped through the doorway. A few seconds later with the Harding family at his heels he again approached it. There he made his second speech. He addressed it to Peter and Junior.

"'Cause she's so little and so scared, I guess the nice lady better go in first, and make up with her. Then onc at a time you can come, so so many strangers won't upset her."

Peter assented heartily, but with a suffocating gesture removed his coat, so Junior followed his example. Mickey cut short something about "extreme heat" on the lips of Mrs. Harding by indicating the door, and opening it. He quickly closed it after her, advancing to Peaches.

"Lily, this is the nice lady I was telling you of who has got the bird singing and the flower-fields——" he began. Peaches drew back, her eyes wide with wonder and excitement, but her mind followed Mickey's lead, for she shocked his sense of propriety by adding: "and the good red berries."

But Mrs. Harding came from an environment where to have "good red berries," spicy smoked ham, fat chickens and golden loaves constituted a first test of efficiency. To have her red berries appreciated did not offend her. If Peaches had said "the sweetest, biggest red berries in Noble Country," the woman would have been delighted, because that was her private opinion, but she was not so certain that corroboration was unpleasant. She advanced, gazing at the child unconsciously gasping the stifling air. She took one hurried glance at the room in its scrupulous bareness, with waves of heat pouring in the open window, and bent over Peaches.

"Won't you come out of this awful heat quickly, and let us carry you away to a cool, shady place? Dear little girl, don't you want to come?" she questioned.

"Is Mickey coming too?" asked Peaches.

"Of course Mickey is coming too!" said the lady.

"Will he hold me?"

"He will if you want him to," said Mrs. Harding, "but Peter is so much bigger, it wouldn't tire him a mite."

Mickey shifted on his feet and gazed at Peaches; as her eyes sought his, the message he telegraphed her was so plain that she caught it right.

"Mickey is just awful strong," she said. "I'll go if he'll hold me. But I want to *see* Peter! I *like* Peter!"

"Why you darling!" cried the nice lady.

"And I like Junior, that Mickey told me about, and your nice little girl that I mustn't ever say no sw——"

Mickey promptly applied the flat of his hand to the lips of the astonished child.

"And you like the little girl and the fat toddly baby——" he prompted.

"Yes," agreed Peaches enthusiastically, twisting away her head, "and I like the milk and the meat—gee, I like the *meat*, only Mickey wouldn't give me but a tiny speck 'til he asked the Sunshine Nurse Lady."

"You blessed child!" cried Nancy Harding. "Call Peter quickly!"

Mickey opened the door and signalled Peter and Junior.

"She likes you. She asked for you. You can both come at once," he announced, holding the door at a narrow crack until they reached it, both red faced, dripping, and fanning with their hats. Peter gasped for air.

"My God! Has any living child been cooped in this all day?" he roared. "Get her out! Get her out quick! Get her out first and talk afterward. This will give her scarlet fever!"

A shrill shout came from behind the intervening lady who arose and stepped back as Peaches raised to her elbow, and stretched a shaking hand toward Peter.

"Gee, Peter! You get your mouth soaped out first!" she cried. "Gee, Peter! I *like* you, Peter!"

Peter bent over her and then stooping to her level he explored her with astonished eyes, as he cried: "Why child, you ain't big enough for an exclamation point!" Peaches didn't know what an exclamation point was, but Mickey did. His laugh brought him again into her thought.

"Mickey, let's beat it! Take me quick!" she panted. "Take me first and talk afterward. Mickey, we just love these nice people, let's go drink their milk, and eat their red berries."

"Well Miss Chicken!" said Mickey turning a dull red.

The Harding family were laughing.

"All right, everybody move," said Peter. "What do you want to take with you Mickey?"

"That basket there," he said. "And that box, you take that Junior, and you take the Precious Child, and the slate and the books dearest lady—and I'll take my family; but I ain't so sure about this, lady. She's sweaty now, and riding is the coolingest thing you can do. We mustn't make her sick. She must be well wrapped."

"Why she couldn't take cold to-day——" began Peter.

"You and Junior shoulder your loads and go right down to the car," said Mrs. Harding. "Mickey and I will manage this. He is exactly right about it. To be taken from such heat to the conditions of motoring might——"

"Sure!" interposed Mickey, dreading the next word for the memories it would awaken in the child's heart. "Sure! You two go ahead! We'll come in no time!"

"But I'm not going to lug a basket and have a little chap carrying a child. You take this and I'll take the baby!"

Mickey's wireless went into instant action so Peaches promptly rebelled.

"I ain't no baby!" she said. "Miss Leslie Moonshine Lady sent me her hair ribbons and I 'spect she's been crying for them back every day; and my name what granny named me is Peaches, so there!"

"Corrected! Beg pardon!" said Peter. "Miss Peaches, may I have the honour of carrying you to the car?"

"Nope," said Peaches with finality. "Nobody, not nobody whatever, not the biggest, millyingairest nobody alive can't ever carry me, nelse Mickey says they can, and he is away off on the cars. I like you Peter! I just like you heaps; but I'm Mickey's, so I got to do what he says 'cause he makes me, jes like he ort, and nobody can't ever tend me like Mickey."

"So that's the ticket!" mused Peter.

"Yes, that's the ticket," repeated Peaches. "I ain't heavy. Mickey carried me up, down is easier."

"Sure!" said Mickey. "*I take my own family*. You take yours. We'll be there in a minute."

Peter and Junior disappeared with thankfulness and speed. Mrs. Harding and Mickey wrapped Peaches in the sheet and took along a comfort for shelter from the air stirred by motion. Steadying his arm, which he wished she would not, they descended. Did she think he wanted Peaches to suppose he couldn't carry her? He ran down the last flight to show her, frightening her into protest, and had the reward of a giggle against his neck and the tightening of small arms clinging to him. He settled in the car and wrapped Lily in the comfort until she had only a small peep of daylight.

Mickey knew from Peaches' laboured breathing and the grip of her hands how agitated she was; but as the car glided smoothly along, driven skilfully by mentality, guided by the controlling thought of a tiny lame back, she became easier and clutched less frantically. He kept the comfort over her head. She had enough to make the change, to see so many strangers all at once, without being excited by unfamiliar things that would bewilder and positively frighten her.

Mickey stoutly clung to a load that soon grew noticeably heavy; while over and over he repeated in his heart with fortifying intent: "She is my family,

I'll take care of her. I'll let them keep her a while because it is too hot for her there, but they shan't *boss* her, and they got to know it first off, and they shan't take her from me, and they got to understand it."

Right at that point Mickey's grip tightened until the child in his arms shivered with delight of being so enfolded in her old and only security. She turned her head to work her face level with the comfort and whisper in glee: "Mickey, we are going just stylish like millyingaire folks, ain't we?"

"You just bet we are!" he whispered back.

"Mickey, you wouldn't let them 'get' me, would you?"

"Not on your life!" said Mickey, gripping her closer.

"And Peter wouldn't let them 'get' me?"

"No, Peter would just wipe them clear off the slate if they tried to get you," comforted Mickey. "We're in the country now Lily. Nobody will even think of you away out here."

"Mickey, I want to see the country!" said Peaches.

"No Miss! I'm scared now," replied Mickey. "It was awful hot there and it's lots cooler here, even slow and careful as Peter is driving. If you get all excitement, and rearing around, and take a chill, and your back gets worse, just when we have such a grand good chance to make it better—you duck and lay low, and if you're good, and going out doesn't make you sick, after supper when you rest up, maybe I'll let you have a little peepy yellow chicken in your hand to hold a minute, and maybe I'll let you see a cow. You'd give a good deal to see the cow that's going on your book, wouldn't you?"

Peaches snuggled down in pure content and proved her femininity as she did every day. "Yes. But when I see them, maybe I'll like a chicken better, and put it on."

"All right with me," agreed Mickey. "You just hold still so this doesn't make you sick, and to-morrow you can see things when you are all nice and rested."

"Mickey," she whispered.

Mickey bent and what he heard buried his face against Peaches' a second and when lifted it radiated a shining glory-light, for she had whispered: "Mickey, I'm going to always mind you and love you best of anybody."

Because she had expected the trip to result in the bringing home of the child, Mrs. Harding had made ready a low folding davenport in her first-floor bedroom, beside a window where grass, birds and trees were almost in touch, and where it would be convenient to watch and care for her visitor. There in the light, pretty room, Mickey gently laid Peaches down and said: "Now if you'll just give me time to get her rested and settled a little, you can see her a peep; but there ain't going to be *much* seeing or talking to-night. If she has such a lot she ain't used to and gets sick, it will be a bad thing for her, and all of us, so we better just go slow and easy."

"Right you are, young man," said Peter. "Come out of here you kids! Come to the back yard and play quietly. When Little White Butterfly gets rested and fed, we'll come one at a time and kiss her hand, and wish her pleasant dreams with us, and then we'll every one of us get down on our knees and ask God to help us take such good care of her that she will get well at our house."

Mickey suddenly turned his back on them and tried to swallow the lump in his throat. Then he arranged his family so it was not in a draft, sponged and fed it, and failed in the remainder of his promise, because it went to sleep with the last bite and lay in deep exhaustion. So Mickey smoothed the sheet, slipped off the ribbon, brushed back the curls, shaded the light, marshalled them in on tiptoe, and with anxious heart studied their compassionate faces.

Then he telephoned Douglas Bruce to ask permission to be away from the office the following day, and ventured as far from the house as he felt he dared with Junior; but so anxious was he that he kept in sight of the window. And so manly and tender was his scrupulous care, so tiny and delicate his small charge as she lay waxen, lightly breathing to show she really lived, that in the hearts of the Harding family grew a deep respect for Mickey, and such was their trust in him, that when he folded his comfort and stretched it on the floor beside the child, not even to each other did they think of uttering an objection. So Peaches spent her first night in the country breathing clover air, watched constantly by her staunch protector, and carried to the foot of the Throne on the lips of one entire family; for even Bobbie was told to add to his prayer: "God bless the little sick girl, and make her well at our house."

CHAPTER XIV

An Orphans' Home

"Margaret, I want a few words with you some time soon," said James Minturn to his sister.

"Why not right now?" she proposed. "I'm not busy and for days I've known you were in trouble. Tell me at once, and possibly I can help you."

"You would deserve my gratitude if you could," he said. "I've suffered until I'm reduced to the extremity that drives me to put into words the thing I have thrashed over in my heart day and night for weeks."

"Come to my room James," she said.

James Minturn followed his sister.

"Now go on and tell me, boy," she ordered. "Of course it's about Nellie."

"Yes it's about Nellie," he repeated. "Did you hear any part of what that very charming young lady had to say to me at our chosen playground, not long ago?"

"Yes I did," answered Mrs. Winslow. "But not enough to comprehend thoroughly. Did she convince you that you are mistaken?"

"No. But this she did do," said Mr. Minturn. "She battered the walls of what I had believed to be unalterable decision, until she made this opening: I must go into our affairs again. I have got to find out where my wife is, and what she is doing; and if the things Miss Leslie thinks are true. Margaret, I thought it was *settled*. I was happy, in a way; actually happy! No Biblical miracle ever seemed to me half so wonderful as the change in the boys."

"The difference in them is quite as much of a marvel as you think it," agreed Mrs. Winslow.

"It is greater than I would have thought possible in any circumstances," said Mr. Minturn. "Do they ever mention their mother to you?"

"Incidentally," she replied, "just as they do maids, footman or governess, in referring to their past life. They never ask for her, in the sense of wanting her, that I know of. Malcolm resembles her in appearance and any one could see that she liked him best. She always discriminated against James in his favour if any question between them were ever carried to her."

"Malcolm is like her in more than looks. He has her musical ability in a marked degree," said Mr. Minturn. "I have none, but Miss Winton suggested a thing to me that Mr. Tower has been able to work up some, and while both boys are deeply interested, it's Malcolm who is beginning to slip away alone and listen to and practise bird cries until he deceives the birds themselves. Yesterday he called a catbird to within a few feet of him, by reproducing the notes as uttered and inflected by the female."

"I know. It was a triumph! He told me about it."

"James is well named," said Mr. Minturn. "He is my boy. Already he's beginning to ask questions that are filled with intelligence, solicitude and interest about my business, what things mean, what I am doing, and why. He's going to make the man who will come into my office, who in a few more years will be offering his shoulder for part of my load. You can't understand what the change is from the old attitude of regarding me as worth no consideration; not even a gentleman, as my wife's servants were teaching my sons to think. Margaret, how am I going back even to the thought that I may be making a mistake? Wouldn't the unpardonable error be to again risk those boys an hour in the company and influence which brought them once to what they were?"

"You poor soul!" exclaimed Mrs. Winslow.

"Never mind that!" warned Mr. Minturn. "I'm not accustomed to it, and it doesn't help. Have you any faith in Nellie?"

"None whatever!" exclaimed Mrs. Winslow. "She's so selfish it's simply fiendish. I'd as soon bury you as to see you subject to her again."

"And I'd much sooner be buried, were it not that my heart is set on winning out with those boys," said Mr. Minturn. "There is material for fine men in them, but there is also depravity that would shock you inexpressibly, instilled by ignorant, malicious servants. I wish Leslie Winton had kept quiet."

"And so do I!" agreed Mrs. Winslow. "I could scarcely endure it, as I realized what was going on. While Nellie had you, there was no indignity, no public humiliation at which she stopped. For my own satisfaction I examined Elizabeth before she was laid away, and I held my tongue because I thought you didn't know. When *did* you find out?"

"A newsboy told me. He went with a woman who was in the park where it happened, to tell Nellie, but they were insulted for their pains. Some way my best friend Douglas Bruce picked him up and attached him, as I did William; it was at my suggestion. Of course I couldn't imagine that out of several thousand newsies Douglas would select the one who knew my secret and who daily blasts me with his scorn. If he runs into an elevator where I am, the whistle dies on his lips; his smile fades and he actually shrinks from my presence. You can't blame him. A man *should be able to protect the children he fathers*. What he said to me stunned me so, he thought me indifferent. In my place, would you stop him some day and explain?"

"I most certainly would," said Mrs. Winslow. "A child's scorn is withering, and you don't deserve it."

"I have often wondered what or how much he told Bruce," said Mr. Minturn.

"Could you detect any change in Mr. Bruce after the boy came into his office?" asked Mrs. Winslow.

"Only that he was kinder and friendlier than ever."

"That probably means that the boy told him and that Mr. Bruce understood and was sorry."

"No doubt," he said. "You'd talk to the boy then? Now what would you do about Nellie?"

"What was it Miss Winton thought you *should* do?"

"See Nellie! Take her back!" he exclaimed. "Give her further opportunity to exercise her brand of wifehood on me and motherhood on the boys!"

"James, if you do, I'll never forgive you!" cried his sister. "If you tear up this comfortable, healthful place, where you are the honoured head of your house, and put your boys back where you found them, I'll go home and stay there; and you can't blame me."

"Miss Winton didn't ask me to go back," he explained; "that couldn't be done. I saw and examined the deed of gift of the premises to the city. The only thing she could do would be to buy it back, and it's torn up inside, and will be in shape for opening any day now, I hear. The city needed a Children's Hospital; to get a place like that free, in so beautiful and convenient a location—and her old friends are furious at her for bringing sickness and crooked bodies among them. No doubt they would welcome her there, but they wouldn't welcome her anywhere else. She must have endowed it liberally, no hospital in the city has a staff of the strength announced for it."

"James, you are wandering!" she interrupted. "You started to tell me what Miss Winton asked of you."

"That I bring Nellie here," he explained. "That I make her mistress of this house. That I put myself and the boys in her hands again."

"Oh good Lord!" ejaculated Mrs. Winslow. "James, are you actually thinking of *that?* Mind, I don't care for myself. I have a home and all I want. But for you and those boys, are you really contemplating it?"

"No!" he said. "All I'm thinking of is whether it is my duty to hunt her up and once more convince myself that she is heartless vanity personified, and utterly indifferent to me personally, as I am to her."

"Suppose you do go to her and find that through pique, because you made the move for separation yourself, she wants to try it over, or to get the boys again—she's got a mint of money. Do you know just how much she has?"

"I do not, and I never did," he replied. "Her funds never in any part were in my hands. I felt capable of making all I needed myself, and I have. I earn as much as it is right I should have; but she'd scorn my plan for life and what satisfies me; and she'd think the boys disgraced, living as they are."

"James, was there an hour, even in your honeymoon, when Nellie forgot herself and was a lovable woman?"

"It is painful to recall, but yes! Yes indeed!" he answered. "Never did a man marry with higher hope!"

"Then what——?" marvelled Mrs. Winslow.

"Primarily, her mother, then her society friends, then the power of her money," he answered.

"Just how did it happen?" she queried.

"It began with Mrs. Blondon's violent opposition to children; when she knew a child was coming she practically moved in with us, and spent hours pitying her daughter, sending for a doctor at each inevitable consequence, keeping up an exciting rush of friends coming when the girl should have had quiet and rest, treating me with contempt, and daily holding me up as the monster responsible for all these things. The result was nervousness and discontent bred by such a course at such a time, until it amounted to actual pain, and lastly unlimited money with which to indulge every fancy.

"In such circumstances delivery became the horror they made of it, although several of the doctors told me privately not to have the slightest alarm; it was simply the method of rich selfish women to make such a bugbear of childbirth a wife might well be excused for refusing to endure it. Sifted to the bottom that was *exactly what it was*. I didn't know until the birth of James that they had neglected to follow the instructions of their doctors and made no preparation for nursing the child; as a result, when I insisted that it must be done, shrieks of pain, painful enough as I could see, resulted in a nervous chill for the mother, more inhumanity in me, and the boy was turned over to a hired woman with his first breath and to begin unnatural life. I watched the little chap all I could; he was strong and healthy, and while skilled nurses were available he upset every rule by thriving; which was one more count against me, and the lesson pointed out and driven home that no young wife could give a child such attention, so the baby was better off in the hands of the nurse. That he was reared without love, that his mother took not an iota of responsibility in his care, developed not a trait of motherhood, simply went on being a society belle, had nothing to do with it.

"He did so well, Nellie escaped so much better than many of her friends, that in time she seemed to forget it and didn't rebel at Malcolm's advent, or Elizabeth's, but by that time I had been practically ostracized from the nursery; governesses were empowered to flout and insult me; I scarcely saw my children, and what I did see made me furious, so I vetoed more orphans bearing my name, and gave up doing anything. Then came the tragedy of Elizabeth. Surely you understand 'just how' it was done Margaret?"

"Of course I had an idea, but I never before got just the perfect picture, and now I have it, though it's the last word I *want* to say to you, God made me so that I'm forced to say it, although it furnishes one more example of what is called inconsistency."

"Be careful what you say, Margaret!"

"I must say it," she replied. "I've encouraged you to talk in detail, because I wanted to be sure I was right in the position I was taking; but you've given me a different viewpoint. Why James, think it over yourself in the light of what you just have told me. Nellie never has been a mother at all! Her heart is more barren than that of a woman to whom motherhood is physical impossibility, yet whose heart aches with maternal instinct!"

"Margaret!" cried James Minturn.

"James, it's true!" she persisted. "I never have understood. For fear of that, I led you on and now look what you've told me. Nellie never had a chance at natural motherhood. The thing called society made a foolish mother to begin with, while she in turn ruined her daughter, and if Elizabeth had lived it would have been passed on to her. You throw a new light on Nellie. As long as she was herself, she was tender and loving, and you adored her; if you had been alone and moderately circumstanced, she would have continued being so lovable that after ten years your face flushes with painful memory as you speak of it. I've always thought her abandoned as to wifely and motherly instinct. What you say proves she was a lovable girl, ruined by society, through the medium of her mother and friends."

"If she cared for me as she said, she should have been enough of a woman——" began Mr. Minturn.

"Maybe she *should*, but you must take into consideration that she was not herself when the trouble began; she was, as are all women, even those most delighted over the prospect, in an unnatural condition, *in so far that usual conditions were unusual*, and probably made her ill, nervous, apprehensive, not herself at all."

"Do you mean to say that you are changing?"

"Worse than that!" she said emphatically. "I have positively and permanently changed. Even at your expense I will do Nellie justice. James, your grievance is not against your wife; it is against the mother who bore her, the society that moulded her."

"She should have been woman enough——" he began.

"Left alone, she was!" insisted Mrs. Winslow. "With the ills and apprehensions of motherhood upon her, she yielded as most young, inexperienced women would yield to what came under the guise of tender solicitude, and no doubt eased or banished pain, which all of us avoid when possible; and the pain connected with motherhood is a thing in awe of which the most practised physicians admit themselves almost stunned. The woman who would put aside pampering and stoically endure what money and friends could alleviate is rare. Jim, pain or no pain to you, you must find your wife and learn for yourself if she is heartless; or whether in some miraculous way some one has proved to her what you have made plain as possible to me. You must hunt her up, and if she is still under her mother's and society's influence, and refuses *to change*, let her remain. But—but if she has changed, as you have just seen me change, then you should give her another chance if she asks it."

"I can't!" he cried.

"You must! The evidence is in her favour."

"What do you mean?" he demanded impatiently.

"Her acquiescence in your right to take the boys and alter their method of life; her agreement that for their sakes you might do as you chose with no interference from her; both those are the acknowledgment of failure on her part and willingness for you to repair the damages if you can," she explained. "Her gift of a residence, the furnishings of which would have paid for the slight alterations necessary to transform a modern home into the most beautiful of modern hospitals, in a wonderfully lovely location, and leave enough to start it with as fine a staff as money can provide—that gift is a deliberately planned effort at reparation; the limiting of patients to children under ten is her heart trying to tell yours that she would atone."

"O Lord!" cried James Minturn.

"Yes I know," said Mrs. Winslow. "Call on Him! You need Him! There is no question but that He put into her head the idea of setting a home for the healing of little children, in the most exclusive residence district of Multiopolis, where women of millions are forced to see it every time they look from a window or step from their door. Have you seen it yourself, James?"

"Naturally I wouldn't haunt the location."

"I would, and I did!" said Mrs. Winslow. "A few days ago I went over it from basement to garret. You go and see it. And I recall now that her lawyer was there, with sheets of paper in his hand, talking with workmen. I think he's working for Nellie and that she is probably directing the changes and personally evolving a big, white, shining reparation."

"It's a late date to talk about reparation," he said.

"Which simply drives me to the truism, 'better late than never!' and to the addition of the comment that Nellie is only thirty and that but ten years of your lives have been wasted; if you hurry and save the remainder, you should have fifty apiece coming to you, if you breathe deep, sleep cool, and dine sensibly," said Mrs. Winslow.

She walked out of the room and closed the door. James Minturn sat thinking a long time, then called his car and drove to Atwater alone. He found Leslie in the orchard, a book of bird scores in her hands, and several sheets of music beside her. Her greeting was so cordial, so frankly sweet and womanly, he could scarcely endure it, because his head was filled with thoughts of his wife.

"You are still at your bird study?" he asked.

"Yes. It's the most fascinating thing," she said.

"I know," he conceded. "I want the titles of the books you're using. I mentioned it to Mr. Tower, our tutor, and he was interested instantly, and far more capable of going at it intelligently than I am, because he has some musical training. Ever since we talked it over he and the boys have been at work in a crude way; you might be amused at their results, but to me they are wonderful. They began hiding in bird haunts and listening, working on imitations of cries and calls, and reproducing what they heard, until in a few weeks' time—why I don't even know their repertoire, but they can call quail, larks, owls, orioles, whip-poor-wills, so perfectly they get answers. James will never do anything worth while in music, he's too much like me; but Malcolm is saving his money and working to buy a violin; he's going to read a music score faster than he will a book. I'm hunting an instructor for him who will start his education on the subjects which interest him most. Do you know any one Leslie?"

"No one who could do more than study with him. It's a branch that is just being taken up, but I have talked of it quite a bit with Mr. Dovesky, the harmony director of the Conservatory. If you go to him and make him understand what you want along every line, I think he'd take Malcolm as a special student. I'd love to help him as far as I've gone, but I'm only a beginner myself, and I've no such ability as it is very possible he may have."

"He has it," said Mr. Minturn conclusively. "He has his mother's fine ear and artistic perception. If she undertook it, what a success she could make!"

"I never saw her so interested in anything as she was that day at the tamarack swamp," said Leslie, "and her heart was full of other matters too; but she recognized the songs I took her to hear. She said she never had been so attracted by a new idea in her whole life."

"Leslie, I came to you this morning about Nellie. I promised you to think matters over, and I've done nothing else since I last saw you, hateful as has been the occupation. You're still sure of what you said about her then?"

"Positively!" cried Leslie.

"Do you hear from her?" he asked.

"No," she answered.

"You spoke of a letter——" he suggested.

"A note she wrote me before leaving," explained Leslie. "You see I'd been with her all day and we had raced home so joyously; and when things came out as they did, she knew I wouldn't understand."

"Might I see it?" he asked.

"Surely," said Leslie. "I spoke of that the other day. I'll bring it."

When Leslie returned James Minturn read the missive several times; then he handed it back, saying: "What is there in that Leslie, to prove your points?"

"Three things," said Leslie with conviction: "The statement that for an hour after she reached her decision she experienced real joy and expected to render the same to you; the acknowledgment that she understood that you didn't know what you were doing to her, in your reception of her; and the final admission that life now held so little for her that she would gladly end it, if she dared, without making what reparation she could. What more do you want?"

"You're very sure you are drawing the right deductions?" he asked.

"I wish you would sit down and let me tell you of that day," said Leslie.

"I have come to you for help," said James Minturn. "I would be more than glad, if you'd be so kind."

At the end: "I don't think I've missed a word," said Leslie. "That day is and always will be sharply outlined."

"You've not heard from her since that note?" he asked. "You don't know where she is?"

"No," said Leslie. "I haven't an idea where you could find her; but because of her lawyer superintending the hospital repairs, because of the wonderful way things are being done, Daddy thinks it's sure that the work is in John Haynes' hands, and that she is directing it through him."

"If it were not for the war, I would know," said Mr. Minturn. "But understanding her as I do——"

"I think instead of understanding her so well, you scarcely know her at all," said Leslie gently. "You may have had a few months of her real nature to begin with, but when her rearing and environment ruled her life, the real woman was either perverted or had small chance. Do you ever stop to think what kind of a man you might have been, if all your life you had been forced and influenced as Nellie was?"

"Good Lord!" cried Mr. Minturn.

"Exactly!" agreed Leslie. "That's what I'm telling you! She had got to the realization of the fact that her life had been husks and ashes; so she went to beg you to help her to a better way, and you failed her. I'm not saying it was your fault; I'm not saying I blame you; I'm merely stating facts."

"Margaret blames me!" said Mr. Minturn. "She thinks I'm enough at fault that I never can find happiness until I locate Nellie and learn whether she is with her mother and friends, or if she really meant what she said about changing, enough to go ahead and be different from principle."

"Her change was radical and permanent."

"I've got to know," said Mr. Minturn, "but I've no faith in her ability to change, and no desire to meet her if she has."

"Humph!" said Leslie. "That proves that you need some changing yourself."

"I certainly do," said James Minturn. "If I could have an operation on my brain which would remove that particular cell in which is stored the memory of the past ten years——"

"You will when you see her," said Leslie, "and she'll be your surgeon."

"Impossible!" he cried.

"Go find her," said Leslie. "You must to regain peace for yourself."

James Minturn returned a troubled man, but with viewpoint shifting so imperceptibly he did not realize what was happening. On his way he decided to visit the hospital, repugnant as the thought was to him. From afar he was amazed at sight of the building. He knew instantly that it must have been the leading topic of conversation among his friends purposely avoided in his presence. Marble pillars and decorations had been freshly cleaned, the building was snowdrift white; it shone through the branches of big trees surrounding it like a fairy palace. At the top of the steps leading to the entrance stood a marble group of heroic proportions that was wonderful. It was a seated figure of Christ, but cut with the face of a man of his station, occupation, and race, garbed in simple robe, and in his arms, at his knees, leaning against him, a group of children: the lean, sick and ailing, such as were carried to him for healing. Cut in the wall above it in large gold-filled letters was the admonition: "Suffer little children to come unto me."

That group was the work of a student and a thinker who could carry an idea to a logical conclusion, and then carve it from marble. The thought it gave James Minturn, arrested before it, was not the stereotyped idea of Christ, not the conventional reproduction of childhood. It impressed on Mr. Minturn's brain that the man of Galilee had lived in the form of other men of his day, and that such a face, filled with infinite compassion, was much stronger and more forceful than that of the mild feminine countenance he had been accustomed to associating with the Saviour.

He entered the door to find his former home filled with workmen, and the opening day almost at hand. Everywhere was sanitary whiteness. The reception hall was ready for guests, his library occupied by the matron; the dining-hall a storeroom, the second and third floors in separate wards, save the big ballroom, now whiter than ever, its touches of gold freshly gleaming, beautiful flowers in tubs, canaries singing in a brass house filling one end of the room, tiny chairs, cots, every conceivable form of comfort and amusement for convalescing little children. The pipe organ remained in place, music boxes and wonderful mechanical toys had been added, rugs that had been in the house were spread on the floor. No normal man could study and interpret the intention of that place unmoved. All over the building was the same beautiful whiteness, the same comfort, and thoughtful preparation for the purpose it was designed to fill. The operating rooms were perfect, the whole the result of loving thought, careful execution, and uncounted expense.

He came in time to the locked door of his wife's suite, and before he left the building he met her lawyer. He offered his hand and said heartily: "My sister told me of the wonderful work going on here; she advised me to come and see for myself. I am very glad I did. There's something bigger than the usual idea in this that keeps obtruding itself."

"I think that too," agreed John Haynes. "I've almost quit my practice to work out these plans."

"They are my wife's, by any chance?"

"All hers," said Mr. Haynes. "I only carry out her instructions as they come to me."

"Will you give me her address?" asked Mr. Minturn. "I should like to tell her how great I think this."

"I carry a packet for you that came with a bundle of plans this morning," said Mr. Haynes. "Perhaps her address is in it. If it isn't, I can't give it to you, because I haven't it myself. She's not in the city, all her instructions she sends some one, possibly at her mother's home, and they are delivered to me. I give my communications to the boy who brings her orders."

"Then I'll write my note and you give it to him."

"I'm sorry Minturn," said Mr. Haynes, "but I have my orders in the event you should wish to reach her through me."

"She doesn't wish to hear from me?"

"I'm sorry no end, Mr. Minturn, but——"

"Possibly this contains what I want to know," said Mr. Minturn. "Thank you, and I congratulate you on your work here. It is humane in the finest degree."

James Minturn went to his office and opened the packet. It was a complete accounting of every dollar his wife was worth, this divided exactly into thirds, one of which she kept, one she transferred to him, and the other she placed in his care for her sons to be equally divided between them at his discretion. He returned and found the lawyer had gone to his office. He followed and showed him the documents.

"What she places to my credit for our sons, that I will handle with the utmost care," he said. "What she puts at my personal disposal I do not accept. We are living comfortably, and as expensively as I desire to. There is no reason why I should take such a sum at her hands, even though she has more than I would have estimated. You will kindly return this deed of transfer to her, with my thanks, and a note I will enclose."

"Sorry Minturn, but as I told you before, I haven't her address. I'm working on a salary I should dislike to forfeit, and my orders are distinct concerning you."

"You could give me no idea where to find her?"

"Not the slightest!" said the lawyer.

"Will you take charge of these papers?" he questioned.

"I dare not," replied Mr. Haynes.

"Will you ask her if you may?" persisted Mr. Minturn.

"Sorry Minturn, but perhaps if you should see my instructions in the case, you'd understand better. I don't wish you to think me disobliging."

Mr. Minturn took the sheet and read the indicated paragraph written in his wife's clear hand:

Leslie Winton was very good to me my last day in Multiopolis. She was with me when I reached a decision concerning my future relations with Mr. Minturn, as I would have arranged them; and I am quite sure when she knows of our separation she will feel that it would not have occurred had James known of this decision of mine. It would have made no difference; but I am convinced Leslie will think it would, and that she will go to James about it. I doubt if it will change his attitude; but if by any possibility it should, and if in any event whatever he comes to you seeking my address, or me, I depend on you to in no way help him, if it should happen that you could. For this reason I am keeping it out of your power, unless I make some misstep that points to where I am. I don't wish to make any mystery of my location, or to disregard any intention that it is barely possible Leslie could bring Mr. Minturn to, concerning me. I merely wish to be left alone for a time; to work out my own expiation, if there be any; and to test my soul until I know for myself whether it is possible for a social leopard to change her spots. I have got to know absolutely that I am beyond question a woman fit to be a wife and mother, before I again trust myself in any relation of life toward any one.

Mr. Minturn returned the sheet, his face deeply thoughtful. "I see her point," he said. "I will deposit the papers in a safety vault until she comes, and in accordance with this, I shall make no effort to find her. My wife feels that she must work out her own salvation, and I am beginning to realize that a thorough self-investigation and revelation will not hurt me. Thank you. Good morning."

CHAPTER XV

A PARTICULAR NIX

Peaches awakened early the following morning, but Mickey was watching beside her to help her remember, to prompt, to soothe, to comfort and to teach. He followed Mrs. Harding to the kitchen and from the prepared food selected what he thought came closest filling the diet prescribed by the Sunshine Nurse, and then he carried the tray to a fresh, cool Peaches beside a window opening on a grassy, tree-covered lawn. Her room was bewildering on account of its many, and to the child, magnificent furnishings. She found herself stretching, twisting and filled with a wild desire to walk, to see the house, the little girl and the real baby, the lawn beyond her window, the flower-field, the red berries where they grew, and the birds and animals from which came the most amazing sounds.

After doing everything for Peaches he could, Mickey went to his breakfast. Mary Harding and Bobbie were so anxious to see the visitor they could scarcely eat. Knowing it was no use to try forcing them, their mother excused them and they ventured as far as the door. There they stopped, gazing at the little stranger, while she stared back at them; but she was not frightened, because she knew who they were and that they would be good to her, else Mickey would not let them come. So when Mary, holding little brother's hand, came peeping around the door-casing, Peaches withdrew her attention from exploration of the strip of lawn in her range and concentrated on them. If they had come bounding at her, she would have been frightened, but they did not. They stood still, half afraid, watching the tiny white creature, till suddenly she smiled at them and held out her hand.

"I like you," she said. "Did you have red berries for breakfus?"

Mary nodded and smiled back.

"I think you're a pretty little girl," said Peaches.

"I ain't half as pretty as you," said Mary.

"No a-course you ain't," she admitted. "Your family don't put your ribbon on you 'til night, do they? Mickey put mine on this morning 'cause I have to look nice and be jus' as good, else I have to be took back to the hot room. Do you have to be nice too?"

"Yes, I have to be a good girl," said Mary.

"What does your family do to you if you don't mind?"

"I ain't going to tell, but it makes me," said Mary. "What does yours do to you?"

"I ain't going to tell either," said Peaches, "but I get jus' as good! What's your name?"

"Mary."

"What's his?"

"Bobbie. Mostly we call him little brother. Ain't he sweet?" asked Mary.

"Jus' a Precious Child! Let him mark on my slate."

Mickey hurried to the room. As he neared the door he stepped softly and peeped inside. It was a problem with him as to how far Mary and Bobbie could be trusted. Having been with Peaches every day he could not accurately mark improvements, but he could see that her bones did not protrude so far, that her skin was not the yellow, glisteny horror it had been, that the calloused spots were going under the steady rubbing of nightly oil massage, so lately he had added the same treatment to her feet; if they were not less bony, if the skin were not soft and taking on a pinkish colour, Mickey felt that his eyes were unreliable.

Surely she was better! Of course she was better! She had to be! She ate more, she sat up longer, she moved her feet where first they had hung helpless. She was better, much better, and for that especial reason, now was the time to watch closer than before. Now he must make sure that a big strong child did not drag her from the bed, and forever undo all he had gained. Since he had written Dr. Carrel, Mickey had rubbed in desperation, not only nights but mornings also, lest he had asked help before he was ready for it; for the Sunshine Lady had said explicitly that the sick back could not be operated until the child was stronger. He was working according to instructions.

Mickey watched. Any one could have seen the delicate flush on Peaches' cheek that morning, the hint of red on her lips, the clearing whites of her lovely eyes. She was helping Bobbie as Mickey had taught her. And Bobbie approved mightily. He lifted his face, put up his arms and issued his command: "Take Bobbie!"

"No! No, Bobbie," cautioned Mary. "Mother said no! You must stay on the floor! Sister will take you. You mustn't touch Peaches 'til God makes her well. You asked Him last night, don't you know? Mother will spank something awful if you touch her. You must be careful 'til her back is well, mother said so, and father too; father said it crosser than mother, don't you remember?"

"Mustn't touch!" repeated Bobbie, drawing back.

Mickey was satisfied with Mrs. Harding's instructions, but he took the opportunity to emphasize a few points himself. He even slipped one white, bony foot from under the sheet and showed Mary how sick it was, and how carefully it must be rubbed before it would walk.

"I can rub it," announced Mary.

"Well don't you try that," cautioned Mickey.

"Why go on and let her!" interposed Peaches. "Go on and let her! After today you said you'd be gone all day, an' if rubbing in the morning and evening is good, maybe more would make me walk sooner. Mickey I ain't ever said it, 'cause you do so much an' try so hard, but Mickey, *I'm just about dead to walk!* Mickey, I'm so tired being lifted. Mickey, I want to get up an' *go* when I want to, like other folks!"

"Well that's the first time you ever said that."

"Well 'tain't the first time I ever could a-said it, if I'd a-wanted to," explained Peaches.

"I see! You game little kid, you," said Mickey. "All right Mary, you ask your mother and if she says so, I'll show you how, and maybe you can rub Lily's feet, if you go slow and easy and don't jar her back a speck."

"Ma said I could a-ready," explained Mary. "Ma said for me to! She said all of us would, all the time we had while you were away, so she'd get better faster. Ma said she'd give a hundred dollars if Peaches would get so she could walk here."

Mickey sat back on his heels suddenly.

"Who'd she say that to?" he demanded.

"Pa. And he said he'd give five hundred."

"Aw-a-ah!" marvelled Mickey.

"He did too!" insisted Mary. "This morning 'fore you came out. And Junior would too. He'd give all in his bank! And he'd rub too! He said he would."

"Well, if you ain't the nicest folks!" cried Mickey. "Gee, I'm glad I found you!"

"Jus' as glad!" chimed in Peaches.

"Mary bring Robert here!" called Mrs. Harding from the hall. Mary obeyed. Mickey moved up and looked intently at Peaches.

"Well Lily," he asked, "what do you *think* of this?"

"I wouldn't trade this for Heaven!" she answered.

"The country is all the Heaven a-body needs, in June."

"Mickey, bring in the cow now!" ordered Peaches.

"Bring in the cow?" queried Mickey.

"Sure, the little red cow in the book that makes the milk. I want you to milk her right here on my bed!"

"Well, if I ever!" gasped Mickey. "Sure, I'll bring her in a minute; but a cow is big, Lily! Awful, great big. I couldn't bring her in here; but maybe I can drive her where you can see, or I don't know what would be the harm in taking you where the cows are. But first, one thing! Now you look right at me, Miss Chicken. There's something I got to *know* if you got in your head *straight*. Who found you, and kept them from 'getting' you?"

"Mickey-lovest," replied Peaches promptly.

"Then who d'you belong to?" he demanded.

"Mickey!" she answered instantly.

"Who you got to do as I say?" he continued.

"Mickey," she repeated.

"Whose *family* are you?" he pursued.

"Mickey's!" she cried. "Mickey, what's the matter? Mickey, I love you best. I'm all yours. Mickey, I'll go back an' never say a word 'bout the hotness, or the longness, or anything, if you don't *want* me here."

"Well I do want you here," said Mickey in slow insistent tone. "I want you right here! But you got to *understand* a few things. You're mine. I'm going to keep you; you got to understand that."

"Yes Mickey," conceded Peaches.

"And if it will help you to be rubbed more than I can rub you while I got to earn money to pay for our supper when we go home, and fix your back, and save for the seminary, I'll let the nice pleasant lady rub you; and I'll let a good girl like Mary rub you, and if his hands ain't so big they hurt, maybe I'll let Peter rub you; he takes care of Bobbie, maybe he could you, and he's got a family of his own, so he knows how it feels; but it's *nix* on anybody else, Miss Chicken, see?"

"They ain't nobody else!" said Peaches.

"There is too!" contradicted Mickey. "Mary said Junior would rub your feet! Well he *won't!* It's nix on Junior! *He's only a boy! He ain't got a family. He hasn't had experience. He doesn't know anything about families! See?*"

"He carries Bobbie, an' I bet he's heavier 'an me."

For the first time Mickey lost his temper.

"Now you looky here, Miss Chicken," he stormed. "I ain't saying what he *can* do, I'm saying what he *can't!* See? You are mine, and I'm going to keep you! He can lift me for all I care, but he can't carry you, nor rub your feet, nor nothing; because he didn't find you, and you ain't his; and I won't have it, not at all! Course he's a good boy, and he's a nice boy, and you can play with him, and talk to him, I'll let you just be awful nice to him, because it's polite that you should be, but when it comes to carrying and rubbing, it's nix on Junior, because he's got no family and doesn't understand. See?"

"Umhuh," taunted Peaches.

"Well, are you going to promise?" demanded Mickey.

"Maybe," she teased.

"Back you go and never see a cow at all if you don't promise," threatened Mickey.

"Mickey, what's the matter with you?" cried Peaches suddenly. "What you getting a tantrum yourself for? You ain't never had none before."

"That ain't no sign I ain't just busting full of them," said Mickey. "Bad ones, and I feel an awful one as can be coming right now, and coming quick. Are you going to promise me nobody who hasn't a *family*, carries you, and rubs you?"

Peaches looked at him in steady wonderment.

"I guess you're pretty tired, an' you need to sleep a while, or somepin," she said. "If you wasn't about sick yourself, you'd know 'at anybody 'cept you 'ull get their dam-gone heads ripped off if they touches me, nelse *you* say so. *Course*, you found me! *Course*, they'd a-got me, if you hadn't took me. *Course*, I'm yours! *Course*, it's nix on Junior, an' it's *nix* on Peter if you say so. Mickey, I jus' love you an' love you. I'll go back now if you say so, I tell you. Mickey *what's* the matter?"

She stretched up her arms, and Mickey sank into them. He buried his face beside hers and for the first time she patted him, and whispered to him as she did to her doll. She rubbed her cheek against his, crooned over him, and held him tight while he gulped down big sobs.

"Mickey, tell me," she begged, like a little mother. "Tell me honey? Are you got a pain anywhere?"

"No!" he said. "Maybe I *was* kind of strung up, getting you here and being so awful scared about hurting you; but it's all right now. You are here, and things are going to be fine, only, will you, cross your heart, *always and forever remember this: it's nix on Junior, or any boy, who ain't got a family, and doesn't understand?*"

"Yes Mickey, cross my heart, an' f'rever, an' ever; an' Mickey, you must get the soap. I slipped, an' said the worse yet. I didn't mean to, but Mickey, I guess you can't *trust* me. I guess you got to soap me, or beat me, or somepin awful. Go on an' do it, Mickey."

"Why crazy!" said Mickey. "You're mixed up. You didn't say anything! What you said was all rightest ever; rightest of anything I ever heard. *It was just exactly what I wanted you to say*. I just *loved* what you said."

"Well if I ever!" cried Peaches. "Mickey, you was so mixed up you didn't hear me. I got 'nother chance. Goody, goody! Now show me the cow!"

"All right!" said Mickey. "I'll talk with Mrs. Harding and see how she thinks I best go at it. Lily, you won't ever, ever forget that particular nix, will you?"

"Not ever," she promised, and lifted her lips to seal the pact with a kiss that meant more to Mickey than all that had preceded it.

"Just how do you feel, anyway, Flowersy-girl?"

"Fine!" said Peaches. "I can tell by how it is right now, that it isn't going to get all smothery an' sweatin's here; whoohoo it's so good, Mickey!"

Mickey bent over her holding both hands and whispered: "Then just you keep right before your eyes where you came from, Miss, and what you must go *back* to, if you don't behave. You will be a good girl, won't you?"

"Honest, Mickey-lovest, jus' as good."

"Well how goes it with the Little White Butterfly?" asked Peter at the door.

Mickey looked at Peaches to slightly nod encouragement, then he slipped from the room. She gave Peter a smile of wonderment and answered readily: "Grand as queen-lady. You're jus' so nice and fine."

Now Peter hadn't known it, but all his life he had been big; handled rough tools, tasks, implements and animals; while his body grew sinewy and hard, to cope with his task, his heart demanded more refined things; so if Peaches had known the most musical languages on earth, she could not have used words to Peter that would have served her better. He radiated content.

"Good!" he cried. "That's grand and good! I didn't take a fair look at you last night. It was so sissing hot in that place and you went to sleep before I got my chores done; but now we must get acquainted. Tell me honey, does any particular place in your little body hurt you? If there does, put your hand and show Peter where."

Peaches stared at Peter, then she faintly smiled at him and laid a fluttering hand on her left side.

"Oh shockings!" mourned Peter. "That's too bad! That's vital! Your heart's right under there, honey. Is there a pain in your *heart?*"

Peaches nodded solemnly.

"Not *all* the time!" she explained. "Only like now, when you are so *good* to me. Jus' so fine and good."

Then and there Peter surrendered. He bent and kissed the hand he held, and said with tears saturating his words, just as tears do permeate speech sometimes: "Pshaw now, Little White Butterfly! I never was more pleased to hear anything in my life. Ma and I have talked for years of having some city children here for summer, but we've been slow trying it because we hear such bad reports from many of them, and it's natural for people to shield their own; but I guess instead of shielding, we may have been denying. I can't see anything about you children to hurt ours; and I notice a number of ways where it is beneficial to have you here. It's surely good for all of us. You're the nicest little folks!"

Peaches sat up suddenly and smiled on Peter.

"Mickey is nice an' fine," she told him. "Not even you, or anybody, is nice as Mickey. An' I'm *going* to be. I'd *like* to be! But you see, I laid alone all day in a dark corner so long, an' I got so wild like, 'at when granny did come, I done an' said jus' like she did, but Mickey doesn't like it. He's scairt 'most stiff fear I'll forget an' say bad swearin's, an' you'll send me back to the hotness, so's I won't get better. Would you send me back if I forget *just once*, Peter?"

"Why pshaw now!" said Peter. "Pshaw Little Soul, don't you worry about that. You try *hard* to remember, and be like Mickey wants you to, and if you make a slip, I'll speak to Ma about it, and we'll just turn a deaf ear, and away out here, you'll soon forget it."

Just then, Mickey, trailing a rope, passed before the window; there was a crunching sound; a lumbering cow stopped, lifted a mouth half filled with grass, and bawled her loudest protest at being separated from her calf. Peaches had only half a glance, but her shriek was utter terror. She launched herself on Peter and climbed him, until her knees were on his chest, and her fingers clutching his hair.

"God Jesus!" she screamed. "It 'ull eat me!"

Peter caught her in his arms, turning his back. Mickey heard, and saw, and realized that the cow was too big and had appeared too precipitately, and bellowed too loudly. He should have begun on the smallest calf on the place. He rushed the cow back to Junior, and himself to Peaches, who, sobbing wildly, still clung to Peter. As Mickey entered, frightened and despairing, he saw that Peter was much concerned, but laughing until his shoulders shook, and in relief that he was, and that none of the children were present, Mickey grinned, acquired a slow red, and tried to quiet Peaches.

"Shut that window!" she screamed. "Shut it quick!"

"Why honey, that's the cow you wanted to see," soothed Mickey. "That's the nice cow that gave the very milk you had for breakfast. Junior was going to milk her where you could see. We thought you'd *like* it!"

"Don't let it get me!" cried Peaches.

"Why it ain't going to get anything but grass!" said Mickey. "Didn't you see me leading it? I can make that big old thing go where I please. Come on, be a game kid now. You ain't a baby coward girl! It's only a cow! You are going to put it on your book!"

"I ain't!" sobbed Peaches. "I ain't ever going to drink milk again! I jus' bet the *milk* will *get* me!"

"Be game now!" urged Mickey. "Mary milks the cow. Baby Bobbie runs right up to her. Everything out here is big, Lily. I ran from the horses. I jumped on a fence, and Junior laughed at me."

"Mickey, what did you say?" wavered Peaches.

"I didn't say anything," said Mickey. "I just jumped."

"Mickey, I jumped, an' I said it, both. I said it right on Peter," she bravely confessed. "Mickey, I said the worst yet! I didn't know I *did*, 'til I heard it! But Mickey, I got another chance!"

Peaches wiped her eyes, tremulously glanced at the window, and still clinging to Mickey explained: "I was just telling Peter about the swearin's, an' Mickey, don't feel so bad. He won't send me back for just once. Mickey, Peter has got 'a deaf ear.' He *said* he had! He ain't goin' to hear it when I slip a swearin's, an' Mickey, I am tryin'! Honest I'm tryin' jus' as hard, Mickey!"

Mickey turned a despairing face toward Peter.

"Just like she says," assured Peter. "We've all got our faults. You'll have to forgive her Mickey."

"Me? Of course!" conceded Mickey. "But what about you? You don't want your nice little children to hear bad words."

"Well," said Peter, "don't make too much of it! It's likely there are no words she can say that my children don't know. Just ignore and forget it! She won't do it often. I'm sure she won't!"

"Are you sure you won't, Miss?" demanded Mickey.

"Sure!" said Peaches, and in an effort to change the subject: "Mickey, is that cow out there yet?"

"No. Junior took her back to the barnyard."

"Mickey, I ain't going to put a cow on my book; but I want to see her again, away off. Mickey, take me where I can see. You said last night you would."

"But the horses are bigger than the cows. You'll get scared again, and with scaring and crying you'll be so bad off your back won't get any better all day, and to-morrow I got to leave you and go to work."

"Then I'll see all the things to-day, an' to-morrow I'll think about them 'til you come back. Please Mickey! If things don't get Bobbie an' Mary, they won't get me!"

"That's a game little girl!" said Mickey. "All right, I'll take you. But you ought to have——"

"Have what Mickey?" she inquired, instantly alert.

"Well never you mind what," said Mickey. "You be a good girl and lie still, so your back will be better, and watch the bundle I'll bring home to-morrow night."

Peaches shivered in delight. Mickey proceeded slowly, followed by the entire family.

"Mickey, it's so big!" she marvelled. "Everything is so far away, an' so big!"

"Now isn't it!" agreed Mickey. "You see it's like I told you. Now let me show you the garden."

He selected that as a safe proposition. Peaches grasped the idea readily enough. Mrs. Harding gathered vegetables for her to see. When they reached the strawberry bed Mickey knelt and with her own fingers Peaches pulled a berry and ate it, then laughed, exclaimed, and cried in delight. She picked a flower, and from the safe vantage of the garden viewed the cows and horses afar; and the fields and sheep were explained to her. Mickey carried her across the road, Mary brought a comfort, and for a whole hour the child lay under a big tree with pink and white clover in a foot-deep border around her. When they lifted her she said: "Mickey, to-night we put in the biggest blesses of all."

"What?" inquired Mickey.

"Bless the nice people for such grand things, an' the berries; but never mind about the cow."

Then Mickey took her back to the house. She awoke from a restful nap to find a basket of chickens waiting for her, barely down dry from their shells. She caught up a little yellow ball, and with both hands clutched it, exclaiming and crying in joy until Mickey saw the chicken was drooping. He pried open her excited little fingers; but the chicken remained limp. Soon it became evident that she had squeezed the life from it.

"Oh Peaches, you held it too tight!" wailed Mickey. "I'm afraid you've made it sick!"

"I didn't mean to Mickey!" she protested.

Mrs. Harding reached over and picked the chicken from Mickey's fingers.

"That chicken wasn't very well to begin with," she said. "'You give it to me, and I'll doctor it up, while you take another one. Which do you want?"

"Yellow," sniffed Peaches, "but please hurry, and Mickey, you hold this one. Maybe I held too hard!"

"Yes you did," laughed Peter. "But we wanted to see what you'd do. One little chicken is a small price for the show you give. It's all right, Butterfly."

"Peter, you make everything all right, don't you?"

"Well honey, I would if I could," said Peter. "But that's something of a contract. Now you rest till after dinner, and if Ma and Mickey agree on it, we'll go see the meadow brook and hear the birds sing."

"The water!" shouted Peaches. "Mickey, you promised——"

"Yes I remember," said Mickey. "I'll see how cold it is and if I think it won't chill you—yes."

"Oh gee!" chortled Peaches. "'Nother blesses!"

"What does she mean?" asked Peter.

Mickey explained.

"Can't see how it would hurt her a mite," said Peter. "Water is warm, nice day. It will be good for her."

"All right," said Mickey, "then we'll try it. But how about the plowing Peter, shouldn't I be helping you?"

"Not to-day," said Peter. "I never allow my work to drive me, so I get pleasure from life my neighbours miss, and I'll compare bank accounts with any of them. To-morrow I'll work. To-day I'm entertaining company, or rather they are entertaining me. I think this is about the best day of my life. Isn't it great, Ma?"

"It just is! I can't half work, myself!" answered Nancy Harding. "I just wonder if we could take a little run in the car after supper?"

"What do you think about it, Mickey?" asked Peter.

"Why, I can't see that coming out hurt her any."

"Then we'll go," said Peter.

"Do I have to be all covered?" questioned Peaches.

"Not nearly so much," explained Mickey. "I'll let you see a lot more. There's a bobolink bird down the street Peter wants to show you."

"'Street!'" jeered Junior. "That's a road!"

"Sure!" said Mickey. "I got a lot to learn. You tell me, will you Junior?"

"Course!" said Junior, suddenly changing from scorn to patronage. "Now let's take her to the creek!"

"Well that's quite a walk," said Peter. "We're not going there unless I carry the Little White Butterfly. You want me to take you, don't you?"

Peaches answered instantly.

"Mickey always carries me. He can! And of course I like *him* the best; but after him, I like you best Peter, so you may, if he'll let you."

"So that's the way the wind blows!" laughed Peter. "Then Mickey, it's up to you."

"Why sure!" said Mickey. "Since you are so big, and got a family of your own, so you understand——"

"What Mickey?" asked Peter.

"Oh how to be easy with little sick people," answered Mickey, "and that a man's family is *his* family, and he don't want anybody else butting in!"

"I see!" said Peter, struggling with his facial muscles. "Of course! But this sheet is going to be rather bunglesome. Ma, could you do anything about it?"

"Yes," said Mrs. Harding. "Mary, you run up to the flannel chest, and get Bobbie's little blue blanket."

Peter lifted the child to his broad breast, she slipped her arms around his neck, and laid her head on his shoulder.

Bloom time was past, but bird time was not, while the leaves were still freshly green and tender. Some of them reached to touch Peaches' gold hair in passing. She was held high to see into nests and the bluebirds' hollow in the apple tree. Peaches gripped Peter and cried: "Don't let it get my feet!" when the old turkey gobbler came rasping, strutting, and spitting at the party. Mickey pointed to Mary, who was unafraid, and Peaches' clutch grew less frantic but she defended: "Well, I don't care! I bet if she hadn't ever seen one before, an' then a big thing like that would come right at her, tellin' plain it was goin' to eat her alive, it would scare the livers out of her."

"Yes I guess it would," conceded Peter. "But you got the eating end of it wrong. It isn't going to eat us, we are going to eat it. About Thanksgiving, we'll lay its head on the block and Ma will stuff it——"

"I've quit stuffing turkeys, Peter," said Mrs. Harding. "I find it spoils the flavour of the meat."

"Well then it will stuff us," said Peter, "all we can hold, and mince pie, plum pudding, and every good thing we can think of. What piece of turkey do you like best, Butterfly?"

Mickey instantly scanned Peter, then Mrs. Peter, and tensely waited.

"Oh stop! Stop! Is *that a turkey bird?*" cried Peaches.

"Surely it is," said Mrs. Harding. "Why childie, haven't you ever seen a turkey, either?"

"No I didn't ever," said Peaches. "Can turkey birds sing?"

Just then the gobbler stuck forward his head and sang: "Gehobble, hobble, hobble!" Peaches gripped Peter's hair and started to ascend him again. Mrs. Harding waved her apron; the turkey suddenly reduced its size three-fourths, skipped aside, and a neat, trim bird, high stepping and dainty, walked through the orchard. Peaches collapsed in Peter's arms in open-mouthed wonder. "Gosh! How did it cave in like that?" she cried.

Peter's shoulders were shaking, but he answered gravely: "Well that's a way it has of puffing itself up and making a great big pretense that it is going to flop us, and then if just little Bobbie or Ma waves an apron or a stick it gets out of the way in a hurry."

"I've seen Multiopolis millyingaires cave in like that sometimes when I waved a morning paper with an inch-high headline about them," commented Mickey.

Peter Harding glanced at his wife, then they laughed together. Peter stepped over a snake fence, went carefully down a hill, crossed the meadow to the shade of a tree, sat on the bank of the brook and watched Peaches as she studied first the clear babbling water, then the grass trailing in the stream, the bushes, trees, and then the water again.

"Mickey, come here!" she commanded. "Put your head right down beside mine. Now look just the way I do, an' tell me what you see."

"I see running water, grassy banks, trees, the birds, the sky and the clouds—the water shows what's above it like a mirror, Lily."

Peaches pointed. Mickey watched intently.

"Sure!" he cried. "Little fish with red speckles on them. Shall I catch you one to see?"

"'Tain't my eyes then?" questioned Peaches.

"Your eyes, Miss?" asked Mickey bewildered.

"'Tain't my eyes seein' things that yours doesn't?"

Mickey took her hand and drew closer.

"Well, it isn't any wonder you almost doubt it, honey," he said. "I would too, if I hadn't ever seen it before. But I been on the trolley, and on a few newsboys' excursions, and in the car with Mr. Bruce, and I've got to walk along the str—roads some, so I know it's real. Let me show you——!"

Mickey slipped down the bank, scooped his hands full of water, and lifted them, letting it drip through his fingers. Then he made a sweep and brought up one of the fish, brightly marked as a flower, and gasping in the air.

"Look quick!" he cried. "See it good! It's used to water and the air chokes it, just like the water would you if a big fish would take you and hold your head under; I got to put it back quick."

"Mickey, lay it in my hand, just a little bit!"

Mickey obeyed while Peaches examined it hurriedly.

"Put it back!" she cried. "I guess that's as long as I'd want to be choked, while a fish looked at me."

Mickey exchanged the fish for a handful of wet, vividly coloured pebbles, then brought a bunch of cowslips yellow as gold, and a long willow whip with leaves on, and when she had examined these, she looked inquiringly at Mrs. Harding.

"Nicest lady, may I put my feet in your water?"

"How about the temperature of it, Mickey?" inquired Mrs. Harding.

"It's all right," said Mickey. "I've washed her in colder water lots of times. The Sunshine Lady said I should, to toughen her up."

"Then go ahead," said Mrs. Harding.

"Peter, may I?" asked Peaches.

"Surely!" agreed Peter. "Whole bunch may get in if Ma says so!"

"Well, I don't say so!" exclaimed Mrs. Harding. "The children have their good clothes on and they always get to romping and dirty themselves and then it's bigger washings and mine are enough to break my back right now."

Peter looked at his wife intently. "Why Nancy, I hadn't heard you complain before!" he said. "If they're too big, we must wear less and make them smaller, and I'll take an hour at the machine, and Junior can turn the wringer. All of you children listen to me. Your Ma is feeling the size of the wash. That means we must be more careful of our clothes and help her better. If Ma gets sick, or tired of us, we'll be in a fix, I tell you!"

"I didn't say I was sick, or tired of you, I'm just tired of washing!" said Mrs. Harding.

"I see!" said Peter. "But it is a thing that has got to be done, like plowing and sowing."

"Yes I know," said Mrs. Harding, "but plowing and sowing only come once a year. Washing comes once and twice a week."

"Let me," said Mickey. "I always helped mother, and I do my own and Lily's at home. Of course I will here, and I can help you a lot with yours!"

"Yes a boy!" scoffed Mrs. Harding.

"Well I'll show you that a boy can work as well as a girl, if he's been taught right," said Mickey.

"I wasn't bringing up any question of work," said Mrs. Harding. "I just didn't want the children to dirty a round of clothing apiece. They may wade when their things are ready for the wash anyway. Go on Peaches!"

Peter moved down the bank and prepared to lower her to the water, but she reached her arms for Mickey.

"He promised me," she said. "Back there on his nice bed in the hot room he promised me this."

"So I did," said Mickey, radiating satisfaction he could not conceal. "So I did! Now, I'll let you put your feet in, like I said."

"Will the fish bite me?" she questioned timidly.

"Those little things! What if they did?"

Thus encouraged she put her toes in the water, gripping Mickey and waiting breathlessly to see what happened. Nothing happened, while the warm, running water felt pleasant, so she dipped lower, and then did her best to make it splash. It wasn't much of a splash, but it was a satisfying performance to the parties most interested, and from their eagerness the watchers understood what it meant to them. Junior sidled up to his mother.

"Ain't that tough?" he whispered.

She bit her lip and silently nodded.

"Look at her feet, will you?" he breathed.

She looked at him instead, then suddenly her eyes filled with a mist like that clouding his.

"*Think they'll ever walk?*" he questioned.

"I don't know," she said softly, "but it looks as if God has given us the chance to make them if it's possible."

"Well say what's my share?" he said.

"Just anything you see that you think will help."

"If I be more careful not to dirty so many clothes, will it help?" he asked.

"It would leave me that much more time and strength to give to her," she said.

"Will all I can save you in any way be helping her that much?" he persisted.

"Surely!" she said. "Soon as he's out of sight, I'm going to begin on her. But don't let them hear!"

Junior nodded. He sat down on the bank watching as if fascinated the feet trying to splash in the water. Mickey could feel the effort of the small body.

"You take her now," he said to Peter. Then he threw off his shoes and stockings, turned up his knee breeches and stepped into the water, where he helped the feet to kick and splash. He rubbed them and at last picked up handfuls of fine sand and lightly massaged with it until he brought a pink glow.

"That's the stuff," indorsed Peter. "Look at that! You're pulling the blood down."

"Where's the blood?" asked Peaches.

Peter explained the circulatory system and why all the years of lying, with no movement, had made her so helpless. He told her why scarce and wrong food had not made good blood to push down and strengthen her feet so they would walk. He told her the friction of the sand-rubbing would pull it down, while the sun, water, and earth would help. Peaches with wide eyes listened, her breath coming faster and faster, until suddenly she leaned forward and cried: "Rub, Mickey! Rub 'til the blood flies! Rub 'em hot as hell!"

"Well, Miss Chicken!" he cried in despair.

Peaches buried her shamed face on Peter's breast. He screened her with a big hand.

"Now never you mind! Never you mind!" he repeated. "Everybody turn a deaf ear! That was a slip! Nobody heard it! You mean Little Butterfly White, 'rub hard.' Say rub hard and that will fix it!"

"Mickey," she said in a faint voice so subdued and contrite as to be ridiculous, "Mickey-lovest, won't you please to rub hard! Rub jus' as hard!"

Mickey suddenly bent to kiss the bony little foot he was chafing.

"Yes darling, I'll rub 'til it a-most bleeds," he said.

When the feet were glowing with alternate sand-rubbing and splashing in cold water, Peter looked at his wife.

"I think that's the ticket!" he said. "Nancy, don't you? That pulls down the blood with rubbing, and drives it back with cold water, and pulls it down, to be pushed back again—ain't that helping the heart get in its work? Now if we strengthen her with right food, and make lots of pure blood to run in these little blue canals on her temples, and hands and feet, ain't we gaining ground? Ain't we making headway?"

"We've just got to be," said Mrs. Harding. "There's no other way to figure it. But this is enough for a start."

Peaches leaned toward her and asked: "May we do this again to-morrow, nicest lady?"

"Well I can't say as we can come clear here every day; I'm a busy woman, and my spare time is scarce; and even light as you are, you'd be a load for me; I can't say as we can do this when Peter is busy plowing and harvesting and Junior is away on the cream wagon, and Mickey is in town at his work; we can't do just this; but there is something we can do that will help the feet quite as much. We can bring a bucket of sand up to the house, and set a tub of water in the sun, and you can lie on a comfort under an apple tree with Mary and Bobbie to watch you, and every few hours we can take a little time off for rubbing and splashing."

"My job!" shouted Junior. "I get a bucket and carry up the sand!"

"I bring the tub and pump the water!" cried Mary.

"Me shoo turkey!" announced Bobbie.

"I lift the tub to the edge of the shade and carry out the Butterfly!" said Peter.

"And where do I come in?" demanded Mickey.

"Why Mickey, you 'let' them!" cried Peaches. "You '*let*' them! An' you earn the money to pay for the new back, when I get strong enough to have it changed, an' the Carrel man comes! Don't you 'member?"

"Sure!" boasted Mickey, taking on height. "I got the biggest job of all! I got the job that really does the trick, and to-morrow I get right after it. Now I must take you back to the house to rest a while."

"Aw come on to the barn with me!" begged Junior. "Let father carry her! Ain't you going to be any company for me at all?"

"Sure!" said Mickey. "Wait a minute! I'd like to go to the barn with you."

He dried Peaches' feet with his handkerchief, stuffed his stockings in his pocket, and picked up his shoes.

"Lily, can you let Peter take you back to rest 'til supper time, so I can see what Junior wants to show me?"

"Yes I can," said Peaches. "Yes I can, 'cause I'm a game kid; but I don't wish to!"

"Now you look here, Miss Chicken, that hasn't got anything to do with it," explained Mickey. "Every single time you can't have your way, 'cause it ain't good for you. If all these nice folks are so kind to you, you must think part of the time about what they want, and just now Junior wants *me*, so you march right along nice and careful with Peter, and pretty soon I'll come."

Peaches pouted a second, then her face cleared by degrees, until it lifted to Peter with a smile.

"Peter, will you please to carry me while Mickey does what Junior wants?" she asked with melting sweetness.

"Sure!" said Peter. "I'm the one to take you anyway, big and strong as an ox; but that's a pretty way to ask, and acting like a nice lady!"

Peaches radiated pride while Peter returned her to the couch, brought her a glass of milk and a cracker, pulled the shade, and going out softly closed the door. In five minutes she was asleep.

An hour before supper time Mickey appeared and without a word began watching Mrs. Harding. Suddenly her work lightened. When she was ready for water, the bucket was filled, saving her a trip to the pump. When she lifted the dishpan and started toward the back door, Mickey met her with the potato basket. When she glanced questioningly at the stove, he put in more wood. He went to the dining-room and set the table exactly as it had been for dinner. He made the trip to the cellar with her and brought up bread and milk, while she carried butter and preserves. As she told Peter that night, no strange woman ever had helped her as quickly and understandingly.

With dishwashing he was on hand, for he knew that Peaches' fate hung on how much additional work was made for Mrs. Harding. That surprised woman found herself seated in a cool place on the back porch preparing things for breakfast, while Mickey washed the dishes, and Mary carried them. Peaches was moved to the couch in the dining-room where she could look on.

Then wrapped in Bobbie's blanket and held closely in Mickey's arms, the child lay quivering with delight while the big car made the trip to the club house, and stopped under the trees to show Peaches where Mr. Bruce played, and then slowly ran along the country road, with all its occupants talking at once in their effort to point out everything to her. No one realized how tired she was, until in calling her attention to a colt beside its mother, she made no response, then it was discovered that she was asleep, so they took her home and put her to bed.

CHAPTER XVI

THE FINGERS IN THE PIE

When Mickey went the following morning to bring water for the inevitable washing, Mrs. Harding said to him: "Is it possible that child is awake this early?"

"No. She is sleeping like she'd never come to," said Mickey. "I'll wait 'til the last minute before I touch her."

"You shouldn't wake her," said Mrs. Harding.

"But I must," said Mickey. "I can't go away and leave her not washed, fed, and fixed the best I can."

"Of course I understand that," said Mrs. Harding, "but now it's different. Then you were forced, this is merely a question of what is best for her. Now Mickey, we're all worked up over this till we're most beside ourselves, so we want to help; suppose you humour us, by letting us please ourselves a trifle. How does that proposition strike you?"

"Square, from the ground up," answered Mickey promptly. "But what would please you?"

"Well," said Mrs. Harding, "it would please me to keep this house quiet, and let that child sleep till the demands of her satisfied body wake her up. Then I'd love to bathe her as a woman would her own, in like case; and cook her such dainties as she should have: things with lots of lime in them. I think her bones haven't been built right; I believe I could make her fifty per cent better in three months myself; and as far as taking her away when this week is up, you might as well begin to make different plans right now. If she does well here, and likes it, she can't be taken back where I found her, till cool weather, if I can get the consent of my mind to let her go then. Of course I know she's yours, so things will be as you say, but think a while before you go against me. If I do all I can for her I ought to earn the privilege of having my finger in the pie a little bit."

"So far as Lily goes," said Mickey, "I'd be tickled 'most to death. I ain't anxious to pull and haul, and wake up the poor, little sleepy thing. Every morning it 'most makes me sick. I'd a lot rather let her sleep it out as you say, but while Lily is mine, and I've got to do the best by her I can, you are Peter's so he must do the best by you he can; and did you notice how he jumped on that washing business yesterday? How we going to square up with Peter?"

"I'm perfectly willing to do what I said for the sake of that child. I've come to be mighty fond of you Mickey, in the little time I've known you; if I didn't like and want to help Peaches I'd do a lot for her, just to please you——"

"Gee, you're something grand!" cried Mickey.

"Just common clay, commonest kind of clay Mickey," said Mrs. Harding. "But if you want to know how you could 'square' it with me, which will 'square' it with Peter—I'll tell you. You may think I'm silly; but as we're made, we're made, and this is how it is with me: of course I love Peter, my children, my home, and I love my work; but I've had this job without 'jot or tittle' of change for fifteen years, and I'm about stalled with the sameness of it. I know you'll think I'm crazy——"

"I won't!" interrupted Mickey. "You go on and tell me! The sameness of it is getting you and——"

"Just the way you flew around and did things last night perfectly amazed me. I never saw a boy like you before; you helped me better and with more sense than any woman I ever hired, and thinking it over last night, I said to myself, 'Now if Mickey would be willing to trade jobs with me, it would give me a change, and it wouldn't be any more woman's work for him than what he *is* doing——"

"Well never you mind about the 'woman's work' part of it," said Mickey. "That doesn't cut any ice with me. It's men's work to eat, and I don't know who made a law that it was any more 'woman's work' to cook for men than it is their own. If there *is* a law of that kind, I bet a liberty-bird the *men* made it. I haven't had my show at law-making yet, but when I get it, there are some things I can see right now that I'm going to fix for Lily, and I'd sooner fix them for you too, than not. Just *what* were you thinking?"

Mrs. Harding went to Mickey, took him by the shoulder, turned him toward the back door and piloted him to the porch, where she pointed east indicating an open line. It began as high as his head against the side of the Harding back wall and ran straight. It crossed the yard between trees that through no design at all happened to stand in line with those of the orchard so that they formed a narrow emerald wall on each side of a green-carpeted space that led to the meadow, where it widened, ran down hill and crossed lush grass where cattle grazed. Then it climbed a far hill, tree crested, cloud capped, and in a mist of glory the faint red of the rising sun worked colour miracles with the edges of cloud rims, tinted them with flushes of rose, lavender, streaks of vivid red, and a broad stripe of pale green. Alone, on the brow of the hill, stood one giant old apple tree, the remains of an early-day orchard. It was widely branching, symmetrically outlined, backed and coloured by cloud wonder, above and around it. The woman pointed down the avenue with a shaking finger, and asked: "See that Mickey? Start slow and get all of it. Every time I've stepped on this back porch for fifteen years, summer or winter, I've seen that just as it is now or as it was three weeks ago when the world was blooming, or as it will be in the red and gold of fall, or the later grays and browns, and when it's ice coated, and the sun comes up, I think sometimes it will kill me. I've neglected my work to stand staring, many's the time in summer, and I've taken more than one chill in winter—I've tried to show Peter, and a few times I've suggested——"

"He ought to have seen for himself that you should have had a window cut there the first thing," said Mickey.

"Well, he didn't; and he doesn't!" said Mrs. Harding. "But Mickey, for fifteen years, *there hasn't been a single morning when I went to the back porch for water*——"

"And you ought to have had water inside, fifteen years ago!" cried Mickey.

"*Why so I had!*" exclaimed Mrs. Harding. "And come to think of it, I've mentioned *that* to Peter, over and over, too. But Mickey, what I started to say was, that I've been perfectly possessed to follow that path and watch the sun rise while sitting under that apple tree; and never yet have I got to the place where there wasn't bread, or churning, or a baby, or visitors, or a wash, or ironing, or some reason why I couldn't go. Maybe I'm a fool, but sure as you're a foot high, I've got to take that trip pretty soon now, or my family is going to see trouble. And last night thinking it over for the thousandth time I said to myself: since he's so handy, if he'd keep things going just one morning, just one morning——"

Mickey handed her a sun hat.

"G'wan!" he said gruffly. "I'll do your work, and I'll do it right. Lily can have her sleep. G'wan!"

The woman hesitated a second, pushed away the hat, took her bearings and crossed the walk, heading directly toward the old apple tree on the far crest. Her eyes were set on the rising sun, and as she turned to close the yard gate, Mickey could see that there was an awed, unnatural expression on her face. He stepped into the dining-room. By the time Peter and Junior came with big buckets of milk, Mickey had the cream separator rinsed and together, as he had helped Mrs. Harding fix it the day before. With his first glance Peter inquired: "Where's Ma?"

"She's doing something she's been crazy to for fifteen years," answered Mickey calmly, as he set the gauge and poured in the first bucket of milk.

"Which ain't answering where she is."

"So 'tain't!" said Mickey, starting the machine. "Well if you'll line up, I'll show you. Train your peepers down that green subway, and on out to glory as presented by the Almighty in this particular stretch of country, and just beyond your cows there you'll see a spot about as big as Bobbie, and that will be your nice lady heading straight for sunrise. She said she'd wanted to go for fifteen years, but there always had been churning, or baking, or something, so this morning, as there wasn't a thing but what I could do as good as she could, why we made it up that I'd finish her work and let her see her sunrise, since she seems to be set on it; and when she gets back she's going to wash and dress Lily for a *change*. Strange how women folks get discouraged on their job, among their best friends, who would do anything in the world for them, 'cept just to see that a little bit of change would help them. It will be a dandy scheme for Lily, 'cause it lets her get her sleep out, and it will be good for you, 'cause if Mrs. Harding doesn't get to sit under that apple tree and watch sunup pretty soon, things are going to go wrong at this house."

Peter's lower jaw slowly sagged.

"If you don't hurry," said Mickey, "even loving her like you do, and loving you as she does, she's going to have them nervous prostrations like the Swell Dames in Multiopolis get when they ask a fellow to carry a package, and can't remember where they want to send it. She's not there *yet*. She's ahead of them now, for she *wants* to sit under that apple tree and watch sunup; but if she hadn't got there this morning or soon now, she'd a-begun to get mixed, I could see that plain as the City Hall."

"Mickey, what else can you see?" asked Peter.

"Enough to make your head swim," said Mickey.

"Out with it!" ordered Peter.

"Well," said Mickey gravely, and seemingly intent on the separator, but covertly watching Peter, "well, if you'd a-cut that window she's wanted for fifteen years, right over her table there where the line comes, she would a-been seeing that particular bit of glory—you notice Peter, that probably there's nothing niftier on earth than just the little spot she's been pining for; look good yourself, and you'll see, there she's just climbing the hill to the apple tree—look at it carefully, and then step inside and focus on what she's faced instead."

"What else does she want?" inquired Peter.

"She didn't mention anything but to watch sunup, just once, under that apple tree," said Mickey. "I don't know *what* she wants; but from one day here, I could tell you things she *should* have."

"Well go ahead and tell," said Peter.

"Will you agree not to break my neck 'til I get this cream in the can, and what she keeps strained, and these buckets washed?" asked Mickey. "I want to have her job all done when she gets back, 'cause I promised her, and that's quite a hike she's taking."

"Well I was 'riled' for a minute, but I might as well hold myself," said Peter. "Looks like you were right."

"Strangers coming in can always see things that folks on the job can't," consoled Mickey.

"Well go on and tell me what you've seen here Mickey!"

Mickey hoisted the fourth bucket.

"Well, I've seen the very nicest lady I ever saw, excepting my mother," said Mickey. "I've seen a man 'bout your size, that I like better than any man

I know, barring Mr. Douglas Bruce, and the bar is such a little one it would take a microscope to find it." Peter laughed, which was what Mickey hoped he would do, for he drew a deep breath and went on with greater assurance: "I've seen a place that I thought was a new edition of Heaven, and it is, only it needs a few modern improvements——"

"Yes Mickey! The window, and what else?"

"You haven't looked at what I told you to about the window yet," said Mickey.

"Well since you insist on it, I will," said Peter.

"And while you are in there," suggested Mickey, "after you finish with that strip of brown oilcloth and the pans and skillets adorning it, cotton up to that cook stove, and imagine standing over it while it is roaring, to get three meals a day, and all the baking, fruit canning, boiling clothes, and such, and tell me if Lily's bed was in so much hotter a place than your wife is, all but about three hours each day."

Mickey listened as intently as he could for the separator he dared not stop, heard not a sound for what seemed a long time, and then came amazing ones. He grinned sympathetically as Peter emerged red faced and raging.

"And you're about the finest man I ever met, too," commented Mickey, still busy with the cream. "You can see what a comfort this separator must be, but it's the *only* thing your nice lady has got, against so many for your work it takes quite a large building to keep them in. Junior was showing me last night and telling me what all those machines were made for. You know Peter, if there was money for a hay rake, and a manure spreader, and a wheel plow, and a disk, and a reaper, and a mower, and a corn planter, and a corn cutter, and a cider press, and a windmill, and a silo, and an automobile—you know Peter, there *should* have been enough for that window, and the pump inside, and a kitchen sink, and a bread-mixer, and a dish-washer; and if there wasn't any other single thing, there ought to be some way you sell the wood, and use the money for the kind of a summer stove that's only hot under what you are cooking, and turns off the flame the minute you finish. Honest there had Peter! I got a little gasoline one in my room that's better than what your nice lady has. The things she should have would cost something, cost a lot for all I know, but I bet what she needs wouldn't take half the things in the building Junior showed me did; and it couldn't be the start of what a sick wife, and doctor bills, and strange women coming and going, and abusing you and the children would cost——"

"Shut up!" cried Peter. "That will do! Now you listen to me young man. Since you are so expert at seeing things, and since you've traded work with my wife, to *rest her* by *changing her job*, suppose you just keep your eyes open, and make out a list of what she should have to do her work convenient and easy as can be, and of course, comfortably. That stove's hot yet! And breakfast been over an hour too! Nothing like it must be going full blast, and things steaming and frying!"

"Sure!" said Mickey.

"Watch a few days, and then we'll talk it over. If it is your train time, ride down with Junior, and I'll stay in the house till she comes. I guess Little White Butterfly won't wake up; and if she does, she'll be all right with me. Mary dresses herself and Bobbie. Is Mary helping her Ma right?"

"Well some," said Mickey. "Not all she could! But her taking care of Bobbie is a big thing. Junior could do a lot of things, but he doesn't seem to see them, and——"

"And so could I?" asked Peter. "Is that the ticket?"

"Yes," said Mickey.

"All right young man," said Peter. "Fix us over! We are ready for anything that will benefit Ma. She's the pinwheel of this place. Now you scoot! I can see her coming."

"It's our secret then?" asked Mickey.

"Yes, it's our secret!" answered Peter gravely.

Mickey took one long look at Peaches and went running to the milk wagon. Junior offered to let him drive, so for the first time he took the lines and guided a horse. He was a happy boy as he spun on his heel waiting a few minutes for the trolley. He sat in the car with no paper in which to search for headlines, no anxiety as to whether he could dispose of enough to keep Peaches from hunger that night, sure of her safety and comfort. The future, coloured by what Mrs. Harding had said to him, took on such a rosy glow it almost hurt his mental eyes. He revelled in greater freedom from care than he ever had known. He sat straighter, and curiously watched the people in the car. When they entered the city and the car swung down his street near the business centre, Mickey stepped off and hiding himself watched for the passing of the boy, on his old route. Before long it came, "I *like* to sell papers," in such good imitation of his tone and call that Mickey's face grew grave and a half-jealous little ache began in his heart.

"Course we're better off," he commented. "Course I can't go back now, and I wouldn't if I could; but it makes me want to swat any fellow using my call, and taking my men. Gee, the kid is doing better than I thought he could! B'lieve he's got the idea all right. I'll just join the procession."

Mickey stepped into line and followed, pausing whenever a paper was sold, until he was sure that his men were patronizing his substitute, then he overtook him.

"Good work, kid!" he applauded. "Been following you and you're doing well. Lemme take a paper a second. Yes, I thought so! You're leaving out the biggest scoop on the sheet! Here, give them a laugh on this 'Chasing Wrinkles.' How did you come to slide over it and not bump enough to wake you up? Get on this sub-line, 'Males seeking beauty doctors to renew youth.'"

"How would you cry it?" asked the boy.

"Aw looky! Looky! Looky!" Mickey shouted, holding his side with one hand and waving a paper with the other. "All the old boys hiking to the beauty parlours. Pinking up the glow of youth to beat Billie Burke. Corner on icicles; Billie gets left, 'cause the boys are using all of them! Oh my! Wheel o' time oiled with cold cream and reversed with an icicle! Morning paper! Tells you how to put the cream on your face 'stead of in the coffee! Stick your head in the ice box at sixty, and come out sixteen! Awah get in line, gentlemen! Don't block traffic!"

When the policemen scattered the crowd Mickey's substitute had not a paper remaining. With his pocket full of change he was running to the nearest stand for a fresh supply. Mickey went with him and watched with critical eye while the boy tried a reproduction of what he called "a daily scream!" The first time it was rather flat.

"You ain't going at it right!" explained Mickey. "'Fore you can make anybody laugh on this job, you must see the fun of life yourself. Beauty parlours have always been for the Swell Dames and the theatre ladies, who pink up, while their gents hump to pay the bill. You ought always take one paper home, and *read* it, so you know what's going on in the world. Now from what I've read, I know that the get-a-way of the beauty parlours is cold cream. And one of the show ladies the boys are always wild over told the papers long ago 'bout how she used icicles on her face to pink it up. Now if you'd a-knowed this like you should, the minute you clapped your peepers on that, 'Chasing Wrinkles,' you'd a-knowed where your laugh came in today, like I've told you over and over you *must* get it. Bet Chaffner put that there on purpose for me. Which same gives me an idea. You been calling the Hoc de Geezer war, and the light-weight champeen of Mexico, and 'the psychological panic' something fine; but did you sell out on them? Not on your topknot! You lost your load on the scream. *Get the joke of life soaked in your system good.* On this, you make yourself see the plutes, and the magnates, and the city officials leaving their jobs, and hiking to the beauty parlours, to beat the dames at their daily stunt of being creamed and icicled and—it's funny! When it's so funny to you that you just howl about it, why it's catching! Didn't you see me catch them with it? Now go on and do it again, and get the *scream* in."

The boy began the cry with tears of laughter in his eyes. He kept it up as he handed out papers and took in change. Satisfied, Mickey called to him: "Tell your sire it's all over but polishing the silver."

He started down the street glancing at clocks he was passing, with nimble feet threading the crowds until he reached the *Herald* office; there he dodged in and making his way to the editorial desk he waited his chance. When he saw an instant of pause in the work of the busy man, he started his cry: "Morning papers! I *like* to sell them!" and so on to the "Chasing Wrinkles." There because he was excited, for he knew that his reception would depend on how good a laugh he gave them, Mickey outdid himself. Reporters waiting assignments crowded around him; Mr. Chaffner beckoned, and Mickey stepped to him.

"Found it all right, did you, young man?"

"The scream lifted the load!" cried Mickey. "War, and waste, and wickedness, didn't get a look in."

"I thought you'd like that!" laughed the editor.

"Biggest scoop yet!" said Mickey. "Why it took the police to scatter the crowd. They struggled to get papers, 'til they looked like the bird on the coin they were passing in, trying to escape the awful things it goes through on the money, and get back to nature where perfectly good birds belong. Honest, they did!"

"Have you any poetry for me yet?"

"No, but I'm headed that way," answered Mickey.

"How so?" inquired the editor.

"Why I've got another kid so he can do my stunt 'til nobody knows the difference, and I've gone into Mr. Bruce's office, and we're after the grafters."

"Douglas Bruce?" queried Mr. Chaffner.

"Yes," said Mickey. "He's my boss, and say, he's the finest man you ever met; and his Joy Lady is nice as he is, and prettier than moonshine on the park lake. I never saw a lady who could hold a candle to Miss Leslie Winton, and they just love to tell folks they're engaged."

Suddenly the editor arose from his chair, gripped his desk, leaned across it toward Mickey, and almost knocked him from his feet with one word.

"*What?*"

Mickey staggered. At last he recovered his breath.

"Mr. Bruce and Miss Leslie don't care if I tell," he defended. "They all the time tell it!"

"*What?*"

"Why that they are going to be married, soon as Mr. Bruce gets the grafter who's robbing the taxpayers of Multiopolis, and collects his big fee. That's what."

As suddenly as he had arisen Mr. Chaffner dropped back, and in a stupefied way still looked at Mickey. Then: "You come with me," Mr. Chaffner said rising, and he entered a small room and closed the door.

"Now you tell me all about this engagement."

"Maybe they don't want it in the papers yet," said Mickey. "I guess I'll let Mr. Bruce do his own talking."

"But you said they told everybody."

"So they do," said Mickey. "And of course they'd tell you. You can call him. His number is 500-X."

The editor made a note of it, studying Mickey.

"Yes, that would be the better way, of course," he agreed. "You have a long head, young man. And so you think Miss Leslie Winton is a fine young lady?"

"Surest thing you know," said Mickey. "Why let me tell you——"

And then in a few swift words, Mickey sketched in the young woman so intelligent she had selected him from all the other "newsies" by a description, and sent him to Mr. Bruce; how she had dolls ready to give away, and poor children might ride in her car; how she lived with "darling old Daddy," and there Mickey grew enthusiastic, and told of the rest house, and then the renting of the cabin on Atwater by the most considerate of daughters for her father and her lover, and when he could not think of another commendatory word to say, Mickey paused, while a dazed man muttered a word so low the boy scarcely heard it.

"I don't know why you say *that!*" cried Mickey.

"Ommh!" said Mr. Chaffner, slowly. "I don't either, only I didn't understand they were *engaged*. It's my business to find and distribute news, and get it fresh, 'scoop it,' as our term is, and so, Mickey, when investigations are going on, and everybody knows a denou—a big surprise is coming, in order to make sure that my paper gets in on the ground floor, I make some investigation for myself, and sometimes by accident, sometimes by intuition, sometimes by sharp deduction we *happen* to land before the investigators. Of course we have personal, financial, and political reasons for not spoiling the game. Now we haven't gone into the City Hall investigation as Bruce has and we can't show figures, but we know enough to understand where he's coming out; so when the gig upsets, we have our side ready and we'll embroider his figures with what the public is entitled to, in the way of news."

"Sure! But I don't see why you act so funny!"

"Oh it's barely possible that I've got ahead of your boss on a few features of his investigation."

"Aw-w-wh!" said Mickey. "Well I hope you ain't going to rush in and spoil *his* scoop. You see he doesn't know who he's after, himself. We talk about it a lot of times. I tell him how I've sold papers, and seen men like he's chasing get their dose, and go sick and white, and can't ever face men straight again; but he says stealing is stealing, and cut where it will, those who rob the taxpayers must be exposed. I told him maybe he'd be surprised, and maybe he'd be sorry; but he says it's got to be stopped, no matter who gets hurt."

"Well he's got his nerve!" cried the editor.

"Yes!" agreed Mickey. "He's so fine himself, he thinks no other men worth saving could go wrong. I told him I wished the men he was after would break their necks 'fore he gets them, but he goes right on."

"Mickey, you figure closer than your boss does."

"In one way I *do*," conceded Mickey. "It's like this: he knows books, and men, and how things *should* be; but I know how they *are*. See?"

"I certainly see," said the intent listener. "Mickey, when it comes to the place where you think you know better than your boss, while it's bad business for me to tell you, keep your eye open, and maybe you can save him. Books and theories are all right, but there are times when a man comes a cropper on them. You watch, and if you think he's riding for a fall, you come skinning and tell me, not over the 'phone, *come and tell me*. Here, take this, it will get you to me any time, no matter where I am or what I'm doing. Understand?"

"You think Mr. Bruce is going to get into trouble?"

"His job is to get other people into trouble——"

"But he says he ain't got a thing to do with it," said Mickey. "He says they get themselves into trouble."

"That's so too," commented Mr. Chaffner. "Anyway, keep your mouth tight shut, and your eyes wide open, and if you think your boss is getting into deep water, you come and tell me. I want things to go right with *you*, because I'm depending on that poem for my front page, soon."

Mickey held out his hand.

"Sure!" he agreed. "I'm in an awful good place now to work up the poetry piece, being right out among the cows and clover. And about Mr. Bruce, gee! I wish he was plowing corn. I just hate his job he's doing now. Sure if I see rocks I'll make a run for you. Thanks Boss!"

Mickey had lost time, and he hurried, but things seemed to be happening, for as he left the elevator and sped down the hall, he ran into Mr. James Minturn. With a hasty glance he drew back, and darted for the office door. Mr. Minturn's face turned a dull red.

"One minute, young man!" he called.

"I'm late," said Mickey shortly. "I must hurry."

"Bruce is late too. I just came from his office and he isn't there," answered Mr. Minturn.

"Well I want to get it in order before he comes."

"In fact you want anything but to have a word to say to me!" hazarded Mr. Minturn.

"Well then, since you are such a good guesser, I ain't just crazy about you," said Mickey shortly.

"And I'm tired of having you run from me as if I were afflicted with smallpox," said Mr. Minturn.

"If your blood is right, smallpox ain't much," said Mickey. "I haven't a picture of myself running from *that*, if it really wanted a word with me."

"But you have a picture of yourself running from me?"

"Maybe I do," conceded Mickey.

"I've noticed it on occasions so frequent and conspicuous that others, no doubt, will do the same," said Mr. Minturn. "If you are all Bruce thinks you, then you should give a man credit for what he tries to do. You surprised me too deeply for words with the story you brought me one day. I knew most of your facts from experience, better than you did, except the one horrible thing that shocked me speechless; but Mickey, when I had time to adjust myself, I made the investigations you suggested, and proved what you said. I deserve your scorn for not acting faster, but what I had to do couldn't be done in a day, and for the boys' sake it had to be done as privately as possible. There's no longer any reason why you should regard me as a monster——"

"I'm awful glad you told me," Mickey said. "I surely did have you sized up something scandalous. And yet I couldn't quite make out how, if my view was right, Mr. Bruce and Miss Leslie would think so much of you."

"They are friends I'm proud to have," said Mr. Minturn. "And I hope you'll consider being a friend to me, and to my boys also. If ever a times comes when I can do anything for you, let me know."

"Now right on that point, pause a moment," said Mickey. "You *are* a friend to my boss?"

"I certainly am, and I'm under deep obligations to Miss Winton. If ever my home becomes once more what it was to start with, it will be her work. Could a man bear heavier obligation than that?"

"Well hardly," said Mickey. "Course there wouldn't likely ever be anything you could do for Miss Leslie that would square *that* deal; but I'm worried about my boss something awful."

"Why Mickey?" asked Mr. Minturn.

"That investigation you started him on."

"I did start him on that. What's the matter?"

"Well the returns are about all in," said Mickey, "and the man who draws the candy suit is about ready to put it on. See?"

"Good! Exactly what he should do."

"Yes exactly," agreed Mickey dryly, "but *who* do you figure it is? We got some good friends in the City Hall."

"Always is somebody you don't expect," said Mr. Minturn. "Don't waste any sympathy on them, Mickey."

"Not unless in some way my boss got himself into trouble," said Mickey.

"There's no possible way he could."

"About the smartest man in Multiopolis thinks yes," said Mickey. "I just been talking with him."

"Who, Mickey?" asked Mr. Minturn, instantly.

"Chaffner of the *Herald*," said Mickey.

"*What!*"

Mr. Minturn seized the boy's arm, shoved him inside his door and closed it. Mickey pulled away and turned a belligerent face upward.

"Now nix on knocking me down with *your* 'whats!'" he cried. "I just been hammered meller with his, and dragged into his room, and shut up, and scared stiff, about twenty minutes ago."

"*The devil you say!*" exploded Mr. Minturn.

"No, I said Chaffner!" insisted Mickey. "Chaffner of the *Herald.* I'm going to write a poetry piece for his front page, some day soon now. I been selling his paper all my life."

"And so you're a friend of Chaffner's?"

"Oh not bosom and inseparable," explained Mickey. "I haven't seen so awful much of him, but when I do, we get along fine."

"And he said——?" questioned Mr. Minturn.

"Just what I been afraid of all the time," said Mickey. "That these investigations at times got into places you didn't *look* for, and made awful trouble; and that my boss *might* get it with his."

"Mickey, you will promise me something?" asked Mr. Minturn. "You see I started Mr. Bruce on this trying to help him to a case that would bring him into prominence, so if it should go wrong, it's in a way through me. If you think Douglas is unlike himself, or worried, will you tell me? Will you?"

"Why surest thing you know!" cried Mickey. "Why I should say I would! Gee, you're great too! I think I'll like you awful well when we get acquainted."

Mickey was busy when Bruce entered, and with him was Leslie Winton. They brought the breath of spring mellowing into summer, freighted with emanations of real love, touched and tinctured with joy so habitual it had become spontaneous on the part of Leslie Winton, and this morning contagious with Douglas Bruce. Mickey stood silent, watched them closely, and listened. So in three minutes, from ragged scraps and ejaculations effervescing from what was running over in their brains, he knew that they had taken an early morning plunge into Atwater, landed a black bass, had a breakfast of their own making, at least in so far as gathering wild red raspberries from the sand pit near the bridge; and then they had raced to the Multiopolis station to start Mr. Winton on a trip west to try to sell his interest in some large land holdings there, the care of which he was finding burdensome.

"Heavens, how I hope Daddy makes that sale!" cried Leslie. "I've been so worried about him this summer."

"I wondered at you not going with him," said Douglas.

"He didn't seem to want me," said Leslie. "He said it was a flying trip and he was forced to be back before some reports from his office were filed; so he thought I wouldn't enjoy it; and for the first time in my life he told me distinctly that he didn't have *time* for me. Fancy Daddy! I can't understand it."

"I've noticed that he has been brooding and preoccupied of late, not at all like himself," said Douglas. "Have you any idea what troubles him?"

"Of course! He told me!" said Leslie. "It's Mr. Swain. When Daddy was a boy, Mr. Swain was his father's best friend, and when grandfather died, he asked him to guide Daddy, and he not only did that, but he opened his purse and started him in business. Now Mr. Swain is growing old, and some of his investments have gone wrong; just when political changes made business close as could be, he lost heavily; and then came the war. There was no way but for

Daddy to stay here and fight to save what he could for him. He told me early last fall; we talked of it again in the winter, and this spring most of all—I've told you!"

"Yes I know! I wish I could help!" said Douglas.

"I do too! I wish it intensely," said Leslie. "When father comes, we'll ask him. We're young and strong, and we should stand by. I never saw Daddy in such a state. He *must* sell that land. He *said* so. He said last night he'd be forced to sell if he only got half its value, and that wouldn't be enough."

"Enough for what?" asked Douglas.

"To help Mr. Swain," said Leslie.

"He's going to use his fortune?" queried Douglas.

"I don't know that Daddy has holdings large enough to deserve the word," said Leslie. "He's going to use what he has. I urged him to; it's all he can do."

"Did you take into consideration that it may end in his failure?" asked Douglas.

"I did," said Leslie, "and I forgot to tell him, but I will as soon as he comes back: he can have all mother left me, too, if he needs it."

"Leslie, you're a darling, but have you ever had even a small taste of poverty?" asked Douglas.

"No! But I've always been curious, if I did have, to see if I couldn't so manage whatever might be my share, that it would appear to the world without that peculiar state of grime which always seems to distinguish it," said the girl. "I'm not afraid of poverty, and I'm not afraid of work; it's dishonour that would kill me. Daddy accepted obligations; if they involve him, which includes me also, then to the last cent we possess, we pay back."

Mickey drew the duster he handled between vacuum days across a table and steadily watched first Douglas, then Leslie, both of whom had forgotten him.

"That should be good enough for Daddy; what about me?" asked Douglas. "If ever I get in a close place, does the same hold good?"

"If I know what you are doing, surely!"

"I knew you were a 'Bearer of Morning' first time I saw you," said Douglas. "But we are forgetting Mickey."

Mickey promptly stepped forward, putting away the duster to be ready for errands.

"How are you this morning?" asked Douglas.

"Fine!" answered Mickey. "I've taken my family to the country, too!"

"Why Mickey! without saying a word!" cried Douglas.

"Well it happened so fast," said Mickey, "and I didn't want to bother you when your head was so full of your old investigation and your own moving."

"Did you hear that Leslie?" he asked. "Mickey dislikes my investigation as much as the man who comes out short is going to, any day now. So you've moved Peaches to the country? You should have told me, first."

"I'm sorry if you don't like it," said Mickey. "You see my room was getting awful hot. I never was there days this time of year, and nights I slept on the fire-escape; all right for me, but it wouldn't do for Lily. Why should I have told you?"

"Because Miss Winton had plans for her," explained Douglas. "She intended to take her to Atwater, and she even contemplated having her back examined for you."

Mickey's eyes danced and over his face spread a slow grin of comprehension.

"Well?" ejaculated Douglas.

"Nothing!" said Mickey.

"Well?" demanded Douglas.

Mickey laughed outright. Then he sobered suddenly and spoke gravely, directly to Miss Winton.

"Thank you for thinking of it, and planning for her," he said. "I was afraid you would."

"Thank me for something you feared I would do! Mickey, aren't you getting things mixed?"

"Thank you for thinking of Lily and wanting to help her," explained Mickey, "but she doesn't need you. She's mine and I'm going to keep her; so what I can do for her will have to be enough, until I can do better."

"I see," said Leslie. "But suppose that she should have attention at once, that you can't give her, and I can?"

"Then I'd be forced to let you, even if it took her from me," agreed Mickey. "But thank the Lord, things ain't that way. I didn't take my say-so for it; I went to the head nurse of the Star of Hope; she's gone to the new Elizabeth Home now; she loves to nurse children best. All the time from the first day she's told me how, and showed me, so Lily has been taken care of right, you needn't worry about that. And where she is now, if she was a queen-lady she couldn't have grander; honest she couldn't!"

"But Mickey, how are you going to pay for all that?" queried Douglas.

"Easy as falling off a car in a narrow skirt," said Mickey. "'Member that big house where things are Heaven-white, and a yard full of trees, and the fence corners are cut with the shears, and the street—I mean the road—swept with a broom, this side the golf grounds about two miles?"

"Yes," said Douglas. "The woman there halted my car one evening and spoke to me about you."

"Oh she did?" exclaimed Mickey. "Well I hope you gave me a good send-off, 'cause she's a lady I'm most particular about. You see I stopped there for a drink, the day you figured instead of playing, and she told me about a boy who was to be sent out by the *Herald* and hadn't come, and as she was ready, and interested, she was disappointed. So I just said to her if the boy didn't come, how'd she like to have a nice, good little girl that wouldn't ever be the least bother. Next day she came to see us, and away Lily went sailing to the country in a big automobile, and she isn't coming back 'til my rooms are cool, if she can be spared then."

"But how are you going to pay, Mickey? Most people only take children for a week——?"

"Yes I know," said Mickey. "But these folks haven't ever tried it before, and they don't know the ropes, so we're doing it our own way, and it works something grand."

"If they are suited——" said Douglas. "That place is far better than where we feel so comfortable."

"We started this morning," said Mickey. "The lady and I traded jobs; she sat on a hill under an apple tree and watched sunrise. I washed the dishes, sep'rated the cream, and scrubbed the porch for her. When Lily wakes up, the lady is going to bathe, rub, feed her, and see to her like she owned her, to pay me back. It's a bargain! You couldn't beat it, could you?"

"Of course if you want to turn yourself into a housemaid!" said Douglas irritably.

Mickey laughed, and Leslie sent a slightly frowning glance toward Douglas.

"You can search me!" cried the boy, throwing out his hands in his familiar gesture. "Why I just love to! I always helped mother! Pay? I'll pay all right; the nice lady will say I do, and so will Peter. It's my most important job to make her glad of me as I am of her. And if you put it up to me, I'd a lot rather have my job than yours; and I bet I get more joy from it for my family!"

"Croaker!" laughed Bruce.

"'Tain't going to be a scream for the fellow who comes short," warned Mickey.

"So you're planning not to allow me to do anything for Lily?" inquired Miss Winton.

"Well there's something you can do this minute if you'd like," said Mickey. "I was going to hurry up and see my Sunshine Nurse, but it's a long way to the new hospital, and you could do as well, if you would."

"Mickey, I'd love to. What is it? And may I see your family? You know I haven't had a peep yet."

"Well soon now, you may," said Mickey. "You see I ain't quite ready."

"Mickey, what do you know about the new Elizabeth Home?" asked Douglas.

"Only that a rich lady gave her house and money, and that my Sunshine Nurse is going to be there after this. I was going for my first trip to-night."

"I wondered," said Douglas. "Mickey, when you get there, you'll find that you've been there *before*."

"My eye!" cried Mickey.

"Fact! Mr. Minturn did put his foot down, and took his boys——" began Douglas.

"Yes he was telling me this morning. That's what I get for stopping at the first page. If I'd a-looked inside, bet I'd have known that long ago."

"He was telling you?" queried Douglas.

"Yes. I guess I must kind of shied at him 'til he noticed it; I didn't *know* I did, but he caught me and told me his troubles by force. We shook hands to quit on. Say, he's just fine when you know him, and there doesn't seem to be a thing on earth he wouldn't do for you, Miss Leslie. Why he said if ever he found happiness again, and his home become what it should, it would be because you were sorry for him, and fixed things."

"Mickey, did he really?" rejoiced the girl. "Douglas, when may Mickey show me what he wants me to do?"

"Right now," he answered. "I got a load of books while he was away yesterday and I haven't started them yet. Now is the best time."

When Mickey made a leap from the trolley platform that night, at what he already had named Cold Cream Junction, he was almost buried under boxes. He stepped high and prideful, for he had collected the money from his paper route and immediately spent some of it under Leslie Winton's supervision.

Pillow bolstered, on the front porch, on his comfort lay the tiny girl he loved. Mickey stopped and made a detailed inspection. Peaches leaned forward and reached toward him; her greeting was indescribably sweet. Mickey dropped the bundles and went into her arms; even in his joy he noted a new strength in her grip on him, an unusual clinging. He drew back half alarmed.

"You been a good girl?" he queried suspiciously.

"Jus' as good!" asserted Peaches.

"You didn't go and say any——?"

"Not ever Mickey-lovest! Not one!" she cried. "I ain't even *thinked* one! That will help, Peter says so!"

"You have been washed and fed and everything all right?" he proceeded.

"Jus' as right!" she insisted.

"You like the nice lady?" he went on.

"Jus' love the nice lady, an' Mary, an' Bobbie, an' Peter, an' Junior, jus' love all of them!" she affirmed.

"Well I hope I don't bust!" he said. "I never was so glad as I am that everything is good for you."

"They's two things that ain't good."

"Well if things ain't right here, with what everybody's doing for you, they ought to be!" cried Mickey. "You cut complaining right out, Miss Chicken!"

"You forgot to set my lesson, an' I ain't had my po'try piece for two days. That ain't complainin'."

"No 'tain't honey," conceded Mickey regretfully. "No 'tain't! That's just all right. I thought you were going to start kicking, and I wasn't going to stand for it. Course I'll set your lesson; course I'll make up your piece, but you must give me a little time. I was talking with Mr. Chaffner of the *Herald, our* paper you know, and he's beginning to get in a hurry about his piece, too."

"I want mine first!" demanded Peaches.

"Sure! You'll get it first! Always! But I'm going to do something for you before I make it, 'cause I won't know how it goes 'til afterward. See?"

"What you going to do?" she questioned. "What's all the bundles? My they look excitements!"

"And so they are!" triumphed Mickey. "Where are all the folks? Do they leave you alone like this?"

"No, they don't leave me alone only when I'm asleep in the room," said Peaches. "They saw you coming an' went away 'cause they know families likes to be alone, sometimes. Ain't they smart to know that?"

"They are!" said Mickey. "First, you come to your bed a little while. I got something for you."

"Ooh Mickey! Those bundles jus' look——!"

"Now you hold on. You wait and see, Miss!"

Mickey carried her in then he returned for the boxes. He opened one and from it selected a pair of pink stockings and slipped them on Peaches; then tiny, soft buckskin moccasins embroidered and tied with ribbons to match the hose. Peaches squealed and clapped her hand over her mouth to muffle the sound; but Mrs. Harding heard and came to the door. Mickey asked for help.

"Young ladies who are going automobiling and taking walks are well enough to have dresses, and things that all *good* girls have," he announced. "But I'm a little dubious about how these things go. Will you dress her?"

"Yes," said Mrs. Harding. "You fill the water bucket and the wood box, and start the fire for supper."

Mrs. Harding looked over the contents of the box and from plain soft pieces of underwear chose a gauze shirt, a dainty combination suit and a tucked and trimmed petticoat, while Peaches laughed and sobbed for pure joy. Then Mickey came, and Mrs. Harding went away. After various trials he decided on a white dress with pink ribbons run in the neck, sleeves, and belt, slipping it on her and carefully fastening it.

"Mickey, I want the glass!" she begged. "Please, oh please hurry, Mickey."

"Now you just wait, Miss Chicken!" said Mickey.

Then he brushed her hair and put on a new pink ribbon, not so large as those she had, but much more becoming. He laid a soft warm little gray sweater with white collar and cuffs in reach, and in turning it she discovered a handkerchief and a pair of gloves in one pocket. Immediately she searched the other and produced a purse with five pennies in it. Then for no reason at all, Peaches began to cry.

"Well Miss Chicken!" exclaimed Mickey in surprise, "I thought you'd be pleased!"

"Pleased!" sobbed Peaches. "Pleased! Mickey, I'm dam—I'm busted!"

"Oh well then, go on and cry, if you want to," agreed Mickey. "But you'd look much nicer to show Mrs. Harding and Peter if you wouldn't!"

Peaches immediately wiped her eyes. Mickey lifted and carried her back to the porch, placing her in a pillow-piled big chair. Then he put the gloves on her hands, set a hat on her head and tied the pink ribbons. Peaches both laughed and cried at that, while the Harding family came in because they could not wait. Mickey raised and put in Peaches' shaking fingers the crowning glory of any small girl: a wonderful little pink parasol. Peaches appeared for a minute as if a faint were imminent.

"Now do you see why I couldn't come with a poetry piece when my head was so full of these things?"

"Yes Mickey, but you will before night?" she begged.

"You want it even now?" he marvelled.

"More 'an the passol, even!" she declared.

"Well you fool little sweet kid!" cried Mickey and choked. He fled around the house as Peter came out. In his ears as he went sounded Peter's big voice and the delighted cries of the family.

"I want Mickey!" wailed Peaches.

He heard her call and ran back fast for fear he might be so slow reaching her that Peter would serve. But to his joy he found that he alone would answer.

"I want to see me!" demanded Peaches.

"Sure you do!" cried Peter. "I'll just hand down the big hall mirror so you can see all of you at once."

He brought it and set it before her. Peaches stared and drew back. She cried, "Aw-w—ah!" in a harsh, half-scared voice. She gripped Mickey with one hand and the parasol with the other; she leaned and peeped, and marvelled, and smiled at a fully clothed little girl in the glass, while the image smiled back. Peaches thought of letting go of Mickey to touch her hat and straighten her skirt, but felt so lost without him, that she handed Peter the parasol, and used that hand, while the other clung to her refuge. When Mickey saw the treasure go in his favour, he swallowed lumps of emotion so big that the Hardings could see them running down his throat. Peaches intent on the glass smiled, grimaced, tilted her head, and finally began flirting outrageously with herself, until all of them laughed and recalled her. She looked at Peter, smiled her most winsome smile and exclaimed: "Well ain't I the——"

"Now you go easy, Miss Chicken," warned Mickey.

"Mickey, if you hadn't stopped me I'd done it sure!" sobbed Peaches, collapsing against him. "'F I had, would you a-took these bu'ful things 'way from me?" "No I wouldn't!" said Mickey. "I couldn't to save me. But I *should!*"

"Mickey, I'm so tired," she said. "Take my hat an' put it where I can see it, an' my passol, an' my coat; gee, I don't have to be wrapped in sheets no more, an' lay me down. Quick Mickey, I'm sick-like."

"Well I ought to had the sense not to spring so much all at once," said Mickey, "but it all seemed to belong. Sure I will, you poor kid!"

"And Mickey, you won't forget the lesson and the po'try piece?" she panted.

"No, I won't forget," promised Mickey, as he stretched her among her treasures and watched her fall asleep even while he slipped the gloves from her fingers.

Next morning she found the lesson and the poetry on her slate. Mrs. Harding bathed and clothed her in the little garments, and showed her enough more for the changes she would need, even two finer dresses for Sunday. She left the coat, hat, and parasol in reach. Then Peaches resolutely took up her pencil and set herself to copy the lines without knowing enough of the words to really understand; but she was extremely well acquainted with one word that Mickey had said "just flew out of his mouth when he looked at her," and in her supreme satisfaction over her new possessions she was sure the lines must be concerning them. Most of all she was delighted with her slippers. A hundred times that morning she looked down, wiggled her toes and moved her feet so that she could see them better. Between whiles she copied over and over:

LILY

Miss L. P. O'Halloran daily went walking,
In slippers so nifty the neighbours were talking.
The minute she raised her gay pink parasol
The old red cow began to friskily bawl.
When they observed the neat coat on her back,
All the guineas in the orchard cried: "Rack! Pot rack!"
She was so lovely a bird flying her way,
Sang "Sweet, sweet, sweet!" all the rest of the day.

Peter came in to visit a few minutes, so she gave him the slate to see if he could read her copy, and by this ruse she found what the lines were. She was so overjoyed she opened her lips and then clapped both hands over them, to smother the ejaculation at her tongue's end. To distract Peter she stuck out her foot and moved it for him to see.

"Ain't that pretty, an' jus' as soft and fine?" she asked.

"Yes," said Peter. "They remind me of a flower called 'Lady Slipper,' that grows along the edge of the woods. It's that shape and the prettiest gold yellow, but little, they'd about fit your doll."

"Oh Peter, could you get me one? I want to see."

"Why I would, but they are all gone now, honey," answered Peter. "Next year I'll remember and bring you some when they bloom. But it's likely by that time you can go yourself, and see them."

"Do you honest think it Peter?" asked Peaches, leaning forward eagerly.

"Yes I honest think it," repeated Peter emphatically.

"But I won't be here then," Peaches reminded him.

"Well it won't be my fault, if you're not," said Peter.

CHAPTER XVII

Initiations in an Ancient and Honourable Brotherhood

"Now father, you said if I'd help till after harvest, I could go to Multiopolis and hunt a job," Junior reminded Peter. "When may I?"

"I remember," said Peter. "You may start Monday morning if you want to. Ma and I have talked it over, and if you're bound to leave us, I guess there'd never be a better time. I can get Jud Jason to drive the cream wagon for me, and I'll do the best I can at the barn. I had hoped that we'd be partners and work together all our days; but if you have decided upon leaving us, of course you won't be satisfied till you've done it."

"Well I can try," said Junior, "and if I don't like it I can come back."

"I don't know about that," objected Peter. "Of course I'd have other help hired; your room would be occupied and your work contracted for——"

"Well I hadn't figured on that," he said. "I supposed I could go and try it, and if I didn't like it I could come home. Couldn't I come home Ma?"

Nancy slowly became a greenish white colour; but the situation had been discussed so often, it worried her dreadfully; now that it had to be met, evasion would do no good. Peter grimly watched her. He knew she was struggling with a woman's inborn impulse to be the haven of her children, her son, her first-born, especially. He was surprised to hear her saying: "Why I hardly think so Junior, it wouldn't be a right start in life. You must figure that whatever kind of work you find, or whoever you work for, there will be things you won't like or think fair, but if you are going to be your own man, you must begin like a man; and of course a man doesn't go into business with his mind made up to run for his mother's petticoats, the first thing that displeases him. No, I guess if you go, you must start with your mind made up to stay till the October term of school opens, anyway."

"Then we'll call that settled," said Peter. "You may go with Mickey on the Monday morning car and we probably won't see you again till you are one of the leading business men of Multiopolis, and drive out in your automobile. Have you decided which make you'll get?"

"Well from what I've learned driving yours, if I were buying one myself, I'd get a Glide-by," said Junior. "They strike me as the best car on the market."

Peter glanced sharply at his son. When he saw that the answer was perfectly sincere, his heart almost played him the trick he had expected from his wife.

"All right Ma, gather up his clothes and get them washed, and have him ready," said Peter.

"I thought maybe you'd take me in the car and sort of look around with me," said Junior.

"I don't see how I am going to do it, with both our work piled on me," said Peter. "And besides, I'm a farmer born and bred; I wouldn't have the first idea about how to get a boy a job in the city or what he ought to do or have. Mickey is on to all that; he'll go with you, won't you Mickey?"

"Sure!" said Mickey. "And you can save a lot by using my room. It is high, but it's clean"—Junior scowled but Mickey proceeded calmly—"and while it gets hot in the daytime, if you open the door at night, and push the bed before the window, it soon cools off, while very hottest times I always take to the fire-escape. It's nice and cool there."

"Of course! That will be the ticket," said Peter heartily. "A boy starting with everything to learn couldn't expect to earn much, and when you haven't Ma and me to depend on for your board you'll be glad to have the bed free. Thank you Mickey, that's fine!"

Junior did not look as if he thought it were. Presently he asked: "How much money ought I to take to start on, Mickey?"

"Hully gee!" said Mickey. "Why your fare in! You're going to make money, kid, not to spend it. If I was turned loose there with just one cent I'd be flying by night, and if I hadn't the cent, I'd soon earn it."

"How could you Mickey?" asked Junior eagerly.

"With or without?" queried Mickey.

"Both!" exclaimed Junior.

"Well, 'without,'" said Mickey, "I'd keep my lamps trimmed and burning, and I'd catch a lady falling off a car, or pick up a purse, or a kid, or run an errand. 'With,' there'd be only one thing I'd think of, because papers are my game. I'd buy one for a penny and sell it for two; buy two, sell for four; you know the multiplication table, don't you? But of course you don't want a street job, you want in a factory or a store. If you could do what you like best, what would it be Junior?"

Junior opened his mouth several times and at last admitted he hadn't thought that far: "Why I don't know."

"Well," said Mickey calmly, "there's making things, that's factories. There's selling them, that's stores. There's doctors, and lawyers, that's professional, like my boss. And there's office-holders, like the men he is after, but of course you'd have to be old enough to vote and educated enough to do business, and have enough money earned at something else to buy your office; that's too far away. Now if you don't like the street, there's the other three. The quickest money would be in the first two. If you were making things, what would you make?"

"Automobiles!" said Junior.

"All right!" said Mickey, "we can try them first. If we can't find a factory that you'd like, what would you rather sell?"

"Automobiles," said Junior promptly.

"Gee!" said Mickey. "I see where we hit that business at both ends. If we miss, what next?"

"I don't know," said Junior.

"Well how am I going to know what to try for, it you don't even know what you want?" asked Mickey.

"I'll make up my mind when I have looked around some" said Junior.

"You can come closer deciding out here, than you can in the rush of the streets," said Mickey. "There, you'll be rustling for your supper, and you'll find boys hunting jobs thick as men at a ball game, and lots of them with dads to furnish their room and board."

Junior hesitated, but Mickey excused himself and without having been told what to do, he accomplished half a day's work for Mrs. Harding, then began some of Peter's jobs and afterward turned his attention to hearing Peaches' lesson and setting her new copy. When Junior paid his fare Monday morning, Mickey, judging by the change he exhibited, realized that both his mother and father had given him, to start on, a dollar to spend. Mickey would have preferred that he be penniless. He decided as they ran cityward that the first thing was to part Junior from his money, so he told him he would be compelled to work in the forenoon, and for a while in the afternoon, and left him to his own devices on the street, with a meeting-place agreed on at noon.

When Mickey reached the spot he found Junior with a pocket full of candy, eating early peaches, and instead of hunting work, he had attended three picture shows. Mickey could have figured to within ten cents of what was left of one of Junior's dollars; but as the cure did not really begin until the money disappeared, the quicker it went the better. As he ate his sandwich and drank his milk, he watched Junior making a dinner of meat, potatoes, pie and ice-cream, and made a mental estimate of the remains of the other dollar. As a basis for a later "I told you so," he remonstrated, and pointed out the fact that there were hundreds of unemployed men of strength, skilled artisans with families to support, looking for work that minute.

"I know your dad signed up that contract with Jud Jason," he said, "'cause I saw him, and that means that he's got no use for you for three months; so you must take care of yourself for that long at least, if you got any ginger in you. Of course," explained Mickey, "I know that most city men think country boys won't stick, and are big cowards, but I'm expecting you to show them just where they are mistaken. I know you're not lazy, and I know you got as much sand and grit as any city boy, but you must *prove it* to the rest of them. You must show up!"

"Sure!" said Junior. "I'll convince them!"

By night the last penny of the second dollar was gone, so Junior borrowed his fare to his room from Mickey, who was to remain with him to show him the way back and forth, and to spend an early hour in search of employment. It was Mickey's first night away from Peaches, and while he knew she was safe, he felt that when night came she would miss him. The thought that she might cry for him tormented him to speech. He pointed out to Junior very clearly that he would have to mark corners and keep his eyes open because he need not expect that he could leave her longer than that. Junior agreed with him, for he had promised Peaches in saying good-bye to keep Mickey only one night. He had understood by her wavering voice and evident anxiety, that with darkness Mickey was expected and essential to her comfort.

He had treated himself to candy and unusual fruits until his money was gone, while by night these and a walk of miles on hot pavement had bred such an appetite that he felt he had not eaten a full meal in years, so when Mickey brought out the remains of the food Mrs. Harding had given him, her son felt insulted. But Mickey figured a day on the basis of what he had earned, what he had expended, what he must save to be ready when the great surgeon came, and prepared exactly as he would have done for himself and Peaches. On reaching the tenement and climbing until his legs ached, Junior faced stifling heat, but Mickey opened the window and started a draft by setting the door wide. While they ate supper, Mickey talked unceasingly, but Junior was sulkily silent. He tried the fire-escape, but one glance from the rickety affair, hung a mile above the ground it seemed to him, was enough, so he climbed back in the window and tossed on the bed.

Junior did his first real thinking that night. He was ravenous before morning and aghast at what he was offered for breakfast. He was eager to find work and he knew for what his first day's wage would go. In justice to his own sense of honour and in justice to Junior, mere common fairness, such as he would have wanted in like case, for the first few days Mickey honestly and unceasingly hunted employment. With Junior at his elbow he suffered one rebuff after another, until it was clear to him that it was impossible for a country boy unused to the ways of the city to find or to hold a job at which he could survive, even with his room provided, while the city swarmed with unemployed men. Everywhere they found the work they would have liked done by an Italian, Greek, Swede, German, or Polander who seemed strong as oxen, oblivious, as no doubt they were, to treatment Junior never had seen accorded a balky mule, and able to live on a chunk of black bread, a bit of cheese, and a few cents' worth of stale beer. When Mickey had truly convinced himself of what he had believed, with a free conscience he then began allowing Junior to find out for himself exactly what he was facing. By that time Junior had lost himself on the way to Mickey's rooms, spent a night wandering the streets, and breakfastless was waiting before the Iriquois.

Mickey listened sympathetically, supplied a dime, which seemed to be all he had, for breakfast, and said as he entered the building: "Well kid, 'til we can find a job you'll just have to go up against the street. If I can live and save money at it, you ought to be smart enough to *live*. Go to it 'til I get my day's work done. You just can't go home, because they'll think you don't amount to anything; the fellows will make game of you, and besides Jud is doing wonderfully well, your father said so. He seemed so tickled over him, I guess the fact is he is getting more help from him that he ever did from Junior boy, so your job there isn't open. Go at whatever you can see that needs to be done, 'til I get my work over and we'll try again. I'll be out about three, and you can meet me here."

Empty and disheartened Junior squeezed the dime and hurried toward the nearest restaurant. But the transaction had been witnessed by a boy as hungry as he, and hardened to the street. How Junior came to be sprawling on the sidewalk he never knew; only that his hand involuntarily opened in falling and he threw it out to catch himself, so he couldn't find the dime. Before noon he was sick and reeling with sleeplessness and hunger. He was waiting when it was Mickey's time to lunch, but he did not come, and in desperation Junior really tried the street. At last he achieved a nickel by snatching a dropped bundle from under a car. He sat a long time in a stairway looking at it, and then having reached a stage where he was more sick, and less hungry, he hunted a telephone booth and tried to get his home, only to learn that the family was away. Gladdened by the thought that they might be in the city, he walked miles, watching the curb before stores where they shopped, searching for their car, and he told himself that if he found it, nothing could separate him from the steering gear until he sped past all regulation straight to his mother's cupboard.

He had wanted ham and chicken in the beginning; later helping himself to cold food in the cellar seemed a luxury; then crackers and cookies in the dining-room cupboard would have satisfied his wildest desire; and before three o'clock, Junior, in mad rebellion, remembered his mother's slop bucket. How did she dare put big pieces of bread and things good enough for any one to eat in feed for pigs and poultry! If he ever reached home he resolved he would put a stop to that. And if he ever got back from the hurry and bustle of the streets, to the quiet of the highway and the delectable autocracy of the cream wagon, where half the neighbours handed him cookies, and dough nuts, and hot bread heels spread with clover butter and honey, he would never again leave it.

He began watching the people to see if he really were the only hungry one in the crowds, and in his study for signs of poverty, he suddenly became shocked and amazed to see the same evidence of suffering, unrest, and mental hunger on the faces of people whose manner of dress and mode of travel indicated wealth.

At three to Mickey's cheerful, "Now we'll find a job or make it," he answered: "No we will find a square meal or steal it," and then he told. Mickey watched him reflectively, but as he figured the case, it was not for him to suggest retreat. He condoled, paid for the meal, and started hunting work again, with Junior silent and dogged beside him. To the surprise of both, almost at once they found a place for a week with a florist.

Junior went to work. After a few tasks bunglingly performed, he was tried on messenger service and started with his carfare to deliver a box containing a funeral piece. He had no idea where he was to go, or what car line to take. In his extremity a bootblack came to his aid. He safely delivered the box at a residence where the owner was leaving his door for his car. He gave Junior half a dollar. Junior met the first friendly greeting he had encountered in Multiopolis, as he reached the street.

Two boys larger than he walked beside him and talked so frankly, that before he reached his car line, he felt he had made friends. They offered to show him a shorter cut to the car line just by going up an alley and out on a side street. At the proper place for seclusion, the one behind knocked him senseless, and the one before wheeled and relieved him of money, and both fled. Junior lay for a time, then slowly came back, but he was weak and ill. He knew without investigating what had happened, and preferring the mercy that might be inside to that of the alley, he crawled into a back door. It proved to be a morgue. A workman came to his assistance, felt the lump on his head, noticed the sickness on his face, and gave him a place to rest. Junior was dubious from the start about feeling better, as he watched the surroundings. The proprietor came past and inquired who he was and why he was there. Junior told him, and showed the lumps behind his ear and on his forehead, to prove his words.

The man was human. He gave Junior another nickel and told him which car to take from his front door. He had to stand aside and see five pieces of charred humanity from a cleaning-establishment explosion, carried through the door before he had a chance to leave it. He reached the florist's two hours late and in spite of his story and his perfectly discernible bumps to prove it, he was discharged as a fool for following strangers into an alley.

On the streets once more and penniless, he started to walk the miles to his room. When he found the building he thought it would be cooler to climb the fire-escape and sit on it until he decided what to do, then he could open the door from the inside. At the top he thrust a foot, head, and shoulders into the room and realized he had selected the wrong escape. He tried to draw back, but two men leaped for him, and as he was doubled in the window he could not make a swift movement.

He was landed in the middle of the room, cursed for a prowling thief, his protestations silenced, his pockets searched, and when they yielded nothing, his body stripped of its clean, wholesome clothing and he was pitched down the stairs. He appealed to several people, and found that the less he said the safer he was. He snatched a towel from a basket of clothes before a door, twisted it around him, and ran down the street to Mickey's front entrance. With all his remaining breath he sped up flight after flight of stairs and at last reached the locked door, only to find that the key was in the pocket of his stolen trousers, and he could not force his way with his bare hands. He could only get to his clothing by trying the fire-escapes again. He was almost too sick to see or cling to the narrow iron steps, but that time he counted carefully, and looked until he was sure before he entered. He found his clothes, and in the intense heat dressed himself, but he could not open the door. He sat on the fire-escape to think.

Presently he espied one of the men who had robbed him watching him from another escape, and being afraid and beaten sore, he crept into the heat, and lay on the bed beside the window. After a while a breath of air came in, and Junior slept the sleep of exhaustion. When he awoke it was morning, his head aching, his mouth dry, and the room cooler. Glancing toward the door he saw it standing open and then noticed the disorder of the room, and of himself, and sat up to find he was on the floor, once more disrobed, and the place stripped of every portable thing in it, even the bed, little stove, and the trunk filled with clothes and a few personal possessions sacred to Mickey because they had been his mother's. The men had used the key in Junior's pocket to enter while he slept, drugged him, and carried away everything. He crept to the door and closed it, then sank on the floor and cried until he again became unconscious. It was four o'clock that afternoon when Mickey looked in and understood the situation. He bent over Junior's bruised and battered body, stared at his swollen, tear-stained face, and darting from the room, brought water, and then food and clothing.

Redressed and fed, Junior lay on the floor and said to Mickey: "Go to the nearest 'phone and call father. Tell him I'm sick, to come in a hurry with the car."

"Sure!" said Mickey. "But hadn't we better wait 'til morning now, and get you rested and fed up a little?"

"No," said Junior. "The sooner he sees the fix I'm in the better he will realize that I'm not a quitter; but that this ain't just the place for me. Mickey, did you ever go through this? Why do I get it so awful hard?"

"It's because the regulars can tell a mile off you are country, Junior," said Mickey. "All my life I've been on the streets so they knew me for city born, and supposed I'd friends to trace them and back me if they abused me; and then, I always look ahead sharp, and don't trust a living soul about alleys. You say the next escape but one? I've got to find them, and get back my things. I want mother's, and Lily and I can't live this winter with no bed, and no stove, and nothing at all."

"I'm sorry about your mother's things Mickey, but don't worry over the rest," said Junior. "Pa and Ma won't ever be willing to give up Peaches again, I can see that right now, and if they keep her, they will have to take you too, because of course you can't be separated from her; your goods, I'll pay back. I owe you a lot as it is, but I got some money in the bank, and I'll have to sell my sheep."

Junior laid his head on his arm and sobbed weakly.

"Don't Junior," said Mickey. "I feel just awful about this. I thought you had a place that would earn your supper, and you had the room, and would be all right."

"Why of course!" said Junior.

Mickey looked intently at him. "Now look here Junior," he said, "I got to square myself on this. I didn't think all the time you'd like Multiopolis, when you saw it with the bark off. Course viewing it on a full stomach, from an automobile, with spending money in your pocket, and a smooth run to a good home before you, is one thing; facing up to it, and asking it to hand out those things to you in return for work you can do here, without knowing the ropes, is another. You've stuck it out longer than I would, honest you have, but it isn't your game, and you don't know how, and you'd be a fool to learn. I thought you'd get enough to satisfy you when you came, but seeing for yourself seemed to be the only way to cure you."

"Oh don't start the 'I told you so,'" said Junior. "Father and mother will hand it out for the rest of my life. I'd as lief die as go back, but I'm going; not because I can't get in the game, and make a living if you can, even if I have to go out and start as you did, with a penny. I'm going back, but not for the reason you think. It's because seen at close range, Multiopolis ain't what it looks like from an automobile. I know something that I really know, and that comes natural to me, that beats it a mile; and now I've had my chance, and made my choice. I'm so sore I can't walk, but if you'll just call father and tell him to come in on high, I'll settle with you later."

"Course if that's the way you feel, I'll call him," said Mickey, "but Junior, let me finish this much I was trying to say. I knew Multiopolis would do to you all it had done to me, and I knew you wouldn't like it; but I *didn't* figure on your big frame and fresh face spelling country 'til it would show a mile down the street. I *didn't* figure on you getting the show I would, and I *didn't* intend anything worse should happen to you than has to me. Honest I didn't! I'm just about sick over this Junior. Don't you want to go to Mr. Bruce's office—I got a key and he won't care—don't you want to go there and rest a little, and feed up better, before I call your father?"

"No I don't! I got enough and I know it! They must know it some time; it might as well come at once."

"Then let's go out on the car," said Mickey.

"I guess you don't realize just how bad this is," said Junior. "You call father, and call him quick and emphatic enough to bring him."

"All right then," said Mickey. "Here goes!"

"And put the call in nearest place you can find and hustle back," said Junior. "I'm done with alleys, and sluggers, and robbers. Goliath couldn't have held his own against two big men, when he was fifteen, and I guess father won't think I'm a coward because they got away with me. But you hurry!"

"Sure! I'll fly, and I'll get him if I can."

"There's no doubt about getting him. This is baked potato, bacon, blackberry roll, honey and bread time at our house. They wouldn't be away just now, and it's strange they have been so much this week."

Mickey gave Junior a swift glance; then raced to the nearest telephone.

"You Mickey?" queried Peter.

"Yes. It's you for S.O.S., and I'm to tell you to come on high, and lose no time in starting."

"Am I to come Mickey, or am I too busy?"

"You are to come, Peter, to my room, and in a hurry. Things didn't work according to program."

"Why what's the matter, Mickey?"

"Just what I told you would be when it came to getting a job here; but I didn't figure on street sharks picking on Junior and robbing him, and following him to my room, and slugging him 'til he can't walk. You come Peter, and come in a hurry, and Peter——"

"You better let me start——" said Peter.

"Yes, but Peter, one minute," insisted Mickey. "I got something to say to you. This didn't work out as I planned, and I'm awful sorry, and you'll be too. But Junior is cured done enough to suit you; he won't ever want to leave you again, you can bank on that—and he ain't hurt permanent, but if you have got anything in your system that sounds even a little bit like 'I told you so,' forget it on the way in, and leave instructions with the family to do the same. See? Junior is awful sore! He don't need anything rubbed in in the way of reminiscences. He's ready to do the talking. See?"

"Yes. You're sure he ain't really hurt?"

"Sure!" said Mickey. "Three days will fix him, but Peter, it's been mighty rough! Go easy, will you?"

"Mickey have you got money——"

"All we need, just you get here with the car, and put in a comfort and pillow. All my stuff is gone!"

Peter Senior arrived in a surprisingly short time, knelt on the floor and looked closely at his sleeping boy.

"Naked and beaten to insensibility, you say?"

Mickey nodded.

"Nothing to eat for nearly two days?"

Another affirmation. Peter arose, pushed back his hat and wiped the sweat from his brow.

"I haven't been thinking about anything but him ever since he left," he said, "and what makes me the sorest is that the longer I think of it, the surer I get that this is my fault. I didn't raise him right!"

"Aw-w-ah Peter!" protested Mickey.

"I've got it all studied out," said Peter, "and I didn't! There have been two mistakes, Junior's and mine, and of the two, mine is twice as big as the boy's."

Peter stooped and picked up his son, who stirred and awakened. When he found himself in his father's arms Junior clung to him and whispered over and over: "Father, dear father!" Peter gripped him with all his might and whispered back: "Forgive me son! Forgive me!"

"Well I don't know what for?" sobbed Junior.

"You will before long," said Peter. He drove to a cool place, and let the car stand while he called his wife, and explained all of the situation he saw fit. She was waiting at the gate when they came. She never said a word except to urge Junior to eat his supper. But Junior had no appetite.

"I want to run things here for a few minutes," he said. "When the children finish, put them to bed, and then let me tell you, and you can decide what you'll do to me."

"Well, don't you worry about that," said Peter.

"No I won't," said Junior, "because there's nothing you can do that will be half I deserve."

When the little folks were asleep, and Mickey had helped Mrs. Harding finish the work, and Jud Jason had been paid five dollars for his contract and had gone home, Junior lay in the hammock on the front porch, while his father, mother and Mickey sat close. When he started to speak Peter said: "Now Junior, wait a minute! You've been gone a week, and during that time I've used my brains more than I ever did in a like period, even when I was courting your Ma, and the subject I laboured on was what took you away from us. I've found out why you were not satisfied, and who made you dissatisfied. The guilty party is Peter Harding, aided and abetted by one Nancy Harding, otherwise known as Ma——"

"Why father!" interrupted Junior.

"Silence!" said Peter. "I've just found out that it's a man's job to be the *head of his family*, and I'm going to be the head of mine after this, and like Mickey here, 'I'm going to keep it.' Let me finish. I've spent this week thinking, and all the things I have thought would make a bigger book than the dictionary if they were set down. Why should you ask to be forgiven for a desire to go to Multiopolis when I carried you there as a baby, led you as a toddler, and went with you every chance I could trump up as a man? Who bought and fed you painted, adulterated candy as a child, when your Ma should have made you pure clean taffy at home from our maple syrup or as good sugar as we could buy? Often I've spent money that now should be on interest, for fruit that looked fine to you there, and proved to be grainy, too mellow, sour or not half so good as what you had at home.

"I never took you hunting, or fishing, or camping, or swimming, in your life; but I haven't had a mite of trouble to find time and money to take you to circuses, which I don't regret, I'll do again; and picture shows, which I'll do also; and other shows. I'm not condemning any form of amusement we ever patronized so much, we'll probably do all of it again; but what gets me now, is how I ever came to think that the only *interesting things* and those worth taking time and spending money on, were running to Multiopolis, to eat, to laugh, to look, and getting little to show for it but disappointment and suffering for all of us. You haven't had the only punishment that's struck the Harding family this week, Junior. Your Ma and I have had our share, and I haven't asked her if she has got enough, but speaking strictly for myself, I have."

"I wouldn't live through it again for the farm," sobbed Mrs. Harding. "I see what you are getting at Pa, and it's we who are the guilty parties, just as you say."

Junior sat up and stared at them.

"I don't so much regret the things I did," said Peter, "as I condemn myself for the things I haven't done. I haven't taught you to ride so you don't look a spectacle on a horse, and yet horses should come as natural as breathing to you. You should be a skilled marksman; you couldn't hit a wash-tub at ten paces. You should swim like a fish, with a hundred lakes in your country; you'd drown if you were thrown in the middle of one and left to yourself. You ought to be able to row a boat as well as it can be done, and cast a line with all the skill any lad of your age possesses. That you can't make even a fair showing at any sport, results from the fact that every time your father had a minute to spare he took you and headed straight for Multiopolis. Here's the golf links at our door, and if ever any game was a farmer's game, and if any man has a right to hold up his head, and tramp his own hills, and swing a strong arm and a free one, and make a masterly stroke, it's a *land owner*. There's no reason why plowing and tilling should dull the brains, bend the back, or make a pack-horse of a man. Modern methods show you how to do the same thing a better way, how to work one machine instead of ten men, how to have time for a vacation, just as city men do, and how to have money for books, and music, and school, instead of loading with so much land it's a burden to pay the taxes. I have quite a bunch of land for sale, and I see a way open to make three times the money I ever did, with half the hard work. We've turned over a new leaf at this place from start to finish, including the house, barn, land, and family. A year from now you won't know any of us; but that later. Just now, it's this: I'm pointing out to you Junior, exactly how you came to have your hankering for Multiopolis. I can see you followed the way we set you thinking, that all the amusing things were there, the smart people, the fine clothes, the wealth, and the freedom—"

"Yes you ought to see the 'amusing things' and the 'happy people' when your stomach's cramping and your head splitting!" cried Junior. "I tell you down among them it looks different from riding past in an automobile."

"Exactly!" conceded Peter. "Exactly what I'm coming at. All your life I've given you the wrong viewpoint. Now you can busy yourselves planning how to make our share of the world over, so it will bring all the joy of life right to the front door. I guess the first big thing is to currycomb the whole place, and fix it as it should be to be most convenient for us. Then we better take a course of training in making up our minds to be *satisfied* with what we can afford. Junior, does home look better to you than it did this time last week?"

"Father," began Junior, and sobbed aloud.

"The answer is sufficient," said Peter dryly. "Never mind son! When, with our heads put together, we get our buildings and land fixed right, I suggest that we also fix our clothes and our belongings right. I can't see any reason why a woman as lovely as Ma, should be told from any other pretty woman, by her walk or dress. I don't know why a man as well set up as I am, shouldn't wear his clothes as easy as the men at the club house. I can't see why we shouldn't be at that same club house for a meal once in a while, just to keep us satisfied with home cooking, and that game looks interesting. Next trip to Multiopolis I make, I'm going to get saddles for Junior and Mickey and teach them what I know about how to sit and handle a horse properly; and it needn't be a plow horse either. Next day off I have, I'm going to spend hauling lumber to one of these lakes we decide on, to build a house for a launch and fishing-boat for us. Then when we have a vacation, we'll drive there, shelter our car, and enjoy ourselves like the city folks by the thousand, since we think what they do so right and fine. They've showed us what they like, flocking five thousand at a clip, to Red Wing Lake a few miles from us. Since we live among what they are spending their thousands every summer to enjoy, let's help ourselves to a little pleasure. I am going to buy each of us a fishing rod, and get a box of tackle, soon as I reach it, and I'm going fast. I've wasted sixteen years, now I'm on the homestretch, and it's going to be a stretch of all there is in me to make our home the sweetest, grandest place on earth to us. Will you help me, Nancy?"

"I think maybe I'll be saved nervous prostration if I can help just a few of these things to take place."

"Yes, I've sensed that," said Peter. "Mickey pointed that out to me the morning you jumped your job and headed for sunup. For years, just *half your time and strength has been thrown away using old methods and implements in your work, and having the kitchen unhandy and inconvenient; and I'm the man who should have seen it, and got you right tools for your job at the same time I bought a houseful for myself and my work.* We must stir up this whole neighbourhood, and build a big entertainment house, where we can have a library suitable for country folks, and satisfying to their ways of life. It's got to have music boxes in it, and a floor fit for dancing and skating, and a stage for our own entertainments, and the folks we decide to bring here to amuse us. We can put in a picture machine and a screen, that we can pay for by charging a few cents admission the nights we run it, and rent films once or twice a week from a good city show. We could fix up a place like that, and get no end of fun and education out of it, without going thirty miles and spending enough money in one night to get better entertainment for a month at home, and in a cool, comfortable hall, and where we can go from it to bed in a few minutes. Once I am started, with Mickey and Junior to help me, I'm going to call a meeting and talk these things over with my neighbours, and get them to join in if I can. If I can't, I'll go on and put up the building and start things as I think they should be, and charge enough admittance to get back what I invest; and after that, just enough to pay running expenses and for the talent we use. I'm so sure it can be done, I'm going to do it. Will you help me, son?"

"Yes father, I'd think it was fine to help do that," said Junior. "*Now* may I say what I want to?"

"Why yes, you might son," said Peter, "but to tell the truth I can't see that you have anything to say. If you have got the idea, Junior, that you have wronged us any, and that it's your job to ask us to forgive you for wanting to try the things we started and kept you hankering after all your life so far, why you're mistaken. If I'd trained you from your cradle to love your home, as I've trained you to love Multiopolis, you never would have left us. So if there is forgiving in the air, you please forgive me. And this includes your Ma as well. I should ask her forgiveness too, for a whole lot of things that I bungled about, when I thought I was loving her all I possibly could. I've got a new idea of love so big and all-encompassing it includes a fireless cooker and a dish-washing machine. I'm going to put it in practice for a year; then if my family wants to change back, we'll talk about it."

"But father——" began Junior.

"Go to bed son," said Peter. "You can tell us what happened when you ain't as sleepy as you are right now."

Junior arose and followed his mother to the kitchen.

"Ain't he going to let me tell what a fool I've been at all?" he demanded.

"I guess your Pa felt that when he got through telling what fools we've been, there wasn't anything left for you to say. I know I feel that way. This neighbourhood does all in its power, from the day their children are born, to teach them that *home* is only a *stopping-place,* to eat, and sleep, and work, and be sick in; and that every desirable thing in life is to be found *somewhere else*, the else being, in most cases, Multiopolis. Just look at it year after year gobbling up our boys and girls, and think over the ones you know who have gone, and see what they've come to. Among the men as far as I remember, Joel Harris went into a law office and made a rich, respectable man; and two girls married and have good homes; the others, many of them, I couldn't name to you the places they are in. This neighbourhood needs reforming, and if Pa has set out to attempt it, I'll lend a hand, and I guess from what you got this week, you'll be in a position to help better than you could have helped before."

"Yes I guess so too," said Junior emphatically.

He gladly went back to the cream wagon. Peter didn't want him to, but there was a change in Junior. He was no longer a wilful discontented boy. He was a partner, who was greatly interested in a business and felt dissatisfied if he were not working at furthering it. He had little to say, but his eyes were looking far ahead in deep thought. The first morning he started out, while Junior unhitched his horse, Peter filled the wagon and went back to the barn where Mickey was helping him.

Junior, passing, remembered he had promised Jud Jason to bring a bundle he had left there, and stopped for it. He stepped into the small front door and bent for the package lying in sight, when clearly and distinctly arose Mickey's voice lifted to reach Peter, at another task.

"Course I meant him to get enough to make him good and sick of it, like we agreed on; but I never intended him to get any such a dose as he had."

Junior straightened swiftly, and his lower jaw dropped. His father's reply was equally audible.

"Of course I understand *that*, Mickey."

"Surest thing you know!" said Mickey. "I like Junior. I like him better than any other boy I ever knew, and I've known hundreds. I tell you Peter, he was gamer than you'll ever believe to hang on as long as he did."

"Yes I think that too," said Peter.

"You know he didn't come because he was all in," explained Mickey. "You can take a lot of pride in that. He'd about been the limit when he quit. And he quit, not because he was robbed and knocked out, but because what he had seen showed him that Multiopolis wasn't the job he wanted for a life sentence. See?"

"I hope you are right about that," said Peter. "I'm glad to my soul to get him home, cured in any way; but it sort of gags me to think of him as having been scared out. It salves my vanity considerable to feel, as you say, that he had the brains to sense the situation, and quit because he felt it wasn't the work for which he was born."

Then Mickey's voice came eagerly, earnestly, warming the cockles of Junior's heart.

"Now lemme tell you Peter; I was there, and I *know*. It *was* that way. *It was just that way exact!* He wasn't scared out, he'd have gone at it again, all right, if he'd seen anything in it he *wanted*. It was just as his mother felt when she first talked it over with me, and the same with you later: that if he got to the city, and got right up against earning a living there, he would find it wasn't what he wanted; and he did, like all of us thought. Course I meant to put it to him stiff; I meant to 'niciate him in the ancient and honourable third degree of Multiopolis all right, so he'd have enough to last a lifetime; but I only meant to put him up against what I'd. had myself on the streets; I was just going to test his ginger; I wasn't counting on the robbing, and the alleys, and the knockout, and the morgue. Gee, Peter!"

Then they laughed. A dull red surged up Junior's neck, and flooded his face. He picked up the bundle, went silently from the barn, and climbed on the wagon. The jerk of the horse stopping at its accustomed place told him when to load the first can. He had been thinking so deeply he was utterly oblivious to everything save the thought that it had been prearranged among them to "cure" him; even his mother knew about, if he heard aright, had been the instigator of the scheme to let him go, to be what Mickey called "initiated in the ancient and honourable third degree of Multiopolis."

Once he felt so outraged he thought of starting the horse home, taking the trolley, going back to Multiopolis and fighting his way to what his father would be compelled to acknowledge success. He knew that he could do it; he was on the point of vowing that he *would* do it; but in his heart he knew better than any one else how repulsed he was, how he hated it, and against a vision of weary years of fighting, came that other vision of himself planning and working beside his father to change and improve their home life.

"Say Junior are you asleep?" called Jud Jason. "You sit there like you couldn't move. D'ye bring my bundle?"

"Yes, it's back there," answered Junior. "Get it!"

"How'd you like Multiopolis?" asked Jud.

Junior knew he had that to face.

"It's a cold-blooded sell, Jud," he said promptly. "I'm glad I went when I did, and found out for myself. You see it's like this, Jud: I *could* have stayed and made my way; but I found out in a few days that I wouldn't give a snap for the way when it was made. We fellows are better off right where we are, and a lot of us are ready to *throw away* exactly what *many of the men in Multiopolis are wild to get*. Now let me tell you——"

Junior told him, and through putting his experience into words, he eased his heart and cleared his brain. He came to hints of great and wonder-working things that were going to happen soon. There was just a possibility that Jud gleaned an idea that the experience in Multiopolis had brought his friend home to astound and benefit the neighbourhood. At any rate Junior picked up the lines with all the sourness gone from his temperament, which was usually sweet, except that one phrase of Mickey's, and the laughter. Suddenly he leaned forward.

"Jud, come here," he said. Junior began to speak, and Jud began to understand and sympathize with the boy he had known from childhood.

"Could we?" asked Junior.

"'Could we?' Well, I just guess we *could!*"

"When?" queried Junior.

"This afternoon, if he's going to be off," said Jud.

"Well I don't know what his plans are, but I could telephone from here and by rustling I could get back by two. I've done it on a bet. Where will we go, and what for?"

"To Atwater. Fishing is good enough excuse."

"All right! Father will let me take the car."

"Hayseed! Isn't walking good enough to suit you? What's the matter with the Elkhart swale, Atwater marsh, and the woods around the head of the lake—

"Hold the horse till I run in and 'phone him."

When he came down the walk he reported: "He wants to go fishing awful bad, and he'll be ready by two. That's all settled then. We'll have a fine time."

"Bully!" said Jud laconically, and started to the house of another friend, where a few words secured a boy of his age a holiday. Junior drove fast as he dared and hurried with his work; so he reached home a little before two, where he found Mickey with poles and a big can of worms ready. Despite the pressing offer of the car, they walked, in order to show Mickey the country which he was eager to explore on foot. Junior said the sunfish were big as lunch plates at Atwater, the perch fine, and often if you caught a grasshopper or a cricket for bait, you got a big bass around the shore, and if they had the luck to reach the lake, when there was no one ahead of them, and secured a boat they were sure of taking some.

"Wouldn't I like to see Lily eating a fish I caught," said Mickey, searching the grass and kicking rotting wood as he saw Junior doing to find bass bait.

"Minnies are the real thing," explained Junior. "When we get the scheme father laid out going, before we start fishing, you and I will take a net and come to this creek and catch a bucketful of right bait, and then we'll have man's sport, for sure. Won't it be great?"

"Exactly what the plutes are doing," said Mickey. "Gee, Junior, if your Pa does all the things he said he was going to, you'll be a plute yourself!"

"Never heard him say anything in my life he didn't do," said Junior, "and didn't you notice that he put *you* in too? You'll be just as much of a plute as I will."

"Not on your bromide," said Mickey. "He is *your* father, and you'll be in business with him; I'll just be along sometimes, as a friend, maybe."

"I usually take father at just what he says. I guess he means you to stay in our family, if you like."

"I wonder now!" said Mickey.

"Looks like it to me. Father and mother both like you, and they're daffy about Peaches." They never made half as much fuss over any of us."

"It's because she's so little, and so white, and so helpless," Mickey hastened to explain, "and so awful sweet!"

"Well for what ever it is, it *is*," said Junior, "and I'm just as crazy about her as the rest. Look out kid! That fellow's coming right at us!"

Junior dashed for the fence, while Mickey lost time in turning to see what "that fellow" might be; so he faced the ram that had practised on Malcolm Minturn. With lowered head, the ram sprang at Mickey. He flew in air, and it butted space and whirled again, so that before the boy's breath was fully recovered he lifted once more, with all the agility learned on the streets of Multiopolis; but that time the broad straw hat he wore to protect his eyes on the water, sailed from his head; he dropped the poles, and as the ram came back at him he hit it squarely in the face with the bait can, which angered rather than daunted it. Then for a few minutes Mickey was too busy to know exactly what happened, and movements were too quick for Junior. When he saw that Mickey was tiring, and the ram was not, he caught a rail from the fence and helped subdue the ram. Panting they climbed the fence and sat resting.

"Why I didn't know Higgins had that ram," said Junior. "We fellows always crossed that field before. Say, there ain't much in that

'Gentle sheep pray tell me why,
In the pleasant fields you lie?'

business, is there?"

"Not much but the lie," said Mickey earnestly.

Junior dropped from the fence and led the way toward a wood thick with underbrush, laughing until his heart pained. As they proceeded they heard voices.

"Why that sounds like my bunch," said Junior.

He whistled shrilly, which brought an immediate response, and soon two boys appeared.

"Hello!" said Junior.

"Hello!" answered they.

"Where're you going?" asked Junior.

"To Atwater Lake, fishing. Where you?"

"There too!" said Junior. "Why great! We'll go together! Sam, this is Mickey."

Mickey offered his hand and formalities were over.

"But I threw our worms at the ram," said Mickey.

"Well that was a smart trick!" cried Junior.

"Wasn't it?" agreed Mickey. "But you see the ram was coming and I had the worms in my strong right, so I didn't stop to think I'd spent an hour digging them; I just whaled away—"

"Never mind worms," said Jud. "I guess we got enough to divide; if you fellows want to furnish something for your share, you can find some grubs in these woods, and we'll get more chance at the bass."

"Sure!" said Mickey. "What are grubs and where do you look for them?"

"Oh anywhere under rotting wood and round old logs," said Jud. "B'lieve it's a good place right here, Mickey; dig in till I cut a stick to help with."

Mickey pushed aside the bushes, dropped on his knees and "dug in." A second later, with a wild shriek, he rolled over and over striking and screaming.

"Yellow jackets!" shouted Jud. "Quick fellers, help Mickey! He's got too close to a nest!"

Armed with branches they came beating the air and him; until Mickey had a fleeting thought that if the red-hot needles piercing him did not kill, the boys would. Presently he found himself beside a mudhole and as the others "ouched" and "o-ohed" and bewailed their fate, and grabbed mud and plastered it on, he did the same. Jud generously offered, as he had not so many stings, to help Mickey. Soon even the adoring eyes of Peaches could not have told her idol from the mudhole. He twisted away from an approaching handful crying: "Gee Jud! Leave a feller room to breathe! If you are going to smother me, I might as well die from bites!"

"Bites!" cried the boys while all of them laughed wildly, so wildly that Mickey flushed with shame to think he had so little appreciation of the fun calling a sting a bite, when it was explained to him.

"Well they sure do get down to business," he chattered, chilling from the exquisite pain of a dozen yellow-jacket stings, one of which on his left eyelid was rapidly closing that important organ. He bowed a willing head for Jud's application of cold mud.

Finally they gathered up their poles and bait and again started toward the lake. The day was warm, and there was little air in the marsh, and on the swampy shore they followed. Suddenly Jud cried: "I tell you fellows, what's the use of walking all the way round the lake? Bet the boats will be taken when we get there! Let's cut fishing and go swimming right here where there's a cool, shady place. It will be good for you Mickey, it will cool off your stings a lot."

Mickey promptly began to unbutton, and the others did the same. Then they made their way through the swamp tangle lining the shore at the head of the lake, and tried to reach the water beside the tamaracks. Sam and Junior found solid footing, and waded toward deep water. Jud piloted Mickey to a spot he thought sufficiently treacherous, and said: "Looks good here; you go ahead Mickey, and I'll come after you."

Mickey was unaccustomed to the water. He waded in with the assurance he had seen the others use, but suddenly he cried: "Gee boys, I'm sucking right down!"

Then on his ears fell a deafening clamour. "Help! Help! Quicksands! Mickey's sinking! Help him!"

Mickey threw out his arms. He grabbed wildly; while a force, seemingly gentle but irresistible, sucked him lower and lower, and with each inch it bore him down, gripped tighter, and pulled faster. When he glanced at the boys he saw panic in their faces, and he realized that he was probably lost, and they were terror stricken. The first gulp of tepid shore water that strangled him in running across his gasping lips made him think of Peaches. Struggling he threw back his head and so saw a widespreading branch of a big maple not far above him. All that was left of Mickey went into the cry: "Junior! Bend me that branch!" Junior swiftly climbed the tree, crept on the limb, and swayed it till it swept the water, then Mickey laid hold; just a few twigs, and then as Junior backed, and the branch lifted higher and higher, Mickey worked, hand over hand, and finally grasped twigs that promised to stand a gentle pull.

Then Jud began to shout instructions: "Little lower, Junior! Get a better grip before you pull hard, Mickey! Maple is brittle! Easy! It will snap with you! Kind of roll yourself and turn to let the water in and loosen the sand. Now roll again! Now pull a little! You're making it! You are out to your shoulders! Back farther, Junior! Don't you fall in, or you'll both go down!"

Mickey was very quiet now. His small face was pallid with the terror of leaving Peaches forever with no provision for her safety. The grip of the sucking sand was yet pulling at his legs and body; while if the branch broke he knew what it meant; that sucking, insistent pulling, and caving away beneath his feet told him. Suddenly Mickey gave up struggling, set his teeth, and began fighting by instinct. He moved his shoulders gently, until he let the water flow in, then instead of trying to work his feet he held them rigid and flattened as he could, and with the upper part of his body still rolling, he reached higher, and kept inching up the branch as Junior backed away, until with sickening slowness he at last reached wood thick as his wrist. Then he dragged his helpless body after him to safety, where he sank in a heap to rest.

"Jud, it's a good thing I went in there first," he said. "Heavy as you are, you'd a-been at the bottom by now, if there *is* any bottom."

Mickey's gaze travelled slowly over his lumpy, purple frame, and then he looked closely at the others. "Why them stingers must a-give about all of it to me," he commented. "I don't see any lumps on the rest of you."

"Oh we are used to it," scoffed Jud. "They don't show on you after you get used to them. 'Sides most all mine are on my head, I kept 'em off with the bushes."

"So did I," chimed in Sam and Junior with one voice.

"I guess I did get a lot the worst of it," conceded Mickey. "But if they only stung your heads, it's funny you didn't know where to put your mud!"

"Well I'll tell you," said Jud earnestly. "On your head they hurt worst of all. They hurt so blame bad, you get so wild like you don't know where you *are* stung, and you think till you cool off a little, you got them all over."

"Yes I guess you do," agreed Mickey.

The boys were slowly putting on their clothing and Junior was scowling darkly. Jud edged close.

"Gosh!" he whispered. "I thought it was only a little spring! I didn't think it was a quicksand!"

"You cut out anything more!" said Junior tersely.

Jud nodded. After a while they started home, walking slowly and each one being particularly careful of and good to Mickey. When he had rested, he could see that it was only an accident; such an astounding one he forgot his bites and could talk of little else. When the frequency and danger of quicksands were explained to him, he was amazed that they would risk wading around the lake shores where there might be one at any step; but they said if it had been any of them they would have known instantly, thrown themselves full length, and rolled, and floated to water where they could swim; so Mickey perceived that it had been because he could not swim, and did not know what to do, that he was in danger; and later remembering that Junior could not swim much, he wondered how he could be so careless.

They made another long pause under a big tree, and Mickey felt so much better as they again started home, that Junior lagged behind, and Jud seeing, joined him. Junior asked softly: "Have any more?"

Jud nodded.

"What?" whispered Junior.

Jud told him.

"Oh that! Nothing in that! Go on!"

So they struck into the path they had followed from the swamp to the woods, when suddenly a warm, yielding, coiling thing slipped under Mickey's feet. With a wild cry he leaped across the body of a big rattlesnake that had been coiled in the path. As he arose, clear cut against the light launched the ugly head and wide jaws of the rattler, then came the sickening buzz of its rattles in mad recoil for a second stroke.

"Run Mickey! Jump!" screamed Junior.

"What is it?" asked Mickey bewildered.

"Rattlesnakes! Sure death!" yelled Jud. "Run fool!"

But Mickey stood perfectly still, and looked, not where the increasing buzz came from, but at them. They had no choice. Jud carried a heavy club; he threw himself in front of Mickey and as the second stroke came, he swung at the snake's head. The other boys collected their senses and beat it to pulp, then the dead mate it watched beside. Junior glared at Jud, but when he saw how frightened he was, he knew what had happened.

Mickey gazed at the snakes in horror.

"Ain't that a pretty small parcel to deal out sudden death in?" he asked. "And if they're laying round like that, ain't we taking an awful risk to be wading through here, this way? Gee, they're the worst sight I ever saw!"

Mickey became violently ill. He lay down for a time, while the boys waited on him, and at last when he could slowly walk toward home, they went on. Jud and Sam left them at the creek, and Junior and Mickey started up the Harding lane. Suddenly Mickey sat down in a fence corner, leaned against the rails, and closed his eyes.

"Gee!" he said. "Never felt so rotten in all my life."

"Maybe that snake grazed you."

"If it did, would it kill me?" asked Mickey dully.

"Well after the yellow-jacket poison in your blood, and being so tired and hot, you wouldn't stand the chance you'd had when we first started," said Junior. "Do you know where it came closest to you?"

"Back of my legs, I s'pose," said Mickey.

"If it had hit you, it would leave two places like needles stuck in, just the width of its head apart. I can't find any-thing that looks like it, thank the Lord!"

"Here too!" said Mickey. "You see if it or the quicksands had finished me, I haven't things fixed for Lily. They might '*get'* her yet. If anything should happen to me, she would be left with no one to take care of her."

"Father would," offered Junior. "Mother never would let anybody take her. I know she wouldn't."

"Well I don't," said Mickey, "and here is where guessing doesn't cut any ice. I must be *sure*. To-night I'll ask him. I'd like to know how it happens that sudden death has just been rampaging after me all this trip, anyway. I seemed to get it coming or going."

Junior did not hide his grin quickly enough.

"Aw-w-w-ah!" grated Mickey, suddenly tense and alert.

He sprang to his feet. So did Junior.

"Say, look here——" cried Mickey.

"All right, 'look here,'" retorted Junior. His face flamed Ted, then paled, and his hands gripped, while his jaw protruded in an ugly scowl. Then slowly and distinctly he quoted: "Course I meant to put it to you stiff; I meant to 'niciate you in the ancient and honourable third degree of the Country all right, so's you'd have enough to last a lifetime; but I only meant to put you up against what I'd had myself in the fields and woods; I was just going to test your ginger; I wasn't counting on the *quicksand*, and the *live* snake, finding its dead mate Jud fixed for you."

"So you were sneaking in the barn this morning, when we thought you were gone?" demanded Mickey.

"Easy you!" cautioned Junior. "Going after the bundle I promised Jud was *not* sneaking——"

"So 'twasn't," conceded Mickey, instantly. "So 'twasn't!"

He looked at Junior a second.

"You heard us, then?" he demanded. "All of it?"

"I don't know," answered Junior. "I heard what I just repeated, and what you said about my being game, and exactly why I came back; thank you for *that*, even if I lick you half to death in a minute—and I heard that my own mother first fixed it up with you, and then father agreed. Oh I heard enough—

"And so you got a grouch?" commented Mickey.

"Yes I did," admitted Junior. "But I got over all of it, after I'd had time to think, but that third degree business; that made me so sore I told Jud about it, and he said he'd help me pay you up; but we struck the same rock you did, in giving you a bigger dose than we meant to. Honest Mickey, Jud didn't know there was a *real* quicksand there, and of course we didn't dream a live snake would follow and find the one the boys hunted, killed, and set for you this morning——"

"Awful innocent!" scoffed Mickey. "'Member you didn't know about the ram either?"

"Honest I *didn't*, Mickey," persisted Junior. "I thought steering you into the yellow jackets was to be the first degree! Cross my heart, I did."

Suddenly Mickey whooped. He tumbled on the grass in the fence corner and twisted in wild laughter until he was worn out. Then he struggled up, and held out his hand to Junior.

"If you're willing," he said, "I'll give you the grip, and the password will be, 'Brothers!'"

CHAPTER XVIII

MALCOLM AND THE HERMIT THRUSH

"Mr. Dovesky, I want a minute with you," said James Minturn.

"All right, Mr. Minturn, what is it?"

"You are well acquainted with Mrs. Minturn?"

"Very well indeed!" said Mr. Dovesky. "I have had the honour of working with her in many concerts."

"And of her musical ability you are convinced?"

"Brilliant is the only word," exclaimed the Professor.

"My reason for asking is this," said Mr. Minturn: "one of our boys, the second, Malcolm, is like his mother, and lately we discovered that he has her gift in music. We ran on it through Miss Leslie Winton, who interested Mrs. Minturn in certain wild birds."

"Yes I know," cried the Professor eagerly.

"When she became certain that she had heard a—I think she said Song Sparrow, sing Di Provenza from Traviata—correct me if I am wrong—until she felt that Verdi copied the bird or the bird copied the master, she told my wife, and Nellie was greatly interested."

"Yes I know," repeated the musician. "She stopped here one day in passing and told me what she had heard from Miss Winton. She asked me if I thought there were enough in the subject to pay for spending a day investigating it. I knew very little, but on the chance that she would have a more profitable time in the woods than in society, I strongly urged her to go. She heard enough to convince her, for shortly after leaving for her usual summer trip she wrote me twice concerning it."

James Minturn tried to keep his face impassive and his voice even as he asked casually: "You mean she wrote you about studying bird music?"

"Yes," said the Professor, "the first letter, if I remember, came from Boston, where she found much progress had been made; there she heard of a man who had gone into the subject more deeply than any one ever before had investigated, and written a book. Her second letter was from the country near Boston, where she had gone to study under his direction. I have thought about taking it up myself at odd times this spring."

"That is why I am here," said Mr. Minturn. "I want you to begin at once, and go as far as you are able, taking Malcolm with you. The boys have been spending much of their time in the country lately, hiding in blinds, selecting a bird and practising its notes until they copy them so perfectly they induce it to answer. They are proud as Pompey when they succeed; and it teaches them to recognize the birds. I believe this is setting their feet in the right way. But Malcolm has gone so fast and so far, that he may be reproducing some of the most wonderful of the songs, for all I know, for the birds come peering, calling, searching, even to the very branch which conceals him. Isn't it enough for a beginning?"

"Certainly," said the musician.

"He's been badly spoiled by women servants," said Mr. Minturn, "but the men are taking that out of him as fast as it can be eliminated. I believe he is interested enough to work. I think his mother will be delighted on her return to find him working at what she so enjoys. Does the proposition interest you?"

"Deeply!" cried the Professor. "Matters musical are extremely dull here now, and I can't make my usual trip abroad on account of the war; I should be delighted to take up this new subject, which I could make serve me in many ways with my advanced Conservatory pupils."

"May I make a suggestion?" asked Mr. Minturn.

"Most assuredly," exclaimed the Professor.

"You noticed I began by admitting I didn't know a thing about it, so I'll not be at all offended if you indorse the statement. My boys are large, and old for the beginning they must make. I have to go carefully to find what they care for and will work at; so that I get them started without making them feel confined and forced, and so conceive a dislike for the study to which I think them best adapted. Would you find the idea of going to the country, putting a tuned violin in the hands of the lad, and letting him search for the notes he hears, and then playing the composers' selections to him, and giving his ear a chance, at all feasible?"

"It's a reversal, but he could try it."

"Very well, then," said Mr. Minturn rising. "All I stipulate is that you allow the other boys and the tutor to go along and assimilate what they can, and that when you're not occupied with Malcolm, their tutor shall have a chance to work in what he can in the way of spelling, numbers, and nature study. Is it a bargain?"

"A most delightful one on my part, Mr. Minturn," said Mr. Dovesky. "When shall I begin?"

"Whenever you have selected the instrument you want the boy to have, call Mr. Tower at my residence and arrange with him to come for you," said Mr. Minturn. "You can't start too soon to suit the boy or me."

"Very well then, I'll make my plans and call the first thing in the morning," said the Professor.

James Minturn went home and told what he had done.

"Won't that be great, Malcolm?" cried James Jr. "Maybe you can do the music so well you can be a birdman and stand upon a stage before a thousand people and make all of them think you're a bird."

"I believe I'd like to do it," said Malcolm. "If I find out the people who make music have gone and copied in what the birds sing, and haven't told they did it, I'll tell on them. It's no fair way, 'cause of course the birds sang their songs before men, didn't they father?"

"I think so, but I can't prove it," said Mr. Minturn.

"Can you prove it, Mr. Tower?" asked Malcolm.

"Yes," said Mr. Tower, "science proves that the water forms developed first. Crickets were singing before the birds, and both before man appeared."

"Then that's what I think," said Malcolm.

"When are they to begin, James?" asked Mrs. Winslow.

"Mr. Dovesky is to call Mr. Tower in the morning and tell him what arrangements he has been able to make," answered Mr. Minturn. "Malcolm, you are old enough to recognize that he is a great man, and it is a big thing for him to leave his Conservatory and his work, and go to the woods to help teach one small boy what the birds say. You'll be very polite and obey him instantly, will you not?"

"Do I have to mind him just like he was Mr. Tower?"

"I don't think you are obeying Mr. Tower because you must," said Aunt Margaret. "Seems to me I saw you with your arms around his neck last night, and I think I heard you tell him that you'd give him all your money, except for your violin, if he wouldn't go away this winter. Honestly, Malcolm, do you obey Mr. Tower because you feel forced to?"

"No!" cried Malcolm. "We have dandy times! And we are learning a lot too! I wonder if Mr. Dovesky will join our campfire?"

"Very probably he'll be eager to," said Mrs. Winslow, "and more than likely you'll obey him, just as you do father and Mr. Tower, because you love to."

"Father, are William and I going to study the birds?" asked James.

"If you like," said Mr. Minturn. "It would please me greatly if each of you would try hard to understand what Mr. Dovesky teaches Malcolm, and to learn all of it you can, and to produce creditable bird calls if possible; and of course these days you're not really educated unless you know the birds, flowers, and animals around you. It is now a component and delightful part of life."

"Do you have to pay him a lot to go with us?"

"It isn t probable that he would go for love only."

"Gee, it's a pity mother isn't here," said Malcolm. "I bet she knows more about it than Mr. Dovesky."

"I bet she does, too," agreed James. "But she wouldn't go where we do. There isn't a party there, and if a mosquito bit her she'd have a fits."

"Aw! She would if she wanted to!" insisted Malcolm.

"Well she wouldn't *want* to!" said James.

"Well she might, smarty," said Malcolm. "She did once! I saw the boots and skirt she was going to wear. Don't you wish she liked the things we do better than parties, father?"

"Yes, I wish she did," said Mr. Minturn. "Maybe she will."

"If she'd hear me call the quail and the whip-poor-will, she'd like it," said Malcolm.

"She wouldn't like it well enough to stay away from a party to go with you to hear it," said James.

"She might!" persisted Malcolm. "She didn't know about this when she went to the parties. When she comes back I'm going to tell her; and I'm going to take her to hear me, and I'll show her the flowers and my fish-pond, and yours and father's. Wouldn't it be fun if she'd wear the boots again, and make a fish-pond too?"

"Yes, she'd wear boots!" scoffed James.

"Well she would if she wanted to," reiterated Malcolm. "She wore them when she wanted to hear the birds; if she did once, she would again, if she pleased."

"Well she wouldn't please," laughed James.

"Well she *might*," said Malcolm stubbornly. "Mightn't she, father?"

"If she went once, I see no reason why she shouldn't again," said Mr. Minturn.

"Course she'll go again!" triumphed Malcolm. "I'll make her, when she comes."

"Yes 'when' she comes!" jeered James. "She won't ever live here! She wouldn't think this was good enough for Lucette and Gretchen! And she gave away our house for the sick children, and she hates it at grandmother's! Bet she doesn't ever come again!"

"Bet she does!" said Malcolm instantly.

"Would you like to have mother come here, Malcolm?" interrupted Mr. Minturn quietly.

"Why——" he said and shifted his questioning gaze toward Aunt Margaret, "why—why—well, I'll tell you, father: if she would wear boots and go see the birds and the flowers—if she would do as we do——Sometimes in the night I wake up and think how pretty she is, and I just get hungry to see her—but of course it would only kick up a row for her to come here—of course she better stay away—but father, if she *would* come, and if she *would* wear the boots—and if she'd let old slapping Lucette go, and live as we do, father, *wouldn't that be great?*"

"Yes I think it would," said James Minturn conclusively, as he excused himself and arose from the table.

"James," said Malcolm, when they went to their schoolroom, "if Mr. Dovesky goes to shutting us up in the study and won't let us play while we learn, what will we do to him to make him sick of his job?"

"Oh things would turn up!" replied James. "But Malcolm, wouldn't you kind o' hate to have him see you be mean?"

"Well father saw us be mean," said Malcolm.

"Yes, but what would you give if he *hadn't?*"

"I'm not proud of it," replied Malcolm.

"Yes and that's just it!" cried James. "That's just what comes of living here. All of them are so polite, and if you are halfway decent they are so good to you, and they help you to do things that will make you into a man who needn't be ashamed of himself—that's just it! How would you like to go back and be so rough and so mean nobody at all would care for us?"

"Father wouldn't let us, would he?" asked Malcolm.

"Hc wouldn't if he could help it," said James. "He didn't used to seem as if hc could help it. Don't you remember he would tell us it was not the right way, and try to have us be decent, and Lucette would tell mother, and mother would fire him? I wonder how she could! And if she could then, why doesn't she now? I guess he doesn't want to stop her party to bother with us; but if she ever conies and wants to takc us back like we were, Malcolm, I'm not going. I *like* what we got now. Mother always said we were to be gentlemen; but we never could be that way. Father and Mr. Tower and Mr. Dovesky are gentlemen, just as kind, and easy, and fine. When we were mean as could be, and acted like fight-cats, you remember father and Mr. Tower only *held* us; they didn't get mad and beat us. If mother comes you may go with her if you want to."

"I wish she'd come with us!" said Malcolm.

"Not mother! We ain't her kind of a party."

"I know it," admitted Malcolm slowly. "Sometimes I want her just awful. I wonder why?"

"I guess it's 'cause a boy is born wanting his mother. I want her myself a lot of times, but I wouldn't go with her if she'd come today, so I don't know *why* I want her, but I *do* sometimes."

"I didn't know you did," said Malcolm.

"Well I do," said James, "but I ain't ever going. Often I think the queerest things!"

"What queer things do you think, James?"

"Why like this," said James. "That it ain't *safe* to let children be jerked, and their heads knocked. You know what Lucette did to Elizabeth? I think she hit her head too hard. She gave me more cake, and said I was a good boy for saying the ice made her sick, but all the time I thought it was hitting her head.

I wouldn't be the boy who said that again, if I had to be shot for *not* saying it, like the French boy was about the soldiers. 'Member that day?"

"Yes I do," said Malcolm shortly.

"You know you coaxed her off the bench, and I pushed her in!" said James, slowly.

"Yes," said Malcolm. "And I kicked her. And I wasn't mad at her a bit. I wonder *why* I did it!"

"I guess you did it because you were more of an animal than a decent boy, same as I pushed her," said James. "I guess I won't ever forget that I pushed her."

"Pushing her wasn't as bad as what I did," said Malcolm. "I guess ain't either one of us going to feel right about Elizabeth again, long as we live."

"Malcolm, we can't get her back," said James, "but if any way happens that we ever get another little sister, we'll take care of her like father *wanted to*."and always got fired."

"You bet we will!" said Malcolm.

Next morning the boys had the car ready. They packed in all their bird books, their flower records, and botanies, and were eagerly waiting when the call from Mr. Dovesky came. At once they drovc to his home for him, and from there to a music store where a violin was selected for Malcolm.

Mr. Dovesky was so big, the boys stood in awe of his size. He was so clean, no boy would want him to see him dirty. He was so handsome, it was good to watch his face, because you had to like him when he smiled. He was so polite, that you never for a minute forgot that soon you were going to be a man, and if you could be the man you wished, you would be exactly like him. Both boys were very shy of him and very much afraid his entrance into their party would spoil their fun.

When they left the music store, Malcolm carefully carrying his new violin, Mr. Dovesky his, and a roll of music, the boys with anxious hearts awaited developments.

"Now Mr. Tower," said Mr. Dovesky, "suppose we drive wherever you are likely to find the birds you have been practising on, and for a start let me hear just what you have done and can do, and then I can plan better to work in with you."

The boys looked at each other. That sounded hopeful. They instantly became a couple of willing and most obliging boys, eager to please and to prove that what they had been doing was wise and instructive. When they reached the brook they stopped to show the fish pools and then entered an old orchard, long abandoned for fruit growing and so worm infested as to make it a bird Paradise. Cuckoos, jays, robins, bluebirds, thrashers, orioles, sparrows, and vireos, nested there, singing on wing, among the trees, on the fences, and from bushes in the corners.

Malcolm and Mr. Dovesky secreted themselves on a board laid across the rails of an alder-filled fence corner, then the boy began pointing out the birds he knew and giving his repetition of their calls, cries, bits of song, sometimes whistled, sometimes half spoken, half whistled, any vocal rendition that would produce the bird tones. He had practised carefully, he was slightly excited, and sooner than usual he received replies. Little feathered folk came peeping, peering, calling, and beyond question answering Malcolm's notes. In an hour Mr. Dovesky was holding his breath with interest, suggesting corrections, trying notes himself, and when he felt he had whistled accurately and heard a bird reply, he was as proud as the boy.

Then a thing happened that none of them had mentioned, because they were not sure enough that it would. A brown thrush, catching the unusual atmosphere of the orchard that morning, selected the tallest twig of an apple tree and showed that orchard what real music was.

The thrush preened, flirted his feathers, opened his beak widely and sang his first liquid notes. "Starts on C," commented Mr. Dovesky softly.

"Three times, and does it over, to show us we needn't think it was an accident and he can't do it as often as he pleases," whispered Malcolm. Mr. Dovesky glanced at the boy and nodded.

"There he goes from C to E," he commented an instant later, "repeats that—C again, falls to B, up to G, repeats that—I wish he would wait till I get my pencil."

"I can give it to you," said Malcolm. "He does each strain over as soon as he sings it. I know his song!"

On the back of an envelope, Mr. Dovesky was sketching a staff of music in natural key, setting off measures and filling in notes. As the bird confused him with repetitions or trills on E or C so high he had to watch sharply to catch just what it was, his fingers trembled when he added lines to the staff for the highest notes. For fifteen minutes the blessed bird sang, and at each rendition of its full strain, it seemed to grow more intoxicated with its own performance. Finishing the last notes perfectly, the bird gave a hop, glanced around as if he were saying: "Now any one who thinks he can surpass that, has my permission to try." From a bush a small gray bird meouwed in derision and accepted the challenge. The watchers could not see him, but he came so close singing the same song that he deceived Mr. Dovesky, for he said: "He's going to do it over from the bushes now!"

"Listen!" cautioned Malcolm. "Don't you hear the difference? He starts the same, but he runs higher, he drops lower, and does it quicker, and I think the notes clearer and sweeter when the little gray fellow sings them, and you should see his nest! Do you like him better?"

"Humph!" said Mr. Dovesky. "Why I was so entranced with the first performance I didn't suppose anything could be better. I must have time to learn both songs, and analyze and compare."

"I can't do gray's yet," said Malcolm. "It's so fine, and cut up, with going up and down on the jump, but I got the start of it, and the part that goes this way——"

"This is my work!" cried Mr. Dovesky. "Is there any chance the apple-tree bird will repeat his performance?"

"Mostly he doesn't till evening," answered Malcolm. "He's pretty sure to again to-morrow morning, but old cat of the bushes, he sings any time it suits him all day. His nest isn't where he sings, and he doesn't ever perch up so high and make such a fuss about it, but I think mother would like his notes best."

"First," said Mr. Dovesky, "I'll take down what Mr. Brown Bird sang, and learn it. I'd call that a good start, and when I get his song so I can whistle, and play it on the instruments, then we'll go at Mr. Cat's song, and see if I can learn why, and in what way you think it finer."

"Oh, it goes from high to low quicker, more notes in a bunch, and sweeter tones trilling," explained Malcolm. Mr. Dovesky laughed, saying in a question of music that would constitute quite a difference. They went to the brook and lunched and made easy records of syllabic calls that could be rendered in words and by whistling. Then all of them gathered around Mr. Dovesky while he drew lines, crossed them with bands and explained the staff, and different time, and signatures, and together they had their first music lesson.

Malcolm whistled the thrush song while Mr. Dovesky copied the notes, tuned the violin, and showed the boy how the strings corresponded to the lines he had made, where the notes lay on them, and how to draw them out with the bow. He could not explain fast enough to satisfy the eager lad. After Mr. Dovesky had gone as far as he thought wise, and left off with music, he wandered with Mr. Tower hunting flowers in which he seemed almost as much interested as the music. Malcolm clung to the violin, and over and over ran the natural scale he had been taught; then slowly, softly, with wavering awkward bow, he began whistling plain easy calls, and hunting up and down the strings for them.

That day was the beginning. Others did not dawn fast enough to suit Malcolm, while the ease with which he mastered the songs of the orchard and reproduced them, in a few days set him begging to be taken to the swamp to hear the bird that sang "from the book." Leslie Winton was added to the party that day. Malcolm came from the land of the tamarack obsessed. James, William, and the tutor did not care for that location, but Malcolm and Mr. Dovesky wanted to erect a tent and take provisions and their instruments and live among the dim coolness, where miracles of song burst on the air at any moment. They heard and identified the veery. They went on their knees at their first experience with the clear, bell-toned notes of the wood thrush. With a little practice Malcolm could reproduce the "song from the book." He talked of it incessantly, sang and whistled it, making patent to every member of the family that what was in his heart was fully as much a desire to do the notes so literally that he would win the commendation of his mother, as to obtain an answer from an unsuspecting bird; for that was the sport. The big thing for which to strive!

They worked to obtain a record so accurately, to reproduce it so perfectly that the bird making it would answer and come at their call. The day Malcolm, hidden in the tamarack swamp, coaxed the sparrow, now flitting widely in feeding its young, he knew not how far, to the bush sheltering him, and with its own notes set it singing against him as a rival, the boy was no happier than Mr. Dovesky.

Mr. Minturn could not quite agree to the camp at the swamp, but he provided a car and a driver and allowed them to go each morning and often to remain late at night to practise owl and nighthawk calls, veery notes, chat cries, and the unsurpassed melody of the evening vespers of the Hermit bird. This song once heard, comprehended, copied, and reproduced, the musician and the boy with music in his heart, brain, and finger tips, clung to each other and suffered the exquisite pain of the artist experiencing joy so poignant it hurt. After a mastery of those notes as to time, tone, and grouping, came the task of perfecting them so that the bird would reply.

Hours they practised until far in the night, and when Malcolm felt he really had located a bird, gained its attention, and set it singing against him, he was wild, and nothing would satisfy him but that his father should go to the swamp with him, and well hidden, hear and see that he called the bird. Gladly Mr. Minturn assented. Whether the boy succeeded in this was a matter of great importance to his father, but it was not paramount. The thing that concerned him most was that Malcolm's interest in what he was doing, his joy in the study he was making, had bred a deep regard in his heart for his instructor. The boy loved the man intensely in a few days, and immediately began studying with him, watching him, copying him. He moved with swift alertness, spoke with care to select the best word, and was fast becoming punctiliously polite.

On their return Mr. Dovesky had fallen into the habit of lunching with the Minturns. The things of which he and the boy reminded each other, the notes they reproduced by whistling, calling, or a combination, the execution of these on the violin, the references Mr. Dovesky made to certain bird songs which recalled to his mind passages in operas, in secular and sacred productions, his rendition of the wild music, and then the human notes, his comparison of the two, and his remarks on different composers, his mastery of the violin, and his ability to play long passages preceding and following the parts taken from the birds, were intensely absorbing and educative to all of them. Then Mr. Tower would add the description and history of each bird in question. Mr. Minturn started the boys' library with interesting works on ornithology, everything that had been written concerning strains in bird and human music; the lives and characters of the musicians in whose work the bird passages appeared, or who used melodies so like the birds it made the fact apparent the feathered folk had inspired them. This led to minute examination of the lives of the composers, in an effort to discover which of them were country born and had worked in haunts where birds might be heard. The differing branches of information opened up seemed endless. The change this work made in the boys appeared to

James Minturn and his sister as something marvellous. That the work was also making a change in the heart of the man himself, was an equal miracle he did not realize.

As each day new avenues opened, he began to understand dimly how much it would have meant to him in his relations with his wife, if he had begun long ago under her tuition and learned, at least enough to appreciate the one thing outside society, which she found absorbing. He began to see that if he had listened, and tried, and had induced her to repeat to him parts of the great composers she so loved, on her instruments, when they reached home, he soon could have come to recognize them, and so an evening at the opera with her would have meant pleasure to himself instead of stolid endurance. Ultimately it might have meant an effective wedge with which to pry against the waste of time, strength and money on the sheer amusement of herself in society. Once he started searching for them, he found many ways in which he might have made his life with his wife different, if indeed he had not had it in his power to effect a complete change by having been firm in the beginning.

Of this one thing he was sure to certainty: that if he had been able to introduce any such element of interest into his wife's residence as he had, through merely saying the word, in his own, it surely would have made some of the big difference then it was making now. He found himself brooding, yearning over his sons, and his feeling for them broadening and deepening. As he daily saw James seeking more and more to be with him, to understand what he was doing, his pride in being able to feel that he had helped if it were no more than to sit in court and hand a marked book at the right moment, he began to make a comrade of, and to develop a feeling of dependence on, the boy.

He watched Malcolm with his quicker intellect, his daily evidence of temperament, his rapidly developing musical ability, and felt the tingle of pride in his lithe ruddy beauty, so like his mother, and his talent, so like hers. The boy, under the interest of the music, and with the progress he was making in doing a new, unusual thing, soon began to develop her mannerisms; when he was most polite, her charm was apparent; when he was offended, her hauteur enveloped him. When he was pleased and happy, her delicate tinge of rose flushed his transparent cheek, while the lights on his red-brown hair glinted with her colour. He shut himself in his room and worked with his violin until time to start to the tamarack swamp. When Mr. Minturn promptly appeared with the car, he found Malcolm had borrowed Mr. Dovesky's khaki suit and waders for him, and on the advice of the boy he wore the stiff coarse clothing, which the tamaracks would not tear, the mosquitoes could not bite through, and muck and water would not easily penetrate—there were many reasons.

When they reached the swamp both of them put on boots and then, following his son and doing exactly what he was told, James Minturn forgot law, politics, and business. With anxious heart he prayed that the bird the lad wished to sing would evolve its sweetest notes, and that his high hope of reproducing the music perfectly enough to induce the singer to answer would be fulfilled. Malcolm advanced softly, slipping under branches, around bushes, over deep moss beds that sank in an ooze of water at the pressure of a step and sprung back on release. Imitating every caution, stepping in the boy's tracks, and keeping a few rods behind, followed his father. He had rolled his sleeves to the elbow, left his shirt open at the throat, while for weeks the joy of wind and weather on his bared head had been his, so that as he silently followed his son he made an impressive figure. At a certain point Malcolm stopped, motioning his father to come to him.

"Now this is as far as I've gone yet," he whispered. "You stay here, and we'll wait till the music begins. If I can do it as well as I have for three nights, and get an answer, I'm going to try to call the Hermit bird I sing with. If a hen answers, I'll do the male notes, and try to coax her where you can see. If a male sings, I'll do his song once or twice to show you how close I can come, and then I'll do the hen's call note, and see if I can coax him out for you. If I creep ahead, you keep covered as much as you can and follow; but stay as far as that big tree behind me, and don't for your life move or make a noise when I'm still. I'll go far ahead as I want to be, to start on. Now don't forget to be quiet, and listen hard!"

"I won't forget!" said James Minturn.

"Oh but it will be awful if one doesn't sing to-night!"

"Not at all!" answered Mr. Minturn. "This is a new experience for me; I'll get the benefit of a sight of the swamp that will pay for the trip, if I don't even see a bird."

By the boy's sigh of relief the father knew he had quieted his anxiety. Malcolm went softly ahead a few yards, and stopped, sheltering himself in a clump of willow and button bushes. His father made himself as inconspicuous as he could and waited. He studied the trunks of the big scaly trees, the intermingled branches covered with tufts of tiny spines, and here and there the green cones nestling upright. The cool water rising around his feet called his attention to the deep moss bed, silvery green in the evening light. Here and there on moss mounds at the tree bases he could see the broad leaves and ripening pods that he thought must be moccasins seeding. Then his eye sought the crouching boy, and he again prayed that he would not be disappointed; with his prayer came the answer. A sweep of wings overhead, a brown flash through the tamaracks, and then a burst of slow, sweet notes, then silence.

James Minturn leaned forward, his eyes on his son, his precious little lad. How the big strong man hoped, until it became the very essence of prayer, that he would be granted the pride and pleasure, the triumph, of success; for his ears told him that to reproduce the notes he had just heard would undoubtedly be the crowning performance of bird music; surely there could be no other songster gifted like that! The bird made a short flight and sang again. Across the swamp came a repetition of his notes from another of his kind, so the brown streak moved in that direction. At its next pause its voice arose again, sweeter for the mellowing distance, and then another bird, not so far away, answered. The bird replied and came winging in sight, this time peering, uttering a short note, unlike its song; and not until it came searching where he could see it distinctly, did James Minturn awake to the realization that the last notes had been Malcolm's. His heart swelled big with prideful possession. What a wonderful accomplishment! What a fine boy! How careful he must be to help and to guide him.

Again the bird across the swamp sang and the one in sight turned in that direction. Then began a duet that was a marvellous experience. The far bird called. Malcolm answered. Soon they heard a reply. Mr. Minturn saw the boy beckoning him, and crept to his side.

"It's a female," whispered Malcolm. "I'm going to sing the male notes and calls, and try to toll her. You follow, but don't get too close and scare her."

The father could see the tense poise of Malcolm, stepping lightly, avoiding the open, stooping beneath branches, hiding in bushes, making his way onward, at every complete ambush sending forth those wonderful notes. At each repetition it seemed to the father that the song grew softer, more pleading, of fuller intonation; and then his heart almost stopped, for he began to realize that each answer to the boy's call was closer than the one before. Malcolm would sleep that night with a joyful heart. He was tolling the bird he imitated; it was coming at his call, of that there could be no question. His last notes came from a screen of spreading button bushes and northern holly. At the usual interval they heard the reply, but recognizably closer. Malcolm raised his hand without moving or looking back, but his father saw, and interpreted the gesture to mean that the time had come for him to stop. He took a few steps to conceal himself, for he was between trees when the signal came, and paused, already so elated he wanted to shout; he scarcely could restrain the impulse. What was the use in going farther? His desire was to race back to Multiopolis at speed limit to tell Mr. Dovesky, Margaret, and Mr. Tower what a triumph he had witnessed. He wanted to talk about it to his men friends and business associates.

Distinctly, through the slowly darkening green, he could see the boy putting all his heart into the song. James Minturn watched so closely he was not mistaken in thinking he could see the lad's figure grow tense as he delivered the notes, and relax when the answer relieved his anxiety as to whether it would come again, and then gather for another trial. At the last call the reply came from such a short distance that Mr. Minturn began intently watching from his shelter to witness the final triumph of seeing the bird Malcolm had called across the swamp, come into view. He could see that the boy was growing reckless, for as he delivered the strain, he stepped almost into the open, watching before him and slowly going ahead. With the answer, there was a discernible movement a few yards away. Mr. Minturn saw the boy start, and gazed at him. With bent body Malcolm stared before him, and then his father heard his amazed, awed cry: "*Why mother!* Is that *you*, mother?"

"*Malcolm! Are you Malcolm?*" came the incredulous answer.

James Minturn was stupefied. Distinctly he could see now. He did not recognize the knee boots, the outing suit of coarse green material, but the beautiful pink face slowly paling, the bright waving hair framing it, he knew very well. Astonishment bound him. Malcolm advanced another step, still half dazed, and cried: "Why, have I been calling *you?* I thought it was the bird I saw, still answering!"

"And I believed you were the Hermit singing!" she said.

"But you fooled the bird," said the boy. "Close here it answered you."

"And near me it called you," said Mrs. Minturn. "Your notes were quite as perfect."

Malcolm straightened and seemed reassured.

"Why mother!" he exclaimed. "When did you study *bird* music? Have you just come back?"

"I've been away only two weeks, Malcolm," she answered, "and if it hadn't been for learning the bird notes, I'd have returned sooner."

"But where have you *been?*" cried the boy.

"At home. I reserved my suite!" she answered.

"But home's all torn up, and pounding and sick people, and you hate pounding and sick people," he reminded her.

"There wasn't so very much noise, Malcolm," she said, "and I've changed about sickness. You have to suffer yourself to do that. Once you learn how dreadful pain is, you feel only pity for those who endure it. Every night when the nurses are resting, I change so no one knows me, and slip into the rooms of the suffering little children who can't sleep, and try to comfort them."

"Mother, who takes care of *you?*" he questioned.

"A very sensible girl named Susan," she answered.

The boy went a step closer.

"Mother, have you changed about anything besides sickness?" he asked eagerly.

"Yes Malcolm," said his mother. "I've changed about every single thing in all this world that I ever said, or did, or loved, when you knew me."

"You have?" he cried in amazement. "Would you wear that dress and come to the woods with us now, and do some of the things we like?"

"I'd rather come here with you, and sing these bird notes than anything else I ever did," she answered.

Malcolm advanced another long stride.

"Mother, is Susan a pounding, beating person like Lucette?" he asked anxiously.

"No," she said softly. "Susan likes children. When she's not busy for me, she goes into the music room and plays games, and sings songs to little sick people."

"Because you know," said Malcolm, "James and I talk it over when we are alone, we never let father hear because he loved Elizabeth so, and he's so fine—mother you were *mistaken* about father not being a gentleman, not even Mr. Dovesky is a finer gentleman than father—and father loved her so; but mother, James and I *saw*. We believe if it had been the cream, it would have made us sick too, and we're so *ashamed* of what we did; if we had another *chance*, we'd be as good to a little sister as father is to us. Mother, we wish we had her back so we could try *again*——"

Nellie Minturn shut her eyes and swayed on her feet, but presently she spoke in a harsh, breathless whisper, yet it carried, even to the ears of the listening man.

"Yes Malcolm, I'd give my life, oh so gladly if I could bring her back and try over——"

"You wouldn't have any person like Lucette around, would you mother?" he questioned.

"Not ever again Malcolm," she answered. "I'd have Little Sister back if it were possible, but that can't ever be, because when we lose people as Elizabeth went, they never can come back; but I'll offer my life to come as near replacing her as possible, and everywhere I've neglected you, and James, and father. I'll do the best there is in me, if any of you love me, or *want* me in the least, or will give me an opportunity to try."

"Mother, would you come where we are? Would you live as we do?" marvelled the boy.

"Gladly," she answered. "It's about the only way I could live now, I've given away so much of the money."

"Then I'll ask father!" cried the boy. "Why I forgot! Father is right back here! Father! Father! Father come quick! Father it wasn't the Hermit bird at all, it was mother! And oh joy, father, joy! She's just changed and changed, till she's *most as changed as we are!* She'll come back, father, and she'll go to the woods with us, oh she will! Father, you're *glad*, aren't you?"

When Nellie Minturn saw her husband coming across the mosses, his arms outstretched, his face pain-tortured, she came swiftly forward, and as she reached Malcolm, Mr. Minturn caught both of them in his arms crying: "My sweetheart! My beautiful sweetheart, give me another chance, and this time I'll be the head of my family in deed and in truth, and I'll make life go right for all of us."

CHAPTER XIX

Establishing Protectorates

"I'm sorry no end!" said Mickey. "First time I ever been late. I was helping Peter; we were so busy that the first thing I knew I heard the hum of her gliding past the clover field, so I was left. I know how hard you're working. It won't happen again."

Mickey studied his friend closely. He decided the time had come to watch. Douglas Bruce was pale and restless, he spent long periods in frowning thought. He aroused from one of these and asked: "What were you and Peter doing that was so very absorbing?"

"Well about the most interesting thing that ever happened," said Mickey. "You see Peter is one of the grandest men who ever lived; he's so fine and doing so many *big* things, in a way he kind of fell behind in the *little* ones."

"I've heard of men doing that before," commented Douglas. "Can't you tell me a new one?"

"Sure!" said Mickey. "You know the place and how good it seems on the outside—well it didn't look so good inside, in the part that counted most. You've noticed the big barns, sheds and outbuildings, all the modern conveniences for a man, from an electric lantern to a stump puller; everything I'm telling you—and for the nice lady, nix! Her work table faced a wall covered with brown oilcloth, and frying pans heavy enough to sprain Willard, a wood fire to boil clothes and bake bread, in this hot weather, the room so low and dark, no ice box, with acres of ice close every winter, no water inside, no furnace, and carrying washtubs to the kitchen for bathing as well as washing, aw gee—you get the picture?"

"I certainly do," agreed Douglas, "and yet she was a neat, nice-looking little woman."

"Sure!" said Mickey. "If she had to set up housekeeping in Sunrise Alley in one day you could tell her place from anybody else's. Sure, she's a nice lady! But she has troubles of her own. I guess everybody has."

"Yes, I think they have," assented Douglas. "I could muster a few right now, myself."

"Yes?" cried Mickey. "That's bad! Let's drop this and cut them out."

"Presently," said Douglas. "My head is so tired it will do me good to think about something else a few minutes. You were saying Mrs. Harding had trouble; what is it?"

Mickey returned to his subject with a chuckle.

"She was 'bout ready to tackle them nervous prostrations so popular with the Swell Dames," he explained, "because every morning for fifteen years she'd faced the brown oilcloth and pots and pans, while she'd been wild to watch sunup from under a particular old apple tree; when she might have seen it every morning if Peter had been on his job enough to saw a window in the right place. Get that?"

"Yes, I get it," conceded Douglas. "Go on!"

"Well I began her work so she started right away, and before she got back in comes Peter. When he asks where she was and why she went, I was afraid, but for her sake I told him. I told him everything I had noticed. At first he didn't like it."

"It's a wonder he didn't break your neck."

"Well," said Mickey judicially, "as I size Peter up he'd fight an awful fight if he was fighting, but he ain't much on *starting* a fight. I worked the separator steady, and by and by when I 'summed up the argument,' as a friend of mine says, I guess that cream separator didn't look any bigger to Peter, set beside a full house and two or three sheds for the stuff he'd brought to make *his* work easier, than it did to me."

"I'll wager it didn't," laughed Douglas.

"No it didn't!" cried Mickey earnestly. "And when he stood over it awhile, that big iron stove made his kitchen, where his wife lived most of her day, seem 'bout as hot as my room where he was raving over Lily having been; and when he faced the brown oilcloth and the old iron skillets for a few minutes of silent thought, he bolted at about two. Peter ain't so slow!"

"What did he do?" asked Douglas.

"Why we planned to send her on a visit," said Mickey, "and cut that window, and move in the pump, and invest in one of those country gas plants, run on a big tank of gasoline away outside where it's all safe, and a bread-mixer, and a dishwasher, and some lighter cooking things; but we got interned."

"How Mickey?" interestedly inquired Douglas.

"Remember I told you about Junior coming in to hunt work because he was tired of the country, and how it turned out?" said Mickey.

"Yes I recall perfectly," answered Douglas.

"There's a good one on me about that I haven't told you yet, but I will," said Mickey. "Well when son came home, wrapped in a comfort, there was a ripping up on the part of Peter. He just 'hurled back the enemy,' and who do you think he hit the hardest?"

"I haven't an idea," said Douglas.

"In your shoes, I wouldn't a-had one either," said Mickey. "Well, he didn't go for Junior, or his Ma, or me. Peter stood Mister Peter Harding out before us, and then didn't leave him a leg to stand on. He proved conclusive he'd used every spare moment he'd had since Junior was in short clothes, carrying him to Multiopolis to amuse him, and feed him treats, and show him shows; so he was to blame if Junior developed a big consuming appetite for such things. How does the argument strike you?"

"Sound!" cried Douglas. "Perfectly sound! It's precisely what the land owners are doing every day of their lives, and then wailing because the cities take their children. I've had that studied out for a year past."

"Well Peter figured it right there for us in detail," said Mickey. "Then he tackled Ma Harding and her sunup, and then he thought out a way to furnish entertainment and all the modern comforts right there at home."

"What entertainment?" said Douglas.

"Well he specified saddles and horses to ride," grinned Mickey, "and swimming, and a fishing-boat and tackle for all of us, a launch on whatever lake we like best, a big entertainment house with a floor for skating and dancing, and a stage for plays we will get up ourselves, and a movie machine. I'm to find out how to run one and teach them, and then he'll rent reels and open it twice a week. The big hole that will cave in on the north side of Multiopolis soon now will be caused by the slump when our neighbourhood withdraws its patronage and begins being entertained by Peter. And you'll see that it will work, too!"

"Of course it will," agreed Douglas. "Once the country folk get the idea it will go like a landslide. So that's what made you late?"

"Well connected with that," explained Mickey. "Peter didn't do a thing but figure up the price he'd paid for every labour-saver he ever bought for himself, and he came out a little over six thousand. He said he wouldn't have wanted Ma in a hardware store selecting his implements, so he guessed he wouldn't choose hers. He just drew a check for what he said was her due, with interest, and put it in her name in the bank, and told her to cut loose and spend it exactly as she pleased."

"What did she do?" marvelled Douglas.

"Well she was tickled silly, but she didn't lose her head; she began investigating what had been put on the market to meet her requirements. At present we are living on the threshing floor mostly, and the whole house is packed up; when it is unpacked, there'll be a bathroom on the second floor, and a lavatory on the first. There'll be a furnace in one room of the basement, and a coal bin big enough for a winter's supply. We can hitch on to the trolley line for electric lights all over the house, and barn, and outbuildings, and fireless cooker, iron, and vacuum cleaner, and a whole bunch of conveniences for Ma, including a washing machine, and stationary tubs in the basement. Gee! Get the picture?"

"I surely do! What else Mickey?" asked Douglas. "You know I've a house to furnish soon myself."

"Well a new kitchen on the other end of the building where there's a breeze, and a big clover field, and a wood, and her work table right where it is in line with her private and particular sunup. There's a big sink with hot and cold water, and a dishwasher. There's a bread-mixer and a little glass churn, both of which can be hitched to the electricity to run. There's a big register from the furnace close the work table for winter, and a gas cook stove that has more works than a watch."

"What does the lady say about it?"

"*Mighty little!*" said Mickey. "She just stands and wipes the shiny places with her apron or handkerchief, and laughs and cries, 'cause *she's so glad*. It ain't set up yet, but you can see just standing before it what it's going to mean for her. And there's a chute from the upstairs to the basement, to scoot the wash down to the electric machine to rub them, and a little gas stove with two burners to boil them, and the iron I told you of. Hanging it up is the hardest part of the wash these days, and since they have three big rooms in the basement, Peter thought this morning that he could put all the food in one, and stretch her lines in the winter for the clothes to dry in the washroom. The furnace will heat it, and it's light and clean; we are going to paint it when everything is in place."

"Is that all?" queried Douglas.

"It's a running start," said Mickey; "I don't know as Peter will ever get to 'all'. The kitchen is going to have white woodwork, and blue walls and blue linoleum, and new blue-and-white enamelled cooking things from start to finish, with no iron in the bunch except two skillets saved for frying. Even the dishpan is going to be blue, and she's crying and laughing same time while she hems blue-and-white wash curtains for the windows. All the house is going to have hardwood floors, the rooms cut more convenient; out goes the old hall into just a small place to take off your wraps, and the remainder added to the parlour. All the carpets and the old heavy curtains are being ground up and woven into rugs. Gee, it's an insurrection! Ma Harding and I surely started things when we planned to dose Junior on Multiopolis, and let her 'view the landscape o'er.' You can tell by her face she's seeing it! If she sails into the port o' glory looking more glorified, it'll be a wonder! And Peter! You ought to see Peter! And Junior! You should see Junior planning his room. And Mickey! You must see Mickey planning his! And Mary and Bobbie! And above all, you should see Lily! Last I saw of her, Peter was holding her under her arms, and she was shoving her feet before her trying to lift them up a little. We've most rubbed them off her with fine sand, and then stuck them in cold water, and then sanded them again, and they're not the same feet—that's a cinch!"

"Is that the sum of the Harding improvements?" asked Douglas, drawing fine lines on a sheet of figures before him.

"Well it's a fair showing," said Mickey. "We ain't got the new rugs, and the music box, and the books; or the old furniture rubbed and oiled yet. When the house is finished, Peter expressly specified that his lady was to get her clothes so she could go to the club house, and not be picked for a country woman by what she *wore*."

"Mickey, this is so interesting it has given my head quite a rest. Maybe now I can see my way clearly. But one thing more: how long are you planning to stay there? You talk as if——"

"'Stay there?'" said Mickey. "Didn't you hear me say there was a horse and saddle and a room for me, and a room for Lily? 'Stay there!' Why for ever and ever more! That's *home!* When I got into trouble and called on Peter to throw a lifeline, he did it up browner than his job for Ma. A *line* was all I asked; *but Peter established a regular Pertectorate—nobody can 'get' us now—*

"You mean Peter adopted both of you?" cried Douglas.

"Sure!" indorsed Mickey with a flourish. "You see it was like this: when we dosed Junior with Multiopolis, the old threshing machine took a hand and did some things to him that wasn't on the program; he found out about it, and it made him mad. When he got his dander up he hit back by turning old Miss Country loose on me. First I tried a ram and yellow jackets; then only a little bunch of maple twigs was all the pull I had to keep me from going to the bottomless pit by the way of the nastiest quicksand on Atwater Lake. Us fellows went back one day and fed it logs bigger than I am, and it sucked them down like Peter does a plate of noodles. Then Junior thought curling a big dead rattler in the path, and shunting me so I'd step right on it, would be a prime joke; but he didn't figure on the snake he had fixed for me having a mate as big and ugly as it was, that would follow and coil zipping mad over the warm twisting body——"

"Mickey!" gasped Douglas.

"Just so! Exactly what I thought—and then some. When I dragged what was left of me home that night, and figured out where I'd been if the big maple hadn't spread its branch just as wide as it did, or if the snake had hit my leg 'stead of my britches—when I took my bearings and saw where I was at, the thing that really hurt me worst was that if I'd gone, either down or up, I hadn't done anything for Lily but give her a worse horror than she had, of being 'got' by them Orphings' Home people, when I should have made her *safe forever*. I took Peter to the barn and told him just how it was, 'cause I felt mighty queer. I wasn't so sure that one scratch on my leg that looked ugly mightn't a-been the snake striking through the cloth and dosing me some, I was so sick and swelled up; it turned out to be yellow jackets, but it might a-been snakes, and I was a little upset. As man to man I asked him what I ought to do for my *family* 'fore I took any more *risks*. A-body would have thought the jolt the box gave me would have been enough, but it wasn't! It took the snake and the quicksand to just right real wake me up. First I was some sore on Junior; but pretty quick I saw how funny it was, so I got over it——"

"He should have had his neck broken!"

"Wope! Wope! Back up!" cautioned Mickey. "Nothing of the kind! You ain't figuring on the starving, the beating, being knocked senseless, robbed of all his clothes *twice*, and landing in the morgue with the cleaning-house victims. Gee, Junior had reasons for his grouch!"

Douglas Bruce suddenly began to laugh wildly.

"Umhum! That's what I told you," said Mickey. "Well, that night I laid the case before Peter, out on the hay wagon in the barnyard, so moon white you could have read the *Herald*, the cattle grunting satisfied all around us, katydids insisting on it emphatic, crickets chirping, and the old rooster calling off the night watches same as he did for that first Peter, who denied his Lord. I thought about that, as I sat and watched the big fellow slowly whittling the rack, and once in a while putting in a question, and when I'd told him all there was to tell, he said this: he said *sure* Lily was *mine*, and I had a perfect *right* to *keep* her; but the law *might* butt in, 'cause there *was* a law we couldn't evade that *could* step in and take her any day. He said too, that if she had to go to the hospital, sudden, first question a surgeon would ask was who were her parents, and if she had none, who in their place could give him a right to operate. He said while she was *mine*, and it was my *right*, and *my job*, the law and the surgeon would say *no*, 'cause we were not related, and I was not of age. He said there were times when the law got its paddle in, and went to fooling with red tape, it let a sick person lay and die while it decided what to do. He said he'd known a few just exactly such cases; so to keep the law from making a fool of itself, as it often did, we'd better step in and fix things to suit us before it ever got a showdown."

"What did he do?" asked Douglas Bruce eagerly.

"Well, after we'd talked it over we moved up to the back porch and Peter explained to Ma, who is the boss of that family, only she doesn't *know* it, and she said for him to do exactly what his conscience and his God dictated. That's where his namesake put it over that first Peter. Our Peter said: 'Well if God is to dictate my course, you remember what He said about "suffering the little children to come to Him," and we are commanded to be like Him, so there's no way to *twist* it, but that it means *suffer them to come to us*,' he said.

"Ma she spoke quick and said: 'Well we've got them!'

"Peter said, 'Yes, we've got them; now the question is whether we *keep* them, or send them to an Orphings' Home.'

"The nice lady she said faster than I can tell you: 'Peter Harding, I'm ashamed of you! There's no question of that kind! There's never going to be!'

"'Well don't get het up about it,' said Peter. 'I knew all the time there *wasn't*, I just *wanted to hear you say so plain and emphatic*. So far as I'm concerned, my way is clear as noonday sun,' said Peter. 'Then you go first thing in the morning and adopt them, and adopt them *both*,' said Ma. 'Lily will make Mary just as good a sister as she could ever have,' said she, and then she reached over and put her arms right around me and she said, 'And if you think I'm going to keep on trying to run this house without Mickey, you're mistaken.'

I began to cry, 'cause I had had a big day, and I was shaking on my feet anyway. Then Peter said, 'Have you figured it out to the end? Is it to be 'til they are of age, or forever?' She just gripped tighter and said fast as words can come, 'I say make it forever, and share and share alike. I'm willing if you are.' Peter, he said, 'I'm willing. They'll pay their way any place. Forever, and share and share alike, is my idea. Do you agree, Mickey?' 'Exactly what do you mean?' I asked, and Peter told me it was making me and Lily both his, just as far as the law could do it; we could go all the farther we wanted to ourselves. He said it meant him getting the same for me and Lily as he did for his own, and leaving us the same when he died. I told him he *needn't do that*, if he'd just keep off the old Orphings' Home devil, that's had me scared stiff all my days, I'd tend to *that*, so now me and Lily belong to Peter; he's our *Pertectorate*."

"Mickey, why didn't you tell me?" asked Douglas. "Why didn't you want me to adopt you?"

"Well so far as 'adopting' is concerned," said Mickey, "I ain't *crazy* about it, with anybody. But that's the *law* you men have made; a boy must obey it, even if he'd rather be skinned alive, and when he *knows* it ain't *right or fair*. That's the law. I was up against it, and I didn't know but I *did* have the snake, and Peter was on hand and made that offer, and he was grand and big about it. I don't love him any more than I do you; but I've just this minute discovered that it ain't in my skin to love any man more than I do Peter; so you'll have to get used to the fact that I love him just as well, and say, Mr. Bruce, Peter is the finest man you ever knew. If you'll come out and get acquainted, you'll just be tickled to have him in the Golf Club, and to come to his house, and to have him at yours. His nice lady is exactly like Miss Winton, only older. Say, she and Peter will adopt you too, if you say so, and between us, just as man to man, Peter is a regular lifesaver! If you got a chance you better catch on! No telling what you might want of him!"

"Mickey, you do say the most poignant things!" cried Douglas. "I'd give all I'm worth to catch on to Peter right now, and cling for much *more* than life; but what I started, I must finish, and Peter isn't here."

"Well what's the matter with me?" asked Mickey. "Have you run into the yellow jackets too? 'Cause if you have, I'm ahead of you, so I know what to do. Just catch on to me!"

"Think you are big enough to serve as a straw for a drowning man, Mickey?" inquired Douglas.

"Sure! I'm big enough to establish a *Pertectorate* over you, this minute. The weight of my body hasn't anything to do with the size of my heart, or how fast I can work my brains and feet, if I must."

"Mickey," said Douglas despairingly, "it's my candid opinion that no one can save me, right now."

Mickey opened his lips, and showed that his brain *was* working by shutting them abruptly on something that seemed very much as if it had started to be: "Sure!"

"Is that so?" he substituted.

"Yes, I'm in the sweat box," admitted Douglas.

"And it's uncomfortable and weakening. What's the first thing we must do to get you out?"

"What I'm facing now is the prospect that there's no way for me to get out, or for my friends to get me out," admitted Douglas. "I wish I *had* been plowing corn Mickey."

The boy's eyes were gleaming. He was stepping from one foot to the other as if the floor burned him.

"Gosh, we must saw wood!" he cried. "You go on and tell me. I been up against a lot of things. Maybe I can think up something. Honest, maybe I can!"

"No Mickey, there's nothing you or any one can do. A miracle is required now, and miracles have ceased."

"Oh I don't know!" exclaimed Mickey. "Look how they been happening to me and Lily right along. I can't see why one mightn't be performed for you just as well. I wish you wouldn't waste so much time! I wish you hadn't spent an hour fooling with what I was telling you; *that* would keep. I wish you'd give me a job, and let me get busy."

Douglas Bruce looked at the valiant figure and smiled forlornly.

"I'd gladly give you the job of saving me, my dear friend," he said, "but the fact is I haven't a notion of how to go to work to achieve salvation."

"Is somebody else getting ahead of you?"

"Not that I know of! No I don't think so. That isn't the trouble," said Douglas.

"I do wish you'd just plain tell me," said Mickey. "Now that I got the *Pertectorate* all safe over Lily, I'd do anything for you. Maybe I could think up some scheme. I'm an awful schemer! I wish you'd *trust*me! You needn't think I'd *blab!* Come on now!"

Suddenly Douglas Bruce's long arms stretched across the table before him, his head fell on them, and shuddering sobs shook him. Mickey's dance steps became six inches high, while in desperation he began polishing the table with his cap. Then he reached a wiry hand and commenced rubbing Douglas up and down the spine. The tears were rolling down his cheeks, but his voice was even and clear.

"Aw come on now!" he begged. "Cut that out! That won't help none! What shall I *do?* Shall I call Mr. Minturn? Shall I get Miss Leslie on the wire?"

Bruce considered the propositions. Then he arose and began walking the floor.

"Yes," he said. "Yes! 'Bearer of Morning,' call her!"

Mickey ran to the telephone. In a minute, "Here she is," he announced. "Shall I go?"

"No! Stay right where you are."

"Hello Leslie! Are you all right? I'm sorry to say I am not. I'm up against a proposition I don't know how to handle. Why just this: remember your father told me in your presence that if in the course of my investigations I reached his office, I was to wait until he got back? Yes. I thought you'd remember. You know the order of the court gave me access to the records, but the officials whose books I have gone over haven't been pleased about it, although reflection would have told them if it hadn't been I, it would have been some other man. But the point is this: I'm almost at the finish and I haven't found what obviously exists somewhere. I'm now up to the last office, which is your father's. The shortage either has to be there, or in other departments outside those I was delegated to search; so that further pursuit will be necessary. Two or three times officials have suggested to me that I go over your father's records first, as an evidence that there was no favouritism; now I have reached them, and this proposition: if I go ahead in his, as I have in other offices, I disobey his express order. If I do not, the gang will set up a howl in to-morrow morning's paper, and they will start an investigation of their own. Did you get anything from him this morning Leslie? Not for four days? And he's a week past the time he thought he would be back? I see! Leslie, what shall I do? In my morning's mail there is a letter from the men whose records I have been over, giving me this ultimatum: 'begin on Winton's office immediately, or we will.'

"Tell them to go ahead? But Leslie! Yes I know, but Leslie—Yes! You are ordering me to tell them that I propose to conduct the search in his department as I did theirs, and if they will not await his return from this business trip, they are perfectly free to go ahead—You are *sure* that is the thing you want said? But Leslie—Yes, I know, but Leslie it is *disobeying* him, and it's barely possible there might be a traitor there; better men than he have been betrayed by their employees. I admit I'm all in. I wish you would come and bring your last letter from him. We'll see if we can't locate him by wire. It's an ugly situation. Of course I didn't think it would come to this. Yes I wish you would! If you say so, I will, but—All right then. Come at once! Good-bye!"

Douglas turned to his desk, wrote a few hasty lines and said to Mickey: "Deliver that to Muller at the City Hall."

Mickey took the envelope and went racing. In half the time he would have used in going to the City Hall he was in the *Herald* Building, making straight for the office of the editor. Mr. Chaffner was standing with a group of men earnestly discussing some matter, when his eye was attracted by Mickey, directly in range, and with the tip of his index finger he was cutting in air letters plainly to be followed: "S.O.S." Chaffner nodded slightly, and continued his talk. A second later he excused himself, and Mickey followed to the private room.

"Well?" he shot at the boy.

"Our subm'rine has sunk our own cotton."

"Humph!" said Chaffner. "I've known for two weeks it was heading your way. Just what happened?"

Mickey explained and produced the letter. Chaffner reached for it. Mickey drew back.

"Why I wouldn't dare do just that," he said. "But I know that's what's in it, because I heard what he said, and by it you could tell what she said. I've told you every word, and you said the other day you knew; please tell me if I should deliver this letter?"

"If you want to give me a special with the biggest scoop of ten years," said Chaffner, "and ruin Douglas Bruce and disgrace the Wintons, take it right along."

"Aw gee!" wailed Mickey, growing ghastly. "Aw gee, Mr. Chaffner! Why you *can't* do that! Not to *them!* Why they're the *nicest folks;* and 'tain't two weeks ago I heard Miss Leslie say to Mr. Bruce right in our office, 'losing money I could stand, disgrace would *kill* me.' You can't kill her, Mr. Chaffner! Why she's the nicest, and the prettiest——She found me, and sent me to the boss, like I told you. Honest she did! Why you can't! You just *can't!* Why Mr. Chaffner, I can see by your nice eyes you can't! Aw gee, come on now!"

Mickey's chin hooked over the editor's elbow, his small head was against his arm, his eyes were dripping tears, but his voice controlled and steady was entreating.

The editor of a big city daily does not give up a scoop like that without a struggle. Mr. Chaffner had his. The boy clung to him and implored.

"You know there's a screw loose somewhere," explained Mickey. "You know 'darling old Daddy' couldn't ever have done it; and if somebody under him has gone wrong, maybe he could make it up, if he was here and had an hour or so. That day, Miss Leslie said he should give all he had for his friend, and he could have all of hers. If she'd be willing for the money to go for her 'dear old Daddy's' *friend*, course she'd be glad to use it for her Daddy, and she's got a lot from her mother, and maybe Daddy has sold the land he went to sell, and all of that ought to be enough; and if it isn't, I know who will help them. Honest I do!"

"Who, Mickey?" demanded Mr. Chaffner, instantly.

"Mr. Minturn! Mr. James Minturn!" said Mickey. "He's Mr. Bruce's best friend, and he *told* me he would do *anything* for Miss Leslie, that day right after I saw you, for if his home ever came right again, it would be 'cause she made it; and she *did* make it, and it is *right*, and he's so crazy happy he can't hardly keep on the floor. *Course* he'd pay Miss Leslie back. He *said* he would. He's the nicest man!"

"Isn't your world rather full of nice men, Mickey?"

Mickey renewed his grip. His eyes were pleading, the white light on his brow was shining, his voice was irresistibly sweet: "You just bet my world is full of nice men, packed like sardines; but they'll all scrooge up a little and make room for you on the top layer among the selects! Come on now! Rustle for your place before we revolve and leave you. All your life you'll be sorry if you make that scoop, and kill Miss Leslie, and shame 'darling old Daddy,' and ruin my boss. Oh I say Mr. Chaffner, you *can't!* You can't ever sleep nights again, if you do! They haven't ever done anything to you. You'll be the *nicest*man of all, if you'll *tell me what to do*. 'Twon't take you but a second, 'cause you *know*. Oh tell me, for the love of God tell me, Mr. Chaffner! *You'll be the nicest man I know, if you'll tell me*."

The editor looked down in Mickey's compelling eyes. He laid his hand on the lad's brow and said: "That would be worth the price of any scoop I ever pulled off, Mickey. Are you going to be a lawyer or write that poetry for me?"

"If I'd ever even thought of law, *this* would cook me," said Mickey. "Poetry it is, as soon as I earn enough to pay for finding out how to do it right."

"And when you find out, will you come on my staff, and work directly under me?" asked Mr. Chaffner.

"Sure!" promised Mickey. "I'd rather do it than anything else in the world. It would suit me fine. That is, if you're coming in among my nice men—"

Mr. Chaffner held out his hand. "This is going to cost me something in prestige and in cash," he said, "but Mickey, you make it *worthwhile*. Here are your instructions: *don't* deliver that letter! Cut for Minturn and give it to him. Tell him if he wants me, to call any time inside an hour, and that he hasn't longer than noon to make good. He'll understand. If you can't beat a taxi on foot, take one. Have you money?"

"Yes," said Mickey, "but just suppose he isn't there and I can't find him?"

"Then find his wife, and tell her to call me."

"All right! Thanks, boss! You're simply great!"

Mickey took the taxi and convinced the driver he was in a hurry. He danced in the elevator, ran down the hall, and into Mr. Minturn's door. There he stopped abruptly, for he faced Miss Winton and Mrs. Minturn, whose paling face told Mickey that he was stamped on her memory as she was on his. He pulled off his cap, and spoke to Mr. Minturn.

"Could I see you a minute?" he asked.

"Certainly! Step this way. Excuse us ladies."

Mickey showed the letter, told what had caused it to be written, and that he had gone to Mr. Chaffner instead of delivering it, and what instructions had been given him there. Mr. Minturn picked up the telephone and called Mr. Chaffner. When he got him he merely said: "This is Minturn. What's the amount, and where does he bank his funds? Thank you very much indeed."

Then he looked at Mickey. "Till noon did you say?"

"Yes," cried Mickey breathlessly, "and 'tisn't so long!"

"No," said Mr. Minturn, "it isn't. Ask Mrs. Minturn if I may speak with her a moment."

"Shall I come back or stay there?" inquired Mickey.

"Come back," said Mr. Minturn. "I may need you."

Mickey stood before Mrs. Minturn.

"Please will you speak with Mr. Minturn a minute?"

"Excuse me Leslie," said the lady, rising, and entering the private room. There she turned to Mickey. "I remember you very well," she said, with a steady voice. "You needn't shrink from me. I've done all in my power to atone. It will never be possible for me to think of forgiving myself; but you'll forgive me, won't you?"

"Sure! Why lady, I'm awful sorry for you."

"I'm sorry for myself," said she. "What was it you wanted, Mr. Minturn?"

"Suppose you tell Mrs. Minturn about both your visits here," suggested Mr. Minturn to Mickey.

"Sure!" said Mickey. "You see it was like this lady. This morning Mr. Bruce's head is down, and if he doesn't get help before noon, he and Miss Leslie and all those nice people are in trouble. I thought Mr. Minturn ought to know, so I slipped in and told him."

"What is the trouble, lad?" asked Mrs. Minturn.

"Why you see Miss Leslie's 'darling old Daddy' is one of the city officials, and of course Mr. Bruce left him 'til last, because he would a-staked his life he'd find the man he was hunting before he got to his office, and he *didn't!*"

"What, James?" said the lady, turning hurriedly.

"Tell her about it, Mickey," said Mr. Minturn calmly.

"Well there ain't much to tell," said Mickey. "My boss he just kept stacking up figures; two or three times he thought he had his man and then he'd strike a balance; and the men whose records he searched kept getting madder, and Mr. Winton went west to sell some land. Someway he's been gone a week longer than he expected; and my boss is all through except him, and now the other men say if he doesn't begin on Mr. Winton's books right away, *they* will, and he told my boss *not to 'til he got back*. A while ago I was in the *Herald* office talking to Mr. Chaffner, whose papers I've sold since I started and I was telling him what nice friends I had, and how Mr. Bruce and Miss Leslie were engaged, and he like to ate me up. When I couldn't see why, he told me about investigations he had his men, like I'm going to be, make, and sometimes they get a 'scoop' on the men appointed to do the job, and he told me he had a 'scoop' on this, and if I saw trouble coming toward my boss, I was to tell him and maybe—he didn't say sure, but *maybe* he'd do something."

"Oh James!" cried Mrs. Minturn.

"Wait dear! Go on Mickey," said Mr. Minturn.

"Well," said Mickey, "the elevated jumped the track this morning when my boss got a letter saying if he didn't go on at once with Mr. Winton's office, somebody else would; and the people who have been in the air ever since are due to land at noon, and it's pretty quick now, and they are too nice for any use. Did you ever know finer people?"

"No I never did," said Mrs. Minturn; "but James, I don't understand. Tell me quickly and plainly."

"Chaffner just gave me the figures," he said, holding over a slip of paper. "If that amount is to Mr. Winton's credit on his account with the city, at the Universal Bank before noon—nothing at all. If it's *not*, disgrace for them, and I started it by putting Bruce on the case. I'll raise as much as I can, but I can't secure enough by that time without men knowing it. Mr. Winton has undoubtedly gone to try to secure what he needs; but he's going to be too late. There never has been a worse time to raise money in the history of this country."

"But if *money* is the trouble," said Mrs. Minturn, "you said you never would touch what I put in your name for yourself, why not use it for him? If that isn't enough, I will gladly furnish the remainder. That I'm not a stranded, forsaken woman is due to Leslie Winton; all I have wouldn't be big enough price to pay for you, and my boys, and my precious home. Be quick James!"

Mr. Minturn was calling the Universal Bank.

Mickey and Mrs. Minturn waited anxiously. They involuntarily drew together, and the woman held the boy in a close grip, while her face alternately paled and flushed, and both of them were breathing short.

"I want the cashier!" Mr. Minturn was saying.

"Don't his voice just make you feel like you were on the rock of ages?" whispered Mickey.

Mrs. Minturn smiling nodded.

"Hello, Mr. Freeland. This is Minturn talking—James Minturn. You will remember some securities I deposited with you not long ago? I wish to use a part of them to pay a debt I owe Mr. Winton. Kindly credit his account with—oh, he's there in the bank? Well never mind then. I didn't know he was back yet. Let it go! I'll see him in person. And you might tell him that his daughter is at my office. Yes, thank you. No you needn't say anything about that to him; we'll arrange it ourselves. Good-bye!"

"Now where am I at?" demanded Mickey.

"I don't think you know, Mickey," said Mr. Minturn, "and I am sure I don't, but I have a strong suspicion that Mr. Winton will be here in a few minutes, and if his mission has been successful, his face will tell it; and if he's in trouble, that will show; and then we will know what to do. Mr. Bruce would like to know he is here, and at the bank I think."

"I'll go tell him right away," said Mickey.

Douglas was walking the floor as Mickey entered.

"You delivered the letter?" he cried.

Mickey slowly shook his head and produced it.

"You didn't!" shouted Bruce. "You didn't! Thank God! Oh, thank God you *didn't!*"

"Aw-w-ah!" protested Mickey.

"Why didn't you?" demanded Douglas.

"Well you see," said Mickey, "me and Mr. Chaffner of the *Herald* were talking a while ago about some poetry I'm going to write for his first page, soon now—I've always sold his papers you know, so I sort of belong—and I happened to tell him I was working for you, and how fine you were, and about your being engaged to Miss Leslie, and he seemed to kind of think you was heading for trouble; he just plain *said so*. I was so scared I begged him not to let *that* happen. I told him how everything was, and finally I got him to promise that if you *did* get into trouble he'd help you, at least he *almost* promised. You see he's been a newspaper man so long, he eats it, and sleeps it, and he had a s'scoop'—"

"'He had a scoop?'" repeated Douglas.

"Yes! A great one! Biggest one in ten years!" said the boy. "He loved it so, that me trying to pry him loose from it was about like working to move the Iriquois Building with a handspike. All he'd promise that first trip was that if I'd come and tell him when I saw you'd got into trouble, he'd *see* what he could do."

"Wanted to pump you for material for his scoop, I suppose?" commented Douglas.

"Wope! Wope! Back up!" warned Mickey. "He didn't pump me a little bit, and he didn't *try* to. He told me nearly three weeks ago just what *would* happen about now, as he had things doped out, and they have. I didn't *think* that letter should be delivered this morning, 'cause you had no business in 'darling old Daddy's' office if he said 'stay out.'" In came Mickey's best flourish. "*Why he mightn't a-been ready!*" he exclaimed. "He had his friend to help you remember, I heard Miss Leslie tell you he did. And she told him to. She told you he could have what she had, you remember of course. He might a-had to use some of his office money real quick, to save a friend that he *had* to save if it took all he had and all Miss Leslie had; and *that* was right. I asked you the other day if a man might use the money he handled, and you said yes, he was *expected* to, if he had his books straight and the money in the bank when his time for accounting came. 'Tain't time to account yet; but you was doing this investigating among his bunch, and so I guess if he did use the money for his friend, he had to go on that trip he was too busy to take Miss Leslie, and sell something, or do something to get ready for you. *That's* all right, ain't it?"

"Yes, if he could *do* it," conceded Douglas.

"Well he can!" triumphed Mickey. "He can just as easy, 'cause he's down at the Universal Bank doing it right now!"

"What?" cried Douglas.

"Sure!" said Mickey. "Back on time! At the bank fixing things so you can investigate all you want to. What's the matter with 'darling old Daddy?' *He's all right!* Go on and write your letter over, and tell them anxious, irritated gents, that you'll investigate 'til the basement and cupola are finished, just as soon as you make out the reports you are figuring up *now*. That will give you time to act independent, and it will give Daddy time to be ready for you—"

"Mickey, what if he didn't get the land sold?" wavered Douglas. "What if his trip was a failure?"

"Well that's fixed," said Mickey, stepping from one toe to the other. "Don't ruffle your down about that. If 'darling old Daddy' has bad luck, and for staking his money and his honour on his friend, he's going to get picked clean and dished up himself, why it's fixed so he *isn't!* See?"

"*It's fixed?*" marvelled Douglas.

"Surest thing you know!" cried Mickey. "You've had your *Pertectorate* all safe a long time, and didn't know it."

"Mickey, talk fast! Tell me! What do you mean?"

"Why that was fixed three weeks ago, I tell you," explained Mickey. "When Mr. Chaffner said you would strike trouble, I wasn't surprised any, 'cause I've thought all the time you *would;* and when you did, I went skinning to him, and he told me *not* to deliver that letter; and he was grand, just something grand! He told me what had to happen to save you, so I kept the letter, and scuttled for Mr. James Minturn, who started all this, and I just said to him, 'Chickens, home to roost,' or words like that; and he got on the wire with Chaffner, and 'stead of giving that 'scoop' to all Multiopolis and the whole world, he give Mr. Minturn a few figures on a scrap of paper that he showed to his nice lady—gosh you wouldn't ever believe she *was* a nice lady or could be, but honest, Mr. Bruce, me and her has been holding hands for half an hour while we planned to help you out, and say, she's so nice, she's just peachy—and she's the *same* woman. I don't know how that happens, but she's the same woman who fired me and the nice lady from Plymouth, and now she *ain't* the same, and these are the words she said: 'All I have on earth would not be enough to pay Leslie Winton for giving you back to me, and my boys, and my precious home.' 'Precious home!' Do you get that? After her marble palace, where she is now must look like a cottage on the green to her, but 'precious home' is what she said, and she ought to know—"

"Mickey go on! You were saying that Mr. Chaffner gave Mr. Minturn some figures—" prompted Douglas.

"Yes," said Mickey. "His precious 'scoop,' so Mr. Minturn showed her, and she said just as quick to put that amount to Mr. Winton's credit at the Universal Bank, so he called the bank to tell them; when he got the cashier he found that 'darling old Daddy' was there that minute—"

"'Was there?'" cried Douglas.

"'*Was there,*'" repeated Mickey; "so Mr. Minturn backed water, and *then* he told the cashier he needn't mention to Mr. Winton that he was going to turn over some securities he had there to pay a debt he owed him, 'cause now that he was home, they could fix it up between themselves. But he told the cashier to tell Mr. Winton that Miss Leslie was in his office. He said 'Daddy' would come to her the minute he could, and then if he was happy and all right, it meant that he had sold his land and made good; and if he was broke up, we would know what to do about putting the money to his credit. The nice lady said to put a lot more than he needed, so if they did investigate they could see he had plenty. See? Mr. Minturn said we could tell the minute we saw him—"

"Well young man, can you?" inquired a voice behind them.

With the same impulse Douglas and Mickey turned to Mr. Winton and Leslie standing far enough inside the door to have heard all that had been said. A slow red crept over Mickey's fair face. Douglas sprang to his feet, his hand outstretched, words of welcome on his lips. Mr. Winton put him aside with a gesture.

"I asked this youngster a question," he said, "and I'm deeply interested in the answer. *Can you?*"

Mickey stepped forward, taking one long, straight look into the face of the man before him; then his exultant laugh trilled as the notes of Peter's old bobolink bird on the meadow fence.

"Surest thing you know!" he cried in ringing joy. "You're tired, you need washing, sleep, and a long rest, but there isn't any glisteny, green look on your face. It's been with you, like I told Mr. Chaffner it's in the Bible; only with you, it's been even more than a man 'laying down his life for his friend,' it was a near squeak, but you made it! Gee, you made it! I should say I *could* tell!"

Mr. Winton caught Mickey, lifting him from his feet. "God made a jewel after my heart when he made you lad," he said. "If you haven't got a father, I'm a candidate for the place."

"Gee, you're the nicest man!" said Mickey. "If I was out with a telescope searching for a father, I'd make a home run for you; but you see I'm fairly well fixed. Here's my boss, too fine to talk about, that I work for to earn money to keep me and my family; there's Peter, better than gold, who's annexed both me and my child; there's Mr. Chaffner punching me up every time I see him about my job for him, soon as I finish school; I'd *like* you for a father, only I'm crazy about Peter. Just you come and see *Peter*, and you'll understand—"

"I'll be there soon," said Mr. Winton. "I have reasons for wanting to know him thoroughly. And by the way, how do you do, Douglas? How is the great investigation coming on? 'Fine!' I'm glad to hear it. Push it with all your might, and finish up so we can have a month on Atwater without coming back and forth. I feel as if I'd need about that much swimming to make me clean, as the young man here suggests; travelling over the west in midsummer is neither cool nor cleanly; but it's great, when things sell as ours did. Land seems to be moving, and there's money under the surface; nobody has lost so much, they are only economizing; we must do that ourselves, but Swain and I are both safe, so we shall enjoy a few years of work to recoup some pretty heavy losses; we're not worth what we were, but we are even, with a home base, the love of God big in our hearts, and doubly all right, since if we couldn't have righted ourselves, our friends would have saved us, thanks to this little live wire on my left!"

"Oh Daddy, if you'd searched forever, you couldn't have found a better name for Mickey!" cried Leslie. "Come on Douglas let's go home and rest."

"Just as soon as I write and start Mickey with a note," said Douglas. "Go ahead, I'll be down soon."

He turned to his desk, wrote a few lines, and sealing them, handed the envelope to the waiting boy.

"City Hall," he said. "And Mickey, I see the whole thing. It will take some time to figure just what I do owe you—"

"Aw-a-ah g'wan!" broke in Mickey, backing away.

"Mickey, we'll drive you to take the note, and then you come with us," said Douglas.

"Thanks, but it would try my nerve," said Mickey, "and I must help Peter move in the pump!"

CHAPTER XX

Mickey's Miracle

That night Mickey's voice, shrill in exuberant rejoicing, preceded him down the highway, so the Hardings, all busy working out their new plans for comfort, understood that something unusually joyous had happened. Peaches sat straighter in her big pillow-piled chair, leaned forward, and smilingly waited.

"Ain't he happy soundin'?" she said to Mrs. Harding, who sat near her sewing. "I guess he has thought out the best po'try piece yet. Mebby this time it will be good enough for the first page of the *Herald*."

"Young as he is, that's not likely," said the literal woman. "There's no manner of doubt in my mind but that he *can* do great newspaper work when he finishes his education and makes his start; but I think Mr. Bruce will use all his influence to turn him toward law."

"Mr. Douglas Bruce is a swell gentl'man," said Peaches, "and me and Mickey just loves him for his niceness to us; but we got *that* all settled. Mickey is going to write the po'try piece for the first page of the *Herald*—that's our paper—and then we are going to make all my pieces into a bu'ful book, like I got it started here."

Peaches picked up a small notebook, scrupulously kept, and lovingly glanced over the pages, on each of which she had induced Mickey to write in his plainest script one section of her nightly doggerel; and if he failed from the intense affairs of the day, she left a blank page for him to fill later. Taken together, the remainder of her possessions were as nothing to Peaches compared with that book. Not an hour of the day passed that it was not in her fingers, every line of it she knew by heart, and she learned more from it than all Mickey's other educational efforts. Peter scraped a piece of fine black walnut furniture free from the accumulated varnish of years, and ran an approving hand over the smooth dark surface, seasoned with long use. He smiled at her. She smiled back, falling into a little chant that had been on her lips much of the time of late: "You know, Peter! You know, Peter! We know somepin' we won't tell!"

Peter nodded, beaming on her.

"Just listen to that boy, Peter, he must be perfectly possessed!" said Nancy.

"He didn't ever sound so glad before!" cried the child eagerly.

Mickey came up the walk radiant. He divided a smile between Mrs. Harding and Peter, and bowed low before Peaches as he laid a package at her feet. Then he struck an attitude of exaggerated obeisance and recited:

"Days like this I'm tickled silly,
When I see my August Lily.
No other fellow, dude or gawk,
Owns a flower that can laugh and talk."

Peaches immediately laughed; so did all of them.

"Peter," asked Mickey, "were you ever so glad that you thought you would bust wide open?"

"I was," said Peter; "I am this minute."

"Would you mind specifying circumstances?"

"Not a bit," said Peter. "First time was when Ma said she'd marry me, and I got my betrothal kiss; second, was the day she said she'd forgive my years of selfish dunderheadedness, and start over. Now you, Mickey, what's yours?"

"The great investigation is over, so far as our commission goes," answered Mickey. "Multiopolis isn't robbed where she was sure she was. Her accounts balance in the departments we've gone over. Nobody gets the slick face, the glass eye, the lawn mower on his cocoanut, or dons the candy suit from our work; but some folks I love had a near squeak, and I got a month vacation! Think of that, Miss Lily Peaches O'Halloran! Gee, let's get things fixed up here and have a party, to show the neighbouring gentlemen what's coming to them, before the weather gets so cold they won't have time to finish their jobs this fall. Some of them will squirm, but we don't care. Some of them will think they won't do it, but they *will*. Kiss me, Lily! Hug me tight, and let me go dig on the furnace foundation 'til I sweat this out of me."

When the children were sleeping that night he sat on the veranda and told Mrs. Harding and Peter exactly what he thought wise to repeat of the day's experience and no more; so that when he finished, all they knew was that the investigation was over, so far as Mr. Bruce was concerned, Mickey had a vacation, and was a happy boy.

As she came to dinner the next day, Mary laid a bundle of mail beside her father's plate. When he saw it, Peter, as was his custom, reached for the *Herald* to read the war headlines. He opened the paper, gave it a shake, stared at it in amazement, scanned a few lines and muttered: "Well for the Lord's sake!"

Then he glanced over the sheets at Mickey and back again. The family arose and hurried to a point of vantage at Peter's shoulder, while he spread the paper wide and held it high so that all of them could see. Enclosed in a small ruled space they read:

Sacred to the memory of the biggest scoop,
That ever fell in MisterChaffner's soup,
And was pitched by this nicest editor-man,
Where it belonged, in the garbage can,
To please his friend, Michael O'Halloran.
Whoop fellers, whoop, for the drownded scoop,
That departed this lifein our Editor's soup!
All together boys, Scoop! Soup! Whoop!

They rushed at Mickey, shook hands, thumped, patted and praised him, when a wail arose to the point of reaching his consciousness.

"Mickey, what?" cried Peaches.

"Let me take it just a minute, Peter," said Mickey, reaching for the sheet.

"Wait a second," suggested Mrs. Harding, picking up a big roll that they had knocked to the floor. "This doesn't look like catalogues, and it's addressed to you. Likely they've sent you some of your own."

"Now maybe Mr. Chaffner did," said Mickey, almost at the bursting point. "Course he is awful busy, the busiest man in the world, I expect, but he *might* have sent me a copy of my poetry, since he used it."

With shaking fingers he opened the roll, and there were several copies of the *Herald* similar to the one Peter held, and on the top of one was scrawled in pencil: "Your place, your desk, and your salary are ready whenever you want to begin work. You can't come too soon to suit me.—CHAFFNER."

Mickey read it aloud.

"Gee!" he said. "I 'most wish I had education enough to begin right now. I'd *like* it! I could just go *crazy* about that job! Yes honey! Yes, I'm coming!"

He caught up another paper, and hurried across the room, quietly but decidedly closing the door behind him, so when Mary started to follow, Junior interposed.

"Better not, Molly," he said. "Mickey wants to be alone with his family for a few minutes. Say father, ain't there a good many newspaper men worked all their lives, and got no such show as that?"

"I haven't a doubt of it," said Peter.

"Mickey must have written that, and sent it in before he came home yesterday," said Mrs. Harding. "I call it pretty bright! I bet if the truth was told, something went wrong, and he was at the bottom of shutting it up. Don't you call that pretty bright, Pa?"

"I guess I'm no fair judge," said Peter. "I'm that prejudiced in his favour that when he said, 'See the cat negotiate the rat' out in the barn, I thought it was smart."

"Yes, and it was," commented Junior. "It's been funny for everybody to 'negotiate' all sorts of things ever since that north pole business, so it was funny for the cat too. Father, do you think that note really means that Mr. Chaffner would give Mickey a place on his paper, and pay him right now?"

"I don't know why Chaffner would write it out and sign his name to it if he *didn't* mean it," said Peter.

"You know he is full of stuff like that," said Junior. "He could do some every day about people other than Peaches if he wanted to. Father, ain't you glad he's in our family? Are you going to tell him to take that job if he asks you?"

"No I ain't," said Peter. "He's too young, and not the book learning to do himself justice, while that place is too grown up and exciting for a boy of his nerve force. Don't you think, Nancy?"

"Yes, I do, but you needn't worry," said Mrs. Harding. "Mickey knows that himself. Didn't you hear him say soon as he read it, that he hadn't the education yet? He's taken care of himself too long to spoil his life now, and he will see it; but I marvel at Chaffner. He ought to have known better. And among us, I wonder at Mickey. Where did he get it from?"

"Easy!" said Peter. "From a God-fearing, intelligent mother, and an irresponsible Irish father, from inborn, ingrained sense of right, and a hand-to-hand scuffle with life in Multiopolis gutters. Mickey is all right, and thank God, he's *ours* If he does show signs of wanting to go to the *Herald* office, discourage him all you can, Ma; it wouldn't be good for him—yet."

"No it wouldn't; but it would be because he needs solid study and school routine to settle him, and make him *great* instead of a clown, as that would at his age. But if you think there is anything in the *Herald* office that could *hurt* Mickey, you got another think coming. It wouldn't hurt Mickey; but it would be mighty good for the rest of them. The *Herald* has more honour and conscience than most; some of the papers are just disgraceful in what they publish, and then take back next day; while folks are forced to endure it. Sit up and eat your dinners now. I want to get on with my work."

"Mickey, what happened?" begged Peaches as Mickey came in sight, carrying the papers.

He was trembling and tensely excited as her sharp eyes could see. They rested probingly a second on him, then on the paper. Her lips tightened while her eyes darkened. She stretched out her hand.

"Mickey, let me see!" she commanded.

Mickey knelt beside her, spreading out the sheet. Then he took her hand, setting a finger on the first letter of his name and slowly moved along as she repeated the letters she knew best of all, then softly pronounced the name. She knew the *Herald* too. She sat so straight Mickey was afraid she would strain her back, lifting her head "like a queen," if a queen lifts her head just as high as her neck can possibly stretch, and smiled a cold little smile of supreme self-satisfaction.

"Now Mickey, go on and read what you wrote about *me*," her Highness commanded.

The collapse of Mickey was sudden and complete. He stared at Peaches, at the paper, opened his lips, thought a lie and discarded it, shut his lips to pen the lie in for sure, and humbly and contritely waited, a silent candidate for mercy. Peaches had none. To her this was the logical outcome of what she had been led to expect. There was the paper. The paper was the *Herald*. There was the front page. There was Mickey's name. She had no conception of Mickey writing a line which did *not* concern her; also he had expressly stated that all of them and the whole book were to be about her. She indicated the paper and his name, while the condescension of her waiting began to be touched with impatience.

"Mickey, why don't you go on and read what it says about me?" she demanded.

Mickey saw plainly what must be done. He gazed at her and suddenly, for the first time, a wave of something new and undefined rushed through him. This exquisitely delicate and beautiful little Highness, sitting so proudly straight, and so uncompromisingly demanding that he redeem his promises, made a double appeal to Mickey. Her Highness scared him until he was cold inside. He was afraid, and he knew it. He wanted to run, and he knew it; yet no band of steel could have held him as this bit of white femininity, beginning to glow a soft pink from slowly enriching blood, now held and forever would hold him, and best of all he knew that. It was in his heart to be a gentleman; there was nothing left save to be one now. He took both Peaches' hands, and began preparing her gently as was in his power for what had to come.

"Yes, Flowersy-girl," he said, "I'll read it to you, but you won't understand 'til I tell you——"

"I always understand," she said sweepingly.

"You know how wild like I came home last night," explained Mickey. "Well, I had reason. Some folks who have been good to us, and that I love like we love Peter and Ma, had been in awful danger of something that would make them sore all their lives, and maybe I had some little part in putting it over, so it never touched them; anyway, they thought so, and I was tickled past all sense and reason about it. It was up to the editor of the *Herald* to decide; and what he did, was what I begged him to. Course left to himself, he would a-done it anyway, *after he had time to think*—"

"Mickey, read my po'try piece about me, an' then talk," urged Peaches.

"Honey, you make me so sick I can't tell you."

"Mickey, what's the matter?"

Peaches' penetrating eyes were slowly changing to accusing. She drew a deep breath, giving him his first cold, unrelenting look.

"Mister Michael O'Halloran," she said in incisive tones, "did you write a po'try piece for the first page of the *Herald, not* about me?"

"Well Miss Chicken," he cried, "I wish you wouldn't talk so much! I wish you'd let me *tell* you."

"I guess you ain't got anything to tell," said Peaches, folding her arms and tilting her chin so high Mickey feared she might topple backward.

"I guess I have!" shouted Mickey. "*I* didn't put that there! I didn't *mean* it to *be* there! If I'd a-put it there, and *meant* it there, and knowed it would *be* there, it would a-been about you, of course! Answer me this, Miss. Any single time did I ever *not* do anything that I said I would?"

"Nothing but this," admitted Peaches.

"There you go again!" said Mickey. "I tell you I *didn't* do *this*, and when I tell you, I tell true, Miss, get that in your system. If you'd let me explain how it was, you'd see that I didn't have a single thing to do with it."

Peaches accomplished a shrug that was wonderful, and gazed at the ceiling, her lips closed. Mickey watched her a second, then he began softly: "Flowersy-girl, I don't see what you mean! I don't know why you act like this! I don't know what's to have a tantrum for, when I didn't *mean* it to be there, and didn't *know* it would be there. Honest, I don't!"

"Go on an' read it!" she commanded.

Mickey obeyed. As he finished she faced him in wonder.

"Why they ain't a damn bit of sense to it!" she cried.

"*Course* there ain't!" agreed Mickey. "Course there *would be* no sense to anything that wasn't about *you!*"

"Then what did you put it there in my place for?"

"I *didn't*! I'm trying to tell you!" persisted Mickey.

Peaches shed one degree of royal hauteur.

"Well why don't you go on an' tell, then?" she ques tioned.

"Aw-w-ah! Well if you don't maneuver to beat a monoplane! I've tried to tell you, and you won't *let* me. If you stop me again, I'm going to march out of this room and stay 'til you bawl your eyes red for me."

"If you go, I'll call Junior!" said Peaches instantly.

"Well go on and call him!"

He turned, his heart throbbing, his eyes burning with repressed tears, the big gulp in his throat audible to Peaches, as her little wail was to him. He whirled and dropping on his knees took her in his arms. She threw hers around his neck, buried her face against his cheek, and they cried it out together. At last she produced a bit of linen, and mopped Mickey's eyes and face, then her own. While still clinging to him she whispered: "Mickey, I'm jus' about *dead* to have it be the *Herald*, an' the *front page*, an' *you*, an' *not* about *me!*"

"Flowersy-girl, I'm just as sorry as you are," said Mickey. "It was this way: I was just crazy over things our editor-man did, that saved our dear boss and the lovely Moonshine Lady who gave you your Precious Child and her 'darling old Daddy' from such awful trouble it would just a-killed them; honest it would Lily! When our editor-man was so great and nice, and did what he didn't *want* to at all, I went sort of wild like, and when I was off for the day and got on the streets, everything pulled me his way. I was anxious just to see him again, and if I'd done what I wanted to, I'd a-gone in the *Herald* office and knelt down, and said: 'Thank you, oh thank you!' and kissed his feet, but of course I knew men didn't do like that, and it would have shamed him, but I had to do something or bust, and I went running for the office like flying, and my mind got whirling around, and that stuff began to come.

"I slipped in and back to his desk, like I may if I want to, and there he sat. He had a big white sheet just like this before it is printed, spread out, and a pencil in his fingers, and about a dozen of his best men were crowding 'round with what they had for the paper to-day. I've told you how they do it, often, and when I edged up some of the men saw me. They knew I had a pass to him, so they stepped back just as he said: 'Well boys, who's got some *big stuff* to fill the space of our departed scoop?' That 'departed' word means lost, gone, and it's what they say about people when they—they go for good. Then he looked up to see who would speak first, and noticed me. 'Oh there is the little villain who scooped our scoop, right now,' he said. 'Let's make him fill the space he's cut us out of.' I thought it was a joke, but I wasn't going to have all that bunch of the swellest smarties who work for him put it clear over me; I've kidded back with my paper men too long for that; so I stepped back and shot it at him, that what's printed there, and when I got to the end and invited the fellows to 'Whoop,' Lily, you could a-heard them a mile. I saw they was starting for me, so I just slung in a 'Thank you something awful, boss,' and ducked through and between, and cut for life; 'cause if they'd a-got me, I might a-been there yet. They are the *nicest* men on earth, but they get a little keyed up sometimes, and a kid like me couldn't keep even. Now that's all there is to it, Lily, honest, cross my heart! I *didn't* know they would put it there. I didn't know they thought it was *good* enough. I wouldn't a-let them for the life of them, if I'd *known* they was going to."

"You jus' said it once, Mickey?" inquired Peaches.

"Jus' once, Flowersy-girl, fast as I could rattle."

"It's twice as long as mine ever are," she said. "I don't see how they 'membered."

"Oh that!" cried Mickey. "Why honey, that's easy! Those fellows jump on to a thing like chained lightning, and they got a way of writing that is just a lot of little twists and curls, but one means a whole sentence—they call it 'shorthand'—and doing that way, they can set down talk as fast as anybody can speak, and there were a dozen of them there with pencils and paper in their fingers. That wasn't anything for them!"

"Mickey, are you going to learn to write that way?"

"Sure!" said Mickey. "Before I go to the *Herald* to take my desk, and my 'signment,' I've got to know, and you ought to know too; 'cause I always have to bring what I write to you first, to see if you like it."

"Yes, if the mean old things don't go an' steal my place again, when you don't know it," protested Peaches.

"Well, don't you fret about that," said Mickey. "They got away with me this time, but they won't ever again, 'cause I'll be on to their tricks. See? Now say you forgive me, and eat your dinner, 'cause it will be spoiled, and you must have a good rest, for there's going to be something lovely afterward. You ain't mad at me any more, Lily?"

"No, I ain't mad at you, but I'm just so—"

"Wope! wope!" cried Mickey softly applying the palm of his hand.

Peaches pulled away indignantly.

"—so—so—so *estremely mad* at those paper men! Mickey, I don't think I'll ever let you be a *Herald* man at all if they're going to leave me out like that!"

"What do you care about an old paper sold on the streets, and ground up for buckets, and used to start fires, anyway?" scoffed Mickey. "Why don't you sit up on the shelf in a nice pretty silk dress and be a book lady? I wouldn't be in the papers at all, if I were you."

"No, an' I won't, either!" cried Peaches instantly. "Take the old paper an' put what you please in it. I shall have all about *me* in the nice silky covered book on the shelf; so there, you needn't try to make me do anything else, 'cause I shan't ever!"

"Course you shan't!" agreed Mickey.

He went back to the dinner table to find the family finished and gone. He carried what had been left for him to the back porch, and eating hastily began helping to get things in place. As always he went to Mrs. Harding for orders. She was a little woman, so very like his mother in size, colouring, speech, and manner, that Mickey could almost forget she was not truly his, when every hour she made him feel her motherly kindness; so from early habit it was natural with him to seek her first, and do what he could to assist her before he attempted anything else. All the help Peter had from him came when he found no more to do for Mrs. Harding. As he washed the dishes while she sat sewing for the renovation of the house, he said to her: "When you dress Lily for this afternoon I wish you'd make her just as pretty as you can, and put her very nicest dress on her."

"Why Mickey, is some one coming?" she asked.

"I don't know," said Mickey, "but I have a hunch that my boss, and Miss Leslie, and her father may be out this afternoon. They have been talking about it a long time, but I kept making every excuse I could think up to keep them away."

But "Why, Mickey?" asked Mrs. Harding, looking at him intently. She paused in her sewing, running the needle slowly across the curtain material.

"Well, for a lot of reasons," said Mickey. "A fellow of my size doesn't often tackle a family, and when he does, if he's going to be square about it, he has got to do a lot of *thinking*. One thing was that it's hard for me to get Lily out my head like I first saw her. I guess I couldn't tell you so you'd get a fair idea of how dark, dirty, alone, and little, and miserable she was. Just with all my heart I was ashamed of her folks, and sick sorry for her; but I can't bear for anybody else to be! I didn't want any of them to see her 'til she was fed, and fatted up a lot, and trained 'til how nice she really is shows plain. It just hurt me to think of it."

"Um-m-uh!" agreed Mrs. Harding, differing emotions showing on her face. "I see, Mickey."

"Then," continued Mickey, "I'm sticking sore and mean on one point. I *did* find her! She *is* mine! I *am* going to keep her! Nobody in all this world takes her, nor God in Heaven!"

"Mickey, be careful what you say," she cautioned.

"I don't mean anything wicked," explained Mickey. "I'm just telling you that nobody on earth can have her, and I'd fight 'til I'd die with her, before even Heaven gets her. I don't mean anything ugly about it. I'm just telling you friendly like, how I *feel* about her."

"I see Mickey," said Mrs. Harding. "Go on!"

"Well, lots of reasons," said Mickey. "She wasn't used to folks, so they scared her. She was crazy with fear about the Orphings' Home getting her, while I wasn't any too sure myself. I flagged one Swell Dame, and like to got caught in a trap and lost her. Then my Sunshine Nurse helped me all I needed; so not knowing how much women were alike, I didn't care to go rushing in a lot on Lily just to find out. She was a little too precious to experiment with.

"That Home business has been a big, grinning, 'Get-you-any-minute devil,' peeping 'round the corner at me ever since mother went. I could dodge him for myself, but I couldn't take any *risks* for Lily. *These Orphings' Homes ain't no place for children*. 'Stead of the law building them, and penning the little souls starving for home and love in them, what it *should* do is to make people who pay the money to run them, take the children in their *own homes* and love and raise them *personal*. If every family in the world that has no children would take two, and them that has would take just one, all the Orphings' Homes would make good hospitals and schools; while the orphings would be fixed like Lily and I are. Course I know all folks ain't the same as you and Peter; but in the long run, children are *safer in homes* than they are in *squads*. 'Most any kind of a home beats no home at all. You can stake your liberty-birds on that."

"You surely can," agreed Mrs. Harding.

"You just bet," persisted Mickey. "When I didn't know what they would do, I didn't want them pestering 'round, maybe to ruin everything; and when I *did*, I didn't want them any more, 'cause then I saw their idea would be to take her themselves, and in one day they would a-made all I could do look like thirty cents. She was mine, and what she had with me was so much better than what she would a-had without me, or if the law got her, that I thought she was doing well enough. I see now she could a-had more; but I thought then it was all right!"

"Now Mickey, don't begin that," said Mrs. Harding. "What you did was to find her, and without a doubt, save her life; at least if you didn't, you landed her in a fairly decent home where all of us will help you do *what you think best for her;* and there's small question but we can beat any Orphans' Home yet in existence. And as for the condition in which I found her, it *was* growing warm in that room, but I'll face any court in the universe and swear I never saw a cleaner child, or one in better condition for what you had to begin on. The Almighty Himself couldn't have covered those awful bones with flesh and muscle, and smoothed the bed sores and scars from that little body; and gone much faster training her right, unless He was going back to miracles again. As far as miracles are concerned, I think from what you tell me, and what the child's condition proves, that you have performed the miracle yourself. To the day of my death I'll honour, respect, and love you, Mickey, for the way in which you've done it. I've yet to see a woman who could have done better, so I want you to know it."

"I don't know the right words to say to you and Peter." he said.

"Never mind that," said Mrs. Harding. "We owe you quite as much, and something we are equally as thankful for. It's an even break with us, Mickey, and no talk of obligations on either side. We prize Junior as he is just now, fully as much as you do anything you've gained."

Mickey polished the plates and studied Mrs. Harding. Then he spoke again: "There's one more obligation I'm just itching to owe you."

"Tell me about it, Mickey," she said.

"Well right in line with what we been talking of," said Mickey. "Just suppose a big car comes chuffing up here this afternoon, like I have a hunch it will, and all those nice folks so polite and beautifully dressed come to see us, I know you are busy, but I'll work afterward to pay back, if you and Peter will dust up a little—course I know the upset fix we are in; but just glorify a trifle, and lay off and *keep right on the job without a second of letting up*, 'til they are gone. See?"

"You mean you don't want to be left *alone* with them?"

"You get me!" cried Mickey. "You get me clearly. I don't want to be left alone with them, for them to put ideas in Lily's head about a nicer car than ours, and a bigger house, and finer dolls and dresses, and going to the city to stay with them on visits; or me going to live with Mr. Winton, to be the son he should have found for himself long ago. I guess I have Lily sized up about as close as the next one; and she has got all that is *good* for her, right now. She'd make the worst spoiled kid you ever saw if she had half a chance. What she needs to make a grand woman of her, like you and mother, is clean air, quiet, good food like she's got here, with bone as well as muscle in it; and just enough lessons and child play with children to keep her brains going as fast as her body, and no silly pampering to make her foolish and disagreeable. I know how little and sick she is, but she shan't use it for capital to spoil her whole life. See?"

"'Through a glass darkly,'" quoted Mrs. Harding laughing. "Oh Mickey, I didn't think it of you. You're deeper than the well."

"That's all right," said Mickey, his face flushing. "Often I hear you say 'let good enough alone.' My sentiments exact. Lily is fine, and so am I. Let us alone! If you and Peter will do me the 'cap-sheaf favour, as he would say, you'll dust up and *spunk* up, and the very first hint that comes—'cause it's coming—at the very first hint of how Miss Leslie would love to take care of the dear little darling awhile, smash down with the nix! *Smash like sixty!* Keep your eyes and ears open, and if you could, dearest lady, beat them to it: I'd be tickled silly if you manage *that*. If you could only tell them how careful she has to be handled, and taken care of, and how strangers and many around would be bad for her—"

"Mickey, the minute they see the shape things are in here, it will give them the chance they are after, so they will begin that very thing," she said.

"I know it," conceded Mickey. "That's why I'd put them off if I could, 'til we were fixed and quiet again. But at *that*, their chance isn't so grand. This isn't worrying Lily any. She saw all of it happen, she knows what's going on. What I want, dearest lady, is for you to get on the job, and spunk up to them, just like you did about Junior going away. I didn't think you'd get through with that, and I know Peter didn't; but you *did*, fine! Now if you and Peter would have a little private understanding and engineer this visit that I scent in the air, so that when you see they are going to offer pressing invitations to take Lily, and to take me, and put me at work that I wasn't born to do; if you'd only have a receiver out, and when your wires warn you what's coming down the line, first and beforehand, *calm* and *plain*, fix things so the nix wouldn't even be needed; do you get me, dearest Mother Harding, do you see?"

"That I do!" said Mrs. Harding rising abruptly. "I'll go and speak to Peter at once, then we'll shift these workmen back, and quiet them as much as we can. I'll slip on a fresh dress, and put some buttermilk in the well, and fix Peaches right away, if she's finished her nap—"

Mrs. Harding's voice trailed back telling what she would do as she hastened to Peter. Mickey, with anxious heart, helped all he could, washed, slipped on a fresh shirt, and watched the process of adjusting Peaches' hair ribbon.

"Now understand, I don't *know* they're coming," he said. "I just *think* they will."

Because he thought so, for an hour the Harding premises wore a noticeable air of expectation. All the family were clean and purposely keeping so; but the waiting was long, while work was piled high in any direction. Peaches started the return to normal conditions by calling for her slate, and beginning to copy her lesson. Mary with many promises not to scatter her scraps, sat beside the couch, cutting bright pictures from the papers. Mickey grew restless and began breaking up the remains of packing cases, while Junior went after the wheelbarrow. Mrs. Harding brought out her sewing, and Peter went back to scraping black walnut furniture. Mickey passed him on an errand to the kitchen and asked anxiously: "Did she tell you?"

"Yes," said Peter.

"Will you make it a plain case of 'nobody home! nobody home?'" questioned Mickey.

"I will!" said Peter emphatically.

Being busy, the big car ran to the gate before they saw it coming. Leslie Winton and Douglas Bruce came up the walk together, while Mr. Winton and Mrs. Minturn waited in the car, in accordance with a suggestion from Douglas that the little sick girl must not see too many strange people at once. Mickey went to meet them, and Peaches watching, half in fear and wholly in pride, saw Douglas Bruce shake his hand until she frowned lest it hurt, clap him on the back, and cry: "Oh but I'm proud of you! Say that was great!"

Leslie purposely dressed to emphasize her beauty, slipped an arm across his shoulders and drawing him to her kissed his brow.

"Our poet!" she said. "Oh Mickey, hurry! I'm so eager to hear the ones in the book Douglas tells me you are making! Won't you please read them to us?"

Mickey smiled as he led the way.

"Just nonsense stuff for Lily," he said. "Nothing but fooling, only the prayer one, and maybe two others."

An abrupt movement from Peaches as they advanced made Mrs. Harding glance her way in time to see the first wave of deep colour that ever had flooded the child's white face, come creeping up her neck and begin tinging her cheeks, even her forehead. With a swift movement she snatched her poetry book, which always lay with her slate and primer, thrusting it under her pillow; when she saw Mrs. Harding watching her she tilted her head and pursed her lips in scorn: "'Our!'" she mimicked. "'Our!' Wonder whose she thinks he is? Nix on her!"

Mrs. Harding, caught surprisedly, struggled to suppress a laugh as she turned to meet her guests. Mickey noticed this. He made his introductions, and swiftly thrust Peaches' Precious Child into her arms, warning in a whisper: "*You be careful, Miss!*"

Peaches needed the reminder. She loved the doll. She had been drilled so often on the thanks she was to tender for it, that with it in her fingers she thought of nothing else, so her smile as Leslie approached was lovely. She held out her hand and before Mickey could speak announced: "Jus' as glad to see you! Thank you ever so much for my Precious Child!"

Nothing more was necessary. Leslie was captivated and would scarcely make way for Douglas to offer his greeting. Mary ran to call her father, while the visitors seated themselves to say the customary polite things; but each of them watched a tiny white-clad creature, with pink ribbons to match the colour in a flawless little face, rounded to the point of delicate beauty, overshadowed by a shower of gold curls, having red lips and lighted by a pair of big, blue-gray eyes with long dark lashes. When Mrs. Harding saw both visitors look so intently at Peaches, and intercepted their glance of admiration toward each other, she looked again herself, and then once more. She had not realized that he child had "fleshed up" so, and the surge of red colouring her face and lips, the light of excitement in her eyes, added to this an indefinable some thing which that instant explained itself.

Peaches spoke with elaborate imperiousness.

"Mickey-lovest, come here and bend down your head."

Mickey slipped behind Douglas' chair, knelt on one knee, and leaned to see what Peaches desired of him. She drew her hankerchief from her waist ribbon, rubbed it across his forehead, looked at the spot with frowning intentness, rubbed again, and then dropping the handkerchief, laid a hand on each side of his head, bent it to her and kissed the spot fervently; then she looked him in the eyes and said with solicitous but engaging sweetness: "*Mickey, I do wish you would be more careful what you get on your face!*"

Mickey drew back thrilled with delight, but extremely embarrassed. "Aw-a-ah you fool little kid!" he muttered, and could not look at his friends.

Watching, Douglas almost shouted, while the flush deepened on Miss Winton's cheeks. Peter began talking to help the situation, so all of them joined in.

"You are making improvements that look very interesting around here," said Douglas to Mrs. Harding.

"We are doing our level best to evolve a sanitary, modern home for all of us, and to set an example for our neighbours," she said quietly. "We always got along very well as we were, but lately, we have found we could have things much more convenient, and when God gave us two more dear children, we needed room for them, and comforts and appliances to take care of our little new daughter right. When we got started, one thing led to another until we are pretty well torn up; but we've saved the best place for her, and the worst is over."

"Yes we are on the finish now," said Peter.

"I did think of taking her and going to my sister's," continued Mrs. Harding, "but Peaches isn't accustomed to meeting people, while Mickey and I both thought being among strangers and changing beds and food would be worse for her than the annoyance of remodelling; then too, I wanted very much to see the work here done as I desired. At first I was doubtful about keeping her, but she doesn't mind in the least; she even takes her afternoon naps with hammers pounding not so far from her—"

"Gee, there is no noise and jar here to compare with Multiopolis," said Mickey. "She's all right, getting stronger every day."

Peaches spread both hands, looking at them critically, back and palm.

"They are better," she said. "You ought to seen them when they was so clawy they made Mickey shiver if I touched him; and first time I wanted to kiss something or go like granny did, he wouldn't let me 'til I cried, an' then he made me put it on his forehead long time, 'til I got so the bones didn't scratch him; didn't you Mickey?"

"Well I wish you wouldn't tell everything!"

"Then I won't," said Peaches, "'cause *I'm* your fam'ly, an' I must do what *you* say; an' *you* are *my* fam'ly, an' you must do what *I* say. Are you a fam'ly?" she questioned Leslie and Douglas.

"We hope to be soon," laughed Leslie.

"Then," said Peaches, "you can look how we're fixing our house so you can make yours nice as this. Mickey, I want to show that pretty lady in the auto'bile my Precious Child."

"Sure!" said Mickey. "I'll go tell her. And the man with her is Miss Leslie's father, just like Peter is ours; you want to show him the Child, don't you?"

"Maybe!" said Peaches with a tantalizing smirk.

"Miss Chicken, you're getting well too fast," commented Mickey in amazement as he started to the car.

Because of what Mr. Winton had said to him the previous day, he composed and delivered this greeting when he reached it: "Lily is asking to show you her Precious Child, Mrs. Minturn, and I want both of you to see our home, and meet our new father and mother. Letting us have them is one thing the law does that makes up a little for the Orphings' Homes most kids get who have had the bad luck to lose their own folks."

"Mickey, are you prejudiced against Orphans' Homes?" asked Mrs. Minturn as she stepped from the car.

"Ain't no name for it," said Mickey. "I'm dead against bunching children in squads. If rich folks want to do something worth while with their money, they can do it by each family taking as many orphings as they can afford, and raising them personal. See?"

"I should say I do!" exclaimed the lady. "I must speak to James about that. We have two of our own, and William, but I believe we could manage a few more."

"I know one I'd like very much to try," said Mr. Winton, but Mickey never appeared so unconscious.

He managed his introductions very well, while again Peaches justified her appellation by being temptingly sweet and conspicuously acid. When Mickey reached Peter in his round of making friends acquainted, he slid his arm through that of the big man and said smilingly: "Nobody is going to mix me with Peter's son by blood—see what a fine chap Junior is; but Peter and I fixed up my sonship with the Almighty, whom my Peter didn't deny, when he took me in, and with the judge of the Multiopolis courts; so even if it doesn't show on the outside, I belong, don't I?"

Peter threw his left arm around Mickey even as he shook hands with his right: "You surely do," he said, "by law and by love, to the bottom of all our hearts."

The visit was a notable success. The buttermilk was cold, the spice cake was fresh, the apples and peaches were juicy, the improvements highly commendable. Peter was asked if he would consider a membership in the Golf Club, the playhouse was discussed, and three hours later a group of warm friends parted, with the agreement that Mickey was to spend a day of the latter part of the week fishing on Atwater.

The Hardings smiled broadly.

"Well son, did we manage that to your satisfaction?" asked Peter.

"Sure!" said Mickey. "I might have been mistaken in what half of that trip was for, but I think not."

"So do I," said Mrs. Harding emphatically. "They were just itching to get their fingers on Peaches; while Bruce and Mr. Winton both were chagrined over our getting you first."

"We feel bad about that too, don't we, Peter?" laughed Mickey.

"Well, I would," said Peter, "if it were the other way around. I didn't mind the young fellow. You'll be with him every day, and he'll soon have boys of his own no doubt; but I feel sorry for Mr. Winton. He looks hungry when he watches you. He could work you into his business fine."

"He's all right, he's a nice man," said Mickey, "but I've lived off the *Herald* all my life 'til this summer, so when school is over I go straight to Mr. Chaffner."

The Winton car ran to the club house; sitting in a group, the occupants looked at each other rather foolishly.

"Seems to me you were going to bring Peaches right along, if you liked her, Leslie," laughed Douglas.

"The little vixen!" she said flushing.

"Sorry you didn't care for her," he commented.

"It is a pity!" said Leslie. "But I didn't 'miss bringing her along' any farther than Mrs. Minturn missed taking her to the hospital to be examined and treated!"

"I'll have to go again about that," said Mrs. Minturn.

"I just couldn't seem to get at it, someway."

"No, you 'just couldn't seem to,'" agreed Douglas. "And Mr. Winton 'just couldn't seem to' lay covetous hands on Mickey, and bear him away to be his assistant any more than I could force him to be my Little Brother. I hope all of us have a realizing sense that we are permitted to be good and loyal friends; but we will kindly leave Mickey to make his own arrangements, and work out his own salvation, and that of his child. And Leslie, I didn't hear you offering to buy any of the quaint dishes and old furniture you hoped you might pick up there, either."

"Heavens!" cried Leslie half tearfully. "How would any one go about offering to buy an old platter that was wrapped in a silk shawl and kept in the dresser drawer during repairs, or ask a man to set a price on old furniture, when he was scraping off the varnish of generations, and showing you wood grain and colouring with the pride of a veteran collector? I feel so silly! Let's play off our chagrin, and then we'll be in condition for friendship which is the part that falls to us, if I understand Mickey."

"Well considering the taste I've had of the quality of his friendship, I hope you won't be surprised at the statement that I feel highly honoured," said Mr. Winton, leading the way, while the others thoughtfully followed.

With four days' work the Harding home began to show what was being accomplished. The song of the housewife carried to the highway. Neighbours passing went home to silent, overworked drudges, and critically examined for the first time stuffy, dark kitchens, reeking with steam, heat, and the odour of cooking and decorated with the grime of years. The little leaven of one home in the neighbourhood, as all homes should be, set them thinking. A week had not passed until people began calling Mrs. Harding to the telephone to explain just what she was doing, and why. Men would stop to ask Peter what was going on, so every time he caught a victim, he never released him until the man saw sunrise above a kitchen table, a line in the basement for a winter wash, kitchen implements from a pot scraper and food pusher to a gas range and electric washing machine, with a furnace and hardwood floors thrown in. Soon the rip of shovelled shingles, the sound of sawing, and the ring of hammers filled the air.

The Harding improvements improved so fast, that sand, cement, and the big pile of lumber began accumulating at Peter's corner of the crossroads below the home, for the playhouse. Men who started by calling Peter a fool, ended by borrowing his plans and belabouring themselves for their foolishness; for the neighbourhood was awakening and beginning to develop a settled conviction as to what constituted the joy of life, and that the place to enjoy it was at home, and the time immediately. Peter's reward was not only in renewed happiness for himself and Nancy; equal to it was his pleasure over the same renewal for many of his lifelong friends.

Mickey started on his day to Atwater with joyful anticipation, but he jumped from Douglas' car and ran up the Harding front walk at three o'clock, his face anxious. He saw the Harding car at the gate, and wondered at Peter sitting dressed for leisure on the veranda.

"Got anxious about Lily," he explained. "Out on the lake I thought I heard her call me, then I had the notion she was crying for me. They laughed at me, but I couldn't stand it. Is she asleep, as they said she'd be?"

Peter opened his lips, but no word came. Mickey slowly turned a ghastly white. Peter reached in his side pocket, drew out a letter, and handed it to the boy. Mickey pulled the sheet from the envelope, still staring at Peter, then glanced at what he held and collapsed on the step. Peter moved beside him, laid a steadying arm across his shoulders and proved his fear was as great as Mickey's by being unable to speak. At last the boy produced articulate words.

"*He came?*" he marvelled.

"About ten this morning," said Peter.

"He took her to the hospital?" panted Mickey.

"Yes," said Peter.

"Why did you let him?" demanded Mickey.

That helped Peter. He indicated the letter.

"There's your call for him!" he said, emphatically. "You asked me to adopt her so I could give him orders to go ahead when he came."

"Why didn't you telephone me?" asked Mickey.

"I did," said Peter. "The woman who answered didn't know where you were, but she said their car had gone to town, so I thought maybe they'd find you there. I was just going to call them again."

"Was she afraid?" wavered Mickey.

"Yes, I think she was," said Peter.

"Did she cry for me?" asked Mickey.

"Yes she did," admitted Peter, who hadn't a social lie in his being, "but when he offered to put off the examination till he might come again, she climbed from the cot and made him take her. Ma went with her."

"The Sunshine Nurse came?" questioned Mickey.

"Yes," said Peter, "and Mrs. Minturn. She sent for him to see about an operation on a child she is trying to save, so when it was over, he showed her your letter. She brought them out in her car, and Ma went back with them."

"She may be on that glass table right now," gulped Mickey. "What time is it? When's the next car? Run me to the station will you, and if you've got any money, let me have it 'til I get to mine."

"Of course!" said Peter.

"Will Junior and Mary be all right?" asked Mickey, pausing in his extremity to think of others.

"Yes, they often stay while we go."

"Hurry!" begged Mickey.

Peter took hold of the gear and faced straight ahead.

"She's oiled, the tank full, the engine purring like a kitten," he said. "Mickey, I always wanted to beat that trolley just once, to show it I *could*, if I wasn't loaded with women and children. Awful nice road—"

"Go on!" said Mickey.

Peter smiled, sliding across the starter.

"Sit tight!" he said tersely.

The big car slipped up the road no faster than it had gone frequently, passed the station, then on and on; Mickey twisted to look back at the rattle of the trolley stopping behind them, watching it with wishful eye. Peter opened his lips to say: "Just warmed up enough, and an even start!"

The trolley came abreast and whistled. Peter blew his horn, glancing that way with a little "come on" forward jerk of his head. The motorman nodded, touched his gear and the car started. Peter laid prideful, loving hands on his machinery; for the first time with legitimate racing excuse, as he long had wished to, he tried out his engine. Mickey could see the faces of the protesting passengers and the conductor grinning in the door, but Peter could not have heard if he had tried to tell him. Flying it was, smooth and even, past fields, orchards, and houses; past people who cried out at them and shook their fists. Mickey looked at Peter and registered for life each line of his big frame and lineament of his face, as he gripped the gear and put his car over the highway. When they reached the pavement, Mickey touched Peter's arm. "Won't make anything by getting arrested," he cautioned.

"No police for blocks yet," said Peter.

"Well there's risk of life and damage suit at each crossing!" shouted Mickey, so Peter slowed a degree; but he was miles ahead of all regulations as he stopped before the gleaming entrance. Mickey sprang from the car and hurried up the steps. Mrs. Minturn arose from a seat and came to meet him.

"Take me to her quick!" begged Mickey.

Silently she led the way to her suite in her old home, and opened the door. Mickey had a glimpse of Mrs. Harding, his Sunshine Nurse, and three men, one of whom he recognized from reproductions of his features in the papers. A very white, tired-looking Peaches stretched both hands and uttered a shrill cry as Mickey appeared in the doorway. His answer was inarticulate while his arms spread widely. Then Peaches arose, and in a few shuffling but sustained steps fell on his breast, gripping him with all her strength.

"Oh darling, you'll kill yourself," wailed Mickey.

He laid her on the davenport and knelt clasping her. Peaches regained self-control first; she sat up, shamelessly wiping Mickey's eyes and her own alternately.

"Flowersy-girl, did you hurt yourself awful?"

"I know something I won't tell," chanted Peaches, as she had been doing for days.

Mickey looked at her, then up at Peter, who had entered and come to them.

"*Did you?*" eagerly asked Peter of the child.

Peaches nodded proudly. "To meet Mickey," she triumphed. "I wouldn't for anybody else *first! The longest piece yet! And it didn't hurt and I didn't fall!*"

"Good!" shouted Peter. "That's the ticket!"

"You look here Miss Chicken, what do you mean?" cried Mickey wonderingly.

"Oh the Doctor Carrel man you sent for, came," explained Peaches, "and you wasn't there, but he had your name on the letter you wrote; he showed me, so I came and let him examination me; but Peter and I been standing alone, and taking steps when nobody was looking. You've surprised me joyful so much, it takes one as big as that to pay you back."

Mickey clung to his treasure, while turning to Peter an awed, questioning face.

"That's it!" said Peter. "She's been on her feet for ten days or such a matter!"

Mickey appealed to Dr. Carrel.

"How about this?" he demanded.

"She's going to walk," said the great man assuringly.

"It's all over? You've performed your miracle?" asked Mickey.

"Yes," said Dr. Carrel. "It's all over, Mickey; but you had the miracle performed before I saw her, lad."

Mickey retreated to Peaches' neck again, while she smiled over and comforted him.

"Mickey, I knew you'd be crazy," she said. "I knew you'd be glad, but I didn't know you could be so—"

Mickey took her in his arms a second, then slowly recovered his feet and a small amount of self-possession. Again he turned to the surgeons.

"*Are you sure?* Will it hurt her? Will it last?"

"Quite sure," said Dr. Carrel. "Calm yourself, lad. Her case is not so unusual; only more aggravated than usual. I've examined her from crown to sole, and she's straight and sound. You have started her permanent cure; all you need is to keep on exactly as you are going, and limit her activities so that in her joy she doesn't overdo and tire herself. You are her doctor. I congratulate you!"

Dr. Carrel came forward, holding out his hand, and Mickey took it with the one of his that was not gripping Peaches and said, "Aw-a-ah!" but he was a radiant boy. and the white light on his forehead shone never so brightly.

"Thank you sir," he said. "Thank everybody. But thank you especial, over and over. I don't know how I'll ever square up with you, but I'll pay you all I have to start on. I've some money I've saved from my wages, and I'll be working harder and earning more all the time."

"But Mickey," protested the surgeon, "you don't owe me anything. I didn't operate! You had the work done before I arrived. I would have come sooner, but I knew she couldn't be operated, even if her case demanded it, until she had gained more strength—"

He was watching Mickey's face and he read aright, so he continued: "I like that suggestion you made in your letter very much. Something 'coming in steadily' is a good thing for any man to have. For the next three months, suppose you send me that two dollars a week you offered me if I'd come. How would that be?"

Mickey gathered Peaches in his arms and looked over his shoulder as he started on the homeward trip.

"Thank you sir," he said tersely. "That would be square."

THE END